THE
VENGEANCE
EQUATION

KENNETH TAM

JAX FURGUS
ADMIRAL (RETIRED), EARTHER NAVY

THE
VENGEANCE
EQUATION

THE SIXTH EQUATIONS NOVEL

KENNETH TAM

ICEBERG

Published in Canada by Iceberg Publishing, Waterloo

Library and Archives Canada Cataloguing in Publication
Tam, Kenneth, 1984-
    The vengeance equation : the sixth equations novel / Kenneth Tam.
ISBN 978-0-9865017-6-0
    I. Title.
PS8589.A7676V45 2010   C813'.6   C2010-900088-9

Iceberg Publishing
55 Northfield Drive East, Suite 171
Waterloo ON N2K 3T6
contact@icebergpublishing.com
www.icebergpublishing.com

First pocket paperback printing: July 2007
Special international edition: January 2010

Cover Artwork: Wesley Prewer
Cover Design: Kenneth Tam

For Peter, my father.

Thanks for the wisdom.
It's at the core of both
sides of this story.

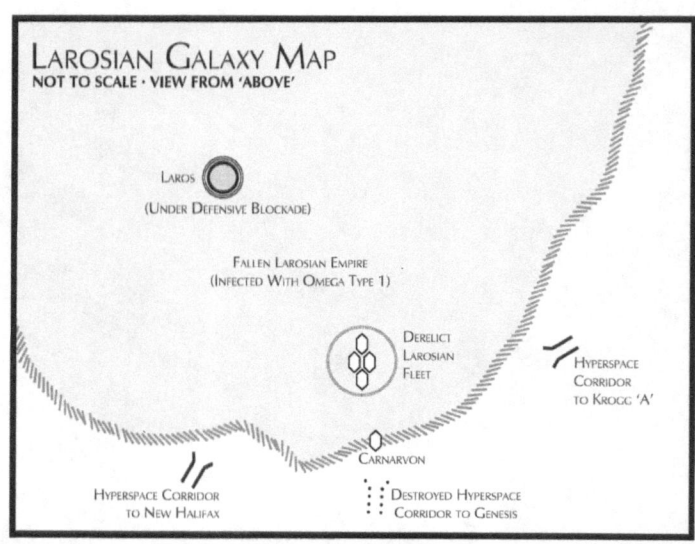

LAROSIAN GALAXY MAP
NOT TO SCALE · VIEW FROM 'ABOVE'

LAROS

(UNDER DEFENSIVE BLOCKADE)

FALLEN LAROSIAN EMPIRE
(INFECTED WITH OMEGA TYPE 1)

DERELICT
LAROSIAN
FLEET

HYPERSPACE
CORRIDOR
TO KROGG 'A'

CARNARVON

HYPERSPACE CORRIDOR
TO NEW HALIFAX

DESTROYED HYPERSPACE
CORRIDOR TO GENESIS

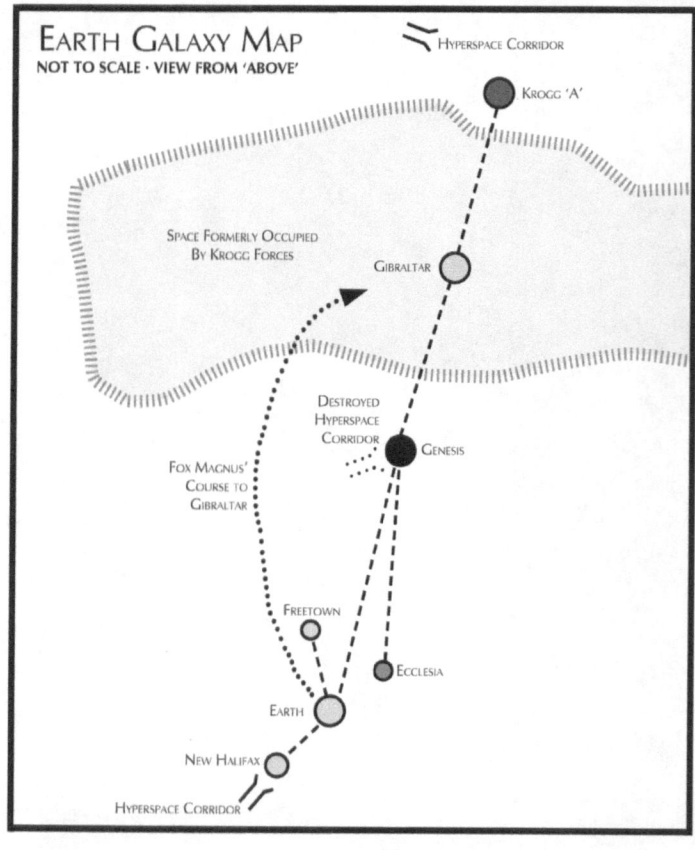

EARTH GALAXY MAP
NOT TO SCALE · VIEW FROM 'ABOVE'

HYPERSPACE CORRIDOR

KROGG 'A'

SPACE FORMERLY OCCUPIED
BY KROGG FORCES

GIBRALTAR

DESTROYED
HYPERSPACE
CORRIDOR

GENESIS

FOX MAGNUS'
COURSE TO
GIBRALTAR

FREETOWN

ECCLESIA

EARTH

NEW HALIFAX

HYPERSPACE CORRIDOR

FOREWORD

So the other shoe has dropped.

Omega's back... and in fact, he never left. He created the Earthers, then their immune systems — systems Omega himself designed to make sure no other plagues could muscle in on his food supply — crippled him, and made him a passive passenger in their blood streams for all their years of do-gooding.

This really irked the plague, because he's a product of our time — he's mean, cynical, and doesn't have much time for do-gooders. The Earthers are much too vanilla for him, and combine that irritation with the fact that they robbed him of his plans for conquest... well, he's just not pleased. And thanks to Krogg biomatter, he has a chance to get his revenge.

When you think about it, his plight actually worked to his advantage: the Earthers unknowingly carried him out to the universe, and gave him the chance to be exposed to the Larosians (see *The Alien Equation*, page 240 in the special edition), who had no immunity to him. Now he's back...

The plan for the return of Omega started very early on in the outlining of this series, when I realized that the Krogg War, in itself, would only go so far in testing the Earthers. A conventional war against other beings was a tough trial for anyone, but the Earthers and their way of life needed a bigger, more head-on challenge.

Challenges don't come much bigger than the plague that created them in the first place.

With no support system — no Larosians, and the humans in chaos — the Earthers are going to go toe-to-toe with their self-professed 'God' in the pages to come, and we'll get to learn a whole lot more about them.

This part of the series is, in many respects, my favorite. Don't mistake me: the Earthers' journey through the Krogg War was very important, and I'm quite proud to have been part of it, but much of the story so far has been centered around the Earthers learning about humanity. Now we turn the attention to the Earthers themselves, building upon their experiences of the Krogg War, and seeing exactly what the humans and Omega think of the idealistic wolves, cats and bears.

Because Omega hails from our time, I find he represents the worst of what we are today — the excess, the self-importance and the angry cynicism that are often celebrated in current times. The Earthers and their innocent philosophy thus get a real challenge when they butt heads with him. The encounter is quite fascinating. And brutal. Very brutal, in fact.

We have certain expectations of what the Earthers can accomplish through feats of arms, but now they're coming off of forty years of peace. How quickly can they mobilize their forces and get into position to protect the most vulnerable points? More to the point, will they be able to protect the vulnerable humans of Freetown, and the refugees from Genesis?

There I go again with the cryptic, skeptical questions — if you've read the forewords to all of the special editions of the *Equations* novels, you'll know how those questions always turn out... but I won't spoil things for you. Omega is mounting an incredible challenge, but with Setter Caine's guidance, and with officers like Lab Forepaw and Fox Magnus running the fleet... you get the idea.

It'll be a hell of a fight, but before we get to it, it's time to offer thanks.

Cody Herauf starts us off once again, because his Kroggs and Larosians still factor into this universe, even if their roles right now are largely tertiary. Nothing that Omega is doing now would be possible without access to those two species. That being the case, I must again thank Cody for providing these fine races to me for the *Equations* novels.

As before, my next acknowledgement must go to Wes Prewer, because his ship art on the covers of these books continues to be excellent. The effort he puts in to get the details right is remarkable, and we're very lucky to have his commitment to this series.

I'm also very pleased that characters he created for *Retaliation* — Ami Cairn (now Ami Dune) and her veterans from the 141st Flying Squadron — have the opportunity in this book to start taking on very important roles within various Earther missions. I remain indebted to Wes for his fine contributions.

Next, I must spend a good deal of time thanking Peter Caron. This is the part of the series where Peter's brilliance really has the chance to shine, because when it came to plotting Omega's offensives, and the way in which the plague would strike out into the galaxy, I needed input. One day in the winter of 2003, Peter and I rented a classroom at Wilfrid Laurier University, drew massive star maps on its white boards, and spent hours discussing how the plague would operate, where he'd go, and how he'd fight. All of this discussion was absolutely indispensable, and Peter's contributions — apt and exceptional — have been incorporated into the plot here.

Without that day of strategizing, and without Peter's superior deconstruction of the way the Earthers fought the Krogg War, this part of the series would have looked very different, and I don't think it would have been as good. Peter put on the 'Omega' hat — he climbed inside the mind of the beast-plague — and he generated a strategy to match. He can't be blamed for some of the more horrid consequences of Omega's strategy (the details are my fault) but his clever approach to the conflict was fundamentally important. So once again, I'm hugely grateful to my friend Peter. Many thanks indeed, sir.

After thanking my friends, I must thank my family.

Jacqui and Peter's ongoing support of this series, and their hard work as partners in Iceberg Publishing, have been indispensable. I think it's actually scientifically impossible to ask for better parents. If you found a way, it'd likely rip a hole in the fabric of space-time. Cheesy, but true.

Finally, Atlas must be thanked.

We're getting into the most severe test of Earther character. Time to see what Omega has in store...

PROLOGUE

The Genesis Fleet exited flux drive several days from Freetown space, its squadrons slowly forming into echelons, waiting for the long line of civilian ships they were escorting to reorganize themselves again. Some of those civilian ships simply couldn't handle the haul from Genesis to Freetown in a single run, so periodic stops were being made to make sure none were left behind.

A week ago, that sort of slow progress and constant starting and stopping would have irritated the officers of the Genesis Fleet. Escorting civilian ships was never a popular job in Naval circles. But now that these ships carried what remained of Genesis civilization, well... it was different. The circumstances of last week no longer applied.

During no period in the history of the human race had so much changed in such a narrow window of time; over the course of the last five days, an entire civilized world had been eliminated... or more precisely, it had been infested... taken over... *seized* by perhaps the most horrifying entity in the galaxy.

Bane of all humanity, destroyer of the Larosian Empire, and, of course, proud creator of the Earther race: Omega had returned.

The plague had been melded to Krogg DNA by a Larosian mistake, and was now a force unlike anything else seen in history. When initially created in the twenty-first century, Omega had been a sentient and deadly bio-weapon, but with the addition of the Krogg DNA to its matrix, its... *his* abilities were unparalleled by anything previously encountered. Any creature that was not protected by Earther DNA could be consumed by him, or infested and controlled by him. Ironically, it was only that Earther biology — designed by Omega himself when he mutated the Earther race into existence to provide him with a food source — that could save humans, Larosians and probably even Kroggs. Treatments with the Earthers' Uniform DNA Regenerative Compound would be necessary to save those other races.

But most of the humans of Genesis had not been protected by such a shield when Omega had arrived on the planet. Omega had taken the Larosian Captain Natosh as its avatar, and crashed into Genesis just as a Church coup attempted to overthrow the united democratic government. He slipped in and took the planet with an ease and efficiency that was simply horrifying.

Only the humans who'd been in orbit of the planet were left untouched... and even some of those people were absorbed into Omega's new legion. The

Genesis orbital stations, longtime defenders of the planet, had been taken before anyone had realized what was going on. Most of the fleet had escaped, and many of the installations hidden in the Genesis asteroid belt had been successfully evacuated, but aside from this body of Genesis Naval officers, only a small number of humans seemed to have made their escape. In transports and cargo haulers, on smaller research and mining stations, or escaping the fighting on Genesis in some other manner of craft, these humans had avoided the plague, and now represented Genesis civilization's only legacy.

Combining Navy and civilian populations, a total of 742,310 Genesis humans remained.

It was a number that was seared into Sarah Manchester's brain.

President Sarah Manchester, she'd been. Head of the civilian government on Genesis, tasked with leading her united people, and counterbalancing the strength of the Church Chancellery in political affairs.

Some job I did.

It was her fault — she was certain of that much. She'd been asleep at the switch — she'd let the Church prepare a coup, and then had failed to remember her priorities once it started. She should never have forgotten the plague threat, the threat the Larosians had warned her about over forty years ago. A Genesis ship should have been blockading the mouth to Genesis' hyperspace corridor, forbidding Omega's ship entry into the system.

Instead, the warring factions had left a field of debris at the corridor's mouth, providing cover that allowed Omega to come through without being noticed until it was too late. And Sarah had stepped onto her presidential pinnace and fled the planet's surface just before Omega landed.

Sarah was certain that her failings were many: she'd let the Church come close to seizing power, she'd failed to protect her race from its most hated historical foe, and she'd managed both of those grievous errors without *dying* for them.

She was alive.

And she didn't want to be.

As *Unity Genesis*, flagship of the Genesis Navy, formed with its squadron and waited for the surviving civilian ships to reorganize themselves, Sarah sat silently on its bridge. Part of her mind was telling her to stand tall, to try to rally her people to the challenge at hand — to staving off Omega, and rebuilding...

Right, because that's the natural reaction I should have, after losing 100 percent of my planet's population to the plague on the first day of a war I had no idea was coming.

No, she didn't have the steel to stand tall, figuratively or literally. She just couldn't. She sat stoically in Graham's chair — that is to say, her dead brother's chair — and let the fleet close with Freetown. She didn't quite know what she'd do when she got to the planet. Someone would tell her something that would make her think, surely.

Until then, nothing. Nothing at all.

Unity Genesis waited for this hodgepodge fleet to assemble itself, and to continue on to Freetown.

CHAPTER 1

ENS Renown seemed to be slowly coming back to life. The *Venerable*-class ship of the line had been battered rather thoroughly by its crash exit from the Genesis corridor, but its Earther construction was demonstrating its resilience. Engineers were putting *Renown's* systems back together quickly, and soon the First Rate would be able to make 3,000 pls under energy drive.

At this moment, though, the vessel floated quietly in space.

Rear Admiral Varnia Lupus (formerly Varnia Broadpaw, daughter of Varnon) was, for her part, optimistic. She'd seen ships in much worse states of disorder put back together by enterprising Earther engineers, and considering the seeming success of their attempt to collapse the corridor, she could afford a certain short-term hopefulness.

Omega was trapped a galaxy away...

Well, that was neither particularly comforting nor precisely true. The new, Krogg-hybrid Omega was stuck back on Genesis, probably even now figuring ways to attack Earth, Freetown, Gibraltar, and Krogg. Meanwhile *Renown* — carrying the only Earther forces to have encountered Omega's military might — was cut off, a galaxy away from the fight.

Indeed, under the best-case scenario, they could be stranded in the galaxy once dominated by the Larosian Empire, but now home only to its burnt-out carcass. All but one of the thousands of worlds of the Empire had been overcome by the original version of Omega — the version that had driven humans from Earth in the twenty-first century, and created the Earthers. Varnia could only hope that somehow her doctors could find a way to cure *that* Omega in Larosians, though at least they knew the old version of Omega couldn't beat the Earther immune system any more than the new Krogg-hybrid version could. She'd take whatever advantages she could get.

As those hopes passed through Varnia's mind, she realized how small they really were. She wasn't even sure *Renown* had made it to the Larosian galaxy; the ship could in fact be trapped in the void between galaxies. There was no telling if this ship of the line would ever get home.

All the more reason to make sure the repairs are done right...

With a sigh, Varnia left her bridge, and began a slow tour of her ship.

• • •

Christine Schaeffer didn't feel altogether well — her head was spinning, she was queasy, she was fairly certain something was broken in her left arm, and she was marooned outside her galaxy on an Earther ship, having just witnessed the extermination of her home planet by a sentient virus in a Larosian body. Her parents were almost certainly dead or enslaved by the plague, and her shocked sister had been left in the care of strangers.

She wasn't having a good week. But despite all that, she knew Graham Manchester was having a much *worse* week.

Because Graham had become the victim of one of Omega's games: the plague had taken over Gillian Hodge — Graham's beloved wife — by infesting their unborn child. That was worse than bad... beyond *sick*...

Everything she'd seen, everything everyone had lost... It was a living nightmare, stabbing Christine with bolts of terror in those moments when she failed in her attempts to remain numb. She had to try not to think about it.

Physical pain actually helped with that effort to ignore, as did the Earther DNA that was swimming through her system, still integrating with her biology. Her crash regen treatment of a few days before was still sinking in — it had protected her from Omega's infection, but was almost as alien to her as the virus would have been.

The regen made her feel strange — there was no better word for it — and its impacts on her body had yet to become fully clear. Not even Doctor Lazarus, *Renown's* surgeon, could completely anticipate the effect of dumping several months' worth of regen injections into a person within the space of fifteen minutes... aside from Christine dying a dozen times during the procedure, to be resuscitated on the table.

Only time would tell what might become of young Christine Schaeffer.

Standing in front of the mirror in her cabin, she busied her mind by checking her body for any visible changes. Her well-toned form was sporting a handsome set of bruises — the legacy first of her fighting at Darymanis City and then of her battle against Omega's minions — but at least she wasn't growing a coat of feline-like fur. And there were no growths, bulges, new joints, or discolored veins.

She looked a battle-weary version of herself... but she just didn't *feel* like she was wearing the same skin as before.

Oh well... she'd best double check, because if she actually stopped being foolish and checking her neck for a lion's mane, she might start thinking about her dead parents. About the way she'd killed a teenaged girl with her saber a few days ago. Or about the fact that she was not only adjutant to her one-time hero, but was now his only human support on this ship.

Come to think of it, she should go look for Graham... make sure he was alright.

So she found some clothes and dressed carefully, focusing on every snap, straightening every crease, and being sure not to reflect on her woes.

Those woes would hit her hard at some point, she knew, and then she'd collapse in on herself.

Maybe she could pencil that in for next week.

Christine left her cabin.

Varnia Lupus walked silently through the corridors of her ship, nodding to the ratings and officers she passed. Every wolf, cat and bear on her crew was working hard to put *Renown* back into fighting trim, and the ship was now starting to show some of the shine it had proudly displayed before the coup. Only two days after being tossed into the great unknown, round the clock work had seen most of the blown relays replaced, most of the scorch marks painted over, and the ship restored to its austere order.

Now they'd have to figure out what to do with the vessel...

"Admiral Lupus?"

Varnia blinked at the call from behind her, snapping her mind from its contemplations and working quickly to identify the speaker. Ah yes, it was—

"Christine, how are you feeling?" Varnia turned with a reassuring smile. Though relatively young, Varnia had commanded ships through her share of dire circumstances, and she knew well that the commanding officer should never be visibly distraught. With that in mind, she made certain her smile was as genuine as possible as the human set eyes upon it.

Christine nodded back as she slowed in the corridor, "I was just looking for Graham... he wasn't in his cabin. Have you seen him at all?"

Varnia narrowed her eyes thoughtfully, "Last time I saw him would have been... last night, on the main observation deck."

A frown crossed Christine's brow at the remark, "That's where I left him yesterday morning."

"Best look there then..." Varnia's mind was preparing some sort of reassuring comment when an instinctive burst preempted it.

The Rear Admiral and the ArcLieutenant locked eyes... Christine's blood crawled and the hair on the back of her neck literally stood up. As that happened, Varnia's own sense of reluctance, dread, and exhaustion was perceived by the young human, and Christine's similar emotions were relayed ponderously — but intentionally — back to Varnia.

Christine froze and Varnia cocked a legitimately fascinated eyebrow, "A side effect of your treatment?"

That was a sentence fragment, which might not have meant anything to another human, but Christine knew that Varnia was referring to what had just happened — an *instinctive* transmission. *Earther* instinct. The non-telepathic and essentially undefinable transmission of understanding between two Earthers.

"Probably," she offered in quiet reply.

Varnia's brow sunk into a frown, but after a second she smiled in understanding, "Don't worry, having fur isn't as itchy as it sounds."

Christine's eyes widened at the remark, even as an instinctive voice in the back of her head told her it was a joke.

"*Not* what I needed to hear..."

Varnia chuckled. It was definitely better to laugh about that sort of thing. Despair or grim depression were the other options, and Varnia was interested in neither.

Standing on the main observation deck, Graham was in no mood to laugh.

He wasn't ignoring all that had happened at Genesis, nor was he dwelling on it.

Stiff professionalism had taken over: pure, inhuman determination to show no weakness, and to feel none. His mind told the fear, the horror, and the deep sense of loss he was experiencing to go away.

And remarkably enough, that approach seemed to be working.

He'd make this discipline last — he'd pledged to himself that he would not lose composure or strength until Omega died or he died. And having lost Gillian, driven Sarah and Pat away, and separated himself from almost all human contact, it seemed likely he'd be able to effectively isolate himself from emotion or weakness.

However, he had a chance to be idle now, and that was dangerous. He had nothing to do on *Renown* — the ship was going nowhere, and its crew was fully capable of handling repairs. Beckett was busy talking to Narosh, and Varnia was concerned with her crew. For Graham there was nothing with which to keep busy, so he simply stayed on the main observation deck, making use of the deck's convenient holo training projectors, looking out at foreign stars, and sealing his mind against grief.

He'd slept for two dreamless hours the night before in the chair just three feet behind him. For several hours, he'd used the training holos that the Earthers had installed in this lounge. For the rest of the day, he'd just paced the same line — a complete circuit of the deck, with its grand windows.

And now, looking out at those stars, he almost walked into Christine.

She'd arrived on the deck without his notice, and her first greeting had managed to go unheard, "Graham, do you *hear* me?"

With a blink he stopped walking and looked at his aide with a neutral expression, "I do. Is everything alright?"

"I was about to ask you the same thing," she countered cautiously. "I'm starting to pick up direct bursts of Earther instincts, but that aside all seems to be rather quiet."

Graham nodded disinterestedly, "Very well. Let me know once we're ready to get under weigh again. I should talk to Varnia then."

That, as far as Graham could figure, was the end of the conversation, but Christine frowned, "Are you just planning to spend your time here?"

He nodded slowly in reply, "That's my intention, yes."

Christine's frown deepened, and she nearly blurted out what she was thinking — *What the hell?* Translating that reaction into a more diplomatic sentence, she countered again, "Well, if you don't mind, I'd suggest you retire to your cabin and get some rest while you can..."

Graham's disinterested expression stopped her words.

He met her eyes with his own stony gaze, inclining his head slightly, "I don't mind you suggesting, Christine. But I fear I won't be doing as you suggest. You should go get your rest though — recover from that regen. Rest would do you well."

"Rest would do us both well..." her words trailed off again, and Graham's head tilted upward.

"I'm quite alright. Thank you. But you best go get some rest. Don't concern yourself with me; I'll let you know as soon as I need you again."

Christine felt that she should say something else, but... but what *could* she say? Graham's eyes weren't cold or harsh, they just *were*.

So she nodded, "As you say, just call me when you need me."

Graham tilted his head again, "Thank you kindly. And good day to you."

His words, though unusually formal, were genial enough, so Christine turned and left the observation deck.

As the door closed behind her Graham spared a contemplative breath, then muttered quietly, "Don't expect me to call, Christine. I won't be needing anything at all."

He went back to pacing.

CHAPTER 2

Admiral (retired and now recalled) Jax Furgus was walking quickly through the corridors of his recommissioned flagship. *Aboukir*, in company with seven other 74-gun ships of the line and a squadron of 44-gun frigates, made up the sum total of the Earther Navy's presence in Freetown space.

And as far as Jax was concerned, that wasn't quite enough.

Like all Earthers, he'd seen Omega's message, and with that sort of nasty megalomaniac of a plague marking the Earthers and humans for annihilation, he wouldn't even begin to feel comfortable until the Earther Navy was properly up to strength again. Decades of peace had left the fleet much smaller than it had been during the Krogg War, even if it was much more advanced. The reduced size meant the Admiralty simply didn't have the ships to fortify Earth, Freetown, New Halifax, Gibraltar *and* Krogg, not until the veterans vessels of the Krogg War were unpacked from their storage crates and rebuilt.

Of course, recommissioning those thousand Krogg War veteran ships would take time, and if Omega was as smart as he was claiming, he'd be moving fast to avoid having to deal with Earther Naval might.

Jax had actually been waiting for some sort of horrid plague fleet to turn up in Freetown space for days — Sarah Manchester's refugee fleet had abandoned the Genesis system a week ago, giving Omega plenty of time to move.

Now, at last, Sarah and her Genesis Fleet were cruising into Freetown space, and as yet there was no indication that Omega was anywhere nearby. He might be following the refugee convoy... he might be only a day or two away... he might be lurking on the periphery of the system, waiting for a chance... he might be going somewhere else entirely...

Might might might... Jax was impatient with himself and his inner doubts. *First time in your career you're spooked, and that's after having six ships shot out from under you, retirement, and fighting a new Church Faithful.*

That, of course, and losing his daughter.

Earthers had a way of ignoring losses like those while duty required their attention, but this was a new sort of loss for Jax. This was his daughter, his beloved cub. He didn't want to think about Joyce, who'd been a Captain of Marines with the Second Battalion, 54th Regiment (2/54th) serving aboard *Renown* at Genesis. Whenever he allowed himself to remember that she was dead, he wanted to stop, and to call his wife, and then to go find Omega and kill him for it. Revenge.

In other words, remembering her loss made him uncharacteristically emotional.

But as an Earther, Jax had the ability to retain control of his emotions, even at times like this. As much as he didn't want it to be the case, he *was* the effective commander at this station... even if Audrey DeBrooke and whoever Sarah had with her happened to be officially senior in the human services.

Omega was an Earther bane, and thus the Earthers would lead the war against him. That plague might fancy himself their God, a creator with the ability to defeat the Earthers in open war, but as much as he'd witnessed (having watched the Krogg War from his hiding place in the blood of every Earther), he'd never seen them so committed to a cause as they were to his destruction.

As far as Jax was concerned, Omega's time in the universe was now quite limited: announcing himself had been a big mistake, because now the Earthers knew he existed, and would eliminate him.

That all being the case, Admiral Furgus, once Second Lord of the Admiralty, was ready to take command of the station at Freetown. While Admiralty House back on Earth scrambled to recommission ships, and decided where the new *Venerables* would go and under whose orders, Jax's force would become the core of a defensive fleet that would keep Omega out of Freetown space.

Now the lion just needed to explain all that to his human counterparts. Because he hadn't exactly let them in on it yet. That was what the coming meeting was for...

The decks he currently trod were winding towards *Aboukir's* main briefing room, where Jax's Flag Captain, the well-known Ronax Hobbes, waited with the commanders of the Freetown and Genesis Fleets. Pacing just behind Jax was Tom Locke, Commodore in charge of Jax's frigates. A little further behind was Alix Tarkam, who'd bailed the Freetown Navy out of a tough spot in their last encounter with the Faithful Navy of Ecclesia.

Jax was going to have quite a few well-regarded Earthers on hand, just in case some of the humans wanted to argue and needed to be convinced that his planned course of action was the correct one. He could be very understanding of human feelings and doubts when he needed to be, but these weren't usual circumstances... and his many years had probably dulled his tolerance. He was a crotchety old cat now, and he was bent on fighting.

The briefing room doors at last appeared in front of him, and slowing himself, Jax took a deep breath. He glanced back to Tarkam and Locke, "Set?"

Both Earthers nodded in turn, and Jax keyed the door and stepped into the room.

His eyes took in the situation immediately... no, actually, his *ears* caught it first... no, in fact, it was the *anger* that managed to pierce his instincts before any of the physical senses detected the strife.

"Gods damn you, this is *our* system — we just paid for it in *blood*! I'm not turning our fleet and our civilization over to you just because you let yours get out of hand!"

That was Audrey DeBrooke, and the sharp, desperate edge in her voice was as obvious when she yelled as it had been in her ordinary conversation during the past few days. Her husband, and co-founder of Freetown, had been killed by the luckiest shot in Church history — James Stanton had been lost with *Archangel Sword's* bridge just before Tarkam could intervene in the Freetown-Faithful engagement.

Audrey had been coping on her own with that loss, and with the threat of Omega, for the past week. Every time Jax had spoken with her, he'd gotten the feeling she wouldn't be pushed too far on matters of her colony and her fleet. He'd come today to convince her that she needed to integrate Freetown's new and advanced warships with his, though by the sounds of it the Genesis officers in the room had started without him.

Jax's eyes fell on the two other humans present. Both wore Genesis Fleet uniforms, but he recognized neither the man nor the woman. Probably young officers — *not* veterans of the Krogg War.

The man with them now bristled, "You have no *concept* of what we've gone through. If your ships hadn't been out here causing trouble and forcing the Earthers to get involved, the Church never would have started the coup and we'd have been in place to stop Omega short of Genesis!"

Audrey's eyes had been hard already, but they turned to steel at that accusation. She almost lunged across the table, but Ron Hobbes — who Jax now realized was standing next to her — had a strong hand on her shoulder.

"Maybe if you could've counted on the *loyalty* of your ships, you wouldn't have been off station anyway. But I suppose your fleet's unity was on the same level as its tactical *skill*. Took you plenty of time to get rid of the traitors, from what I hear!" Audrey lashed back.

The Genesis woman fielded that one, and although Jax heard the door open behind him, he found himself compelled to watch the young ArcLieutenant-General's snarled reply, "I hear *you* divided your fleet in the face of an unknown enemy and got ambushed by the *Church*. You renegades don't get to talk about skills after a screw up like that, especially now that you're reliant on Earther technology to keep up with us–"

Jax was done with this garbage, "I think that's *quite enough*!"

His roar caused the human heads to whip around, and his eyes narrowed as he looked at each of them in turn, "Now perhaps we can behave with some civility. I grant you we've all had a *very* bad week, and speaking as an Earther who just lost his daughter to a plague that's been using my race as a Trojan horse for seven centuries, I'm in no mood for this sort of infighting. Were President Manchester here, I doubt she'd be impressed."

"I might need Captain Tarkam to restrain someone if I hear another word, in fact."

Jax's ear twitched as he immediately recognized Sarah's voice. He didn't turn, but his eyes narrowed further, "Are we ready to *talk* then, ladies and gentlemen?"

There was silence for a moment, and Ron Hobbes was able to half-gesture, half-push the human fleet officers into chairs at the table. None looked too happy. Turning back to Sarah, Jax ground his jaw and bobbed his eyebrows, "Good to see you again, madam President. Just wish for better circumstances, of course."

Sarah nodded slowly, "Just so. I think... we'll have much work ahead of us."

Jax's head tilted a bit, "You could call it that... anyway, let's sit."

The Earthers and the President of Genesis found seats, and slowly the atmosphere over the table seemed to calm down — just a little, at least. There was no pretense that Audrey was pleased with her guests' candor, and Alix Tarkam had taken a seat between the two groups in case of a scuffle. He'd been a great hand-to-hand specialist in his heyday, and his skills might be needed if the humans became any less agreeable.

As far as Jax was concerned, tension was understandable... but again, his patience for irrational yelling was nonexistent. The humans' tendency to snap at each other when under stress had never made much sense to the lion, and today he wouldn't accept much of it before he hammered the table. There needed to be focus in this room.

For her part, Sarah agreed entirely, though she certainly didn't feel like her old self. Once upon a time, she'd have simply commanded the meeting, brought order through force of personality. That wasn't a card she felt she would be able to play anymore — it would require confidence, and she wasn't entirely sure she had any of that left.

But she wouldn't reveal that to her officers, and even if the Earthers noticed they'd have the sense not to point it out. Not now. Not when the Genesis survivors needed a place to settle, and all terrestrial species needed to establish a safe frontier.

As the leader of the people of Genesis, she needed to take responsibility for a lot of that work. Gods help her.

She was still seeing flashes of her chaotic capital city in her mind's eye. Her hurried escape, and the terror and chaos. Everything she'd already failed to *stop*, everything the Church had gotten away with...

Not the time, Sarah. For Gods' sake, not the time.

And if she could help it, there wouldn't be a time. Not for quite a while, anyway.

Realizing that Jax had just cast a prompting glance in her direction, she offered a quick nod, "Very well, let's try to get something sorted out here. Audrey, I'd hoped to speak to James about finding a place to settle our survivors on Freetown — there are a lot of civilians, I know, but not so many as there... *might* be."

Audrey DeBrooke's face tightened and she swallowed. As her eyes met Sarah's, the President realized suddenly that something was wrong, "James?"

The question drew a jerked nod from Audrey, "Fluke shot. Faithful put a missile into his bridge..."

Sarah hadn't read that report yet, a fact she now regretted. She'd been given one... but honestly she hadn't thought that any small action between Faithful and Freetown Fleets could be of much interest given the circumstances. She wasn't a fleet commander any more, after all. And she'd spent the whole trip trying to sort out the list of survivors, figuring out supply situations, and admittedly staring aimlessly at walls and floors, hoping to make her mind accept the loss of her planet.

But she couldn't afford to stray down the brooding path...

Audrey struggled with a similar determination. She'd lost her husband of four decades with one brutal missile — a missile that shouldn't have gotten through, but did. It was a freak occurrence, a barely possible shot... and it had connected.

So she was left alone, with a colony of free humans looking for leadership, and reasonably assuming that because Audrey was co-founder that'd be her role. She'd save them, surely, but she didn't feel any more up to that task than Sarah did to hers. And unfortunately, the Freetown constitution wasn't helping too much — it was vague, riddled with thirty-ear-old loopholes that were supposed to have been closed, but which they'd never gotten around to working on.

Now the government scrambled, and Audrey was obliged to take this meeting — to deal with these haughty ArcGenerals, who had never fought the Kroggs, and who were in little better psychological state than she was. This was one of those situations, laden with shock, that wasn't destined to turn out well.

Jax saw that plainly enough, "Right now Freetown is facing a constitutional crisis, so Audrey has stepped in until somebody can figure out what exactly is supposed to happen. Sarah, I hate to say this, but you're a President without a... well, *coping* with what's just happened. And–" he turned and scowled at the ArcGenerals "–I don't even *know* who you two are."

The male ArcGeneral's eyes found Jax's very briefly, "ArcLieutenant-General John Togo, sir."

Grinding her jaw, the woman took her turn, "ArcLieutenant-General Kelly Rozhestveski, sir."

Sarah leaned forward in her chair, "With Graham... gone..."

She'd managed to avoid thinking about her brother. The scope of the loss of Genesis could mask a lot, but now as she said his name she felt a twinge in her stomach. She almost winced, but forced her words forward.

"They're sharing fleet command. John has the cruisers, Kelly the capital ships. Overall command hasn't been an issue since we left Genesis space... I've been holding down any central work that's needed to be done."

"Indeed," Jax leaned back in his chair and scratched at his wiry mane. "Looks like everything around here is ship-shape, doesn't it."

To everyone's surprise — including, to an extent, Jax himself — there was a sizable sum of impatience in the words. Sarah's eyebrows shot up, and all the humans turned to stare at him. Hobbes frowned at Locke, and Locke at Tarkam.

"That seems just a little insensitive, Jax," Sarah began, but the Earther held up his hand.

"It does, probably. But I'm not going to try to be as enlightened as most of my fellows right now, and say something comforting and philosophical. I know you and Audrey will find a way to survive this, because that's what people like you do. I don't know anything about you two ArcGenerals, and I know that Ron, Tom and Alix here are all rather surprised at me. But I wasn't the king diplomat when I got this job, and like the rest of the people at this table, I think I'm in a state of shock. So you'll forgive me for getting right to it."

The exhausted and frustrated humans gaped at the Earther Admiral. He peered back at them with a baleful expression and a crotchety stare.

"Now, none of you are in any state to pull together the defense of Freetown, and I'm not going to sit here and watch Omega roll in and take over because you all refuse to stop blaming each other," his eyes shifted from Sarah to the ArcGenerals to Audrey, and he leaned forward. "I'm taking command of this system, until I'm relieved by a commanding officer more capable than me. Which means no one in this room."

The three other Earthers at the table sat back awkwardly — Jax wasn't being very delicate with these humans, and after all that had happened...

Togo lurched forward in his own seat, "You have no *right*! The Genesis Fleet is ours, we got it out of Genesis, *we* command it..."

"Which is great. You've got your cruisers, and Kelly's got her battleships. Peachy. But you're going to put them where and when I tell you, ArcLieutenant-General. Because if I leave you all here to fight about it some more, Omega will arrive, and your ships will become *his*," Jax's tone was unimpressed.

Rozhestveski now bristled, "Look Admiral, you don't know what we've just been through–"

Jax cut her off impatiently, "Lost your planet, families, and so on. I know, because I lost *my* daughter at the same time. I also know what Omega has done. Which means something professing to be *my* God, something I carried out into the cosmos, is responsible for billions of deaths. I won't pretend that all qualifies as even close to the same, but I am feeling a bit displeased myself. Enough so that I'm not going to try to tolerate your inane inabilities to work together unsupervised. Finger pointing gets us nowhere right now. If you don't work with the Freetowners it'll be as good as giving this system up to Omega. Take my meaning?"

Audrey realized her mouth was open, but she couldn't think of anything suitable to say. If Jax took fleet command in system, she'd have time to sort out the situation on Freetown without having to worry that some green-gilled ArcGeneral would leave her colony open to invasion. She slowly began to nod as the thoughts processed.

Jax noticed her out of the corner of his eye, his instincts picking up on her positive reaction, but kept his glare fixed on the young ArcGenerals.

Togo's face was twisted with a mix of anger and desperation, "Madam President, it isn't his place to…"

Sarah was shocked by Jax's take-charge move, and by his lack of diplomacy in explaining why none of the humans at the table was better suited than he was for the job. However, unlike her junior fleet commanders, she knew that this was how Earth functioned: Earthers who knew they were fit for a job did it, or acquiesced if someone even better qualified came along. It wasn't ego-stroking or vanity, they simply wanted things done.

Personally, she feared she wouldn't have the nerve to lead this battle fleet into a fight with Omega, even if doing so was technically her job. Jax would look after things until someone better arrived… or she recovered…

"No… it is his place. He is quite right. Our best chance now is to unify command, and we cannot afford infighting. Not with so few of us alive, John. Jax taking command will allow me time to find a place for our civilians, Audrey the chance to sort out her constitutional position, and you and Kelly the chance to work with the Earther and Freetown Navies on equal terms. I endorse his decision."

Common sense! These new kids are too young to understand some things… Jax allowed himself a thankful smile as he nodded to Sarah, then looked back to everyone else.

"For now, I think we cut this meeting short. Cool our heads a little. Sarah, you have a lot to sort out… I might even recommend you head to Earth to talk this over with Setter and Varnon. I honestly don't know what the overall strategy is going to be, but you should be in on shaping it. Audrey, could you give Ed Jeffries fleet command, at least temporarily?"

Slowly processing the Admiral's words, Audrey nodded.

"Good. Then let's have him, John and Kelly back aboard in say… three hours. Meantime, we'll get the civilian ships out from the midst of the Genesis Fleet, put them somewhere safe."

There were absent nods as Jax delivered his orders, and as he saw the humans slowly process them, he came to his feet, "Good. That's it for now."

Turning on his heel, Jax Furgus left the room.

Despite his tactless assumption of command, people felt better for his leadership.

CHAPTER 3

Recently recalled Vice Admiral Artie Tigar was fairly pleased with his Naval headquarters. It was familiar and comfortable... owing to the fact that it was actually his office.

The same office from which he ran his museum, which happened to be his same old office aboard his former flagship, the 150-gun *Agamemnon* — one of the dozen ships he and his museum maintained.

All the great ships from the Krogg War were here at the museum. Orbiting New Halifax's second moon, one could find *Orion, Agamemnon, Endymion, Algenon, Atlas, Vulcan, Cerberus, Inferno, Flame, Joseph Barron*, and a couple of others, all hitched to a central docking column that hung above the moon's unoccupied surface.

It was a great museum, seeing tens of thousands of visitors a year, with enough interest to more than justify the upkeep of these forty-year-old warships.

And, to keep things simple, Artie ran his museum affairs from his old ship, *Agamemnon*. He kept an apartment on the first moon of New Halifax, but more often than not he stayed aboard ship when the museum closed. He was very fond of *Agamemnon*, though his habit of spending time alone in an aging First Rate convinced some that he was insane. He was keen on keeping his rapport with the old veteran intact, though he didn't know quite why he'd need to...

But then, present circumstances were making that desire to remain close to *Agamemnon* seem less foolish, because he was about to run up his colors on *Agamemnon*'s transponder. The New Halifax squadron would soon be under his direct control.

Sitting in his office-cabin, Artie looked over the statistics of the fleet here at New Halifax, and was fairly pleased with what he saw. New Halifax, and more particularly the nearby hyperspace corridor, were constantly watched by a sizable Earther force, including sixteen *Champion*-class ships of the line, eight *Cerberus*-class frigates and eight *Active*-class sloops.

Those ships were organized into two equal forces, each taking week-long shifts at the blockade station before rotating in to New Halifax for some rest. The need to support that blockade force had helped the once-tiny colony in the system grow to a remarkable size, and it now boasted 175 million Earthers in a number of surface settlements and in orbital accommodations.

Artie was taking command of the forty-eight ship New Halifax Squadron, and Lab Forepaw had already promised him a solid recommissioned force in support. In addition to what was already at the museum, eighty-eight ships were on the way, fifty-six of them of the line. The number of guns at New Halifax would be substantial enough — no Omega scheming would go unchecked on Earth's flank.

Artie just needed to pull all these disparate vessels together into a cohesive force, probably centering around the mini-*Venerables* — properly known as the *Champions*. Those sixteen ships weren't as powerful as the vessels that made up the front line force of the Earther Navy, but they packed a sizable punch all the same. Though they only had 100 guns, each carried sixty boats, making them easily on par with the likes of *Orion* in terms of overall firepower.

Yes, this should work out well enough... with the First Rate squadron I'm getting from recommissions, I'll have three full heavy capital ship units, backed with plenty of 74s... I suppose the only question is what I'm supposed to do with them all...

And that was indeed the question. Artie certainly didn't mind holding New Halifax, but somehow it seemed unlikely that the planet would come under much threat from Omega — at least not at first. The corridor would be of interest, but to get to it the plague would have to run up awfully close to Earth, and Lab Forepaw had three squadrons of *Venerables* and countless 74s at his disposal — it didn't seem too prudent for Omega to just come blazing this way.

Still, no one quite knew what a self-professed God was going to do...

There was a chime, and Artie blinked and looked up from his notes, "Come on in."

The doors parted and a young Rear Admiral stepped into the cabin. Artie came to his feet and nodded to the nominal commander of the New Halifax Squadron, one lioness by the name of Minnie Maximane. Daughter of Draco Maximane — the creator of the Earther gunboat service, and a lion with a singular sense of humor when it came to naming his only daughter — she had been with the Navy for about thirty years, and had proven herself as clever as her father in war-games for that entire time. With the Navy being so relatively small, and with so many of the Krogg War officers retired, she'd risen up the promotion ladder quickly, and the blockade battle group had been her charge for two years now.

Of course, Artie was about to relieve her of command — battle experience had to supersede war-gaming credentials when things got as chaotic as Omega was trying to make them. She didn't feel at all slighted, as it was rather obvious that a legend of the Krogg War was better suited to combat command than she was.

"My squadron just rotated in off the rift blockade, thought you might need to talk to me," she stood opposite Artie but the tiger waved them both to comfortable armchairs.

"Yes... I'm guessing Lab sent you a pod about the change in command?"

She nodded, "Got it two days ago. Command is yours, and rightly so."

Artie shrugged, "Alright, but I still want you commanding your battle group. I'm thinking we'll split our fleet when the recommissions arrive — I'll fly my flag from *Agamemnon*, and you stay aboard *Galahad*. Then I'll take overall command, as well as direct command of the recommissions, and we can operate that way. Whatever happens, I'll want your newer ships serving as the vanguard — I'm sure the modernized 74s will be up to a fight, but you'll be much more mobile."

Maximane nodded slowly, "Sounds good. Will we be moving everyone up to the corridor for the blockade?"

Artie leaned back in his chair and 'hmmed' thoughtfully. He'd been wondering about that for the past couple of hours — the corridor was a good seven hours outside the New Halifax system, and another forty-eight hours from Earth. If he didn't have enough force at its mouth, and Omega somehow started trying to force the breach, the smart money said he wouldn't be able to bring up reinforcements in time.

But to leave nothing but good luck in orbit of New Halifax seemed no better...

"I have to ponder that some more, I suppose. Right now, I'll worry about getting volunteer crews for these ships called up from the colony... I'm thinking I'll send most of the museum ships up to Earth, and keep the rest of them here. Having *Orion* in Earth space might be a morale boost for Setter, Andra and Sarah."

Maximane nodded, "Sounds fair. For now I suppose we'll just wait for the reinforcements to arrive."

Artie blinked thoughtfully, "I don't like having your force split, Minnie... why don't you call in everything save for a sloop or two to keep an eye on the corridor. Right now if Omega starts launching assaults, he'll run up against strong forces in all our systems. If he's got enough strength to overwhelm us or Earth, half your task force wouldn't be able to stop him at the mouth of the corridor."

Offering another nod, Maximane slowly stood, "I'll head back to *Galahad* and send a pod. You want to save one of your pods and send your dispatches along to Admiralty House with mine?"

Raising an eyebrow, Artie shrugged, "Your pods are probably faster than the old ones *Agamemnon's* carrying anyway. I'll make sure my messages are in your database by the time you get back aboard."

Maximane bobbed her head a last time, then began to turn away. A thought stopped her in mid-movement, and she looked back to Artie, "You expect we'll really see action out here?"

Artemis Tigar looked thoughtful for a brief second, then grinned, "Now that you've said it, I'm pretty sure there's no getting away from it."

Her eyebrows rose, and then with a slight shrug and a sigh, Rear Admiral Maximane left.

Artie watched the door close and wondered about her question.

Would Omega come this far?

"Well you're not going to have a clue 'til he does or doesn't," Artie muttered to himself.

He started looking for a pad on which to write dispatches.

CHAPTER 4

"So we have no idea what Omega will try first."

Supreme Consul Setter Caine sat back in a briefing room chair aboard *ENS Venerable* and nodded in reply to the statement. The other Earthers in the room mirrored his gesture, and as they did, the speaker — First Lord of the Admiralty Labrador Forepaw — acknowledged them with a shallow nod of his own.

Looking from veteran to veteran, neither Setter nor the First Lord could see any expressions revealing insight — and that in itself was startling, given the company they were in.

There was Varnon Broadpaw, First Consul and nominally the civilian leader of Earther society, only recently superseded by Setter's self-appointment as Supreme Consul. The wolf had fought the Krogg War from start to finish, was always formidable with a battle fleet, and was one of surprisingly few high-ranking Earther Admirals to make it out of the siege of Krogg. Names like Draco Maximane and, of course, Savanna Felix came to mind with that thought.

The Comptroller of the Navy, Dran Nightclaw, was perhaps the greatest cruiser officer the Earther Navy had ever seen — only Andra Ursla could contest him for that title — and he sat back in his own chair impassively, projecting his usual calm.

Finally there was the biggest Admiral in the Navy's history — literally *biggest*, of course — Andra Ursla herself. She scarcely needed introduction, having led the Second Fleet through the entire Krogg War, and destroying her foes more times than any average observer could recall. Now she sat back next to Caine with steepled fingers and slowly shook her head, "Lab, you've been through both levels of the Admiralty staff with this, we're not going to have anything more for you right now."

Setter looked from his bear friend to his once-Flag Captain and nodded in agreement, "Sorry Lab, but believe me, I've been trying to figure Omega out... and nothing."

Forepaw tilted his head and let out a breath, "I figured as much... just about now I'd take *any* ideas as to how to deploy, but you're right, it's impossible to get the measure of this enemy without having faced him... so we're just going to have to come up with deployments that maximize our strength."

Despite his somber mood, Varnon looked up at the remarks, "The Admiralty have the plans drafted yet?"

His tone lacked its usual jovial, optimistic, and friendly qualities — it was flat, *dead* even, and he knew it.

Almost as dead as my daughter and my son-in-law, he thought, but immediately put a stop to that musing.

Like Jax Furgus, Varnon had much to mourn with the loss of *Renown*. Varnia skippered that ship well, and she'd done the right thing in closing the corridor to Omega, but the sensor readings from *Unity Genesis* were conclusive: the corridor's collapse had annihilated all matter within.

Varnon wasn't a parent anymore.

He was pressing on with his job, and his overall performance as First Consul wasn't suffering because of his sadness. However, the upbeat, friendly Varnon that so many of his colleagues had come to rely on was gone.

Setter hoped they'd see a happy Varnon again, but thinking of how he'd feel if Phealan had died in such a way to such a foe, the Supreme Consul couldn't imagine rebounding from the loss.

For his part, Lab ignored the darkness in Varnon's tone, and merely nodded in answer to the question, "I've got two basic plans with a number of variations for us to play with... they were tailored to deal with different potential styles of opposition, but since we have no way of knowing which style it'll be, I want to go over it with you four."

Ursla raised an eyebrow, glanced sideways to Setter, then nodded, "Let's see it."

Coming to his chair at the head of the briefing table, Lab tapped the room's holo projectors to life, "Alright, the two basic variations first: Home Fleet either stays home or goes to Freetown."

Two identical starmaps appeared over the briefing table, one showing the white transponders of Home Fleet stationary in Sol, the other moving them through space to the privateer colony.

"Either case, I want to keep as many recommissions in system as I can," Forepaw went on. "Fox took the four squadrons of *Chimeras* with him, with fourteen squadrons of Krogg War ships in boxes to be put together when he gets to Gibraltar. They're an even split, seven squadrons of the line, seven squadrons of frigates and sloops. He'll be in good shape out there when he combines with Garvin and Karl at Gibraltar."

Just after receiving first word of Omega, Fox Magnus, the intrepid First Space Lord (the officer who represented the First Lord of the Admiralty in space, allowing Forepaw to stay in Sol to run the fleet), had shipped straight for Gibraltar and Krogg with reinforcements. The thirty-two *Chimera*-class ships of the line he commanded were even older than the *Champions*, and were essentially third line units. But between those ships and the Krogg War veteran vessels they were towing in hundreds of giant crates, Fox had a mighty force at his disposal. As Lab had said, when he got to Gibraltar and met up with Garvin Jardaw's fleet

— which included numerous first line units, *Venerables* not least of them — that front could be considered reasonably secure against Omega's advance.

Or so they hoped.

That was the problem. No one really knew what Omega would come out with, just that the plague would do everything in its power to overcome Earther resistance. That prospect was unsettling, to understate it wildly.

"We're recommissioning ships about twice as fast as expected," Nightclaw put in smoothly. "The yard crews are well aware of the gravity of the situation — we'll have about eighteen squadrons by the middle of next week, and that's in addition to what we've already committed to New Halifax."

As Comptroller of the Navy, Nightclaw's job was to maintain the machinery of the fleets — ships, crews and stations. Anything about the service not related to deployment and strategy usually crossed his desk, and given the circumstances, the Navy was very lucky to have such an officer in control of the remobilization.

Varnon, Ursla and Setter exchanged quick glances and then looked curiously to Forepaw. With so much social discomfort after Omega's announcement last week, neither of the Consuls, nor the retired Admiral had been briefed on the Admiralty's commitments to New Halifax. But Forepaw was well ahead of the questions, and the ships being sent now scrolled through a window floating in the map projection.

"I'm giving Artie Tigar a lot of support," Lab said quietly, "I hope he won't have to use it, but I think it's best we make the commitment. Frankly, I wouldn't expect Omega to go for New Halifax, but because I don't expect him to, I almost think he will... to try to take us off guard... but then I start second-guessing."

"Actually, that's already second-guessing," Ursla said with a subdued smile, and Lab looked from the maps to his old comrade.

For a moment the First Lord frowned, then a small smile formed on his face, "Yes, I suppose it is. See the dilemma?"

The mild humor lightened the atmosphere just a bit — there had been little of the last war's optimism lately. Not that, thinking back to the days of the war against the Kroggs, Setter would have considered himself very optimistic... it was just that in those early days, the Earthers had been *younger*, fresher.

These were the same leaders dealing with a new war — for humans a forty-year gap between wars might be considered long, but it fell essentially within the same generation for the Earthers. And this time it was against Omega.

So no one was able to elevate the morale to a particularly high level — Ursla's joke had just slammed into the glass ceiling on good moods that seemed to be holding everyone in their darkened state. Only action, and the belief that they were doing some good, might alleviate the overriding tension.

"Well, Artie aside," Ursla's smile now faded, "we need to think about Freetown. I'd advise against sending out the Home Fleet right away — as long as we're strong in all three systems, I think our defense is pretty solid. It'd be too easy for Omega to slip past Freetown and hit Earth undefended if you ship out."

"Best wait to see what Sarah thinks of the state of her fleet. Without Graham especially," Varnon's words were in the same grim monotone — Graham had been a good friend, as had Gillian Hodge, the ArcGeneral's now-Omega wife.

Lab offered nods to all the comments, "I tend to agree. If we send anything, it probably should be recommissioned too — they're going to have the Freetown Fleet and the Genesis Fleet in system as it is."

"Assuming they get along... I heard Jax was going to try to take command. Any word from him yet?" Setter scratched his chin thoughtfully, recalling the ample strain that had existed between the privateers and the Genesis Fleet during the old days, and even between the wars.

Lab shook his head, "I got that message yesterday too, but no pod yet telling me how it went. Though knowing Jax, I imagine he's running the show out there by now. He'll be setting everything up as best he can... once we hear from him we'll be in a better position to deploy."

Again, slow nods rounded the table, and silence returned. Setter looked to Ursla with a raised eyebrow, then glanced at the other three Earthers, "So is that it then, Lab?"

Forepaw frowned, then tilted his head, "For now I suppose it is. Not as many updates as I thought I had, for some reason. I'll probably head back down to Admiralty House soon, just to check in on things..."

Setter smiled, "Awful tempting to run the show from your ship, isn't it?"

Lab shrugged, "I hear the last guy who did wasn't half bad. But I also hear his Flag Captain was much more handsome and charismatic than he was."

Caine grinned at the remark, and Ursla chuckled.

"Fair point," Setter slowly came to his feet, "and enough to drive me out of the room. I'm sure I can find something to do. Coming Varnon?"

The First Consul nodded and stood as well, "Indeed. We should probably start preparing for an influx of Genesis refugees... just in case."

As the Consuls stood, Ursla came to her feet as well, "I'm going to catch a ride with them too."

Lab and Nightclaw, the only serving Naval officers in the room, both nodded, the First Lord speaking up, "Alright. I'll keep you up to speed."

As the trio of veterans filed out, a thought crossed Forepaw's mind, "Andra..."

Ursla stopped and turned, "Yes?"

"When I start sending ships to Freetown, I'm probably going to want you at their head, if you don't mind. Jax will undoubtedly need all the help he can get, dealing with the humans and whatnot."

With another slow nod, Ursla smiled, "Humans? My specialty."

With that, she left, and Lab and Dran Nightclaw talked fleet business.

CHAPTER 5

Unity Genesis was making a solid 2,985 cee on its run towards Earth, and at that relatively blistering speed, the Superdreadnought was about thirteen hours out of the Sol system. On the bridge of the ship, sitting again in her brother's old chair, Sarah watched the clock tick.

Now that she was away from the refugee fleet, she almost wanted to be back with them in Freetown... but there wasn't anything for her to do there until Audrey sorted out the situation of government in the young republic. There was no way she would land the survivors at Freetown if they were only going to get limited assistance from bitter renegades.

Perhaps that was harsh, but Sarah was somewhat unsure of the population of Freetown. She knew Audrey well, and would trust the co-founder of Freetown with her very life... but the population of the colony had been suspicious of Genesis ever since the Church had started flexing its muscle in Congress after the Krogg War.

The Earthers, on the other hand, would never turn away people in need, which meant Sarah needed to talk to Varnon and see if he could reopen a couple of the human towns on Earth that had been closed down over the past few decades.

Immediately after the Quest, millions of humans had come to call Earth home, but with the Krogg War raging and with the privateers opening their colony, most of the Naval officers who'd taken up residence alongside the Earthers had left to help build Freetown. The Crusaders who'd stayed on Earth had moved back to Genesis at the request of Harvey Bingham — they constituted the millions of moderates he'd used to soften the ranks of the Crusaders for two decades, until most of them retired.

Unfortunately, none of the moderate Crusaders had been able to get regen — none who'd undergone the treatment were allowed into the Crusader ranks by the Chancellery, and of course, the Church had gotten the process banned on Genesis, even over Bingham's objections.

The moderates were all long dead, and Earth's human population numbered in the tens of thousands. But if Sarah got her way, that would soon change.

Unity Genesis was carrying her to Earth to petition the Earthers for sanctuary, while her ArcGenerals Rozhestveski and Togo tried to shake the Genesis Fleet back into fighting condition, under Jax Furgus' watchful eye.

So much uneasiness... so much shock...

Well, Sarah decided silently, she'd just have to keep dealing with it.

That was the same decision she'd made about half an hour before, and half an hour before that, and before that, and before that...

So far, simple determination was the best she could manage. She'd hold fast to it.

Patrick Conroy sat silently in his chair, staring at the book in his hands.

He wasn't actually reading it, of course — he was on the same page now that he'd been on two weeks prior. While he'd been known to rarely go anywhere without a book, he was frankly surprised he'd even thought to take this one along with him during the evacuation of Genesis.

How could he care about history at a time like this?

Well, he was a bestselling historian, and that probably explained why he would try to look to the past to try to make sense of all that had happened. But why was he trying to read right *now*, while his wife sat rigidly on the bridge, trying to determine the fate of Genesis society? It was a question he kept asking himself, even though the answer was quite evident.

Lying on the couch across from his chair was a teenage girl, damned near catatonic with shock and in no condition to be left alone. She was Claire Schaeffer, and after he'd abided by the pleas of her father to take her off Genesis in Sarah's pinnace, he'd watched the girl's downward spiral into darkness. At first Christine — the elder Schaeffer sister and Graham's assistant — had been there to ease Claire's pain, but then she'd gone off with Graham and died.

Claire's response to all this had been to shut down.

She'd eat occasionally, sleep irregularly, and spend much of her time just doing nothing. While Sarah tried to save her people, Pat found himself in the awkward position of trying to save this girl — and he was painfully aware that he was horribly unqualified for the task.

He'd tried just about everything he could to bring her around, from nattering on about music and films, convincing her to join him on walks in the ship arboretum... but nothing was getting through. She seemed to Pat to be like the living dead, feeling nothing because if she dared to come out of her shock the pain would be too much to bear. Pat could hardly blame her for her unresponsiveness. She'd lost everything but her life.

After a week in transit from Genesis, a couple of days in Freetown and now another day and a half on the way to Earth, he'd given up trying to engage her with activities. In bygone times he might've been more enterprising... but his enthusiasm was finite, and he was trying to save enough to remain the optimist with Sarah.

Someone on this ship needed to act as though this was just another problem for them to deal with — someone had to avoid thinking of the genocide. Pat wasn't sure if that was possible for a human, but he had to try. At least until the Earthers handed Omega his ass and they could really start putting everything behind them...

So Pat had relegated himself to the role of companion. Sitting, apparently reading, fixing crude but effective meals on the rare occasions when Claire seemed hungry, and basically staying nearby in case her status changed somehow.

At times he worried she'd attempt suicide. She'd been virtually silent since the fleet had left Genesis space, acknowledging only when necessary and either with gestures or monosyllabic words. Her inactivity and shock were deeply disturbing... every night as he watched her head into her bedroom and went back across the hall to his cabin, he wondered if he'd turn up the next morning and find her with wrists slit in the bathtub.

Ooh, really good with the cheery thoughts.

To his own credit, he'd been enterprising enough to plant a health-sensor in Claire's cabin that would set off an alarm in the medical section if her vitals dropped to critical, and she'd probably be saved. It would thus take a very unlikely series of coincidences for her to kill herself, but then, it took a huge number of vicious coincidences for Omega to capture Genesis. Pat couldn't rule anything out anymore. He still worried.

To be fair, though, Claire hadn't taken any drastic action at all. She just sat, lay down, stood, and stared.

For now, that was better than many of the alternatives.

Pat just wanted to figure out how to get her out of that loop on the positive side — surely it had to be possible. She *had* to be able to move on... somehow... after the murder of her whole family...

Right, that seemed highly likely.

Again with the optimism — better watch it, or you'll start sounding like an idealist.

Pat almost frowned at himself, but managed to hide any change in expression behind his book. He glared at the pages, and reread the page number again. It was neither insightful nor useful in any conceivable way.

He wanted an answer to this — he wanted this burden gone. He'd be ashamed to say it, but he needed to get Claire off his mind as much as he wanted her to feel better about the situation. He had Sarah to support, he couldn't handle helping her *and* Claire at the same time. Not for much longer. And as much as he wanted to help Claire, Sarah came first.

But what to do? Claire would need many weeks to recover, so he'd have to move her to someone else's care. He couldn't simply hand off a vulnerable teenage girl to somebody for counseling — he wouldn't trust anyone, not with Claire in this state. Some well-meaning therapist would find a way to worsen things, Pat was sure of that.

So what other options were there? He had this cruise to Earth to figure things out — by the time *Unity* returned to Freetown after Sarah's meeting with the Earther Consulate, Claire would have to be ready to move down to that planet. Combat was on the horizon, there was no way she should be aboard ship for a fight.

Well the answer might be obvious, and staring Pat in the face, but he didn't see it. All he saw was his miserable book — one he'd marveled at two weeks earlier. It was a history of Earthers, in fact, and was now focusing on the first generation of Earthers, including the leader and scholar, Alpha Caine, who, on this page 122, was setting up an estate on the island of Newfoundland.

Pat hadn't been to Alpha's estate, but it was reputedly near Setter's, where the Irishman had spent much time. Maybe he'd visit again, while they were at Earth. Maybe, if he could talk to Setter, he could figure out this situation with Claire.

Maybe... for now she stared at the coffee table, and Pat pretended to read his book.

Unity Genesis hurtled through space.

CHAPTER 6

Audrey DeBrooke sat silently in a chair at the end of *Aboukir's* briefing table, rubbing her head slowly. It ached, and had for days. Nothing the doctors had given her had really gotten rid of the pain — it was as though her mind *wanted* the ache... a physical manifestation of the loss she'd suffered, to make sure it stayed firmly with her.

As though I could forget...

Well, whatever her subconscious was trying to pull, there was too much going on for her to simply sleep, try to recover, reenergize... mourn, maybe... No, there wasn't time for that, and she probably couldn't have slept if there was.

Limited progress was being made on the constitutional issues, with the Freetown Executive Council sorting through articles she and James had written up hastily forty years ago — articles neither had really expected to have to apply to the number of people now in Freetown.

All their work had built what was proving to be a very fragile system...

Her advisors were saying that if there wasn't a constitutional answer to the leadership question by the end of the day, they'd have to go to a plebiscite tomorrow, and the citizens of Freetown could amend the constitution and put someone in charge... or give the power of appointment to Audrey, or the Executive Council...

They'd work out the options later tonight, if it came to that.

More likely than not, it *would* come to that too...

But right now she had different concerns. Technically, she still ran the Freetown Navy, even though she'd handed control of the mobile fleet over to newly-minted Commodore Ed Jeffries. Her control of the service meant that she had to be present at this meeting, with Ed, Togo, Rozhestveski and Jax Furgus. It wasn't going to be fun.

Last night they'd sorted out the combined operations side of things — Jax had been granted overall command of the fleets in system, and now he apparently was ready to start issuing deployment orders. They'd have to meet and approve everything, of course, since this was a strategic matter instead of a tactical one... and Audrey hoped that no one would resist the lion's wisdom.

During the Krogg War, Jax Furgus had had more ships shot out from under him than he could count on one hand, but he'd also managed to lead aged units of 64-gun Fourth Rates to stunning victories between the large battles. With such a haphazard force assembling here at Freetown, his style of aggressive operations could be very useful.

Well, against the Kroggs it would've been. Against Omega… Gods only know.

Rubbing her eyes now, Audrey let out a long breath, and managed not to hear the door open. Her headache was dimming her senses, too, it seemed, and she only realized she wasn't alone when Jax dropped ungraciously into the chair across the table from her.

"How are you, Audrey. How's the pain?"

Lowering her hands slowly, the human blinked a couple of times, "Passable. And you?"

"Old, grumpy… just like yesterday I suppose," Jax leaned back in his chair. "No one else is coming. I commed Ed and told him you could handle this one, and Togo and Rozhestveski are going to meet with me in an hour."

A few more blinks signaled Audrey's inability to quite process that statement — or more precisely, to grasp the logic behind it, "*What*? Why are we meeting now, then?"

Jax smiled, "I'm not grumpy with you, Audrey. We're in similar situations, so I figured we should minimize the agitation as much as possible. I'll deal with the Genesis kid-ArcGenerals so you won't have to yell at them."

"You get along with Ed well enough, why'd you keep him out?" Audrey's brow creased and she leaned forward in her chair. "Is this going to turn into a heart-to-heart thing? I'm not ready for that sort of healing garbage right now, alright. I've got a job–"

Jax held up his hand, and Audrey stopped as his aged eyes met hers, "Remember who you're talking to. I don't coddle, and I know you don't. I need to talk to you frankly about the Freetown Navy, and about the Genesis Fleet."

Audrey cocked her eyebrow, "What about us, exactly?"

"I'm kicking you out of the system. There's no way we can keep you in such close space with these Genesis crews and not have more arguments like the one yesterday. If you guys got into it verbally, I don't want to think about what happens when one of their Destroyers gets in the way of your maneuvers, or some damned thing. You won't go off, but I'll bet your crews' frustration will climb."

To that Audrey had no reply. Jax Furgus' first strategic act was to kick the Freetown Fleet out of its own system?

"What… where do you want to send us?"

Jax leaned forward and tapped the table's holo to life. A star chart of the three remaining Allied systems and Genesis appeared, and the gold markers of the Freetown Fleet were out of the system, deployed in a picket position near the main Genesis-Earth space line.

"I want you where you can see Omega if he runs at us. I'll be moving about a third of Togo's cruisers out as well, but I'm going to spread you in a broad pattern that walls a fair section of the route between here and Genesis, and Genesis and Earth."

Audrey frowned, "But there's no way fifty ships can effectively blockade that much space... Omega could easily go right around us."

"Could, but I'm willing to bet Omega's going to be fairly direct with whatever ships he has... and it'll give our crews something tangible to do. I'm saving most of my squadrons' e-hyper pods to serve as two-way communications with the pickets, and I won't post you more than two hours out of the system. But any warning we get will be useful."

"And," Audrey's words were tired but thoughtful, "if Omega starts probing to see what we're holding in Freetown space, or even wants to start raiding us, we've got cruisers all over the place. And *Republic* there in case we need teeth."

Jax nodded slowly. He'd thought this plan through at length today, and had discussed it Hobbes and Locke. Both officers — despite their radically different approaches to carrier operations — had consistent ideas about the situation here at Freetown. They all agreed the area would be in more danger if all the human factions in the system were left to brood and argue.

A picket line was probably going to be of only marginal use — the Allies had found out many times in the Krogg War that trying to seal open space against any possible travel route was simply impossible. Last time they'd tried, Gibraltar had almost fallen, and Jax was pretty sure he'd left a hand or something on the wreck of his ship that day.

In any case, putting the ships out there was, at least from Jax's perspective, an invitation to Omega to go around, or worse, to start picking them off piecemeal. But the defensive arrangements at Earth, New Halifax, and to a certain extent even in Freetown, wouldn't change. Each system would still have a powerful fleet on station, ready to hit any Omega-ship that came out of the black of space, whether Omega danced around the pickets or not. This just gave the Allies a better chance to see him coming.

And maybe — just maybe — if Omega thought this picket frontier was serious, he'd underestimate the readiness in each system, and rush haphazardly into a slaughter.

No, Jax didn't expect it to happen, but nothing was gained by *not* trying. Scattered pickets wouldn't be so vulnerable, and keeping a watch for approaches would give the humans something important to do.

Audrey, too, could see these potential weaknesses of a deployment, but she couldn't deny the appeal of getting her ships and some of the Genesis Fleet out of the system — heads needed to cool.

There'd be no great risk — if Omega picked off a few pickets, the rest would simply come in, and both Freetown and Earth would be ready and waiting when the plague ships turned up to fight.

"Sounds good," she said at last. "I'll tell Ed, then. He'll take *Republic* out."

Jax nodded, recalling the large dark-skinned officer — a Krogg War veteran, and long ago one of Sarah Manchester and Pat Conroy's Battlecruiser skippers. He'd do well on the picket, no doubt.

"Sounds good. So you go and let him know, and I'll talk to Togo and Rozhestveski," Jax slowly came to his feet, and Audrey felt compelled to match his action.

"I'll have the government situation sorted out tomorrow... though with Ed looking after the fleet I won't have to rush it, which is good..."

Her words trailed off, and as Jax met her eyes he recognized her expression. Exhaustion. And his instincts could recognize veiled desperation mixed in there too. Audrey was fighting hard to retain control of her mind and faculties, and she was winning, but the effort was taking its toll.

She was going day-to-day, rising to every occasion, and it was wearing her out.

Not unreasonable at all, under the circumstances.

"Look..." Jax rounded the table so silently Audrey didn't hear him, and he surprised her with a gentle hand on her shoulder, "once you get the government taken care of, you should find somewhere to get a night's sleep... maybe two. You don't want to run yourself down — we'll need you in fighting trim when Omega comes calling."

Audrey blinked twice to get her mind to focus on the words, and her expression shifted to one of near-futility, "I don't know if I can sleep like that, Jax. They could drug me, knock me out, stasis me... I don't believe I can settle my mind enough right now. I only hope that's temporary."

Sliding his hand off her shoulder, Jax nodded in understanding, "I'm not sleeping well at all myself... but I'm old, so I'm used to being up a lot at night. I just wish nowadays I was getting up for snacks and the use of facilities, instead of hauntings. Do what you can... we'll have to wait to see if this all will really pass."

Audrey nodded slowly, "Yes. And for now we work."

Jax replied with a shallow nod, and Audrey took a deep breath. Without another word, she stepped past Jax and out the door.

As the Admiral stood alone in the room, he thought of his command, his picket, and his situation here in Freetown.

And then he thought of his daughter, and that lasted for ten minutes at least.

After that he left to await the arrival of the ArcGenerals.

CHAPTER 7

"Reactors four and six, coming online… *now*."

A low hum slowly began to fill *Renown's* engine deck, and from the core of the ship, energy flowed. Four other reactors were already running, and seven and eight had been cannibalized to get these last two working, but at least life was finally being breathed into this marooned Earther ship of the line.

Renown, with fully three quarters of its main power grid reactivated, could now fight and fly without threatening to overload its power systems, and without losing systems in dangerous situations. Options were open again.

For his part, Beckett Lupus was just getting his legs back under control — the regen treatments had fully reconnected his spine, but as was always the case after restoration from paralysis, there was a little bit of lag time in the motor skills. The connecting pathways through the spine never knit together exactly the same way twice, so his mind had to get used to a very subtle difference in his reaction time.

Well, that was fine — he could walk normally, just not spar as skillfully as he might have liked. Which was fine too, since there weren't many people keen on sparring right now. The marines of 2/54th had been helping with the reconstruction of the ship, and clearing up the mess in the boat bays. Obviously, the Navy crew had been busy doing much the same.

Indeed, Beckett's only company for the past few days had been an alien friend from forty years back, one Admiral-of-a-Fleet Narosh.

Narosh was recovering well from his lost hand and lost eye — Earther regen tanks were growing replacements for both even now. Doctor Lazarus had things well under control there, and Narosh would have new parts developed from his own DNA's schematics by the end of the week.

And he was looking forward to having them back.

Narosh hadn't felt perfectly Larosian before he'd been carried to Genesis by Omega — indeed, through the whole siege of Laros, the Earther drugs injected into him forty years earlier had dwelled in his blood, and sharpened his mind. Now, he'd benefit from both that heightening of instinct, and from replacement limbs. While the Earthers could probably have grown him a replacement hand and eye had he not had the UDRC in his system, the presence of the compound virtually removed fears of rejection.

But for now, he wore an eye patch and his handless arm rested in a sling at his chest. His silver Larosian armor, shattered as it had been by the ministrations of Omega, had been replaced by a newly-manufactured Earther replica, straight from *Renown's* machine shop. For a warrior who had thought his death was imminent, Narosh felt quite fortunate.

Beckett, standing next to the Larosian as they watched the engineers revive *Renown's* power grid, sensed that feeling of good fortune from Narosh, but he decided not to comment.

"Impressive work, though it does not surprise me at all. Your crews always shared skill and discipline in high measure," Narosh spoke to Beckett, but was purposefully loud enough to allow every Earther nearby to hear him.

The General smiled in reply, "You picked a pretty good ship to get stuck on."

Narosh nodded slowly, then inclined his head toward the hatch behind them, "I expect your wife will be deciding our course now. Shall we head up?"

Beckett smiled, "I'm a soldier, not a spacer. But I'm sure your expertise will help with decisions… who knows, you might even recognize some constellations, if we've got long-range scans online again."

With something that approximated a shrug, Narosh turned to the hatch, and the duo left the engineering deck.

Varnia stood at *Renown's* main battle plot, arms crossed and a frown dominating her brow. The computer had no idea where they were — and if the computer didn't know, it was inevitable that the Cruising Master, the navigator, the First Lieutenant… the entire *bridge crew* didn't know.

Even with the benefit of their long-range detection gear, there was nothing on the scope that could tell them their location.

Their best shot was Narosh — hopefully this space was somehow familiar to the alien. Of course, all the short-range scans they'd shown him so far had yielded nothing conclusive, but the Rear Admiral had to hope things would improve.

Turing to the Third Lieutenant, Varnia opened her mouth to order the Admiral-of-a-Fleet paged to the bridge, but over the young bear's shoulder she caught sight of both Narosh and her husband stepping through the hatch. Good timing.

"We still don't recognize anything," she said as the pair closed with the battle plot. "Narosh, if you could give us *anything*, I'm sure you realize it'd be greatly appreciated."

Coming to a stop next to Varnia, the Larosian nodded. The holo tank had been cycling through scans in front of him, but was blank for the moment, as the Sensor Chief piped a new feed into its computer. The Admirals and the General stood by and waited.

After a moment, Varnia frowned and looked up at the rating behind the sensor panel.

"Sorry ma'am," he shrugged, "we're still reconnecting the relays. Transfer is moving at about half speed."

"It's coming up..." Beckett leaned forward and frowned as clusters of constellations appeared in the plot, and all eyes shifted to the floating fields of stars.

Though she wanted to avoid looking over-eager, Varnia's eyes darted from the constellations to Narosh's impassive face and back. She couldn't tell whether his one good silver eye was shifting its focus or not...

She was actually feeling impatient, and nervous, though the latter emotion was buried as deep as possible. It was odd how tense she'd become over the past hours, as the promise of getting her ship under weigh grew closer and closer to reality.

She really needed the universe to give *Renown* a break.

"Do we know where we are yet?"

The voice came from behind, and both Varnia and Beckett turned to see Graham striding towards the plot. "I heard the reactors come online from the observation deck. I take it long-range sensors have been restored?"

Varnia quickly assessed her human counterpart, and she was surprised by what she saw. For a man living out of an observatory, Graham looked every inch the professional officer. His uniform was crisp, he was clean and well-shaven... maybe Christine had dragged him back to his cabin at sword-point... or not, it didn't matter.

Shaking her head in answer to the question, "By the looks of it, we're as completely lost as I expected we'd be."

Graham came to a stop next to her, studying the constellations with a reserved disdain, "We shall have to come up with a means of dead reckoning, I suppose. Otherwise, we are lost."

"I was born in this system here," Narosh's hand entered the plot abruptly, pointing to a constellation. "And this is definitely the Son's Cluster. That's the human colony in our galaxy. And if I'm not mistaken, this faint star here is Laros' sun. I'd guess we're about a day outside the outer border of the old Empire, assuming travel at 2,700 pls."

Yes, someone could have dropped a pin, and it would have been heard rushing loudly through the air on its way to the floor. Every Earther and human eye on the bridge settled on Narosh. For a moment the Larosian didn't notice, then he looked up, and with his one eye managed a sort of blink-twitch, "I'm sorry, did I say something wrong?"

Varnia cocked an eyebrow, "Did all that regen twist your sense of humor, or are you serious?"

Narosh again managed his shrug, "I'm quite serious, I just couldn't recognize any of it before you got long-range scans back. We're not all that far from the actual exit of the corridor we collapsed... we can make it to the Empire quickly enough, and to our choice of corridors back to your galaxy as well."

As his words faded, a slow sense of triumph began to spread. They had *options*, and they could go *home*...

Of course, fate's sense of good drama couldn't let the positive reign without a nasty counterweight. As the plot blanked again, and slowly glowed back to life, there was a beep. It sounded like a friendly beep, because as far as the computer was concerned, the ships it saw were friendly.

They were Genesis Fleet ships, after all.

But the only Genesis ships that could be out here were ones under the control of Omega — the ones that had chased *Renown* into the corridor just before the Earther ship had fired its hyper charges.

"Ma'am!"

Varnia was already turning to the plot, and she nodded, "Range?"

There was a pause, and the battle plot shifted its focus and zoomed in on the group of Omega ships.

Relative to the Larosian frontier, these ships were 'behind' *Renown*... but there were five of them. And though the sensors weren't getting a clean read on their class, Varnia's happiness of the moment prior quickly vanished, and serious concern took over again.

"They're cruising at 1,400 pls, and they're two days away from our position at that speed. I don't think they've got the sensor range to have seen us, but they're headed in this direction."

Varnia nodded slowly at the report, blinking a few times she did. This complicated matters immensely.

Omega — the *new* Omega — was here too, dammit all.

"Well," Graham said in a strikingly disinterested tone, "I suppose we shall have to do something about them."

Varnia, Beckett, and Narosh nodded slowly in reply.

CHAPTER 8

In Gibraltar space, ships of all sorts clustered together in anchored formations. Around the powerful orbital stations, and near the many portable shipyards, Earther Navy ships and Earther survey ships, mixed with a few human freighters and a number of Earther cargo haulers, sat in almost stunned silence.

They'd remained on station at Gibraltar for just over a week now — since the warning about Omega had come from *Renown*. Gibraltar station was the most powerful Earther position in existence, arguably as well fortified as Earth itself. From this base, ships under Earther and friendly colors could launch expeditions across the vast frontier, just as they had during the Krogg War. These days, though, such expeditions weren't mounted by Battle and Flying Squadrons; they were carried out by ships of the Earther Survey Service.

The Earthers had years ago begun discovering the fate of the planets once occupied by the Kroggs, trying to restore whatever they could, leaving much to recover on its own. Ships had been going out for the past three decades, usually old converted 64-gun vessels with guns removed, gunports locked, and plenty of survey and bio equipment aboard. They were a new Earther fleet — one tasked with a much more pleasant mission than the original one that had brought them out here during the war.

Of course, Gibraltar was also a buffer against Krogg... and Genesis. If either system suddenly began to act up again, the fifteen *Venerables* and forty-eight frigates assigned to the region would be well-placed to deal with the trouble. Hence the continued Naval presence and potency at Gibraltar — it was a deterrent base, and it was under the command of a number of veteran officers whose records alone were a warning to potential aggressors.

Well, that's what was said about them, but for his part, Admiral Garvin Jardaw wasn't so sure that such boasts were warranted. He had never been an overconfident sort of fellow — not back in his first days aboard the 64 *Highlander*, not in his time serving with Draco Maximane aboard *Apollo*, and not even when he was with the old First Carrier Group. He'd held command at this station on and off for twenty years, rotating back to Earth for intervals at home every four years or so. He was actually nearing the end of his most recent five-year term in command, and was slotted to head home to Earth for a few years...

Not that he'd be doing that now. No, he had rather more important things to look after.

Standing in the central C&C of *Gibraltar One*, the same veteran station that had been set up to orbit the granite-covered Gibraltar planetoid decades ago, he studied the glowing battle plot in the centre of the great room. In it floated the most up-to-date telemetry from Earth's e-hyper pod: Lab Forepaw had now begun reinforcing New Halifax in case of an end run to the corridor there, and Freetown seemed to be bustling with ships from all Navies.

But as yet, no one knew what Omega was up to.

The tragedy of all that had happened was still being absorbed at Gibraltar — from Omega's overwhelming of Genesis to the death of James Stanton, everything took a toll on the Earthers and humans at the base. But despite that, Garvin felt he was reasonably secure; he was in a good position here, and soon he'd be in a better one.

In the battle plot, a set of icons marked the Gibraltar-bound relief force under First Space Lord Fox Magnus. The wily old warrior was bringing thirty-two *Chimera*s and 128 *Krogg War* ships in crates, ready to be pieced together in the Gibraltar yards, then taken over by crews of reservists drawn from the Survey Service.

Fox would be at Gibraltar in just about two more weeks — he was taking a wide arc around Genesis to avoid allowing Omega a glimpse of the strength that was going to appear on his flank. Hopefully the plague wouldn't even notice this great Earther convoy's cruise... *hopefully*...

Well, that wasn't up to Jardaw. All that he could do was continue recalling the survey fleet.

"What news from Earth?"

Jardaw's ear twitched at the abrupt question from behind him, and he recognized the voice immediately. Rear Admiral Lang Sandpelt, once of *Flame*, a good friend of both Fox Magnus and Chronos Claw, and now commander of the Gibraltar Squadron, was just entering the C&C.

Jardaw turned to him as he approached, "Not a great deal. Looks like Jax Furgus is taking the lead in Freetown, and Artie Tigar is getting strongly reinforced at New Halifax."

Sandpelt came to a stop next to his commanding officer and the pair studied the holo plot quietly. Not much had changed since yesterday's update, then.

"I'll have our reply pod ready to launch in half an hour," Vice Admiral Karl Kandam spoke as he descended the stairs from the C&C's signal station. The great panda was the longtime commanding officer of the *Gibraltar* space stations, and the administrative Port Admiral in the system.

Slowing on the other side of the plot, he looked up at the glowing holo, then cast his gaze down through the blue light to Jardaw, "We've just gotten word in from the 73rd Survey Squadron. They're on their way in, ETA three days."

Both Jardaw and Sandpelt nodded slowly in reply. Pods and dozens of sloops had gone out to collect the 100-odd Survey Service missions that were spread across the frontier, but even after a week only about half had sent word back acknowledging the recall. Only seven had actually reached Gibraltar thus far, though many more were coming.

The perpetual fear was that the survey ships, which were crewed by both humans and Earthers, would get caught out there by Omega. Jardaw couldn't risk sending out the entire Flying Squadron — or *any* of his frigates — to defend the survey ships. Everything had to be concentrated in case Omega moved against Gibraltar.

So the Admirals at the base were forced to wait and wonder... or to *hope*, actually... to *hope* the ships of the Survey Service could get in safely.

"And we still don't have any idea what Omega's doing?"

Sandpelt's question was sharp — after the loss of *Renown*, a ship detached from his own Third Battle Squadron, he'd been eager to find Omega and bring action. He knew he couldn't rob Gibraltar of its mobile protection without a good indication of where Omega was deploying, and what the plague had at its disposal ship-wise, so he'd been anxiously awaiting any telemetry on Genesis itself.

Unfortunately, none of the e-hyper scout drones they'd sent into the system had come back... and they'd sent plenty, from both Gibraltar and Earth. Omega had evidently learned something from his time inhabiting Earther blood — he was robbing them of information, and doing it rather well.

"Nothing yet," Jardaw gave the obvious answer. "Hopefully Fox will be able to get a good look as he passes by. If not, we'll have to figure something else out."

Sandpelt and Kandam offered slow nods in reply, and Jardaw's eyes shifted away from Genesis to the other planet Gibraltar was supposed to be watching.

"Has Chronos' drone come in yet?"

Kandam frowned, "He's always late with it. We'll probably see it in a few minutes."

And sure enough, a few minutes later the e-hyper daily pod from Krogg rushed into Gibraltar space.

The *Venerable*-class ship of the line *Formidable* sat at anchor above the planet Krogg, and in the flagship's main briefing room, Vice Admiral Chronos Claw was having an interesting conversation.

With a Peacelord named Kragran.

A *Peace*lord, not a *War*lord, and yes, a *Krogg*.

A Krogg with whom Chronos had had many interesting conversations — about civilizations, aspirations, tactics, strategy, lifestyle, technology, and today...

"Iced cream?"

Claw nodded with a smile at the Peacelord's curiously raised brow. The Krogg had only one eye and a protruding ridge above it that could be considered a 'brow', which almost made the expression impossible to read, but Chronos was getting a lot of practice. Kragran enjoyed conversation — and just about everything else Earther — and he was leading the Kroggs down a path that was thoroughly Earther-izing them.

It was even harder to believe than it sounded.

And it sounded *very* hard to believe.

For his first three years commanding this station, Chronos hadn't bought any of it. He'd watched the Krogg *government* establish itself along the lines of the Earther Consulate, with Kragran and the other Peacelords — all survivors of the war — at its head, advocating a more Earther-like society.

Naturally, Chronos had monitored most of the first year of that effort through the gunports of his squadron — literally, since he'd kept the eight *Venerables* he had in system hanging in orbit over the Krogg planet, with at least one broadside aimed at the council buildings on the surface. After all, the Kroggs had started up this new Consulate after thirty-five years of seemingly idle existence on the surface — it was suspicious to say the least.

But, now, five years later, Chronos and many of his officers, marines and ratings had been down to the surface, where they'd been given free access to *everything*, and done thorough analyses of how the Krogg race had evolved in the absence of their Queen. Theirs was no longer a warlike society — even the old soldiers who'd survived the war carried themselves differently.

Chronos' instincts no longer screamed when he was on Krogg, or when he sat in a room with Kragran. He still wasn't entirely comfortable... but he was beginning to foresee a time when he might be.

But getting back to the conversation, "Yes indeed, *ice cream*."

Kragran's voice had changed remarkably from its hiss of bygone days, and now was almost crisp in its formation of English words, "Your ice cream, this is a delicacy dessert?"

Chronos shrugged, "Yep. Now, I also like cake... sometimes I'll have ice cream *on* my cake. That's good."

Kragran moved his head in a slow nod, "I suppose the combination would be pleasing. I do enjoy putting Targ Intestine with Eyes of Mergok occasionally. Soaked in Gornett blood, if I can find it."

Chronos blinked. As much as the Kroggs were Earther-izing, there was still a rather large gap in some regards. Best to dodge commenting on that delightful-sounding Krogg dessert, "Why are we talking about food, anyway, Krag?"

The Peacelord blinked his single eyelid, "You said you were hungry, and I suggested we dine."

Oh right, that had been the start of it, "And I said I was craving dessert, not a meal... right."

Kragran looked curiously at his counterpart.

For a second Claw didn't notice, then he blinked twice and looked up, "What?"

"You haven't told me whether we're going to eat, my friend."

"Ah, right. What Earth foods are you cleared for?"

Kragran tilted his head, "I've had my DNA resequenced to accept all terrestrial foods — I presume that includes your *iced cream*."

A smile formed on Chronos' face, "We're going to the mess then. Now, we'll have to talk flavors on the way..."

The pair of leaders left *Formidable's* briefing room, a testament to the calm in the Krogg system.

CHAPTER 9

Unity Genesis decelerated smoothly from flux, and almost immediately the Superdreadnought found itself passing a squadron of gunboats and a sloop. As the human ship's main screens came to life with detailed sensor pictures of the Sol system, Sarah instantly recognized the Earther deployments. There were pickets everywhere along the Pluto Orbital Plane, each one made up of a sloop and an escorting squadron of gunboats.

Deeper in system, at Io, a squadron of 74s was shaking down — likely having just been reassembled — and then well in-system, orbiting Earth, Sarah recognized the pennant of Labrador Forepaw, and noted the icons of the entire Home Fleet.

As it had been when she arrived on the bridge of *Warlock Prophet* over forty years earlier, this solar system was abuzz, waiting for what seemed an inevitable return. A return even less welcome and far less expected than the one she'd been part of.

"We're being queried by Admiralty House, ma'am."

Though Sarah technically wasn't a member of the fleet hierarchy, the report had been directed right over the head of *Unity's* ArcColonel to her seat. She nodded slowly, and turned her eyes to the main screen.

After a few seconds the screen divided, and as sensor diagrams of the system swirled on monitors all around the main screen, First Lord Lab Forepaw appeared, "Sarah, it's very good to see you again."

The First Lord's tone was somber but somehow comforting, and Sarah took a deep breath and inclined her head, "Likewise, Lab. Glad to see your preparations are going so well."

Forepaw smiled thinly, "We're... doing alright. I'll detail a squadron of boats to you for your cruise in. Mind coming down to Admiralty House when you make orbit?"

"Glad to. See you in an hour."

At first Pat had been determined to go down to Admiralty House with Sarah, but as *Unity* proceeded in-system and Earth loomed closer, he realized there was a complication.

Claire Schaeffer was sitting on the couch, staring out the view port at Earth. She wasn't asking any questions about where they were — she'd probably seen the planet in many movies by now anyway. She was just staring.

He certainly couldn't leave her aboard a Superdreadnought while he went to look for an Earther who could tell him how to help her. Well, he *could*, but it wouldn't be right. So he'd have to wait for Sarah aboard ship and start contacting his Earther friends.

With that in mind, Pat paced over to the desk in Claire's quarters and began calling up the signal grid. He wasn't sure if *Unity's* ArcColonel had opened the grid for general comm traffic yet — as CO of the ship, the ArcColonel had the right to determine if or when the crew could start sending non-military messages. Usually restrictions on such traffic came when it was likely going to be profuse, but it seemed unlikely that *Unity's* crew would be calling too many people on Earth...

As the screen for ship comm came up, the lockout screen flashed. Well that was fine, Pat would just have to call up to the bridge and get a pass–

"Can we go down there?"

Pat was frowning and not particularly thinking, "Well, I'd thought to call instead, but the damned–"

And then it clicked. Pat's head whipped up, "Um... yes. I think we can arrange that. I'll... ah... go get ready. You should too... wear something warm I think — I'm pretty sure it's cool in London."

Forcing himself abruptly to his feet, he hurried out from behind the desk.

For the first time in days Claire had taken the initiative and said something... she wanted to go down to Earth — a convenient two-birds-one-stone arrangement. He could even introduce her to some Earthers, see if their instincts gave them any insight into dealing with her.

This was going to be excellent!

He turned and headed out of the room.

Having forgotten to open the door first, he smacked into the alloy hatch with a pleasant thud, stifled a swear, opened it and walked out.

Sarah sat silently aboard her pinnace, watching through the side windows as the small craft descended towards London and Admiralty House. She hadn't been to Earth for many years now... she'd have liked to visit more, to spend time with the Earther officers and with Elandra Caine, but it hadn't worked out as she'd wished.

She also wished her planet hadn't been infested by a malicious plague. Wishes obviously weren't helping too much lately...

Sarah's grief was intense, underlying everything she thought. It hadn't dulled with time, only been pushed farther beneath the surface of her consciousness. There was no way to be rid of it, nor would she ever want to be rid of it. At least not any time soon... for now she would have to simply force it aside.

Setter could help with that. Setter, Andra and Elandra would each surely have something to say that would help clear her head, make it easier to cope. They always did, didn't they?

If not... well, she'd have to figure something out. She would have to be ready to lead her people again.

And as that thought crossed her mind, Sarah's eyes shifted from the windows to the girl sitting across the isle from her. Claire Schaeffer, a young woman Sarah knew almost nothing about, sitting and staring blankly out the window.

Just as Sarah's gaze settled on the pinnace's unusual passenger, Claire's eyes swept from the window to the President, and locked with Sarah's own. They held the gaze for a moment, and almost unthinkingly Sarah struggled to don a reassuring smile. Claire's gaunt face and empty eyes did not show any response.

"That would be the Atlantic, right there. Not at all acidic, you could swim in it if you liked... though at the more southern latitudes, if you don't like the cold," Pat's gaze hadn't shifted from the window, and he was trying now to capitalize on Claire's interest in this alien planet.

The teenager broke her gaze with Sarah, looking back out the window as a brief spell of turbulence buffeted the pinnace.

Sarah found she'd stopped breathing. Forcing a quick inhalation, she glanced again out the window and at last saw the British Isles. The pinnace was just banking to make the run to London, across the thinly forested countryside of southern England.

"Back in the days before Omega, England didn't look much like this, from what I've read," Pat continued his tour guide explanations. "The Earthers haven't needed much land for cultivation, so they've let whatever would normally grow sprout out here."

Moving at such speeds as they were, London was beneath them in an abrupt flash, and Sarah found herself wanting to get off the pinnace — to get away from the haunted girl. Innocent young Claire was just another reminder of what had been lost... and worse than that, Sarah didn't want to be near someone who'd try to console her, as Pat would as soon as he lost his distraction.

Dammit, that fear of being comforted, of being weak... I have to get past it...

The pinnace slowed and circled as the great Admiralty House compound appeared beneath it. Rebuilt London was in full view all around — glorious and bright, bustling and friendly. It was a major Earther centre, not entirely unlike its predecessor, the city that had been destroyed in the chaos leading up the end of Earth's humanity.

Descending smoothly, the pinnace passengers got a good view of it all, and Sarah watched blankly. Earth was so alive, like all the cities and towns on Genesis had been... bright and crisp, rich and clear...

Come on Sarah, this will do you no good. You must stop yourself.

There was a slight jar as the pinnace's landing feet came down on the Admiralty House fields, and Sarah used the sensation to jerk her mind back to the present. She focused on not hitting her head when she stood up, then watched as Pat stood gingerly and ushered Claire out of the ship.

Then she walked with a façade of assuredness to the exit hatch.

Lab had decided against any fanfare for Sarah. She probably wouldn't have appreciated him turning out the marines for her — he surely wouldn't have wanted them, especially at a time like this.

So instead he stood next to Dran Nightclaw on the pad, watching as the human pinnace settled on its legs, and the hatch swung open. Heavy footsteps came from behind, and he looked back over his shoulder to see Ursla approaching.

"Sorry I'm late," she said with a thin smile, "I was halfway to *Venerable* when I realized you were meeting them here."

Lab nodded, "Sorry, we came down to brief civil defense."

Ursla shrugged absently, "No problem. Where's Setter?"

Lab raised an eyebrow, "Last I heard he was at home, but he wasn't in when I left a message."

"He and Phealan are probably out hiking somewhere," Ursla said thoughtfully, eyes shifting from Forepaw to the pinnace. "He said he was going to take some time now that the initial shock's worn off and Varnon has a handle on things."

"A good idea," Forepaw nodded. It wasn't as though Supreme Consul had a clear job description — the role had simply been invented by Setter so that he could be in position to take leadership if he was needed. That time hadn't come yet.

"I'm sure he'll be here soon enough," Nightclaw put in smoothly, and then the first person emerged from the pinnace.

The three Earthers on the pad were all suddenly very still, their eyes drawn to the unfamiliar young human with the gaunt features and the blank expression. Their instincts reached out next, and immediately the deep wounds in the human's psyche were evident. She seemed tortured, desperate. Who was she?

Pat came out closely behind her, and as they both descended the ramp to the tarmac, he automatically reached his hand out, ready to grab her in case she fell.

Instincts shifted, and now the three Earthers began trading perceptions of the stranger Pat seemed to be looking after... and then they studied Pat. Tired, weary, yet determined as ever to be a source of stability. For both this girl and for Sarah.

Ah yes, and there was Sarah. At the top of the ramp, moving slowly, determinedly, with her mind on the verge of collapse but held fast by sheer willpower. If she didn't take time to deal with all she'd seen, her condition would almost inevitably bring either a breakdown or a long-term detachment from all emotion.

The Earthers' moods darkened quickly — not that they'd been feeling overly optimistic to begin with. As Pat and the stranger waited at the bottom of the ramp for Sarah, Lab forced himself not to stare, but Ursla found her eyes locked with those of the girl.

This youngster didn't seem frightened by Ursla's height or bulk... she didn't seem to care much at all about anything, except the great tear within her soul.

Ursla didn't need instincts to see great pain in the girl's expression.

Sarah passed her two traveling companions and approached Lab. As she came close enough, she extended her hand to the Comptroller of the Navy and to the First Lord in turn.

"Good to see you," Lab said quietly, and Nightclaw nodded to mirror the comment before stepping out of Ursla's way.

The great retired Admiral bent at the waist and gingerly hugged her old human friend — *very* gingerly — and despite herself Sarah managed to awkwardly return the embrace. She even managed to keep her composure, as much as she might not have wanted to.

"We have much to discuss," she said in a cool tone, and Lab nodded.

"Is there anything we can do for... your guest?" Ursla bobbed her head at Claire, and Sarah looked immediately to Pat.

The Irishman smiled up at Ursla with as much enthusiasm as he could manage — a remarkable amount, on Ursla's scale, "Claire Schaeffer... Claire, this is Andra Ursla, Lab Forepaw, Dran Nightclaw. You've probably seen them in movies."

Claire just stared at them.

Pat noted the awkwardness but pushed past it, "I'd like to take Claire around and show her the planet. She'd very much like to see Earth."

Ursla forcibly kept herself from cocking an eyebrow — *Claire* didn't seem to be in a state to do anything of the kind, and that certainly was no fault of her own. But if Pat thought it would help...

"I know a place, and some people who do well with this sort of situation."

Pat's smile seemed to change slightly, and he nodded thankfully to Ursla, "That's what I was hoping to hear."

Ursla nodded, gesturing for the pair to follow her, then looking to Lab, Nightclaw and Sarah, "I'll be in presently. I'll just get them a ship."

The trio nodded, then turned to head inside. Ursla would look after Pat and Claire — or more precisely, she'd send them where help would be available.

Well Setter, here's a job for a Supreme Consul...

They walked to the Earther pinnace that had carried Andra to Admiralty House, sitting nearby on the tarmac.

CHAPTER 10

Phealan Caine knew the woods of his family's estate very well. As a youngster, he'd wandered for many days out in this bush, sometimes alone, sometimes with his parents, and on rare but pleasant occasions, with the local wolves — the members of the species *canis lupus*, the *real* wolves that still existed in their original four-legged form. There was a pack that frequented the estate, and genetic tests had shown it was distantly related to the Caines. The original Caine, a great Earther leader named Alpha, had come from the pack, and now, almost as though successive generations recognized the connection, the wolves remained in the area of the Caine estate.

Today Phealan and Setter had run across them on their hike. The pack's leader and all its members had welcomed the Earthers with the serene and friendly air that always surrounded interactions between the Earthers and their ancestors, and for two hours they'd kept each other company, hiking and introducing themselves to the younger pups, only months old now.

It was a glorious day — unusually consistent in its pleasant weather, at least by Newfoundland standards — and it had thus far served its purpose well.

Phealan had made a pact with his father: today would be a day away from it all. They would hike and talk about regular things. As though Omega wasn't out there. As though Setter was still retired, and all was right with the universe.

Such escapism was hardly typical of the Earther philosophy, let alone the Caine mindset, but on this occasion Setter could hardly have been more enthusiastic about the chance to distract himself. He would stand at the head of his people until the crisis passed... but for the moment he had no real duties to perform. The Consulate was a very efficient government; the Consuls hardly needed him stepping on their toes as the days passed. His specific duty was difficult to quantify, but ultimately Caine had to be ready to step to the front when the Consuls hit a powerful obstacle, or when his unique experience would be needed in the decision-making process. He had the authority to walk into the Consulate and take total control, but until the situation demanded such action, he would not. It simply wasn't his way.

So for now he felt like a fifth wheel. A part of him hoped it would remain that way, because if he remained on the outside it would mean that Omega had been dealt with effectively, without the need for extraordinary sacrifice. Setter knew that would not be how Omega ended, though. He just *knew*.

But he did not want to dwell on that at this moment: today he and his son were hiking.

And Setter was relaxed — happy even. These woods had been home to his own childhood as much as they'd played host to Phealan's. This was *home*, and *peace*. Omega wasn't here now, and if he came, he would have to fight hard to take this place from the Caines... and Earth from the Earthers, for that matter.

But Caine halted that line of thought. There would be no mental war against Omega today.

"So mom's moving her offices to London, you said?"

Phealan was a few meters ahead of his father, descending a relatively steep and perilous slope with ease. There was no trail to follow — Earthers didn't use the same routes through the woods frequently enough to leave trails — but the young Caine, and indeed his father, found no trouble in traversing the rocky and spongy turf.

As they both reached the bottom of the ridge, the elder nodded, "Yes. She was working on the Omega research down at Fengate, but now that she's getting close to something she wants to be nearer to Admiralty House. If we're going to cure humanity, we're going to have to use the Navy as the delivery system... and if the cure can be used as a weapon against Omega, the Navy needs to know."

Phealan hadn't been seeing much of his mother at all lately — she'd been spending long days in her office in Australia, carefully analyzing Earther blood samples to isolate the Omega cells that floated harmlessly through Earther veins. It was through that blood that Omega had been spread to vulnerable hosts, but if a way could be found to cleanse the blood of Omega, a cure for the plague was almost certainly close at hand.

And as one of Earth's leading geneticists, that was where Elandra Caine came in.

Phealan honestly didn't mind her absence today — spending time alone with his father was a treat.

"Well, I'm thinking I might start writing something soon," Phealan's tone didn't change as he used two steps to climb over a fallen tree. "Just don't know what."

Setter smiled at his son's remark, "Well, it's not going to be about romance, is it?"

Phealan chuckled, "She was polite when she turned me down, dad. Cut me some slack."

"Excluding Jax Furgus, name one Earther who *isn't* polite when they say no, son," Setter grinned, and Phealan groaned. With a laugh of his own, Setter traversed a bog hole, "Hey, when I was your age I wasn't doing too bad you know."

"Yes, well good for you father dear," Phealan grinned. "Doesn't change my luck... not right now anyway. I'll get to it in good time..."

Setter glanced at his son with a smile, "Should I have posters made up with 'Desperate' as the headline?"

"I can make my own, thank you very much," Phealan was about to laugh when something stopped him.

The atmosphere had changed — actually, considering they were in Newfoundland and weather systems changed all the time, that wasn't the right way to put it. No, the mood in the woods was abruptly much darker than it had been.

"We have visitors at the house," Setter's face was already sobering. So much for the day off...

Phealan was nodding when his eye caught a furry figure moving through the woods to the left... one of the junior females of the pack, leading the wolves cautiously towards the house to investigate.

Setter saw them too, and began to move forward with a quickened pace — the wolves wouldn't move so cautiously if Earthers had come to visit, so that probably meant there were humans here. Sarah and Pat had been due in sometime today... it was most likely to be them.

But the thought that it was Omega — somehow here already — did cross Setter's mind.

Phealan followed his father at the faster pace, and the last two kilometers to the house disappeared quickly.

Pat cupped his hands around his eyes and pressed his face up to the glass, trying to see inside the Caine house.

"Hello?" he called again loudly, but there was no movement inside.

Ursla had said they might be hiking, and sure enough, it seemed they were. Well that was just dandy then — he and Claire would have to sit on the deck and wait until Phealan and Setter got back. Leave it to the Caines to be enjoying inner peace in the midst of this mess... well, that was why he'd brought Claire to this house. If any Earthers could help her, it was the Caines. Setter and Elandra between them had done so much for Pat and Sarah, the Irishman didn't even know where to begin.

"Well, we'll just have to sit and wait. Sorry about this... they must be out for a hike. I'm pretty sure there's still a table and chairs out back for outside entertaining... back being a relative term, I know, since it's a round house..." Pat was babbling, perfectly coherent thought escaping him. "Anyway, just watch out for the local wildlife, and we'll head back there."

As the big Irishman turned and looked down the stairs to address Claire directly, two amber eyes narrowed at him. *Not* Earther eyes.

He managed not to jump in surprise at the black-coated wolf sitting on the deck staring up at him... almost *sternly*, if Pat had to put an adjective into play.

"Well... uh... hi. Good to see you... though we haven't met."

Of course it didn't make sense to talk to the wolf as if it was an Earther, but it was all that came to mind. But what about Claire–

Pat rocked slowly up onto the balls of his feet and looked down the stairs. Claire had already crossed the deck and descended the stairs, and was now sitting at the bottom, with a couple of wolves lying contentedly at her feet. She was petting them both. *Petting wolves*. One of those things that generally came with a 'don't try this at home' warning.

"Okay, this is way too disturbing," Pat muttered to himself. The wolf's eyes narrowed a little further, and Pat looked back to them, "What? I know you haven't had humans hunting you to the brink of extinction lately, but I've watched the tapes of the old conservationist efforts. You're supposed to be friendly enough, but not *this* friendly or this *therapeutic*."

"Where do you think *we* get it from?"

Pat again almost jumped, thinking for the briefest instant that the wolf had spoken. But then, with a rush of relief, he recognized the voice — the wolf wasn't *talking* to him, it was Setter.

"Well, I don't know that I'd call your bad humor therapeutic," Pat switched immediately into friendly banter mode, turning slowly to smile at the Caines as they came around the deck.

With a last glance at the black wolf, he stepped towards the Earthers, extending his hand, "It's wonderful to see you both. And I mean that — Gods wept, it's been a rough week."

Setter cocked an eyebrow with a mild smile, and as Phealan shook the Irishman's hand he twitched his ear and replied, "A bit of an understatement, but I don't expect revising it would be a good idea."

Pat shook his head, "No... no I really don't think I'll be ready to deal with the scope of that understatement for a long time."

As the Irishman's eyes shifted from Phealan back to Setter, he realized the elder Caine had spotted Claire. For a second, both Earthers digested all their instincts had to tell them about the girl, and then they both looked back to Pat, who shrugged and half shook his head.

"That'd be Miss Claire Schaeffer. Sister to a young lady who'd become Graham's new aide. It was sheer chance we ran into her and her father when we were evacuating Genesis... now she has no parents and no sister, and you both know me, I'm surely not a very good substitute," Pat's low voice betrayed his own distress.

Setter blinked a few times and looked down the stairs at the girl. Pat had brought her here for a reason then... probably to get her some advice that would help her cope with her loss. She was in a terrible mental place, gripped by shock and deeply-rooted anguish that were all too obvious to his instincts. Could he help? Could his Earther philosophies help a battered young human who literally felt she had nothing left to live for?

"I don't know that we can fix anything, Pat. We can try, but I don't have an Earther heal-all for the sort of pain she's feeling," Setter said quietly, then glanced back at his son.

Phealan was frowning now, and he looked from the girl to Pat, "What do you know about her personality-wise... likes, dislikes... favorite food?"

The Irishman shrugged, "I think Christine... that's her sister... said something about journalism. But I really didn't know her before the whole thing started. She was with Beckett when they got out of Darymanis City, and that was a pretty bloody mess... hasn't spoken much since."

Phealan nodded thoughtfully, "Alright."

Pat was about to prod for clarification of what the younger wolf meant, but Phealan was already walking past him. As the younger Caine passed the black wolf on the deck, they exchanged wordless and somewhat amused glances — the Earther and the animal almost seeming to share a silent chuckle along the lines of 'I scared the human but *good*.' Then Phealan descended the steps quickly, and sat down on the opposite side of the broad stairway from the human girl.

She didn't seem to take a great deal of notice, but a couple of the wolf pups bounded over, insisting that Phealan play. He busied them with his hands, and glanced over at Claire Schaeffer, "Pat says he doesn't know you all that well, but he thinks you were interested in journalism."

Claire's head tilted slightly at the remark, but her eyes stayed on the white wolf lying lazily at her feet, enjoying her attention.

"Well," Phealan continued, "I'm thinking I might like to get into writing, though we're not very well versed in journalism out here..."

She gave no indication she'd heard his words, and Phealan's eyes narrowed thoughtfully. The rest of the pups now followed their siblings to play, and he added one foot to the mix to keep them all happy.

"Alright, I know that you know I'm trying to get you to talk, to open up and all that. And I'm guessing you really don't want to, which is actually fine by me. But there's one thing Pat said that I'm not comfortable with at all. Something about you I mean."

For the first time, Claire turned her head and eyes to look at the junior Caine, though she said nothing.

Getting some eye contact at last, Phealan donned a thoughtful frown, "He said he doesn't know what your favorite *food* is. Now it's an Earther tradition to eat much and to enjoy it, and so whether you want to talk or not, I think we should figure out what food you like before you leave here. Alright?"

She sort of nodded.

"Good. I'm Phealan, by the way..." he lifted his arm to shake her hand, but two pups came off the ground with it and he thought better than to drop them on her.

Setter and Pat watched this dialogue with interest — the elder Caine proud of his son's initiative and his balanced way handling of the situation, and Pat grimly elated that Claire was responding.

So as the two youngsters came to their feet, Setter bobbed his head towards the woods, "Let's you and I go talk. I need to know how Sarah's doing. And you too."

Pat nodded slowly, looking away as Phealan and Claire climbed the stairs to the deck and then entered the house.

"Oh and next time wait in the living room, Pat. You know better than to think we have locks on our doors," Setter offered a kind smile to his friend, and Pat snorted a laugh.

As the two turned to head away, Pat caught the gaze of the black wolf, and again the animal's yellow-amber eyes narrowed at him sternly.

"Damn your pack is strange, Setter," he muttered.

As the duo paced around the deck, Pat could have sworn he heard dismissive growling.

CHAPTER 11

Omega loved life.

He also loved the entrails of human teenagers — particularly females. It was best when he kept the girls alive on the table, slit their stomachs and began slowly extracting and eating the organs. He kept them alive so they could watch. Technology was a beautiful thing.

And it was amusing to listen to them try to scream with their diaphragm ligatures lying in a bloody mess on their stomachs.

That sort of thing just *never* got old.

Well, it would eventually. Frankly, all carnage would get old. There were only so many entertaining ways to kill humans, but he was going to find every possible one of them. He had two good reasons for this sadistic pleasure: first it pleased him, and second (and much more importantly) it would horrify the Earthers.

The fucking boy scout Earthers, his creations that had become everything he hated. Omega was recording every grizzly death, and was getting a nice care package together to send them. See how they liked watching a field full of children being eaten alive by their parents. That would be his gift to the Earthers. He'd make them *watch* him. Because now they knew *they* had carried him out to the stars, and given him the chance to do this. They had failed the humans, and they'd get to see Omega's gruesome, almost theatrical carnage in action. Just out of spite, he'd torture billions, and then render their dead bodies into biomatter that he could put to other uses.

That thought brought a smile to the face of Omega-Natosh (the Natosh avatar of the plague). Dabbing his chin with a napkin, he stood up from behind his dining table, then pushed the half-empty corpse of what had been a suitably lovely girl onto the floor for his minions to clean up.

He flashed a bloody-mouth smile at the uninfected humans trapped behind glass in an adjacent chamber, and enjoyed the screams of terror, roars of anger, and whimpering. It was worth keeping some around unchanged just for the entertainment value.

God they were fun to toy with.

As Omega-Natosh left his dining hall, he continued to bask in the feeling of being alive. There was nothing like torture and murder to give him a buzz, *and* he could use it against the Earthers. Talk about your win-wins.

Pacing down a corridor of his central building — one that had once been some sort of government building on Genesis — he thought of some of those vids... ah they made him giddy! Some of his favorites involved skinning. He'd perfected that — taking strips an inch wide and a foot long randomly from the body while it lay on a tray full of iodized salt... it took effort to keep his playthings conscious and alive, but it was *worth* it.

The Earthers were going to *love* it.

By which, of course, he meant be horrified by it. Worse even... it'd just be mind-numbing. The plague's old cattle were so civil, so goody-goody. The only way to counter that sort of over the top goodness was to be even more over the top with carnal viciousness.

Omega-Natosh kept walking through the corridors of his capital, heading to a room for more torture of one sort or another. Minions milled around the corridors, moving uninfected humans, some of whom were screaming, some of whom had given up and could do no more than whimper.

The minions were probably the 'lucky' ones. They had all been human, but their conversions, while excruciating, were relatively quick. Once they were turned into minions, they were little more than extensions of Omega's will. Like fingers on a hand — billions of fingers on a huge hand — none of them thought, they simply acted according to the direction of the greater Omega plague. Avatars like Omega-Natosh were more advanced, thinking minions, used for interaction with humans and Earthers, but the vast majority of minions were essentially just appendages.

Of course, Omega could reconfigure a minion to be an avatar whenever he wished. All his minions possessed infected cells, and it was the telepathic link between these cells that allowed the plague to be a single great mind made up of billions of separate parts. He could retask any one of these parts with ease, and turn it from minion to avatar to a piece of living ship hull. He just liked to keep the number of avatars down — too many could conceivably overcomplicate his mind, so it was better to keep them few and the minions numerous. Besides, fewer, more vicious avatars suited his twenty-first century bred sense of drama and theatre.

In other words, to maximize shock value. To maximize the distress those bastard Earthers would feel when he sent them vids of all that was happening.

Ah, life was good.

Ooh, he could even produce a movie trailer. Humans of Genesis still had movies, just like humans of the twenty-first century. The men and women who'd created him had loved to watch the senseless, unrealistic violence of movie films. Triumph and glory through actors on a screen... Omega could package up some stuff that would make humans realize what violence truly could be.

"Why just shoot them when you can skin their loved ones in front of them, then eat their entrails as they watch?" he muttered to himself matter-of-factly, then frowned. "I better be careful not to seem unbelievable…"

Not that they'd be able to argue with the visual evidence he was recording. Ah, vid was a fantastic medium. So he'd best stop being distracted and get back to his carnage…

Omega-Gillian studied Gillian Hodge's body in the mirror in her quarters aboard what had once been a Genesis Superdreadnought, but now barely resembled a human ship. It was a prototype, with growths of Krogg-type flesh (rendered from the biomatter of dead humans) patched onto it and random bits of other ships thrown on for purposes that were clear only to the plague.

And Omega-Gillian was riding it towards Freetown.

But of course, multitasking was key. No need to focus on just traveling, this was going to be a great segment in the video. Sometimes you had to go big with your torture, sometimes you needed to go small and abhorrent. Omega loved both types.

So Omega-Gillian stripped out of her uniform and found a nice mother-like sun-dress that'd been in her quarters on *Genesis One* — a nice red dress that she could wear to a summer picnic. She fixed her hair, drained the black pigment from the whites of her eyes, then started up the cameras and sat on her couch.

Another of Omega's selves — a lowly minion human spacer sort — then led an eight-year-old girl into the room. As the minion left, Omega-Gillian opened her arms, "Come here honey, it's okay. I'm going to take you to your mommy."

The little girl ran to Omega-Gillian and sobbed as she accepted a big hug. Omega-Gillian smiled and stroked her hair, making sure to make eye contact with the camera as she let the black color creep back into her eyes. Then she bared her teeth in a chilling smile.

"Ah, Graham will love *this*," Omega watched Omega-Gillian's progress with relish, and enjoyed the tastes and sounds and smells.

Omega was also in a human Captain… pardon, *ArcColonel* — wherever the hell they'd gotten that stupid title — named Corbett, in a ship approaching what appeared to be a Freetown picket line. Ooh, whoever was in Freetown was playing mean, sending out pickets… *perfect*.

This demoralization effort was going to go well.

Omega loved being a monster.

ArcBrigadier Kari Peltier sat silently on the bridge of the Genesis Navy Battlecruiser *Paladin Saint*, her flagship, and the fourth Genesis vessel to carry that storied name. With her was a squadron of the best Battlecruisers in the fleet, which were serving as the extreme left flank of Jax Furgus' Freetown picket line, watching for Omega.

There was stress involved with the job, but more than that, there was anger. *Plenty* of anger.

Because her home was gone and the Earthers weren't letting Kari do a damned thing about it. She had one of the best squadrons in the Genesis Navy under her command — people had been calling her the next Pat Conroy for years. She could go home, look around, find out what Omega was up to and help lay the groundwork for an assault.

But no, Jax Furgus was saying wait, and no human in the higher ranks was willing to tell the old Earther to shut up. Kari had once admired the Earthers, but now she was starting to think that, despite what Pat's books had suggested, they were really cowards.

She wanted to fight, but instead she was on the extreme flank. Out in deep space, way off the regular transit routes to Genesis from Freetown, all the action she'd see would involve floating dust...

"Ma'am?"

Kari blinked and shifted her gaze to the officer of the watch. The ArcLieutenant was frowning over the shoulder of one of the sensor technicians, "We've got something on the scope... it's a fluctuation or something. About the size of—"

Paladin Saint was seized.

Omega cheered as the Genesis Battlecruiser squadron seemed to freeze in shock, then desperately tried to scatter. They had no idea what was really going on, they just saw plague-commanded vessels falling onto the hull of their flagship. If they'd been Earthers, they would have started shooting, intent on saving the ship, but like true humans these cowards were instead trying to run away.

None made it to flux drive.

As more of Omega's minions moved their craft to seize the rest of the squadron, Omega-Gillian left her quarters to be suitably cleaned and to supervise the absorption of the new ships into the greater collective.

Omega basked again in life and victory, looking forward to Freetown... to *everything* in this galaxy. And to everything in the other one. Which reminded him, he needed to find the Larosian planets, to start converting all those suffering from his 'Type 1' version so they could join up with his new, 'Type 2' consciousness. It was a shame they weren't compatible without genetic revision, but life couldn't be perfect.

Once they blended, though, it'd be a family reunion. There'd have to be a feast...

Omega-Natosh licked the blood off his lips and smiled to himself.

It was great to be unspeakably evil. Let the universe be shocked and awed.

• • •

For some reason, sitting across the galaxy in his living room, talking to Pat Conroy and watching his son coax some information out of Claire Schaeffer, Setter Caine shivered.

CHAPTER 12

"We can outrun them... well, I'm pretty sure we can, anyway."

Varnia raised an eyebrow at the remark, glancing from her Chief Engineer to her Flag Captain and back, "Pretty sure? Something wrong with the reactors?"

The Engineer wasn't looking at her as she asked the question, but now his eyes shifted from the holo plot to the Admiral, "No, no. That's not it... I'm just not sure what those ships are capable of pulling. I spent an hour looking at the drive signatures you sent down, and the emissions on a couple of them are awfully high."

There were murmurs of concern among the assembled senior officers. They were briefing on *Renown's* bridge, watching the Omega ships in the holo tank while the Engineer reported on the ship's restored combat capacity.

As far as anyone knew, the *Venerable*-class ship was back up to fighting trim... running wasn't usually what an Earther ship did, but it should still be *able* to...

Varnia frowned, "You think that means they have more powerful drives than ours?"

With a brief shrug the Engineer nodded, "I've also been talking to Doc Lazarus. She's of the opinion that these new humans Omega reconfigured could *potentially* have Krogg carapace structure all through them. Now I don't know too much about Kroggs, but if Omega's as smart as he's letting on, I think he might find a way to augment his humans' bodies so they could survive massive acceleration in enhanced ships."

Varnia's eyebrows climbed and then she nodded slowly. They had to figure out exactly what they were going to do about the Omega forces that had made it to the Larosian galaxy — running had been an option... but now the Engineer was skeptical for *biological* reasons. Back in the Krogg War days, when enemy ships had been alive, there'd been a lot of crossover between biology and engineering. Now it was surfacing again.

"The question doesn't seem too complicated, Varnia," Graham's tone was cool as he spoke, and eyes shifted to him as he peered into the plot. He didn't look up, but he kept speaking, "I should think we either make a stand in a system of our choosing, or make a direct run for Laros."

Narosh tilted his head at that remark, "If we inoculate the homeworld, what remains of my fleet can come out and do battle with these Omega ships at will. We could muster at least thirty ships for work in this part of the Empire, I'm sure of it."

There was a thoughtful pause, the eyes of the officers assembled at the plot shifting from Varnia to Narosh to Graham to Beckett, and then back to the plot. The strobing black icons of the Omega ships were edging closer to *Renown's* position, though the First Rate was jumping ahead of them every hour, just to keep out of sight...

Graham was right, though. It wasn't too difficult a question. Fight or flee... it was one of the basic primal choices.

And *Renown* was Varnia's flagship, it was her call. She cast a quick glance to Beckett. He gave her a supportive look, then smiled, which after thirty-nine years of marriage she knew meant *I trust you!*

"We're heading to Laros then. Make it top cruising speed... what can you give us Engineer?"

The aged cougar frowned thoughtfully for a second, eyeing the distance from *Renown's* present position to Laros, "I can give you 3,375 pls for that run, I think."

"Make that your speed, Cruising Master," she nodded.

As informally as it had begun, the gathering of senior officers slowly disbanded, the Chief Engineer heading to the hatch to return to his engines, the Cruising Master barking orders, Narosh and Beckett stepping back to stay out of the way, and Varnia staring again at the plot.

"And what of the Omega ships. Shall we let them run around unchecked in our absence?"

Varnia hadn't even realized Graham was standing next to her, and his quiet question caught her off guard. She blinked and glanced sideways at him, "You think we could lose them?"

Graham's tone still hadn't changed, and as his own gaze turned to meet Varnia's she almost caught an instinctive chill, "It's a big Empire. I shouldn't like to leave them out here, if we can help it."

It was a cryptic enough statement, and a confusing one. *Renown* couldn't be in two places at once...

Graham turned to Narosh and waved the Larosian over. With an approximation of a frown, the alien stepped back to the plot, "Something up, Graham?"

The ArcGeneral bobbed his head sideways thoughtfully, then stretched his hand into the plot, pointing to a silver icon, "I noticed that on sweeps this morning. It appears to be an abandoned Battleship, based on what long-range telemetry tells me."

Leaning towards the plot curiously, the Admiral-of-a-Fleet bobbed his head, "It is. The Battleship *Carnarvon*. A very early loss, as I recall, from the Second Fleet-of-War. I received the report of its abandonment before the entire Second was infected. It was racked by the plague, left to drift."

The silver dot in question was less than a day ahead at full speed, well inside the borders of the Larosian Empire, and plans had begun forming in Graham's mind from the first moment he'd seen it.

"Will my plan work, Narosh? Feel free to dive into my mind, it will be clearer that way," the ArcGeneral's eyes remained on the silver icon, and his mind tingled just slightly as Narosh reached out and read his thoughts.

The Larosian was thoroughly surprised... for two reasons. The plan itself was daring — extremely so — and the mind that had conceived of it was remarkably controlled. Narosh had scanned many human minds, none had been so controlled, so cold.

"Well *done*, Graham. You're quite right, our ships do keep well in the void. A team of engineers might have it back online within a day, if all is found to be in order."

Varnia glanced between them, "And we're sharing this little plan with the group..."

Narosh smiled in his Larosian way, "Graham believes that a duly reactivated Battleship could serve as an interdictor ship, to keep track of Omega and perhaps do him some damage."

The explanation was loud enough for most people on the bridge to hear, and all eyes shifted to the ArcGeneral, who didn't seem to notice. Instead he met Varnia's gaze, "It would make sense to divide our strength at virtually no cost, perhaps give Omega something to worry about that he hadn't foreseen."

"In a forty-year-old plague ship?" Varnia frowned as she tried to determine whether the junior Manchester had become unhinged. "There's no telling whether that ship could be put to rights, and even if it was, how could you run the combat systems, assuming they're intact? You wouldn't be anything more than a nuisance to those Omega ships, then they'd blow you out of the stars."

Graham blinked, "A distinct possibility. But what if some of the crew is still alive? I must talk to Doctor Lazarus, but I do wonder what UDRC would do to their infection with the original Omega. There are a number of possibilities there, Varnia. And if I can get that ship into action, with some of the original crew or just a few volunteers, I can keep Omega in sight."

"But one Battleship, Graham?" Beckett stepped forward. "I'm no Naval expert, but without support I still think those odds are tight..."

Graham offered a short nod, "They could be, but *Renown* has the ability to add firepower without being present. For the plan to work I'd have to insist we arm that ship ourselves."

"Arm it?" Varnia paused in thought, her mind quickly sorting through *Renown's* armaments. The ship mounted 250 guns, 42 carronades, and carried 115 gunboats...

Aha.

"You want my boats?"

Graham offered a slow nod, "Give me sixty, and I can turn that ship into a scratch carrier. We'd have FTL capability once we got hyper online, and Omega certainly wouldn't be expecting us. While you get to Laros, we could distract our pursuers, and try to keep them from spreading the new plague."

Varnia's eyes shifted to the plot, and to the silver icon floating there, now temptingly. Graham had a point, but to give up half her boats and their crews was no minor concern. *Renown* was an incredible gun platform, but its boats increased its firepower half again, and added important anti-corvette capabilities if she ran across hostile Kroggs...

As if that's a pressing issue right now. And Graham could really do something with them...

Yes. Yes he could... and perhaps a return to active duty could help him sort out his personal affairs... perhaps...

"Alright. Let's look into this."

Graham nodded, Narosh tilted his head, and *Renown* accelerated to 3,375 pls.

CHAPTER 13

"London's so beautiful."

Varnon Broadpaw's eyebrow rose at the remark, and standing on the lawn of Admiralty House, he looked up again just to confirm that it was indeed raining. Yep, he was getting drenched.

But standing without a coat or umbrella, her usually-perfect presidential hair drooping ungraciously in wet jagged angles down to her shoulders, Sarah *loved* it. She didn't know why, but the cold rain from the sky — a rarity on Genesis — was soothing.

Earthers walking down the street beyond the lawn avoided staring. They all immediately recognized Sarah — most had lived through the Krogg War, and those too young to have experienced it would have seen holos. And of course, they all knew what had happened to Genesis. So whatever the President needed to do to ease her mind for a moment was fine...

"I don't mind getting soaked," Varnon said quietly after a moment, "it does tend to cool the mind."

Sarah nodded, "It does. It does indeed."

The brief meeting between the leaders of the Earther government and military had broken a few minutes earlier, and the conclusions had been fairly straightforward: the Genesis Fleet was going to protect Freetown, and refugees from Genesis would come immediately to Earth.

Sarah wished she could say she'd been the one to recommend those things, but really it had been Lab and Varnon giving the advice. They were keeping it together better than she was, and even with his daughter gone, Varnon was truly *leading* his people in a way Sarah could not.

The Earthers never stopped being remarkable, it seemed.

But Sarah was willing to give herself some credit; she had asked the right questions, made sure the arrangements wouldn't cause the Earthers too much trouble, that suitable accommodations could be provided, and so on. Her mind was still lagging, but at least it seemed to be moving now.

Earth had that effect on her, apparently. And more importantly, *Earthers* had that effect on her.

The rain stopped before Sarah realized her eyes were closed — she was facing the sky, her back arched and her arms outstretched in a pose that must have looked ridiculous. It had been so wonderful to feel cold rain, she hadn't been thinking at *all*...

The rain had suddenly stopped. She opened her eyes slowly, curiously.

Ursla stared straight down at her.

The big retired Admiral was leaning over the President with her hands on her hips, "You feeling alright there, Sarah?"

For a moment the President didn't know what to say. Then she smiled, "I'm not alright, but I imagine I'm better than I was."

As the two friends straightened their posture, Ursla stopped shielding Sarah from the rain, and it began to fall on the President again. Varnon quietly stepped up next to them. "Lab and Elandra are probably waiting for us by now. We best set off."

Elandra Caine, Earth's leading geneticist, mother of Phealan and, of course, wife of Setter, laid her tray on a table and settled in her seat. Lab Forepaw followed her, placing his tray next to hers and sitting slowly.

"They should be here soon," he said as he hefted his fork, and Elandra nodded.

She'd agreed to leave the office for lunch to meet Sarah. The President needed to know everything Earther scientists had figured out about Omega, and taking her to the lab might be a bit too stressful right now.

So instead, lunch — and a good lunch too — at one of London's best restaurants. Six kinds of salmon, lots of fries, and enough pie and cake to keep Ursla very happy. Like all Earther restaurants it was buffet style, and of course it was absolutely free to everyone. Elandra would've liked to eat at this particular place — *Barklay's Buffet* — every day, but it was a long walk from her lab, and she'd specifically moved her work up to London to increase productivity, not spend all her time eating.

Somebody had to find a cure for the new strain of Omega...

"So how's Setter holding up, really?" Lab's question might have seemed impertinent, but he'd introduced young Elandra to young Setter over a century ago... in a round about way, anyway. He was one of the family's best friends — he had a right to know.

For her part, Elandra shrugged, "You know, he's really dealing with it rather well. He and Phealan are spending a lot of time together, he's coming to terms with everything, and I think he's actually getting to the point where he feels we can take Omega on directly."

Forepaw was nodding when a tray twice as big as his own dropped onto the space on the table facing him. Ursla lowered herself onto her seat with a smile, "Haven't had *Barklay's* since yesterday. Figure I'm due for a top-up."

Elandra and Forepaw laughed and nodded to the new arrival, and then Elandra got quickly to her feet as Varnon and Sarah approached. The President's tray seemed almost empty compared to the Earthers', but that was of course due to comparative metabolisms. One of Elandra's colleagues was working on a pill for that — one that would let the humans set their own eating tempo without risk of excessive weight gain. Freetown had been all for it... before the current situation it had even been a priority.

But that was immaterial now. Elandra smiled at Sarah and stood up to offer a hug as soon as the President's tray came to rest on the table, "I'm *very* happy to see you, Sarah."

Despite being dripping wet, Sarah accepted the big hug from Elandra, and felt warmed by the greeting, "You have no idea how glad I am to see you, El."

Elandra was, to Sarah anyway, something of a miracle worker. Of course, long ago she'd replaced Liz Hastings' leg, and since then she'd developed UDRC and regen. Much more importantly, though it had been Elandra's advice that had really helped Sarah, both with her own personal losses and with her relationship with Pat. Sarah would be forever indebted to the wolf for that.

Now Elandra probably held the key to surviving Omega, and curing the humans already taken by the plague.

As everyone settled down at the big restaurant table, and Sarah tried to take measure of the mound of food on Ursla's tray — at least twenty-five centimeters high, and being stabbed with a pitchfork — Elandra slowly began her informal briefing.

"Well, I wanted to make sure you know what we know about Omega. Now I don't have a cure for the new strain yet, that's going to be complicated. Attacking it is tough because it has Krogg-based defenses on the cellular level, and cracking those is *not* easy. But we do have the vaccine — that is, it can't affect anyone with Earther antibodies of any sort in their system."

Sarah nodded slowly at Elandra's casual words — the doctor seemed to have the issue so well in hand, as though Omega was just another problem to solve.

"Also of interest, I'm pretty sure we're all carriers of old Omega — humans and Earthers. That's what infected the Larosians, and I'm fairly certain it's curable with a targeted compound..."

Elandra halted as Sarah's eyes widened and she blurted, "*Humans* are carriers?"

Ursla and Elandra traded glances quickly, and the bear suggested the wolf slow down a bit — for every Earther at the table, this was all review, but for Sarah it was *very* new.

"Sorry, let me back up here. We all have Type 1 Omega in our blood. It doesn't seem to have any effect on us. Type 2 is the one we know, and it's a different sort because it's blended with Krogg biology. It's... *he's* not able to get past our biological defenses, but we can't get past his either," Elandra tried to make sure she didn't speak more slowly than normal — she didn't want to seem condescending.

Sarah wasn't even trying to eat, "So... somehow Type 1 infected the Larosians, and they hit it with Krogg cells and it mutated and became Type 2. Can the two types communicate?"

Elandra arched an eyebrow at the question — it had been the first thing Varnon, Lab, Dran, Andra, and Setter had asked her. Tactical minds, all of them...

"Not as far as we know. Communication seems to be telepathic, but based on the scans I got from Doctor Lazarus on *Renown*, the receptors on the new Omega cells don't match those on the old ones. I have to run this question by someone with a better grasp of telepathic broadcast laws, but I don't believe the two can integrate."

Varnon was chewing evenly as he listened, but now he paused to intercede, "Bottom line is the Omega who took your planet is Type 2. Type 1 is in our blood. And we have no idea what Type 2 is planning."

"I'm working on a new compound that will scrub the Omega cells from our blood. I'm also hoping UDRC can cure Larosians infected with Type 1. We'll use both as the basis for a cure to Type 2," Elandra continued before she began eating again.

Sarah's mind struggled but still managed to drag those facts together... "So inoculations for my refugees... just as simple as some UDRC?"

Elandra nodded, "We've got a stockpile waiting for their arrival. Infection won't be a problem any more... with certain exceptions, perhaps."

For a moment Sarah frowned, but then her sister-in-law came to mind. She didn't voice that thought. She wanted to eat.

"Alright... that's all good to hear," Sarah picked up her fork and stared at her plate for a while. The Earthers continued to eat at an even pace... then Ursla stood and headed to the dessert line.

"Well," Sarah tried again to say something, but it would've been just inane small talk.

She stopped herself and looked up briefly, eyes shifting from Earther to Earther. There was no need to make conversation. Theirs wasn't an awkward silence.

So they ate.

CHAPTER 14

Jax Furgus frowned as he stood at the plot on *Aboukir's* bridge, with Captain Ronax Hobbes standing next to him.

"That's exactly an hour overdue now," Ron Hobbes was carefully watching a ticking chrono, and Jax nodded at his Flag Captain's observation.

A report was supposed to have come in sixty minutes ago from Kari Peltier and *Paladin Saint.* They were on a picket station off on the extreme flank... surely the entire squadron hadn't been eliminated. There wasn't too much that could wipe out a Battlecruiser squadron without allowing a single warning to get off. Last time Jax could remember having heard about such a loss, it had been Pat Conroy's famed 'Pirates', and they'd encountered a Krogg Fleet about 100 times too powerful for them to deal with.

More likely than that, Kari was just late filing her report, which was nigh unforgivable for a whole host of reasons, under the circumstances.

Or perhaps she was shadowing an Omega force, and was under a comm blackout to avoid detection...

"Well, I'll give her two more hours, and then I'm sending someone out looking for her," Jax said quietly after his thoughtful pause, and Ron Hobbes nodded in reply.

It would take two hours to get one of the other human squadrons ready to cruise out there as it was, so Jax would give Peltier more time. He hoped it was a comm problem or a shadowing exercise... he wasn't confident it was either.

Aboukir continued to float in easy orbit over Freetown.

First Space Lord Fox Magnus was more than a little restless. *ENS Chimera* should have been nearing the end of its long journey between Earth and Gibraltar, but the run wasn't proving as fast or as easy as he'd first hoped.

Omega had infected ships out all across Fox's course to Gibraltar, and it was taking every scrap of creative instinct the First Space Lord had to keep the long line of almost seventy Earther ships from being detected.

Of course, he had more than enough firepower with him to handle most of the pickets he was finding; Lab had assigned all four of the slightly older squadrons of *Chimera*-class ships of the line to escort the cargo ships hauling reserve vessels to the distant Earther strong point. But even with that much punch at hand, Fox couldn't hazard being seen — Omega had to think that

Gibraltar was going unsupported. That way he'd get a nasty surprise if he went after the base.

The Earther Fleet in Gibraltar usually numbered some 127 ships, including fifteen *Venerables*, but in addition to the thirty-two *Chimeras* he was bringing, Fox had 128 packed Krogg War ships in the holds of his cargo convoys, and the nucleuses of reserve crews for all of them.

In other words, if Omega came to Gibraltar he'd find the system protected by over twice as many ships as he'd expect to see — so long as Fox got through to the distant base undetected and quickly enough to get the ships reassembled before Omega arrived.

That might be easier said than done, though...

"I don't see us making it through that net, Fox."

With a blink, the First Space Lord looked from the main battle plot to the Vice Admiral tasked with the command of his *Chimeras* — a rather familiar fox named Thena (Venus) Magnus, once Captain of *ENS Vulcan* and, of course, his wife.

"You don't think so?" he asked slowly, almost seeming to have to process his own question.

She nodded, "There's no way they'd miss a drive anomaly our size."

The 'they' she referred to was a substantial one; some sixty ships that Fox had to assume were infected now swept out in a long a net across their base line of advance. They had the space lane to Gibraltar and most of the immediate surrounding space under the eyes of deep-range sensors, and Thena was correct: there was no a way to get through their grid. Omega was obviously taking precautions against the Earthers getting around his flank.

Even with fields out at 350 percent, their convoy was just too big to be missed.

"So we go around. The long way if we have to..." Fox's tone wasn't particularly enthused.

"If we make the deep space run we'll have to do it by dead reckoning... could take us a week or two to figure out the way," Thena replied in her own soft tone.

Fox offered a slow nod, "So it adds two weeks to the trip... but it's worth it if it gets us there undetected. Even without ships unpacked we increase the capital ship force in Gibraltar by 200 percent... as long as Gibraltar is still there when we arrive."

Thena's jaw clenched and she nodded slowly, "And we can't send a drone to warn Earth or Gibraltar that we're overdue."

"Nothing to betray our position... they'll probably think we've been caught and destroyed by the time we arrive... but nothing we can do about that. Maybe we could fire off a pod when we get far enough out of the space lane for it to be unnoticed... but then it might not find its way back. We'll just have to play it by ear," Fox wasn't pleased by the proposition of dropping off the map, but it looked as though that would be precisely what his force would have to do.

There was nothing else for it, they couldn't afford to be detected.

So as Thena gave quiet orders to *Chimera's* Cruising Master, and Fox relayed a message through the Signal Officer, the ship of the line and its compatriots began a sharp turn to starboard.

Admiral Garvin Jardaw rubbed his forehead, continuing to stare at the icons in the main battle plot in *Gibraltar One's* C&C. The Gibraltar Fleet, the second most powerful formation of Earther warships in space — behind only the Home Fleet — wasn't as concentrated as it needed to be.

Jardaw had all his capital ships in system, but despite the risks, most of his frigates and sloops were now out on missions to bring home the dozens of survey ships that still filled star systems all across the old front lines of the Krogg War. He hadn't wanted to scatter his frigates, but he'd wanted the Survey Service ships to get jumped by Omega even less.

And those ships were literally all over the place...

Over the last three decades, investigation of the Krogg-occupied worlds had been drawing many ships to this side of Genesis, in hopes of learning about some of the civilizations the Kroggs had overwhelmed in their earlier days, as well as providing information on the way the Kroggs had evolved over their campaigns against different species.

It was enlightening research, and it demanded having ships all across the old war frontier between Gibraltar and Krogg. He had to bring all those ships in, and he didn't want to e-hyper pod warnings to the many unescorted survey ships out there in case Omega was able to track the pod flights and somehow got ships out to attack the vulnerable vessels.

He'd already used e-hyper pods to call in all of the 'escorted' survey teams — some sloops and frigates had gone out with survey ships when asteroid belts or other obstacles posed a potentially gun-worthy problem — but over thirty ships were still out there, and they all had to brought in.

"Pod just came back from Liz on *Grimbold*, she's bringing her team home now."

Jardaw blinked and looked through the tank at Vice Admiral Karl Kandam as he stepped over from the main signals center, "That's eleven coming in, then?"

Kandam nodded, "Four more pods out there, so we should be hearing from more ships soon... as long as Omega hasn't been there already."

The two bears shared a sigh at that possibility — they couldn't be certain of what Omega might try. This enemy was even more devious than the Kroggs. But how they'd cope with him wasn't a matter to worry about today. They needed everyone safe under Gibraltar's guns. No fleet could break through the system's massive defense grid, even if it was a leftover from the Krogg War. There were enough battle stations and asteroids seeded with energy drive rams here to turn an invading force of 5,000 ships into a floating debris field. That was why the Earthers maintained the station — it was the first bastion against a Krogg resurgence.

And now the last bastion against Omega's push towards Krogg, if such an assault ever came.

"Did I hear you say Liz Hastings was coming in?" perfectly timed to join the meeting, Rear Admiral Lang Sandpelt came to a stop next to Jardaw, having just arrived on the deck.

Kandam offered a slow nod and Jardaw's eyes narrowed just a little. One unadvertised benefit of the survey fleet was the opportunity its missions offered to old spacers to get out into the void during peacetime. Many of the survey crews were made up of Earther reservists, which meant Gibraltar would have extra crews for the ships Fox Magnus was bringing in. A number of others were partially or entirely made up of humans who'd elected to leave Genesis and hadn't taken well to Freetown. Liz Hastings was one prime example — regenerated and tired of her political life on Genesis, she'd relocated to Freetown, and had left that planet shortly thereafter for a retirement on Earth.

Then *Grimbold*, a Krogg War 64-gun Fourth Rate, had been half converted to a deep-range surveyor, and she'd asked for command. She'd been grounded too long, it seemed, and needed a deep-range mission or two to restore her balance.

That was fifteen years ago, and *Grimbold* had been back to Earth only eleven times since, never for more than six months at a time. With over 120 years left to live, Liz was apparently basking in the opportunity to command a ship in peacetime.

But it wasn't peacetime any more, and the thirty guns that *Grimbold* still had available — albeit disarmed on their tracks — weren't enough to make the ship dangerous until they were reactivated by the Gibraltar yards, and reinforced by the missing thirty-four. As soon as Liz got here... if she got here...

"She's five days out," Jardaw said finally.

Sandpelt's eyes had already settled on the star charts in the tank, "And we still don't know what Omega has, or where?"

Kandam shook his head, "None of the recon pods we've sent have survived in Genesis space long enough to let us know. Still no reports of activity from the ships we have out, and our last pod from Lab says the Earth side seems clear. Omega's probably saving up for something... the question is *us* or *them*."

Jardaw ground his jaw silently, and Sandpelt frowned, "I could take the *Venerables* in for a look. They wouldn't be able to shoot us down as easily as a pod, surely."

Kandam raised an eyebrow, "You want to chance our battle line on a recon?"

With a slight frown Sandpelt shrugged, "It could do us some good to know where they are... but no, you're right. If we passed their incoming attack fleet in space I'd be leaving Gibraltar without a mobile line, and minus 2,000 boats."

With a murmur of agreement, Jardaw glanced at the Rear Admiral, "For now we all stay put. Job one is getting the survey ships back... though that might take three weeks. If Omega moves on us we'll have to counter, but I'm confident we're in a strong enough position here to beat him if he comes. If he moves against Earth or Freetown we might have a chance to attack his flank — I don't imagine he'll be thinking too clearly about the danger from both front and rear, so you keep your ships ready for that trip, alright Lang?"

Sandpelt nodded slowly — conservatism made sense, even if it was a bit frustrating. Having spent the Krogg War in *Flame*, Sandpelt was accustomed to engaging in daring cruiser-style warfare, even with ships of the line.

But not yet. That would be for a different chapter of this struggle... hell, it might be in another volume. So everyone would have to wait until the time came.

In the meantime, Gibraltar remained restless.

CHAPTER 15

Christine walked quickly through the corridors of *Renown*. Part of her was trying to decide if the small of her back was actually itching, part was wondering whether the rumors about Graham's plan were true, and part was still staying dark and repressed.

There were things that she still refused to think about, and that seemed reasonable enough to her.

As she absently pushed her hand up under the back of her shirt and scratched at the itch, thoughts of *Carnarvon* were taking precedence. If scuttlebutt was right — and on Earther ships it invariably seemed to be, because the Earthers didn't understand the word to mean 'salacious rumor', just 'unannounced news' — then Graham wanted to reactivate a Larosian Battleship to turn it into a provisional Carrier.

Which was either a brilliant plan or his attempt to fulfill a death wish, because Omega ships weren't far behind.

Renown was only six hours from the stricken old Larosian ship, and the Omega vessels were said to be about twenty hours behind *Renown*, though for now the ship of the line was pulling steadily away from its unknowing pursuers.

Scuttlebutt also said the Omega ships might somehow have known that *Renown* was out here — they seemed to be following the First Rate's flight path fairly closely, though no one really knew if that was because they could see some sort of 'wake', or if it was a simple bad luck coincidence. They'd be at *Carnarvon* soon after *Renown*... and the Battleship would likely just be a hulk, at best boasting partial power and no weapons.

Graham was either planning something brilliant, or his dark mood of late had gotten to him...

What the hell am I doing?

Christine came to an abrupt halt as she realized she'd hiked her shirt halfway up around her midriff while scratching fervently at her back. She was hardly looking professional, and with that same weird instinctive connection, she could get a mild sense of what the Earthers walking past her were feeling as they saw her pacing through the corridors scratching her back.

"Damned regen," she muttered, forcibly taking her hand away and straightening her shirt while she consciously tried not to turn red. She needed to figure out what was going on with her system — her sensitivity to a number of things now seemed heightened... it wasn't fun.

Funny perhaps, but not fun.

She'd have to see the doctor... which was just as well, because scuttlebutt said Graham was talking to Doc Lazarus already. And scuttlebutt on an Earther ship was always right...

Graham tilted his head dispassionately as Doctor Celia Lazarus, *Renown's* chief physician and a formidable medical professional, pointed him to his wife's severed hand.

Wife, of course, was becoming a relative term in Graham's vocabulary. That was the hand of Gillian Hodge, the woman he loved, but when Christine had lopped it off, it had really been Omega's hand. And now it was Lazarus' best hope of trying to isolate a cure that would kill the savage plague, and hopefully restore the universe to rights.

Hopefully.

"I've been running tests on it since we got main power back, Graham," Lazarus came to a stop before the perfectly preserved appendage. "The new Omega cells are shielded by some sort of Krogg cellular defense mechanism I can't crack... yet, anyway. But if you look at the actual Omega cells themselves..." she keyed up a holo of one of Omega's new cells, and then had the computer peel the Krogg defenses from it "...it's actually almost exactly the same as a common cell that's present in all human and Earther bloodstreams."

Graham's eyes narrowed, "So we all have an immunity to it then?"

Lazarus nodded, "*We* do... to the original form, and we carried it. But the Larosians don't have the protection, obviously. Narosh was alright only because I pumped him full of UDRC at Krogg, so he had our immunities grafted in."

"So why can new Omega infect humans then?" Varnia had been standing quietly to one side, Beckett next to her.

Lazarus sighed as she looked to the two wolves, "It's the Krogg cell... it's a strange mechanism and I'm still trying to get a handle on it, but it looks like it's able to manipulate the natural defenses of a human... I hate to use the terms, but it seems to *hack* unprotected human DNA. Earther sequences seem to have some sort of regenerative block that it can't decrypt, so we're safe... I'm still trying to figure out how it works, but I think Omega created a shield with that Krogg cell. Something that protects him from our immune systems."

"So to the point, then," Graham drew Lazarus' attention again, "will a shot of UDRC cure Larosians infected with the old version of Omega?"

Lazarus bobbed her head sideways, "Simulations suggest it'll be that easy... but keep in mind, that's only if they have the original form. If the new form reached them, there's no reversing it... not yet, anyway. I'm still working on something to crack that Krogg cellular shield, but I really doubt I've got the resources aboard. It's more a project for the likes of Elandra Caine anyway…"

"You're doing a fine job, Celia," Beckett offered the reassurance, and Lazarus shrugged.

"Yes, I know," she agreed almost dismissively, but just as she opened her mouth to continue her comments the sickbay door opened and Christine entered.

The young human wasn't paying attention to what she was doing, and her shirt was pulled up again as she feverishly scratched the small of her back.

"Ah Graham, I've been…"

She came to a stop as the ArcGeneral's curious expression focused on her, and Beckett and Varnia exchanged amused glances.

Then she realized what she was doing and dropped her hand again, turning bright red, "Sorry, I'm *itchy*. Actually Doc, can you have a look… I haven't been able to stop scratching."

"I don't know, Christine, I think the short-shirt style suits you," Beckett chuckled. "Saves on the cloth too…"

Christine scowled, and Varnia and Beckett laughed as Lazarus picked up a couple of instruments and went around to examine the young human's back.

Lieutenant Colonel Cadmus Howler, the wolf in charge of 2/54th, stood next to Beckett Lupus half an hour later. Christine was sitting on a nearby bed, an Earther medic applying some sort of paste to the small of her back, and Graham was standing next to her. Doctor Lazarus was manipulating several canisters of liquid UDRC, transferring them under high pressure into a half-meter cylinder transport container.

"This'll come out as an aerosol now. I'm fairly certain you can release it and expect everyone who breathes it to be cured… it'll just take a few minutes, I think. But I'll give you UDRC injector guns too, just in case this doesn't work."

The hatch opened as she spoke and Narosh slipped into the room. He stepped towards Lupus, his active eye settling briefly on Christine, who waved at his confused expression, before he came to a stop next to the General.

"We have UDRC loaded up as an aerosol. Doc here thinks any Larosian who inhales it will be cured of the old form of Omega *and* immunized against the new one," Beckett said, and the Admiral-of-a-Fleet nodded slowly.

"Excellent," his word was thoughtful, as he eyed the container holding the gaseous cure. "There is a central environmental control center in the Battleship. If this was released into the main atmospheric ducts, it could circulate through the ship within an hour."

"Wouldn't they have closed the ventilation when a plague broke out, Narosh?" Graham's words were again cool and professional, his expression impassive.

The Larosian paused thoughtfully, then offered another nod, "A distinct possibility. The system controls are in that center... but the power systems draw on the main reactor. We'd need to bring that back online, or at least patch a generator into the power grid, to get that system running."

Beckett's ear twitched thoughtfully and he glanced sideways at Howler, "Two objectives then. Two teams... you with one and me with the other?"

Howler nodded slowly, "Sounds reasonable. Can you give us specifications for the Battleship, Narosh?"

The Admiral nodded, "I have them committed to memory... somewhere in there, I'm sure. I'll put together a map for you both, and I should like to come with you. If some of the crew is restored, I'll be able to orient them quickly."

Beckett frowned, "You can't handle a sword, can you?"

The Admiral-of-a-Fleet shook his head, "I was never really trained with one, and my attempt to use one against Omega didn't work out for the best... but I imagine rifles will be enough in this case. I will just need the good doctor to restore my hand so that I may use one."

Lazarus offered her own nod, "It's ready, I can attach it when we're done here. And rifles should work, I think. The Krogg cells are the ones that allow for genetic rewriting. Original Omega can't biologically change the Larosians, only manipulate things like neuro-transmission and telepathy. I don't *think* you'll have to face any Krogg carapace."

Narosh looked to the doctor with a smile, "Exceptional work, as ever, Doctor."

Again she shrugged, "It's not that hard to–"

"Now my *wrist* itches."

Christine hadn't even thought before she blurted out the complaint, and the medic with the paste looked to Lazarus with a concerned expression. The Earther physician approached Christine slowly, frowning as she did, "Your wrist?"

Christine held up her arm in frustration and pointed, "Right here."

It was getting less and less amusing, and embarrassment wasn't even coming to mind any more. The itching just wouldn't stop...

"There something sinister at work here, Celia?" Graham almost — *almost* — sounded concerned, and the fact that he came so close gave Christine a little comfort.

Lazarus took up a few more instruments and ran a scanner over Christine's wrist. The doctor shook her head, "Nothing on the scope. Your skin is clean. I'm thinking it must be some sort of ultra-sensitivity... your nerves are overactive. It's probably a symptom of the regen — it should pass. Don't worry about it for now."

"I *can't* not worry about it," she protested in reply, but Lazarus already had a small patch in one hand and box in the other.

"Stasis patch," the doctor said as she approached the ailing human. "It has a full body field, with variable settings, and a remote, too."

Lazarus gently applied the five-centimeter square silver patch to the side of Christine's neck. As soon as more than three quarters of its surface came into contact with a surface with a bio signature, it stuck.

"To remove it you just need to rotate it clockwise. Now, for the time being I'm going to set the field to about five percent. That should dull the itch but leave feeling for you... and I'm going to localize it around your back and your wrist..."

Lazarus keyed the remote and suddenly the itching was gone. As Christine sat more upright in surprise, the doctor handed her the slim silver box with a screen.

"Don't run the field up over sixty percent in any area or you'll completely lose feeling. It's only a temporary fix... so check how you feel with it off every now and then. I imagine the itching will clear up — it's just surface nerves getting too much attention from your brain, I think. But keep me apprised."

Examining the silver box briefly, Christine nodded and slid forward off the bed, "Sounds good... thank you kindly, Doc. Now I can go with these gentlemen to *Carnarvon*."

There were exchanged glances, but no one objected.

The Earthers and humans left sickbay to start planning the operation, while Lazarus led Narosh into a surgery bay to have his hand reattached.

CHAPTER 16

Sarah glanced up at the graying sky as she paced through the woods towards the Caine house. They'd finished what they'd needed to do at Admiralty House, and the arrangements for Genesis refugees to come to Earth were already being made. *Unity Genesis* would have to boost back to Freetown very soon, and once she returned, Sarah would personally assume command of the Genesis Fleet.

There was really nothing left for her to govern, and given her notoriety as a hero of the Krogg War, it would probably be better for the morale of the survivors of Genesis if she was wielding a battle fleet against Omega.

So she wanted to pay her respects to the Supreme Consul, collect Pat and Claire, and get off the planet. Hopefully she'd live long enough to come back one day.

Caine's house emerged through the trees ahead, and Sarah saw it just as several wolves in the trees around her caught her attention — the local pack was evidently visiting as well. Sarah continued to ignore the four-footed watchers, keeping her pace as they shadowed her to the house's clearing.

Pat and Setter were sitting on the deck outside, talking quietly as she came into view. Caine noticed the wolves' heightened interest before Pat saw his wife, and thus the Supreme Consul glanced towards her and then slowly came to his feet. Pat followed his gaze and then mirrored his action, descending the stairs as she approached.

She tried to smile at her husband, but that didn't quite work. He didn't smile either. Instead he slid his arm around her waist and fell into step with her as the pair paced up onto the deck.

Caine did smile at his new guest, and gauging her spirits he decided to go so far as to offer her a hug. Sarah didn't turn down the offer — she almost felt like she was seeing her own father, and under the circumstances... She stepped in close and hugged the wolf, taking some comfort in his seeming calm.

After a moment she moved away and took a centering breath, then dropped into a chair next to Pat. Determined as always to lighten the mood, the Irishman finally drummed up a smile of his own, "See, if you didn't happen to be married, Setter, that sort of thing might get you in trouble!"

His tone was playful and Caine chuckled, "It's just the fur coat. Hugs are irresistible. I thought that was why you grew the beard..."

The Irishman snorted a laugh but decided not to fire back, instead shifting his gaze to Sarah, "So everything set for the refugees?"

She nodded slowly, glancing from husband to fath... stupid slip, from husband to *great old friend*, and nodded, "Indeed. We shall send the convoy of survivors back once we get back to Freetown. We'll want to get them out of there before Omega attacks that system."

"You'll be taking command of the Genesis Fleet?" Setter asked softly, and she again nodded.

"Togo and Rozhestveski have the fleet right now... and though I'm sure they're both quite good, I don't trust either of them under these circumstances. We need more experience than they have, I think... and since Graham won't be available..."

She let her words trail off and then set her jaw. Fair enough, her brother was dead. Moving on...

"So we should head up to *Unity* soon, Pat. How's Claire — will she be ready to leave with us?"

The Irishman looked back across the table to the wolf with a quizzical expression, then bobbed his head in the direction of the house. Sarah hadn't even looked through the glass panels yet, so she shifted forward in her seat and peered through the window.

Claire and Phealan Caine were talking. Eating ice cream and talking.

Talking.

"We're going to ask her if she wants to stay with us," Setter said as Sarah's mouth fell open at the sight. "She's not laughing or pouring out her emotions by any means, but Phealan's got her talking, which from what I hear is a bit of a coup in itself. I don't know what we can do for her in the long run, but for now we don't mind looking after her."

Sarah nodded very slowly, closing her mouth with some effort. So she wasn't the only one who found being with the Earthers comforting... peaceful.

Well, if they could help that girl in *any* way, it'd be worth leaving her to them...

"If you don't mind, that'd be excellent, Setter. She'd probably just end up getting put on a ship to come back here with the convoy anyway... and someone ought to start healing after all this."

Setter smiled thinly and his ear twitched, "No one's ready to start healing yet. But she's probably better off here, you're right."

Looking back from the conversing youngsters to the Supreme Consul, Sarah studied the look in Caine's eyes... he didn't seem unduly distraught... but then she'd be in no position to tell. Earthers held their emotional cards close. Though if he didn't seem upset to her, he wouldn't seem upset to Claire...

"Better off here. Yes."

The three sat silently for a few moments, Sarah taking deep breaths of fresh air, and after a moment indulgently closing her eyes as she breathed in. The atmosphere on Earth was so comforting... she didn't want to leave. She didn't want to go back. She didn't want to be the fleet commander...

"You take over your fleet, and help Andra see Omega off," Setter said slowly, reassuringly. "There's nothing more you can do than your job, Sarah. Just use that excellent tactical mind of yours, and don't let yourself get caught up asking questions about what might have been. What might have been isn't what has been, there's no changing that now."

Sarah slowly opened her eyes and looked across the table at Setter. His earnest gaze pierced her own and she felt a tear slide down her cheek — just one tear — as Pat gently eased her head onto his shoulder, then leaned his head against hers. She closed her eyes again and let out a long sigh.

It was good advice, and from Setter it came with a lot of weight. She just had to do her job.

"And don't worry," Setter added more quietly. "He won't beat us. He won't beat you. We're going to win, it'll just take time."

Sarah nodded as her head rested on Pat's shoulder, but she didn't open her eyes. Setter's words and Pat's shoulder were the comfort she needed. Setter was the only person in the universe who could understand the tremendous weight she felt she was bearing at this moment, and what he said was true.

She'd take his comfort, and forge on. She had to.

An hour later *Unity Genesis* made ready to return to space. Aboard the Superdreadnought, Pat quickly collected everything Claire had taken aboard with her, handed it to a waiting ArcEnsign, and sent that runner on to the flight deck to hand the kit off to the crew of an Earther pinnace that sat waiting on the deck to collect the baggage.

After watching the ArcEnsign leave the girl's cabin, Pat turned to the window. Earth loomed large off the ship's port quarter, and the island of Newfoundland was still in sight. Hopefully being down there would do that poor girl some good...

Pat let a certain sadness simmer in him for a moment — but only for a moment.

This was it. The mourning period was over for now. Action had to start. Sentiment could no longer be permitted.

It was time to get into this Gods-damned war.

The civilians would get to Earth, find out-of-the-way places to settle, and let the fleets go to work. When Omega came he'd meet the fury of veteran Genesis officers, fierce Freetown fighters, and the unholy, righteous fire of Earther might.

"Let's see if you're ready for it all, you bastard," he whispered.

Then Pat left the cabin.

•••

President Sarah Manchester had taken off her suit, and thus considered herself President no more.

No, instead she was something entirely more comfortable.

Tightening her belt over her hips, she examined her familiar green uniform in the mirror of her cabin. She'd taken this one set of her old fatigues with her when she'd left Genesis, and she'd pull more sets from *Unity's* stores.

It was time for *ArcGeneral* Manchester to take command of this human war effort. Audrey DeBrooke would respect that move, having fought at Sarah's side in the past, and some of the pressure on Jax would be relieved.

And somehow, being in the comfortable old tunic, pulling her hair back into the same old tight ponytail, and setting her jaw in the same old way gave her strength.

This was what she did for a living — she may not be perfect at it, but she would be a hell of a lot better at it than at politicking.

"Here I come, Omega."

With that utterance, she checked her crisp appearance once more in the mirror, took a centering breath, and left the cabin.

Unity Genesis accelerated into flux drive ten minutes later.

Standing silently on the deck of their house hours after *Unity Genesis* departed, Phealan and Setter Caine watched the stars. The sky was clear, the wind was up a bit, and the night was peaceful. The wolves were lying all around the house, and on the couch just visible through the glass in the living room, young Claire Schaeffer was fast asleep.

"So you'll deal with her?" Setter asked in quiet tones, and Phealan nodded.

"She definitely needs some attention. I can't say I'm a particular expert in humans, but hopefully I can help her sort herself out..." the younger Caine's voice trailed off for a moment, and his instincts connected with his father's. "You're going to start governing, aren't you? No more time off?"

Caine was pleased by his son's intuitiveness, "Sarah and Pat both expected me to be a bastion of wisdom in all of this. Obviously I'm not... but it's my job to look like one. I'll stay out of Varnon's way, but I'll have to step forward more."

"Because you've got the most experience. Even if it's not with Omega in particular," Phealan agreed softly. "So we're really going to start this war now, aren't we? Time to shake off the shock?"

Setter blinked thoughtfully and then nodded, "We have no choice. We'll mourn again after it's over... for now, we go to war."

The Caines sighed simultaneously, and their eyes remained fixed on the stars.

The bloodletting would start soon.

CHAPTER 17

Renown emerged from energy drive a few minutes off the port beam of the floating Larosian Battleship *Carnarvon*. The venerable old silver warship was drifting through space, a very gentle yaw turning it a few degrees an hour in its almost-stagnant place.

"We're definitely getting intermittent life signs, skipper."

As the report reached *Renown's* Captain, Varnia raised an eyebrow with interest. Graham had called it correctly then... his plan might just turn out for the best...

"About... sixty life signs I think."

Varnia's other eyebrow went up to join the first. From a crew of 1,500, that wasn't much of a survival rate... though that said, she couldn't imagine spending forty years alive in a derelict ship. Well, hopefully those Larosians were sane, and maybe there were more alive, just masked from the sensors by the Omega filling their blood. Who knew what that plague could do if it put its... well, *mind* to it.

"Close to docking range and bring us right alongside," Varnia spoke while she considered the possibilities of life on the ship. She then keyed the intercom, "Bridge to airlocks. We're coming alongside now... three minutes to hard dock."

Several decks below the bridge, Graham Manchester smoothly checked his energy rifle. The weapon was in good operating order, as he'd expected, so he let it fall to his side as Varnia's words came through.

Keying the intercom panel next to him, he offered a clipped reply, "Very good."

"Ready back here," Beckett's voice came through the speakers. He and Narosh were taking charge of the team headed for the Battleship's engineering department. The Larosian's expertise would be needed down there to connect the Earther generator to the ship's power grid, so Graham and Howler's party would be responsible for releasing the cure.

Hopefully the infected Larosians would be weak and passive after forty years adrift, but in case they weren't, the entire 2/54th was ready to contain them on their ship, and to punch its way to its two objectives. Graham and Howler thus had an entire platoon coming with them, under Lieutenant Ellen

Arbear, and Joyce Furgus' company was waiting in the corridor right behind them in case of trouble.

Swords had been slung for this operation — they weren't expecting any problem dropping infected Larosians with energy rifles, though the blades were near at hand if things went awry.

Renown steadily closed the distance to *Carnarvon*, the Cruising Master watching with narrowed eyes as the coxswain pushed the massive First Rate towards the equally robust Larosian ship.

"Boarding anchors in five... four... three..."

Boarding anchors were a post-Krogg War addition to all Earther ships, as were the combat airlocks *Renown* was using to mate with the Larosian vessel. After the ad hoc boarding of Krogg ships in the battle for Krogg 'A', it had seemed prudent to build Earther ships with the ability to mate easily with other vessels — even hostile alien ones.

Varnia was pleased as she watched the system at work.

And hopefully *Carnarvon* would be much more passive than the Krogg Superdreadnought she'd bumped *Algenon* up against forty years ago...

Graham watched the silver Larosian ship's lock fill the view port on the outer door, and waited as *Renown* gently rubbed up against the alien vessel. There was a hum as the lock extended and connected with its Larosian counterpart, then a second hum as atmospheric shields mated the two vessels.

The inner lock opened, then the outer lock. Howler nodded to Graham, and then he stepped though the first door with Lieutenant Arbear.

Graham watched the marines of 2/54th file into the chamber and wait for *Renown's* computer to open the Battleship's alien airlock with Narosh's command codes. It was taking longer than he'd expected, so he cast a glance at Christine.

His young aide was hefting a rifle of her own, and to her regret she found the weapon altogether too familiar. It was just like the one Beckett had given her in Darymanis City... but she wasn't going to think about that right now.

She didn't even realize Graham's eyes had settled on her until the clang of the opening Larosian airlock grabbed her attention. She blinked, looked to Graham quickly, and offered what she hoped was a confident smile.

The ArcGeneral's impassive gaze remained, but he nodded to her, "Itching gone, then?"

Christine nodded, glancing briefly past him as the Earther platoon began to step across the bridge to *Carnarvon*, "The patch works like a charm."

"Very good. Just warn me before scratching if any indiscreet areas get itchy," Graham's tone didn't change, nor did his expression.

That had almost sounded like a *joke*...

But before Christine could say anything, the junior Manchester had stepped around the corner, into the lock.

Carnarvon loomed ahead...

Beckett Lupus looked carefully down his barrel as he swung into *Carnarvon's* corridor, and Narosh followed closely, covering the other direction with his own Earther-built weapon.

The corridors were dark, and empty.

It took only a few seconds for Beckett's eyes to adjust to the dimness, and then he waved the rest of his marines forward into the broad corridor. The platoon fanned out carefully, covering both directions with their trusted old rifles.

Nothing...

No wait, there was *something*.

Beckett's instincts weren't quite screaming at him, but they were unsettled — it felt almost as though a storm was on the way, or something...

Something.

His headset was live, so he decided to inquire, "Varnia, how many life signs?"

There was a pause, then she replied with some uncertainty, "We thought about sixty... but now that we're closer we're thinking more. It looks like the sensors are having a hard time distinguishing between individuals — Omega's making their readings muddle."

"Hmm... sounds a bit–"

He stopped, and now his instincts *did* scream.

A Larosian came around a corner a dozen meters down the corridor from him, its limbs randomly flailing, its motions jerky and undisciplined. It stopped there, staring at Beckett and the marines for a moment. None of the Earthers moved.

"Narosh..."

The Admiral-of-a-Fleet was ahead of Beckett's strained request, reaching out with his mind towards the seeming plague-carrier. Indeed, the poor fellow's mind was aflame...

"I can't reach him," Narosh said after only a second. "And if he fits the pattern we've seen, he won't remain passive..."

As if on queue, the Larosian opened its mouth and *hissed* loudly, like a Krogg.

"Not a good sign," Narosh carefully lined his good eye up along his rifle's barrel and drew a bead on the Larosian's chest.

Ten more infected Larosians came around the corner.

"Well damn..." Beckett sunk to one knee and the marines quickly found targets.

"What's going on down there, Beckett?" Varnia's question coincided with the lunge of the Larosians — they surged ahead like flailing animals, and the Earthers clamped down on their triggers.

It was a somewhat pleasant surprise when the bursts of energy actually did accomplish what they were meant to, dropping the Larosian crew into comas with clean shots... but then more threw themselves around the corner.

"What's going on?" Varnia sounded even more concerned the second time.

Gritting his teeth, Beckett dropped two more infected Larosians, "I'm betting there are more than sixty, dear. And... well, did I ever show you those crazy zombie movies from the early twenty-first century?"

There was silence on the line for a second, then Varnia almost seemed to verbally shrug, "Umm... no."

Firing again, Beckett gritted his teeth, "Never mind. Suffice it to say it's very disturbing down here..."

The Larosians kept coming.

CHAPTER 18

Howler was the first of his team to see the surge of infected Larosians coming up the corridor, and he immediately opened fire. Lieutenant Arbear quickly waved her squad into formation across the hallway, and by the time Graham and Christine emerged into the dim alien ship, piles of comatose Larosians were building up in the corridors.

"We'll need to advance from this position soon, unless you want to wait here until they spend themselves," Graham brought his rifle sight up to his eye as he spoke, and Howler nodded quickly to him between bursts.

"They don't seem to be too threatening, just plentiful," shifting his attention away from the corridor, he looked back to the chute to *Renown*. "Joyce, we're going to force our way to environmental control. Get people into position to keep them out of the lock, but leave the doors open. If there's some sort of power failure I don't want to be trapped in here."

"Understood, moving into position now," Jax Furgus' daughter was one of 2/54th's best officers — she wouldn't compromise *Renown's* safety, and she wouldn't leave the disembarked marines cut off. If it looked like those two objectives were going to conflict with each other, she'd find a way to make sure they *didn't*.

"Alright, Ellen, let's get moving."

Arbear, the first marine officer to have met Omega's new soldiers aboard *Genesis One*, nodded, waving her squad forward down the corridor. Behind sheets of energy, the Earthers and humans began to make their way to the environmental control center.

Narosh found himself somewhat shaken as he pushed ahead, stepping over the fallen. No Larosian had ever been as close to the plague-carriers as he was now. The chaos in their minds was startling and bordering on gruesome. Even in his original form, Omega was quite a compelling telepathic captor.

Well, Omega would be expelled from these noble warriors soon enough.

"If I'm following the directions correctly we're about a hundred meters away now," Beckett managed to unclench his jaw to speak.

No more great tides of infected Larosians were appearing — only a half dozen individuals here and there. So long as the ones they'd already shot stayed down until the power got hooked up and the UDRC started pumping, things would be okay.

Wait a second, did I just think *that...? Oh damn, they're going to start waking up now, aren't they?*

Yep, one grabbed his foot as he tried to step around it.

"Dammit, they're waking up!"

Beckett's rifle swung down to catch the Larosian in the chest, but already a new rush from the rear had the marines' full attention. Had the Larosians just played possum to get the boarding party isolated away from the lock?

"Alright that's it, bring up the reserves. Keep a company in *Renown*, and then I want the rest of the battalion in here to keep them out of the way. If it gets physical don't *kill* them, they'll be ours again soon..."

Christine was firing fast, dropping Larosians repeatedly as they surged up behind her.

"No, they're definitely not staying down," she said quickly as one she'd shot repeatedly lunged again. The Omega-riddled aliens were pressing close to the rear of the squad, and for all the Earthers did to try to stay ahead of them, it seemed impossible with Omega driving the Larosians' bodies so fast...

"It's still clear up here," Howler barked, swinging out of his position with the front group to come alongside Graham in the rear. Both officers clamped down on their triggers, as did another dozen marines, but the Larosians were shrugging off the blasts now.

"Omega must be keeping them out of the coma somehow, Cadmus," Sergeant Ernile Cuttar, another of the veterans from Lupus' old Krogg War recon squad, made the observation. "I think we'll need to go hand-to-hand, and I don't know that there'll be any other way to put them down but to kill them."

Howler nodded in agreement; they couldn't keep this up forever, even with the rest of the battalion flooding the ship. Eventually one side would start killing...

"Alright. Ellen, I have to ask you and the squad to run interference for us. Pick some corridor space and hold it, with fists if you have to. Graham, Christine and I will move ahead and get the canister in place and ready to go."

Graham and Christine exchanged glances, and as Howler took the pack with the half-meter cylinder off the back of the cat who was carrying it, Arbear came up next to him, "Not a problem. Can we start trying the injection guns if we get close enough? That might put them down."

Howler blinked, "Indeed, glad you remembered them!"

Both squads were carrying the UDRC injectors Doc Lazarus had provided, in case the aerosol didn't end up working. At this rate they might actually start curing Larosians before their intricate plan got into place.

"We're moving. Good luck, Ellen."

The Lieutenant nodded to her Colonel, then picked a piece of Larosian deck and set her feet firmly. She didn't intend to move... she just hoped these Omega victims didn't fight as viciously as the infected humans she'd encountered on *Genesis One*. As the first lunging Larosian came at her, she activated her second shield and settled her balance.

Larosians hurled themselves at Earthers.

Beckett and Narosh had adopted Cadmus Howler's idea, and now they ran the last fifty meters to the engineering section with their squad well to the rear, holding back the tide of Larosians.

So far it looked as if none were ahead of them...

"Get the generator prepared, Beckett!" Narosh kept his rifle at the ready as they neared the hatch to the ship's propulsion section.

Swinging his pack deftly over his shoulder, Beckett opened its top flap and flipped open the upper casing on the generator. He started keying the device to standby as they both slid to a stop just short of the hatch, and Narosh began stripping the door panel and exposing its external power interface. As the outlet appeared in the dim light, Beckett handed him the transfer cable from the Earther generator, and the Larosian quickly hooked the two together.

The door motors hummed, and Narosh tripped the opening circuit.

"Here's the part of the zombie movie where we realize the biggest and baddest alien of them all is hanging out in the engine room..." Beckett said just a little jovially, and he swung his pack back over his shoulder, disconnecting the exchange cable. He steadied his bag with his left hand while hefting his rifle with his right, then the pair stepped into the darkened engine section.

"Why do you keep referring to *zombie* movies? My people here aren't dead," Narosh gave a Larosian frown as he edged into the seemingly empty corridor, and Beckett narrowed his eyes thoughtfully in reply.

"Well... hmm... valid point..."

No! No you must close it or we will all die!

Narosh froze — that was a *proper* telepathic Larosian voice.

Who is this? I am Admiral-of-a-Fleet Narosh, who is speaking to me?

A Larosian rushed around a corner just ahead and slid to a stop as he saw Narosh and Lupus silhouetted against the dim corridor lights.

No, they are through the barricade! Seal the secondary, I will try to slow them before I fall victim to it!

Beckett was already drawing a bead on the Larosian when Narosh realized the wolf couldn't hear the telepathic conversation, "He's not infected Beckett! We have to inject him now!"

The sound of a hatch sealing around the corner from which the Larosian had emerged now clanged through the air, but as the Larosian moved forward to attempt to challenge the two seeming intruders in his corridor, Beckett recognized the coherence of his steps.

"I'm Beckett Lupus, Earther Marine Corps!" he barked loudly, laying his rifle down quickly and pulling his injection gun from the holster on his hip. "Just stay put — we've got a cure for the plague..."

It is already driving me mad! It says it is Admiral-of-a-Fleet Narosh and an Earther with a cure. Do not let me break the barricade, my honorable fellows. May Praaxus protect you all...

"He thinks we're hallucinations brought on by infection," Narosh reported quickly as he eavesdropped on the thought.

Beckett nodded quickly, then shifted into a combat stance as the Larosian closed to fighting distance. Convinced he was going mad, the poor fellow simply threw himself at the General in a tackle, but the wolf sidestepped, and in a blinding motion managed to press the injection gun against the alien's neck as he passed in midair.

Landing with a thud on the floor, the Larosian clutched in disbelief at the injection site. He had *felt that...*

It's not Omega, my friend. I am Admiral-of-a-Fleet Narosh. And this is General Lupus. Now we must get to engineering, to open the vents of the atmospheric system and release the cure we just gave you into the ventilation system.

The Larosian, unsurprisingly, was dumbfounded. He was well beyond thinking, and obviously he wasn't ready to talk. Taking a certain amount of command prerogative, Narosh thus reached into the survivor's mind, pulling together scattered thoughts of the past *forty* years.

With sixty comrades, this Larosian — the Chief Engineer of *Carnarvon* — had managed to seal off the engineering section of the ship, closing its vents and isolating them from the infection. They had lived carefully on the massive stockpile of stores kept in the rear cargo bays, and had eked out an existence in the dark hull, hoping against hope for rescue.

And after all that time, they remained disciplined Larosians, ready to sacrifice themselves for each other.

Narosh was most proud, but that was for another time. He looked more carefully into the Engineer's... *Neytosh's* mind. They had only manually closed the vents to this section — the rest of the ship's environmental ducts remained *open*.

"They only closed the vents in this section," Narosh said quickly, and his comm carried the words across *Carnarvon* to Graham, Christine and Howler.

"We're at the Environmental Center now..." Howler's report was clipped as he came to a quick stop outside the door of the desired chamber. "How do we get this hatch overridden again?"

Before Narosh could answer the question, Graham had keyed the safety off his rifle and leveled it at the door. In a rather cliché fashion, he blew the heavy hatch right out of the way.

Howler tipped his head, "Never mind, Graham remembered."

Leading the trio into the relatively small, unoccupied chamber, Graham's eyes quickly traced the walls and found the device Narosh had shown him in his mind's eye: the filtration assembly. This chamber was the central recycling point for the ship's atmosphere, so if they could just open the duct work above that filter they could release the high-pressured aerosol into the ship.

"We'll still need power to activate the circulation pumps," Christine was closely following Graham's own line of thought, already stepping forward to open the filtration cowl.

"We're on it. Come on Mister Engineer Neytosh, we need to reactivate the power grid, *now*," Beckett's voice came back over the headset.

Ellen Arbear ducked low as a Larosian lunged at her head, then stood upright as the fellow passed over her back, flinging him sideways before he fell heavily to the floor. Her injection gun found his head before he could rise again, and with that introduction, he was reduced to convulsions on the deck.

Ellen still hadn't moved from the place she'd chosen in the corridor — as a bear she had more than enough body weight to use as an anchor. She just had to hold on.

"My injector just ran out," one of her marines said quickly. They hadn't carried enough UDRC for this sort of melee... they needed the aerosol...

The infected Larosians pressed over piles of their half-cured fellows and attacked again.

The Engineer was still stunned as Beckett and Narosh helped him hobble down the corridor. After forty years, Narosh certainly couldn't blame this poor fellow for his condition... he just wished *Neytosh* would stabilize and help them get the grid online.

I am sorry Admiral-of-a-Fleet... I was suffering disbelief. You need to interface an Earther generator with the power grid?

"Indeed," without thinking, Narosh answered verbally, and Beckett glanced sideways at him.

Neytosh took the cue, forcing himself to recall the process for using his ill-attended vocal cords, "We... we can work from the auxiliary chamber. There is no need for full power to run the pumps. This cure... it will cleanse the infected, and protect my crew?"

"Seems to have worked for you," Beckett said quickly. "Where's the auxiliary chamber?"

The Engineer paused, getting his bearings, "Ten meters behind us. Sorry, I was not paying attention."

Beckett stifled a groan and helped the hobbling Larosian back to the appropriate hatch.

...

"I hear them outside," Howler straightened and narrowed his eyes. "I'll hold them off, you get this thing hooked into the system."

Graham and Christine both nodded as the Colonel laid the aerosol cylinder on the deck and pulled his injection gun from his hip, then turned for the door.

"Cadmus," Graham halted him quickly, then drew his own injection gun and tossed it to the marine. The wolf nodded in thanks, then disappeared beyond the hatch.

Christine looked to Graham, then at the silver cylinder on the floor, "We need to get this into the duct... how heavy do you think it is?"

Graham's expression still hadn't changed, even with all the fighting, all the insanity, "Very pertinent question..."

He looked from the cylinder to the now open duct line, "Not too heavy. Do you think we should open it before we slide it in there?"

"Makes sense..." Christine knelt slowly next to the cylinder, then gingerly hefted it up onto its end. "It's pretty light, you're right... now..."

Flipping up the top cowling, her eyes narrowed at the controls. As always, Earther buttons were clearly labeled, just for days like this one...

An infected Larosian got past Cadmus Howler in the hall, and launched himself into the room. Without a weapon in hand, and with the only remaining injection gun left on Christine's hip, Graham opted to tackle it short of the cylinder, using a great thrust of his legs to get his shielded shoulder into the alien's waist.

The Larosian slammed into the wall, but having gone almost head-first into an armored Larosian's torso, Graham was the more stunned of the two. Christine's right hand went quickly to her injection gun, and then without thinking her left went to the 'Open' button on the cylinder.

An invisible, high-pressured mist of UDRC erupted from a previously invisible slit on the top of the cylinder, blowing directly into her face before she could twist away. Ignoring the odd taste in her mouth, she tipped the container towards the Larosian. He hit the invisible wall of aerosol and immediately went into convulsions, falling just as Graham regained his feet.

Still the ArcGeneral's expression failed to change, but as the hiss of the escaping UDRC reached his ears, he rushed to Christine's side and helped her heft the cylinder into the duct, and shut the flap.

As if on cue, the pump started humming, "We just got environment exchangers online down here, Graham. The aerosol spraying?"

"Indeed," Graham said coolly, and as he looked to Christine she offered a smile.

"Nice tackle."

His reply was stoic, "A throwback to my days of sport. I saw you got a blast of UDRC in the face there?"

Christine frowned, "Yes, doesn't taste great..."

Then she stopped.

There was a tingling now... it was about to become another itch...

"Oh great, I'm getting itchy..." she started to smile in spite of herself when *sensation* stabbed her.

Every nerve in her body seemed to tingle abruptly, and for a second she thought the dose of UDRC had somehow thrown her senses into a fit of pleasure...

A single gasp escaped her, but then it got much more intense. Every nerve in her body began to *burn* — to feel literally as though it were on fire. And the fire got *worse.*

And it didn't stop getting worse.

The stasis patch wasn't even slowing it down.

When she realized she'd only begun feeling the tingling three seconds earlier, her mind tried to shut down. It was receiving burning signals from all over... as though she was caught in a fire... being burned alive.

Christine went into shock, but for some reason she wasn't able to lose consciousness.

"Burning..." she rasped in a second, her eyes screwing shut.

And then she screamed, because fire was consuming her nerves.

She fell backwards before Graham could move to catch her, but his mind was already racing. As she screamed and writhed on the floor he stepped quickly forward, pulled the control of her stasis patch off her belt, and turned it up to full.

She stiffened and froze.

A second later, Howler reentered the room with a smile on his face and pointed back at convulsing Larosians, "Looks like it's working..."

Graham stood and turned to the Colonel, his expression still not having changed. Even his eyes hid any sign of concern.

"We have a problem here," the ArcGeneral said softly.

Looking from Christine to Graham and back, Howler's smile faded, and he called for a medical team.

Omega had been evicted from *Carnarvon.*

CHAPTER 19

Jax Furgus wasn't entirely pleased.

Kari Peltier's cruisers had been out of contact for fourteen hours, which seemed a bad sign to the grizzled old lion — Omega might be out here, near Freetown. If that was the case, the plague was moving damned quickly. He'd need more information before he could be absolutely certain of that, though, which was why another squadron was out there looking for Peltier even now...

"ArcBrigadier Lutjens' Dreadnoughts should be arriving at the picket line in ten minutes," Ron Hobbes had been standing at *Aboukir's* main battle plot, but now he turned and paced back to his chair next to Jax.

Jax nodded in reply, "Let's hope he's a bit luckier... or that this has all just been a signaling failure. But I swear, if Peltier is just off station because she wants to stir up trouble, *I'll* have words with her."

Hobbes smiled, "You make it sound as though that'd be menacing."

"I'm a curmudgeon, of course it'd be menacing," Jax grumbled and rested his chin in the palm of his hand.

The two cats waited.

Nine Genesis Dreadnoughts slid through space towards the assigned picket coordinates of Kari Peltier's squadron. Sitting on the bridge of the flagship of this squadron, ArcBrigadier Henry Lutjens was being cautious. He wasn't sure whether it was a show of confidence or of disdain that Jax Furgus had tasked him with finding out what was going on in this section of the picket line, but he wasn't about to take any chances — these were ships the Fleet really couldn't afford to lose.

Knowing that Kari Peltier's ships might have met with a rapid demise, Lutjens was determined to take great care in his maneuvers on this mission. Though he was a new officer, both his parents had served in combat ships during the Krogg War, and he'd learned from them the importance of prudence and good tactics. At twenty-nine, he was young for his rank, (young officers were much more uncommon in this modern peacetime fleet than they had been in Sarah Manchester's and Pat Conroy's days of war and casualties), and he was thought to have the makings of a great Fleet Commander one day.

Of course, he wasn't exactly counting on 'one day' any more, because it seemed rather likely that Omega was going to get a twist on Freetown before the Earthers could manage a heavy counter. And like all humans in his Naval service, Lutjens knew damned well that only the Earthers had the power and leadership to hold back Omega.

He'd just have to do what he could today — find out what was going on out here and get word back to Jax Furgus at Freetown. It could be Omega... even if he saw friendly ships, they could be Omega.

"Preparing to decelerate from flux, sir," *Saint Walter Zai's* ArcColonel turned from the bridge's screens to his ArcBrigadier, and Lutjens nodded.

"Alright, let's get the squadron to General Quarters. Sensors, you warn me the minute you see anything. Comm, order *Saint Thomas Southerby* to remain back from the squadron — tell ArcColonel Narayan she's to run immediately for Freetown if there's trouble, no waiting."

As Lutjens spoke, the lights in his Dreadnought made a melodramatic shift to the red side of the visible spectrum, warning the crew of impending action. The Helm Officer read the change in flux output from her panel and reported, "Deceleration at your order, sir."

Looking to Lutjens, *Walter Zai's* ArcColonel managed to hide his own hesitation.

This crew had only been in battle once, against the Church traitors, but that had been a completely different enemy than the one they might be facing right now...

But Lutjens maintained an air of unflappability — one of the things his parents had impressed upon him was the importance of the appearance of calm. Abiding by that advice, the young ArcBrig looked to his ArcColonel, "Squadron to decelerate, battle order."

Omega watched the Genesis ships come from the bridge of the lead Battle-cruiser he'd captured earlier. The entire squadron was floating alongside that ship, ready to draw the newcomers in... and those Dreadnoughts were indeed coming. Unlike the old days, in this era they were actually pretty efficient at maintaining formation while exiting flux.

That was dandy, because it was always more fun to tear up a nice formation than to watch a disorderly rabble come apart.

As a vicious plague with a taste for the macabre, Omega enjoyed a good destruction of order now and then.

But of course, that came after he messed with them a bit...

It was seemingly ArcBrigadier Kari Peltier who ordered *Paladin Saint's* comms to spin up, but it was in fact Omega-Kari sitting in her command chair. Same body — and what a body, Omega was pleased! — but different owner.

Omega-Kari wiggled to get more comfortable in her chair, then smiled.

The Dreadnoughts were approaching slowly, with the tubes loaded and their lasers ready. One was hanging well back, obviously ready to run and tell the Earthers what was happening out here. Well that would never do...

While the Genesis Battlecruisers turned off their patrol station in good formation to meet the newcomers, some other Omega avatars, including Omega-Gillian, waited nearby, but they were small and unseen...

"Any signals, Comm?"

Lutjens sat frowning in his chair, and the ArcLieutenant watching for comm traffic shook her head, *"Paladin Saint's* comm is spun up, but I hear only static."

This was certainly unsettling — either it was a massive comm failure, or those ships didn't belong to Genesis anymore. Better to get them in the crosshairs in case they tried to cause trouble... if that was really Kari Peltier, Lutjens could apologize later.

"Alright, squadron to target the Battlecruisers. All ships to stand by..."

And then, rather abruptly, the Battlecruisers flushed their tubes at the Dreadnoughts.

"What the *hell?" Walter Zai's* ArcColonel was already walking toward the bridge's fire control section, and the ArcLieutenant there was quickly turning the AI against the incoming missiles.

"Point defense lasers active, armor fully charged... those missiles aren't emitting any tracking signals — looks to me like they're flying on dead reckoning, sir," the bridge Sensor Officer reported quickly.

Lutjens scowled at the report — most missiles maneuvered and chased their targets, but those Battlecruiser missiles had been fired like over-glorified bullets... he should easily be able to get around them.

But what did this mean? It had to be Omega. The Battlecruisers were somehow under the plague's control. Lutjens didn't know how a plague could cross space and infect a sealed ship, but the bastard must have found a way...

"Squadron to evade, orders to ArcColonel Narayan to report to Freetown that Omega has infected this section of the picket. We'll deal with him as best we can, but recommend recalling the line until inoculations of the fleet are complete..."

They'd started using the surplus of UDRC and other Earther compounds on Freetown to inoculate marines against Omega, since in case of a boarding, the marines would best able to stop the spread of the plague. That had actually made little sense to Lutjens — when Togo had given the order, the ArcBrigadier wondered whether the ArcGeneral realized that the marines would be the only uninfected members of the crew left if a boarding took place.

But orders were orders, and besides that, there hadn't been enough Earther compound on hand to inoculate more than the Superdreadnoughts attached to the Genesis Fleet.

His crews had no protection — save, of course, the atmospheric isolation of their ships in the void.

By the look of things at this moment, though, Omega had found a way through the void... perhaps boarding craft...

"Point defense concentrating on incoming missiles, sir," the ArcLieutenant at fire control spoke somberly, and Lutjens nodded.

"Squadron to maneuver out of missile range. Open fire as soon as solutions are locked."

There was some calm on the bridge. This was all Omega had to offer? A squadron of poorly coordinated Battlecruisers?

"Ah, but here falls the other shoe," Omega-Gillian's mouth twisted into a smile.

Omega was seeing through Lutjens' plans fairly easily, and was mildly amused by the young ArcBrig's thinking. He'd be more amused if he made the man cut off his own fingers and then fed him his own eyeballs.

Ah, that *never* got old...

So as Omega-Gillian's eyes watched *Saint Thomas Southerby* explode in a silent but bright fireball under her lasers — long before it even got *close* to getting away in flux — she smiled.

"Sir!"

Lutjens turned his chair quickly to the sensor section as *Thomas Southerby* exploded, and immediately his mind raced.

"New track! Drive signatures all around us! Some large ships, many small craft... can't identify... they're closing with us, ballistic courses!" the Sensor Officer sounded genuinely — and understandably — panicked.

This was a very, *very* good trap, Lutjens realized abruptly. He had to get something away to warn Freetown, but his Dreadnoughts wouldn't have a chance now. If they ran for flux, all these ships that were popping up on the screen around the squadron would destroy them before they got out of range.

"All ships, dump logs into e-hyper pods and launch them for Freetown and the other blockade squadrons. Activate self destructs and put them on a three-minute timer... we won't give up our ships to this damned plague."

The realization that he'd just condemned his squadron to infection and then death didn't immediately register with Lutjens, though the sound of a small craft hitting his ship's hull did.

So much for a promising career. Have you ever eaten your own eyeballs?

Lutjens froze in his chair as a foreign thought entered his head. Where had–

Not the time for dumb questions, is it now? Oh look, pods for me to shoot down...

As six pods erupted from each remaining Dreadnought, shots from the ships closing all around his squadron destroyed them.

See I've got actual combat experience, you're just an amateur. So now you've failed, just enjoy the ride. Oh, and by the way, don't you think I know how to disable an auto destruct? Nobility gets you nowhere these days...

Lutjens was frozen in his chair, trying for a desperate few seconds to keep calm, but as Omega heckled him, he panicked. Those Battlecruiser missiles' guidance systems — which had been offline when they were fired — suddenly activated, and their maneuvering drives spun up. They started dancing around the Dreadnought squadron, drawing all of the ships' point defense crews' attention while the rest of Omega's small craft came in to dock.

Mmm... Dreadnoughts...

Jax Furgus frowned and scratched his chin.

"What's that now, an hour overdue?"

Ron Hobbes glanced at the nearest chronometer and nodded, "He should have gotten there ninety minutes ago. So with half an hour's grace for recon, he's still awfully late."

Jax ground his jaw and nodded. So much for being able to rely on the Genesis Fleet — not that Jax didn't respect the determination of that service, he just had no faith left in its picket skills right now. Crews were too inexperienced, and Omega was likely *very* clever.

Coming to his feet he let out a lean growl, "Alright, let's recall the entire picket line. Get the senior officers together so we can prepare a better recon squadron. And get a pod ready for Earth, let Admiralty House know we're dealing with an unknown concentration of force out here."

Ron Hobbes nodded, and *Aboukir's* bridge came to life as the 74 redirected its Admiral's orders through the fleet.

They'd be ready for Omega next time.

CHAPTER 20

Setter Caine, Supreme Consul of the Earther government, sat in a pinnace as it smoothly rose through the atmosphere of his homeworld. It was still early in the day, Newfoundland time, though Admiralty House had been fully awake since a few famed old ships returned to Earth space six hours earlier.

Artie Tigar had decided to send some of his museum pieces back to Earth to join the recommissioning march, and they'd arrived just in time to be integrated into the force Lab Forepaw was putting together to support Freetown.

Visible just beyond the view port now were the famous 74s *Atlas* and *Vulcan*, both ships painstakingly maintained and ready to take on crews from the wealth of Earther Naval reserves. Caine was glad to see such renowned vessels back in the line — it was good of Artie to send them along instead of requisitioning them for his own force.

Of course, the larger veterans lay in higher orbit, and as the pinnace climbed faster they came into view just beyond Caine's window. The great old First Rates, *Endymion* and *Algenon*, the former once the ship of Kella Felar, rebuilt extensively after her loss at Gibraltar, and the latter being Varnon Broadpaw's longtime flagship. Both oversized First Rates would feel at home in the battle line with *Venerables* — they were as tough as the new ships, if relatively lightly gunned for their size.

But these vessels weren't Caine's destination, nor was the diminutive but proud little sloop *Flame* that floated just beyond them. No, Setter Caine was on this pinnace heading to a reunion — not with a person, but with a ship. One he'd been away from for far too long.

Of course that ship was... *wait for it...*

The 175-gun First Rate ship of the line *Orion*. Perhaps the most famous Earther ship ever built, it was the only one Caine had ever gone to war in, and he was most glad to see its glistening hull come into view. Fit to lead a battle line even today, the titanic veteran was just slightly smaller than a *Venerable*, and it was being restored to fighting trim by a crew of the very best reservists.

Soon it would be heading to Freetown, to serve as the flagship for the Allied forces there.

But not under his command...

"Andra, I'd prefer not to be squished."

Andra Ursla was leaning over her old friend's head to get a better look at

Orion, and as Setter sunk in his seat to avoid being crushed, she chuckled, "You were right, I should've taken the window seat. Sure you don't mind me taking it out?"

As soon as *Orion* had come in under a skeleton crew from New Halifax, Ursla had requested the veteran ship for her flag, for both sentimental and practical reasons. She'd been *Orion's* Flag Captain for many years, after all, and the ship remained formidable. She had fought the Krogg War from the bridge of *Agamemnon*, but Artie had kept that First Rate as his own flagship, and she had nearly as many sentimental connections to *Orion* from the years before the war. It would feel right to go to Freetown aboard the 175-gun ship.

Setter was pleased that Andra would be taking the First Rate too. He had as many sentimental attachments to his old flagship as anyone, so he wouldn't want to see it relegated to just any Earther. It was right that a veteran and someone nearly as close to the ship as he was would be sitting in his old command chair on the bridge.

Well, they'd have to replace his old chair with a bigger one, but the idea was the same.

"You'll look after it, I'm sure," Caine smiled at last in reply to his friend as Ursla shifted back into her seat.

"Well, it'll give us a major advantage. Last I heard Jax had a picket long overdue out there, and he'd sent Dreadnoughts to have a look, so it sounds like something's brewing. That's why Lab's sending us so soon."

Caine nodded slowly — he hadn't stopped by Admiralty House yet this morning to get the full reports, but he'd spoken briefly with both Varnon and Lab, and he'd received an abridged version of Jax's latest dilemma.

"So, you taking them all out with you, or is Lab keeping a reserve?"

Ursla scratched her ear thoughtfully, "He's actually giving me the lot of them. I'll have *Endymion*, *Atlas*, and *Vulcan* all together in an irregular squadron, and Barty Stowt's flying his flag from *Algenon*. We'll be boosting with about 115 ships total. Should be able to bolster Freetown fairly well."

Indeed she would. The Earther Fleet was coming alive again, with veteran officers like Vice Admiral Bartemius Stowt, once the Flag Captain of Ami Cairn's 141st Flying Squadron, in command. Reservist spacers were returning to duty and fitting out ships at a rate of dozens per day. Ursla's force was made up of the latest conglomeration of veteran Krogg War ships. Once they left, Earth would again be temporarily stripped, its only defense the Home Fleet... but within a week an entirely new fleet of packed ships would be recommissioned and crewed, ready to operate against Omega.

Operating against Omega?

Caine shook his head gently. Operating against Omega was for the moment a pretty passive concept. There had been so little relative activity... aside from a missing picket squadron, there was no indication of where the fight was going to come. Had this been the Kroggs they were facing, Caine would've been inclined to suggest that the missing picket was a portent of bad things in Freetown's future... but this was Omega. He could be baiting them with a lost picket and aiming to hit Gibraltar for all anyone knew.

They had to sit and wait. They couldn't take the first bait Omega threw at them.

Orion was growing to eclipse the pinnace now, and as the small ship made its turn to port to enter the great First Rate's main bay, Caine watched with interest. Little seemed to have changed in his old ship — it had been modified slightly to be more appropriate for carrying gunboats just after the war, when he was still flying his flag from its bridge, but other than that, even the paint was the same.

Well done, Artie.

The cavernous bay swallowed the pinnace, and Caine's eyes narrowed as they settled on the honor guard awaiting him and Ursla. As the craft lowered itself slowly to the deck, settling on its landing feet, Ursla slid out of her seat first, and Caine followed. The hatch was already open and the ramp lowering as they reached the craft's front, and Ursla proceeded down the walkway to the deck, with Setter close behind.

For her part, Ursla felt an incredible sense of calm wash over her as her boots thudded down on the landing bay's deck. She had never fought a war from the deck of this particular ship, but it was still a good home. The bosun's pipes twittered as she stepped forward towards the ratings and marines drawn up to meet her.

Stopping at the appointed place before those Earthers, she offered a crisp salute, which the assembled honor guard matched smartly, then gave the formal greeting, "Permission to come aboard, Captain?"

The Captain was the veteran skipper Esther Arbear, who'd distinguished herself many times during the Krogg War, and whose daughter had been lost with 2/54th on *Renown*.

Esther's professionalism was unaffected by that tragedy, of course, "Granted. And it's an honor to have you, Admiral."

With a smile, Ursla took her hand, "It's mine to be aboard. Lab didn't tell me who he'd gotten to take the Captain's chair, but I'm rather glad to see you, Esther."

"Thank you, ma'am..." Captain Arbear paused as Caine came to a stop next to Ursla. He'd been eclipsed from view by Ursla's large frame, and out of sight of the honor guard, had become distracted by his old ship. As he appeared from behind Ursla's broad torso, the honor guard snapped back to attention.

As the boots of 300 bear marines struck the deck in unison, Setter's nostalgia was shaken, and he blinked and looked up, "Oh at ease, please. I'm not in the service anymore."

The Earther marines slipped to their at rest positions, some veterans of the service smiling at the once-First Lord's gaze as it shifted around his old landing bay, then settled on Captain Arbear, "You're looking after *Orion*, I see, Esther."

With a smile Arbear nodded down to him, "It's an honor to, sir. We'll take good care of this ship."

Caine raised an eyebrow, "I know you will. And I was sorry to hear about Ellen, I have to say. Very sorry."

He remembered that detail, despite all that he'd read and seen in the past days, because he was... well... Setter Caine. He remembered such things.

Arbear smiled sadly, "Thank you, sir."

With a short sigh, Caine shook his head, "We... no. No, never mind. Think you're ready for Omega?"

Two long blinks prefaced Arbear's answer, "I miss my daughter."

Caine nodded slowly — that was all the answer he needed. Looking around a last time, he glanced up at Ursla, "Alright, I've said my hellos. I'll leave you to weigh anchor, and Lab will let Jax know you're coming."

Ursla smiled again and nodded, "You look after things around here. I'll see to Freetown."

"And take care," Setter said with a quiet smile. "See you... afterwards."

Ursla nodded, and then Caine turned and walked back to the pinnace ramp.

An hour later *Orion* led the recommissioned Earther force out of the system.

CHAPTER 21

Grand Chancellor Gregory Paine stared at the orange Ecclesia sky.

He had not slept in two days, but the Gods were making certain he did not feel fatigue — they had sent stimulants to him through his doctor, and with the drugs' help he remained alert and ready to act.

And act he would have to... because surely the new Freetown Fleet, supported by those heathen Earthers, had to be close to attacking Ecclesia by now. It had been almost two weeks since Chancellor Leo had returned his partially crippled fleet to the docks of the Commonwealth of the Faithful. Ecclesia space was abuzz with fear and expectations that the unholy demons were coming to carry the last bastion of sanctity away from the Gods.

The silence from Genesis did not help, either. High Chancellor Pious had not been in touch with Paine for all this time, and many feared that his demise was thus certain. The Church coup must have failed, despite the Holy whirlwind that had been its driving force, and that left Ecclesia and its Faithful in a precarious position.

With just a handful of ships capable of combat, with no working Carrier and no effective capital ships, the Faithful were vulnerable even at home. There were, of course, many orbital defenses available for the protection of the planet, but these would not withstand a concerted strike by Freetown's modern bastard ships.

So why had the Naval scum not arrived already?

Sensor logs that had survived in ships returning to Ecclesia had suggested that the flagship of the old Freetown Fleet had lost its bridge — perhaps the action had killed the Freetown leadership... DeBrooke or Stanton, or both. But if that was the case, why then would the Earthers wait?

It was conceivable, of course, that the Earthers would not attack, but would instead wait and trick the Faithful into believing there would not be an assault... perhaps draw Faithful ships out for scouting missions where they could be destroyed with little risk of Earther loss. The Genesis Fleet — if it was under Naval control — could do the same...

But somehow Paine believed that neither was quite the case.

No, something more sinister was at work beyond the limits of this Faithful system.

You got that right, Paine boy.

Gregory Paine stiffened as an alien thought entered his mind, and something compelled him to cast his gaze skyward.

Chancellor Leo dropped unceremoniously into his chair on the bridge of *Saint Tobias Janus*, the least-crippled of the Dreadnoughts remaining in the Faithful Fleet. It was a ship that had propulsion but no armor, missiles but no lasers, and that still had some sixteen sections of forward hull open to space; it was in poor fighting condition.

And from what was appearing on the flickering screen at the front of the bridge, *Tobias Janus* would be of little use to the Faithful, especially since it would undoubtedly be obliterated in a few minutes...

Eight Genesis Dreadnoughts and twelve Battlecruisers were decelerating from flux at the edge of the system, and Leo had only seven ships that were in any way capable of opposing them. Nothing available to him had the firepower of those Dreadnoughts, though, and even the Battlecruisers were likely more than a match for his ships. They were all modern — brand new warships built in Genesis yards for the heathen Navy.

Damn them...

"All capable ships make ready at battle stations. We will stay in orbit and attempt to combine our firepower with that of the stations. Ask that all the Faithful citizens begin to pray."

No need to pray Leo... Damn that sounds like an Earther *name, too bad you're not as smart as one... Anyway, no need to pray, like I said. See, your God is here.*

The alien thought filled Leo's brain, and he stiffened in his chair. What was this?

Oh here we go, the religious types getting all prayer-ish with me.

Leading Omega's Battlecruisers was *Paladin Saint*, with Omega-Kari grinning in her chair on the ship's bridge. Close behind those ships was *Saint Walter Zai*, with Omega-Henry Lutjens.

I'm like Napoleon returning from Elba... everyone they send to stop me becomes me... now I get some more Church to add to the collection!

Before any Faithful humans could truly react, Ecclesia had fallen.

"We need to know what's happening out there," Jax Furgus leaned back in his chair in *Aboukir's* briefing room, and the assembled humans, as well the Earthers Ron Hobbes, Tom Locke, and Alix Tarkham, offered nods of agreement.

Jax was none too pleased by the loss of two picket squadrons. He'd recalled the rest of the patrolling human ships and now, with Sarah only about six hours away from the system, and Ursla only five hours behind her, there was a chance to get a real force together to go looking.

"So... what then?" ArcLieutenant-General Togo leaned forward in his chair. "If Omega got Kari, then my cruisers aren't going to do you a hell of a lot of good — she was my very best, Admiral Furgus."

Jax cocked an eyebrow, "And what about Lutjens, Kelly? He your best too?"

ArcLieutenant-General Rozhestveski nodded, "I had him marked for a Generalship, sir. He wouldn't have been caught out by an ambush."

"Evidently he wasn't as good as you thought," Ed Jeffries thinly masked his disdain. "Jax, I think we should head out there. You and me — I'll take the Strike Fleet and you can come with, and between us we should be able to reconnoiter in force without losing anyone–"

"Now wait a godsdamned minute," Togo's eyes shifted quickly to glare at the dark-skinned Freetowner. "Just because we happen to be younger than you batch of renegades doesn't mean you're any better than us at *not* getting caught. I'll guarantee you Omega's got a strong force out there–"

"You're not in a position to guarantee anything, son! Now why don't we stop pretending that the fight you folks had against the traitors was anything like the experience my people had in the war. I'm not sending you all out to die when we need your ships here to–"

"You want to go hunting for *glory* and leave us to watch hearth and home? You need a priority check if you–"

As Rozhestveski joined the debate, Jax rubbed his brow. These particular humans weren't doing as well in the top spots as their predecessors had... though Ed was admittedly only saying what Jax was thinking. The Genesis Fleet was lacking seriously in experience right now, and without Graham or Sarah at its head, it was a liability.

So until the Manchester sister returned, Jax wouldn't let them go anywhere — the Genesis ships would stay and protect Freetown.

But he still had to tell *them* that. Unfortunately, they weren't ready to listen. Now they were yelling at Ed. Now they were trading expletives. Togo was shaking his fist... Rozhestveski was *pointing*...

Glancing sideways at Alix, Jax bobbed his eyebrows, and the Captain nodded.

Tarkham then very carefully put his fist through the table.

The crunching sound as the tabletop gave way to Tarkham's iron-like fist instantly stopped the younger humans. Jax had to hand it to Caine, the fist-through-the-table technique sure did work.

The lion leaned forward, "Alright, so I'm afraid I'm siding with Ed on this one, John, Kelly. I'm not risking any of your ships or you out there now. Not without Sarah to give the okay and not until you get your crews inoculated. Freetown crews are cleared to go since, for the past forty years, they've been using our drugs. Ed, I want your fleet to get untied and ready to cruise. I'm going to send Tom out with you, and I'll keep my Battle Squadron here. Go find out what's going on out there. I'll wait for Andra, and then if you need more help, we'll get more 44s and some 74s to you. Clear?"

There was angry silence, but Jax was feeling just a bit too unimpressed to care — Sarah would have to give these young humans some instruction as to how briefings worked... and to be fair, he'd have to tell Ed not to get the kids started.

But for now the humans nodded and quieted.

Alix pulled his fist back out from the underside of the table, and Jax stood, "Good. Now go different ways to the landing bay please, or I'm going to call the marines to escort you."

No one responded directly to that comment, but the two ArcLieutenant-Generals left immediately, and Ed a few seconds thereafter. Alix and Tom followed them discreetly, just in case, leaving Ron and Jax to exchange fatigued glances.

"Think Ed's up to it, then?" Ron asked quietly, and Jax sighed.

"I hope he is."

CHAPTER 22

Graham's expression hadn't changed.

The whole three hours he stood in *Renown's* sickbay, Celia Lazarus hadn't seen his mouth twitch or his ambivalent expression waver. But he *did* stay there, standing and occasionally pacing, his arms alternately folded across his chest and held behind his back as he waited.

Christine was unconscious on one of the sick beds, and was completely surrounded by Earther medical equipment. It looked complicated even to Lazarus, and she'd set most of it up herself. But Graham had remained patient and impassive for all this time, not asking questions, not sitting, not doing anything to get in the way...

It all seemed very unnatural.

Beckett Lupus had been by for an hour to keep the ArcGeneral company, but the duties of rounding up infected Larosians in *Carnarvon* had called him away, along with almost all Lazarus' support staff. She'd be on that Larosian Battleship herself, trying to save as many of the infected as she could, were Christine's problems not so critical.

What was going on in this poor human's DNA?

First Lazarus had looked for some sort of allergic reaction to the UDRC. But no, the surface signs all came up negative — nothing at the allergic level could explain the abrupt over-sensitivity. So she'd gone back to the first sites of itching — the small of Christine's back and her wrist. Still, topical scans revealed nothing.

That had taken two hours.

Then Lazarus had reluctantly turned to the next logical cause of the problem: the rapid regeneration treatment Christine had received in Genesis orbit after her injury. And damn, that had been it.

Though she'd been monitoring Christine's regenerated biology reasonably closely, Lazarus hadn't been marking every change it caused in the young woman's system. During the thirty years of using regen there had never been adverse side-effects in humans, and after the initial shock of the crash treatment had worn off, Lazarus assumed Christine's system would simply respond the same way everyone else's had.

Well that definitely *wasn't* the case, and as Lazarus came to terms with that fact, she restrained a verbal self-scolding. She should never have made the assumption, but she'd been distracted working on Omega.

It seemed that the residual regen in Christine's system had stayed very subtly active, and that due to a miscue in the genetic blueprints they were following, the compounds were acting to make her nerves more sensitive. By itself this shouldn't have caused more than that itching Christine had been feeling... but apparently the UDRC — a milder version of the regen compound — had magnified the process.

Suddenly Christine's surface nerves had been over-sensitized at the genetic level. They were sending her brain about six times the signal it should be receiving, so essentially everything from a gentle breeze to a sharp punch was producing the same blindingly painful sensation.

Lazarus needed to find a cure, but for the past hour she'd had little success with that effort. She still didn't actually understand *how* the regen and UDRC were creating this change — she could see the effect, but so much of Christine's DNA seemed in flux that she couldn't identify what part of which compound was doing the changing... or if it was both... or if it was something latent in Christine's own genetic code that had been reactivated...

All she could do for now was run more tests, and hope the triggering factor made itself apparent.

Having finished one such scan, Lazarus turned from the sick bed and nearly walked into Graham, who'd apparently stopped pacing and had been standing woodenly right behind her.

Casting a quick glance back to Christine's unconscious body, she nodded, "I've confirmed it, Graham. The mix of regen and UDRC has started another recode to her DNA. Looks like her genetic structure hadn't fully stabilized after the crash regen, and now she's in some sort of flux that I've never seen before. Genetically she has surface nerves almost as sensitive as mine, but her brain hasn't adapted to the new signals."

The ArcGeneral offered a slow nod, "Very well. An unexpected complication, I doubt it would have been possible to predict."

His cool words served as some comfort, but Lazarus simply shrugged, "Right now I'm most concerned with reversing it, but I'm not sure how to do that. I can't simply attempt to recode her with UDRC, since UDRC obviously started the flux... I might be able to create a counter-regen compound, but that might disrupt her recovery from the original injury."

"It seems to be a complicated problem," Graham commented distantly.

With a very slow nod, Lazarus tilted her head, "It is. And Graham, it might not be safe for me to try. I don't have a full genetic suite aboard — I'd normally want to send her to Gibraltar or even Fengate Hospital for work like this. I'm fairly well versed in the area, but the only one I know with the expertise to really rewrite her code and undo this is Elandra Caine herself."

"Ah," Graham's simple reply again showed no change in emotion. Despite her focus on Christine, Lazarus was becoming quite concerned about this man. He was seriously repressing, and she could only imagine that if he kept this up, he'd also wind up as her patient.

Of course, Lazarus had spent the last couple of weeks studying the alien plague that was living in his wife's severed hand, while he'd been thinking about the woman who'd lost that hand because she'd been infested through their first unborn child…

Lazarus could certainly understand repression.

"I'll have another look at the data, Graham, but my instinct right now is that stasis is going to be the only way to keep her nerves in check. And I'm not sure if a patch will be finely tuned enough to do that without rendering her immobile."

The ArcGeneral nodded again, "Investigate the options, Celia. I trust you'll come up with an adequate solution."

The doctor resisted shrugging in response to that comment, then turned her head towards her console and stepped past Graham, "Perhaps you should sleep, Graham. This is going to take me at least a couple of hours."

"I'll be quite alright here."

As he began to pace the deck again, Lazarus shook her head and moved behind her desk, calling up holos of genetic strands.

Narosh walked through one of *Carnarvon's* empty cargo bays with a sense of pure dread.

Some 611 Larosians, only hours before plague infested but alive, now lay dead in this bay, the shock of the UDRC aerosol proving too much for their systems. All but six of the crew they'd injected with the UDRC guns had died as well — the cure, it seemed, had proved more deadly than the disease.

According to medics who were now combing the ship for crew, it was not technically Omega that had killed these fine warriors — they were so malnourished that their systems had collapsed when the Omega cells had been crippled by Earther DNA. Some violent seizures had killed the more thoroughly infected, but for the most part the cause of death had been delayed starvation.

But, including the survivors who had managed to isolate themselves in the engine sections of the ship, some 214 of the aerosol-inhaling crew survived, and those who remained were recovering. Enough perhaps…

"Narosh."

The Admiral-of-a-Fleet came to a halt and turned as the familiar voice called to him, and Beckett Lupus stopped just short of his alien friend, "Varnia's looking for you… she's wondering about getting this ship back into fighting order. The Engineer isn't as used to dealing with us as you are…"

Narosh nodded, "Indeed, I'll be along presently. I'm just considering some of the same questions. With so many dead…" The Larosian paused in silence, and as his silver eye tracked across the room full of bodies, Beckett took a breath and looked over the fallen aliens as well. After Lazarus examined them, all these Larosians would be cremated and buried in space, according to Larosian tradition. There were so many of them... but it could have been much worse.

"Well, we can run this ship on a skeleton crew if we must," Narosh said softly, then turned. "Let's get to it."

The pair left the cargo bay.

"Engines... core power systems... no, I fear not Admiral Lupus," Engineer Neytosh nodded, forgetting which head movement meant 'no' just now. "We dismantled many of these systems to maintain our localized power, they will need to be rebuilt entirely."

"And you don't have the parts?" Varnia stopped herself from frowning, even though she wasn't sure the Larosian would have recognized the expression's meaning.

"We used up our replacement parts before actually dismantling the grids, ma'am. We thought at first our rescue might come quickly. Local generators became more important as the years wore on, though — we had to use them to bolster the auxiliary grid, to maintain basic life support."

Varnia took a deep breath and then looked to her own expert, "The machine shops can probably knock together the parts they need, eh Norm?"

Renown's Second Lieutenant and former Chief Engineer, a cougar named Norm Catwright, nodded, "But it'll take us at least two days, ma'am. Sorry, but I had a look at some of their kit, and I'm actually going to have to *retool* number three shop to produce compatible joins. And I'm still not certain about an alloy."

"We've got five hours... six tops. We need *something* out of *Carnarvon* by then, folks..." Varnia scratched her chin anxiously as she spoke, but the two engineers slowly shook their heads.

"Sounds bad..." heads turned as Beckett stepped onto *Renown's* bridge and advanced towards the plot, Narosh just a step behind.

Varnia nodded to her husband, "Looks like *Carnarvon's* going to be dead in space when the Omega ships get here. We need to do something... I'm honestly not sure what, though. Where's Graham?"

Beckett frowned, "I imagine he's still with Christine. I'll go get him."

Varnia nodded, and then Narosh stepped forward and began to consider the problem as Beckett headed to the sick berth.

When Christine awoke, all she could remember about what had happened was the *burning...* and screaming... but as her eyes fluttered open, she was pleasantly surprised to find she wasn't in flames or in pain. Her face felt a bit singed, but she could deal with that so long as she couldn't feel the rest of her...

Wait, she *couldn't feel the rest of her body*.

"Help..." she almost gurgled the word as her vocal chords only partially responded to her mind's order.

"Whatss happning to..."

Graham's face was set as he appeared in the space above her. He leaned in slightly so Christine could see him better, "I'm afraid we've had to put your entire body into full stasis. Regen is overacting thanks to that concentrated dose of UDRC you inhaled."

"Whatss it doin... hairry...?"

She was even hearing her slur now — her face was still partially in stasis, it seemed.

For a second Graham's lips almost twitched upward... or perhaps she'd just imagined that.

"No fur, Christine," he said in his same smooth tone, "just nerves six times too sensitive transmitting signals from your skin to your brain. Doctor Lazarus is working on the problem right now, but she doesn't want to keep you awake as she works. I just wanted to let you know what's going on before she brings stasis back to full. Next time we wake you up she should have something to treat you."

Oh, well then. Super-active nerves... that sounds painful.

Christine wanted to wince at the blatant foolishness of her internal monologue, but found her eyelids were moving too sluggishly.

"Thaanks for telllin me... seee yoou sooooon I guessss..."

Graham nodded very slowly as the stasis patch returned to full and Christine blacked out.

Looking to Lazarus, Graham offered a nod, "Keep me apprised please, Celia."

She nodded, "I will."

With that, Graham turned and nodded to Beckett. The pair left the sickbay and Celia Lazarus to contemplate just precisely what could be done for Christine Schaeffer.

Omega was only five and a half hours away.

CHAPTER 23

Graham emerged silently onto *Renown's* bridge, already having put the plight of his unfortunate young aide out of his mind. She'd pull through — here or back on Earth, someone would have a solution to her problem.

In the meantime, there was a much greater concern to be dealt with...

As he came closer to the battle plot, Graham let his eyes narrow and shift between the markers in the glowing blue holo tank.

"Well, they're already making 3,200 pls, Varnia — they clearly aren't regular Genesis ships anymore. And I don't know how well Omega handles ship-to-ship action..." Narosh paused as he detected the seeming telepathic abyss he'd come to associate with Graham. Only when Graham invited the Larosian in were there any thoughts to be read.

Varnia was nodding at the Admiral-of-a-Fleet's comment when her eyes shifted to the approaching human, "Just in time, Graham. With their increases in speed the Omega ships have managed to cut ETA to about five hours. There's no way to get *Carnarvon* fully online before they arrive, so we're trying to decide what to do..."

"I maintain, sirs, ma'ams, that I might be able to reestablish some combat systems, but not main power. We will in no way be maneuverable."

Graham's eyes dashed quickly from the plot to the unknown Larosian who'd spoken, and then he commented, "It should be all or nothing. I don't believe we should let Omega know that we have the ability to reactivate a Larosian warship if it can't be of immediate use to us — the advantage of surprise might prove important later."

Beckett raised an eyebrow, "That's true, but we're still looking at five enhanced ships, Graham — extra firepower might be useful..."

Varnia nodded slowly, "There are two Dreadnoughts in that group, Graham. I don't know what they'll be capable of, but I don't want to learn the hard way that *Renown's* outgunned. Our obligation is to relieve Laros with the formula for inoculation, then get back to our own galaxy... two things we can't do if we're crippled or destroyed."

Narosh offered his own brief bow-nod in agreement and Graham let out a short, thoughtful sigh. He didn't even know quite what had spawned the idea to stop here at *Carnarvon*, but surely even an immobile ship could serve them somehow...

But from what he saw on the plot, *Renown* appeared helpless. Tethered to a plague ship with only five gunboats roaming space as a combat patrol, helping cure survivors on the Larosian Battleship while they licked their wounds from...

We look vulnerable.

It was one of the few thoughts that Narosh could actually detect as it entered Graham's mind, and it was so abrupt and unexpected that even Narosh picked it up from the other side of the plot. He blinked a long blink with his good eye, then looked to Varnia.

She frowned at him, "What? Not telepathic, remember."

Narosh opened his mouth but Graham had already locked eyes with the Earther, "We might be able to lure them into close action if we appear vulnerable. Mask our long-range sensors, stay tethered to *Carnarvon*, and make it seem like we're attempting to take off survivors."

Varnia's eyes narrowed in thought as she envisioned *Renown* sitting at anchor as five enemy ships bore down...

"That way Omega doesn't realize we can fix *Carnarvon*," Beckett added softly. "When we jump him, he just sees it as an ambush... presuming, of course, the same Omega that's in Genesis is somehow in communion with these ships."

"Indeed," Varnia's eyes shifted to her husband. "So... we spring our trap as soon as he's in close enough."

Beckett tilted his head for just a second... the remaining question was what trap *Renown* had to spring, aside from *Carnarvon*.

Graham looked back to the plot with his same impassive gaze, and Narosh quickly lifted the idea from his mind.

"Gunboats," the Admiral-of-a-Fleet said quietly.

Beckett blinked. Oh right, *those*.

"We put *Carnarvon* between us and Omega's approach vector, and then put all our boats but for the patrol in its shadow. Omega closes, we untether in a seeming panic, and as his ships come right at us, to hit us before we can run for it, the boats jump them early."

Varnia was already nodding to herself as she spoke, and Beckett shrugged, "Sounds fine to me."

Narosh bow-nodded again, "Certainly."

Graham stiffly inclined his head, "We should see about the arrangements."

The commanders left the battle plot.

Lieutenant Vern Grange was *Renown's* senior boat officer, and unlike many of the ship's officers he was actually a newcomer to the Earther Navy — he'd joined during peacetime, and had distinguished himself as a Midshipman and then a Lieutenant in regular war-gaming. With his posting to *Renown* he'd entered a different branch of the service, eager to get a sense of how gunboats could supplement a battle line, and again he'd rapidly earned promotion based on his handiness with *Renown's* boats.

His orders during the mission over Darymanis City had led to the shredding of a Church mechanized brigade, and here in this new galaxy it would seemingly be his boats that stopped the first wave of the new Omega.

Not bad, the coyote thought to himself as he and his Squadron Lieutenants waited in *Renown's* Boat Ops Room for the arrival of Admiral Lupus. They were a maverick bunch, though not quite in the tradition of past characters like Fox Magnus. Boats were too closely tied to their base ships to allow quite the adventurism Fox Magnus was famous for, so these cats and canines tended to be daring, but always with an eye to the security of *Renown*.

Garth Badger, Grange's second-in-command and the only bear officer in *Renown's* flight wing, was probably the most conservative of them all — and he'd lit up a jungle full of Crusaders back over Darymanis.

So this was a fairly combat-effective group; with 111 boats ready to fly, they had about 150 cannon and plenty of pulsars to use against Omega... they'd just have to get the drop on his ships...

Or so the rough structure of the plan seemed to dictate. They'd get a better sense of exactly how the positioning would work once Varnia arrived to brief them.

"So, bit of a step up from air strikes against Crusaders, eh Vern?"

Grange blinked and glanced at Garth Badger. The black bear was grinning at his senior, and Grange nodded and shrugged slightly, "Seems so. But I'm sure we'll be alright."

With a thoughtful smile, Badger replied, "I'm inclined to think so."

The room full of Earther officers waited for the Admiral.

"I'll need to shore up the tethers before we begin turning with *Carnarvon*," *Renown's* Chief Engineer said quickly as he paced alongside Varnia on the way to the Boat Deck.

She nodded, "Very well, get right to it. We'll need to be in position soon."

The Engineer mirrored her nod and split off from Varnia's group at the next corridor. Only Graham and Narosh remained now, and as she thought more about the riskiness of this plan she glanced sideways from one to the other.

For the first time in her career she wasn't comfortable with how she was handling her ship.

Hell, she'd felt better about leaving Savanna Felix alone on *Tonnant's* bridge a very long time ago. And she'd felt *very* bad about that.

There was just something about fighting Omega that unsettled her — he wasn't like a Krogg...

But that was nothing she didn't already know. She'd just have to do her best and get her ship and crew through this. And these gunboat officers would be instrumental to that effort. They were her ace in the hole — something Omega hadn't seen too much of in the last war.

In Draco Maximane's day, only Carriers had held this sort of firepower in boats. Now dedicated Carriers like *Engadine* were relics, relegated to museums, and ships like *Renown* doubled as both Carrier and ship of the line.

Omega was about to get a dose of that new combined reality... hopefully he wouldn't be ready for it.

Varnia and her company slowed as the Boat Ops Room appeared ahead. These young officers, none of them veterans of the Krogg War, would have to come up with something new to beat Omega.

As she entered the room, Varnia forced away any doubt that suggested they wouldn't be equal to the task.

They were Earthers, they'd get the job done.

CHAPTER 24

The modern ships of the Freetown Navy decelerated quickly from flux drive as they came to the picket station that had already swallowed two squadrons of Genesis ships.

Still flying his flag from the bridge of the Battlecruiser *Savanna Felix*, the first of the six specially designed ships built for the Freetown fleet, Commodore Ed Jeffries was more than a little anxious at being out here.

He had *Felix, Caine, Ursla, Broadpaw,* and *Magnus*, along with the fleet's pride, the assault carrier *Republic*... he really didn't want to lose them to a quick strike by some unseen enemy...

"Talk to me, Sensors. What do you see out there?"

There was some delay as *Savanna Felix's* sensors adjusted to the new space around the squadron, but the main battle plot at last shifted its glowing projection to reveal the spinning wreckage of a Dreadnought. One of Lutjens', no doubt. Someone, some*thing* had caught him out.

But where was the rest of his squadron? Here on the extreme flank of the picket line, there were countless possible directions for those ships to have gone... back to Genesis, over towards Freetown, even off towards Ecclesia...

"All clear, sir. Getting nothing on scopes... wait, a distortion off to port, sir. Can't get a clear read on it, but it's definitely not friendly."

Felix's sensors were Freetown-designed and Earther-built, and while they weren't quite as finely tuned as Earther-designed models, they were much more sensitive than Genesis patterns. Perhaps that would give the Freetown Fleet an unexpected edge...

Ed was about to order his ships to beat to quarters when he realized they were already at action stations, so he skipped to the next order, "Get *Republic* under our lee, and give me a line abreast for the Battlecruisers."

The orders were relayed immediately through *Felix's* Signal Officer, and the five agile Battlecruisers quickly placed themselves in a line in front of their flagship, weapons coming to bear on the strange readings ahead.

"Carronade range?" Ed came out of his chair and advanced to the plot.

"Fifteen seconds, sir."

Nodding now, the veteran Commodore turned to his bridge's weapons' section, "As soon as we're in range put a shot into it. And prepare for multiple targets." He turned now to the pilot section, "Master, let's get ready for some hard maneuvering."

The equally experienced Cruising Master nodded back to her Commodore, "Aye, sir."

Time seemed to slow as the pride of the Freetown Navy closed on its unknown foe.

How very interesting... I hadn't expected them to see me this quickly... but alas, I'm still here to be seen.

Omega-Gillian was lounging in her chair on the bridge of the ship in that anomaly, watching as the smart little Freetowners moved closer and closer to her hiding spot. She'd have to make this look good, but she couldn't afford to destroy them all...

Interesting that the Earthers were still sending humans out here though — he'd frankly been hoping to see some Earther frigates for this gambit. But these advanced humans would just have to do...

"Coming out of its stealth, skipper," one of the ratings at Sensors barked abruptly, and then frowned as a strangely mutated Dreadnought with no transponder appeared out of the distortion in the main battle plot.

"Orders to *Republic*, launch ready wing and prepare to be hit from the rear."

"Sir! Six ships just came out of nowhere from behind — they're heading for *Republic*... twenty seconds out of weapons range..."

Yep, this was Omega playing dirty. Damn...

"Pod to Freetown with that stealth signature, quickly now! Order *Magnus* and *Broadpaw* around to aid *Republic*," Ed's eyes narrowed as they settled on the six ships bearing down behind him — four were military ships, one was a passenger ship and one was a yacht. This was the force that had cowed Lutjens' Dreadnought's and Peltier's cruisers?

The streaking icons of a wing of BSF-19A Gorgons appeared from *Republic*. These new boats had been developed specifically for operations off the Carrier, and they ferociously hurled themselves out of the ship's bays, their strike missiles already almost in range of the Omega ships. Even as the Gorgons launched, a wing of the much-vaunted FSF-192C Basilisk interceptor boats hurtled out after them, ready to cover their heavier compatriots on their runs.

"Range on the Dreadnought, skipper!"

Ed didn't even think as he turned to his Second Lieutenant commanding the gunners, "Fire as you bear!"

Felix and *Ursla* were first into range, and both Battlecruisers vented their missiles at the hulking Dreadnought, their long carronades reaching out and stabbing at the now-alien ship.

The Dreadnought shuddered with the impacts, but the carronades seemed to slide off its hull and the ship's point defense cut most of the missiles out of space.

"Fighting well, are you..." Ed muttered to himself as he turned back to the plot.

"Sir, the boats!"

His eyes shifted from the Dreadnought to a line of exploding Basilisk interceptors, and then a ripple of explosions ran down the line of Gorgon strikers. They'd been wiped from space by... lasers?

Felix abruptly bucked under Ed's feet, and as he grabbed the edges of the plot table to hold himself upright, his eyes whipped up to the Sensor Officer.

"Major range improvement on their lasers, sir!"

"Shields holding, skipper!"

Ed grunted to himself and steadied his feet.

Republic's long carronades and missiles came into action as he regained his balance, lashing out at the biggest aggressors now approaching it as *Magnus* and *Broadpaw* fell into flanking positions around the Carrier. Their combined firepower was formidable, and even Omega's cargo ship showed it respect, trying to maneuver beyond its range.

"Dreadnought's pulling back, sir... looks like we did get the drop on it!"

Ed frowned then. The Dreadnought was pulling back, flux drives charging... that was far too easy.

"Knock out its drives, quickly!"

The gunners weren't slow to answer the order, and their tubes recycled and immediately targeted the drive section of the hulking ship. It looked as though the engine components of the vessel were in the usual places... though perhaps Omega had shielded them more completely...

As the warheads launched from *Felix's* tubes, Ed again shifted his eyes to *Republic*. The three advanced Freetown ships fighting on that side appeared to be holding their own...

Then the Omega ships surged forward, the military vessels firing lasers at what once would have been impossibly long range, and the civilian ships diving at *Republic* at high speed.

It took a few seconds for Ed to figure out precisely what those civilian ships were doing, and then as they got well within a reasonable firing envelope, he watched *Republic's* maneuver drives flare in an attempt to push out of their path. It almost worked — the cargo ship was too slow at the helm and it dove right past the strike Carrier.

Then the yacht slammed into *Republic's* bridge.

As *Magnus* and *Broadpaw* swung around quickly and sent a salvo of missiles into the cargo ship, blasting its main drives apart, *Republic* yawed in space without control. The members of *Felix's* bridge crew collectively found themselves breathless, wondering if their prized flagship was about to explode.

But *Republic's* Chief Engineer was a veteran, and she held the ship's reactors in check against overload, while the auxiliary control stations all over the ship took over its operations.

That was two Freetown flagships that had lost bridges now — one to Omega, the other to the Faithful.

Ed was too stunned to give orders for the next few seconds, and as he blinked past his growing anger he prepared to order the destruction of the Dreadnought before him. But it had accelerated into flux and was hurtling away... into deep space.

The remaining warships did the same, following their larger compatriot out into the void at some 3,000 pls.

They were probably heading in a direction meant to mislead any pursuers, but Ed had to know where they'd end up.

"Download sensor logs into a pod and send it to Freetown. *Magnus* to remain with *Republic* and escort it back to Freetown as well. Everyone else, set pursuit course. Let's find out where they're headed."

Seconds later, a Carrier and a Battlecruiser short of its former strength, Ed Jeffries' squadron surged back into flux, following the Omega ships...

...on a wild goose chase.

Omega felt rather pleased — the humans had done as expected, taking the bait and rushing out into the depths of space to discover just where the concentration of his ships lay. And they'd even been fool enough to leave a serviceable infected ship behind.

As *Republic* and *Fox Magnus* accelerated into a low flux and left the hauler in their wake, Omega cheered their foolishness. Then he carefully activated the auxiliary flux drive in the massive wounded cargo ship and contemplated what use his distraction would be. They hadn't even thought he might be operating from Ecclesia... this little plan was working out marvelously.

So as the cargo hauler entered flux and began to crawl to its new (once Faithful) home base at an admittedly ponderous 1,105 pls, Omega was pleased with his action. The Allies were chasing his ships one direction, he was setting up to hit them from the other.

It was working perfectly.

"Its vector suggests Ecclesia, Tom. But that could be a feint."

Commodore Tom Locke nodded as his Flag Captain reported, avoiding a sigh. They'd sacrificed the Freetown Carrier to allow this little operation to go ahead. Now, with drives fields stretched to almost 300 percent, Locke's 44s were ready to follow the crippled hauler to its real home port.

But it could be a misdirection... Omega could have seen them...

Well, hopefully he was trading mistakes with the Earthers, not leading them on a wild goose chase.

"Alright, order *Demeter* to stay back until we're out of range and then to report directly to Freetown by pod. If they can catch up with us after that it'll be appreciated, but if we veer off expected course and they can't find us they should head back to Freetown. Let's see where Omega's really going."

The orders reached out from Locke's Signal Officer in *Charybdis* to his squadron, and then the Earther frigates accelerated gently behind the slow hauler.

Omega wasn't the only wily one out there...

CHAPTER 25

Graham Manchester stood silently on *Renown's* bridge, watching as the five icons of the boat patrol crossed space ahead of *Carnarvon* again. The Omega ships were well within sight of long-range sensors now, and they'd changed course to come after the two Allied battleships, but with the detection gear set to passive, *Renown's* battle plot wasn't showing their approach with the same smooth projection he was accustomed to seeing.

Every thirty seconds the icons would jump a little further, but there was no smooth straight-line advance through the plot.

"They're about fifteen minutes out, ma'am."

Varnia was standing opposite Graham at the plot, and she offered a short nod, "Very good."

Carnarvon's power grid had been completely shut down and its redundant batteries disconnected, so everything on the ship was weightless. Nothing about the battlewagon seemed alive — hopefully it would indeed appear that the Earthers were just picking up survivors. Omega couldn't be allowed to suspect that the old Larosian ships, once cured, could return to the fight.

Graham hoped *Carnarvon* could be put to rights, and sent on to Laros while *Renown* went home. It would maximize the Allied effectiveness in this galaxy — the Earthers could head straight for New Halifax, while the Larosian ship could begin the reconstruction here.

The more he thought about it, the more Graham was determined to stay with *Carnarvon*. He wanted a ship of his own, and a separate war against Omega. And he didn't want to go home. Not after all that had happened.

Yes, he was fully aware that he would be running from both reality and responsibility if he took that course. So he was still debating it... mainly so that he could *say* he was still debating it. He truly did not want to go back. They'd want him to assume responsibilities, fight the good fight, when all he wished to do was kill the plague.

But that was a decision for another time.

"Report from Lieutenant Grange, ma'am. The boats are now heaving to beneath *Carnarvon*."

Graham blinked as the report went to Varnia, and as she nodded, both commanders' eyes turned to the plot. Standing on a third side of the great holo tank, Narosh tapped a closer view of the Larosian warship up into a separate window, and the markers of the boats were clear.

The question was whether they'd be detected by the enemy. They were holding position close to the Battleship's hull, trying to drift as though they were debris just below the great ship's engine pylons. With luck they wouldn't be seen.

"Alright then," Varnia turned away from the plot towards her First Lieutenant, "Let's beat to quarters. Take the port broadside's power down to minimal. Keep output as low as you can until I give the order."

The Lieutenant nodded, and Varnia turned to her Master, "When the time comes we'll need to make a quick and clean break from *Carnarvon*."

As the Master offered a nod in reply, Varnia turned to Graham, "All set?"

The ArcGeneral's expression, for all the thoughts swirling in his head, remained static, "Indeed."

Renown waited, playing possum.

Garth Badger had direct command of Number Three Gun Squadron, and he was also the second in command of the entire strike wing. Since they'd turned out every boat for this operation, he had to help Vern Grange coordinate over 100 boats while his crew worried about firing the two Mark XXIV cannon slung low in the small craft's hull.

Badger wasn't the sort who actively sought out these sorts of assignments — he was inclined to go wherever he was needed, and to do whatever was asked of him, but he wasn't one to hunt command.

He had it now, though, so he was committed to doing a good job with his allotment of fifty-seven boats. Hopefully Omega wouldn't be expecting such a prompt response...

"Omega ships preparing to decelerate," the Boat Officer reported over the comm from *Renown's* bridge. "Stand by."

Badger looked to his copilot and nodded, then keyed open the comm channel to his other boats, "Alright folks. You know the routine, stay on my flank until I give the word. Make them count."

Lifting his finger from the button, Badger brought the combat systems of his boat to full power, his fellow pilot helping him put the boat's propulsion systems into a state of readiness. The window at the head of the cockpit had a Heads Up Display floating over it, and as the Omega ships entered local space, *Renown's* scans were projected into the holo.

Garth Badger took a deep breath, "Get ready..."

Varnia cocked an eyebrow, "This mightn't be as bad as we thought."

Narosh glanced curiously at his comrade, but then Graham's mind offered the immediate answer to his question; one of the Omega ships — once a Genesis Heavy Cruiser — had almost collided with one of the Dreadnoughts as it decelerated.

Maybe Omega was less well-honed than any of the Earthers had expected...

No. What had looked like a near-collision was just the first maneuver in an elaborate weave — the Omega ships were curling forward in a serpentine double line.

"Weapons range in twenty seconds."

Varnia nodded, "Alright Master, let's look uncomfortable. Have guns ready to fire as they bear."

Renown busily set about its panicked split from *Carnarvon*, with airlocks breaking contact almost violently while the *Venerable*-class ship's shields started to rise. As the intentional lessening of the ship's power signature was incrementally relieved, the ship took on the guise of a surprised animal getting ready for a panicked fight.

And Omega seemed keen on this hunt...

Haha, taking off survivors are they? A shame that my earlier version left any alive at all... ah well, I was younger and less experienced.

It wasn't as easy as Omega would have liked to command ships several galaxies away — even telepathy between his constituent cells could face temporal interruption when crossing galaxies. Next time he'd have to send more of himself out there. In order to master the ships he had, he'd been required to use all the humans aboard them as either operators or biomatter — they either worked the ship systems or were rendered and resequenced into raw Krogg-type material to augment them. He had no real avatars to help focus his telepathic energy.

But if he captured some of the Larosians infected with his older self, he could upgrade them to his new Krogg-hybrid version, and then have enough bodies to turn some into proper avatars. That way he'd have a stronger connection between the two galaxies.

But as it was, even though seeing anything at this great distance was like looking out the corner of a human eye, he could squash this *Venerable*.

He was Omega, after all. In one galaxy, Omega-Gillian was leading a wild goose chase, Omega-Paine was being turned into a new avatar, and Omega-Natosh was eating infants in front of their parents. In another galaxy, Omega himself — even without a specific avatar through which to act — was reaching out to smash the Earther ship of the line.

Talk about multitasking. Being a decentralized, kick-ass plague really rocked.

Yes *rocked*, not that anyone alive in this century would know what he meant when he thought that. Omega took pride in being a twenty-first-fucking-century plague — colloquialisms and profanities included.

Now he'd see these Earthers learned the sort of vicious lessons that twenty-first century life had taught him...

What the fu–

As the first of Omega's Dreadnoughts closed on *Carnarvon*, it launched missiles at *Renown*. The larger Earther warship was shifting out of the shadow of its defenseless consort, so the missiles were in no danger of hitting the Larosian vessel.

No, as was the plan, everything was headed for the Earther ship.

As a smile graced Varnia Lupus' face, gun crews who would not have been at their posts had *Renown* truly been surprised, lined up their sights on the missile spread. About 130 missiles made up the first launch, and another 250 followed in a thick wave as the rest of Omega's ships — another Dreadnought, two Battlecruisers and a Heavy Cruiser — closed the range.

"Canister, I think," Varnia hadn't finished her comment by the time *Renown's* Gun Captains loosed the ship's port broadside — and loosed it with canister, as she would have liked.

They were veterans of the Krogg War, they didn't need to be told to fire canister at a moment like this.

"Full power now, let's not waste surprise. Roll on the lead Dreadnought, starboard guns fire as they bear," Varnia felt a familiar calm as her words smoothly flowed — she hadn't been in a fight quite like this since... since she'd joined her father in *Algenon* at Krogg 'A'.

Well, she didn't know how to ride a bike, but Pat had once told her that she wouldn't forget how if she ever learned. This, it would seem, was like that.

"Ready for firing, ma'am," the First Lieutenant bobbed his head to Varnia, and as he did, the Master rolled *Renown* and kicked the ship's speed up from 55 pls to 97 pls.

The Dreadnought was caught out as so many enemy ships had been in past — few were ready to deal with the mass and agility of Earther warships. Guns crashed back along their tracks on *Renown's* starboard side, and the shot sliced through the Dreadnought's hull with near impunity.

That Dreadnought was hammered until it died in a violent white explosion, but more were coming fast.

Well, that was clever. A bit more ready than average — must've seen me coming after all.

Omega wasn't really disappointed.

Ah well, I suppose they can't all be easy prey.

Omega-Natosh shrugged to himself at that overriding thought, as he continued to chew on some human on Genesis.

Throat flesh always tastes the best... Omega concluded, tasting what Omega-Natosh tasted. At the very same moment, Omega was reacting to the Earthers.

He was everywhere at once...
I am such a God!
Now let's kill these Earthers...

Even with the loss of a Dreadnought, Omega's remaining ships still posed a serious conventional threat to the Earther vessel, so *Renown* dropped backward past *Carnarvon* in a delicate but prudent maneuver.

New flights of human missiles were vomited into space, and as the great *Venerable* made its apparent retreat, the Omega ships drove directly after it, going right past *Carnarvon*, ignoring the plague ship.

That was exactly what the Earthers had been counting on, and as Garth Badger watched the leading pair of Omega vessels pass 'over' the ship he was hiding 'under', he looked briefly to his copilot, then keyed his comm.

"Badger to second group, let's move."

Renown's gunboats darted out from beneath *Carnarvon's* hull, space filled with death.

Death for *Omega*.

CHAPTER 26

What the hell...
Omega's focus shifted sluggishly across the telepathic bands between Ecclesia and the events surrounding *Carnarvon* galaxies away. It was proving more difficult that expected, operating over such distances without an avatar there to serve as a node for his telepathic energy. After he crushed *Renown*, he'd have to take the time to convert one of the minions in that region.

This was probably why dinosaurs had kept extra brains in their tails.

Except dinosaurs were stupid, and I'm not...

He focused hard now. Focus could overcome the lack of an avatar...

"We're about to put an end to this," Garth Badger said quietly, and though his copilot nodded in reply, he knew he'd essentially made the comment for his own benefit.

His boat leapt out from under *Carnarvon*, and with it the entire flight of *Renown's* gunboats surged ahead. Their cannon were fully charged, and as they slashed abruptly towards the Omega Dreadnought, they met no resistance.

The screening cruisers, if they could still be called that, were out of conventional formation, and weren't even close to being in position to intercept.

So as Badger's Three Gun Squadron reached optimum firing range, shot from the pair of guns mounted in each of its boats hurtled towards the Omega capital ship's undefended flank. Some 100 bursts of concentrated energy joined the salvo, as the rest of the gunboat squadrons loosed their own firepower at the hulking Genesis-built vessel.

Had the ship been under the control of its builders, the salvo would surely have proven its end, but Omega was far faster than most humans when it came to ship-handling. He'd observed enough during the Krogg War to know just how important handy ships were to victory, and while he hadn't exactly prepared his Genesis provisionals for a gunboat ambush, the evasion principle held true.

With an ease at the helm that came from the ability to control every member of the ship's crew as though they were fingers on some sort of giant hand, Omega threw the Dreadnought wildly off course, reversing its starboard drives and bringing its tubes quickly to bear on *Renown*.

Most of Badger's squadron's shot sailed right past its target.

"They're moving quickly. Squadrons break formation, I'll bet we're faster."

The tide of boats shattered abruptly, *Renown's* squadrons suddenly forming a host of claw-shaped formations as they drove in closer to the Omega ships.

"Three Gun, keep with us," Badger continued his orders. "Let's make a run for that Dreadnought's drives."

As laser fire started to slice out from the massive Dreadnought, Badger's boats dove through the fray, closing fast with the aft section of the ship. They'd just need a clean stern-on shot for their guns to tell…

But one of Omega's Battlecruisers arced back over its large compatriot, and coming bow-on at Three Gun Squadron, the wedge-shaped ship split the gunboat claw short of its target.

Lasers from that ship lashed out and batted two of Three Gun's boats on the pass, too. Badger ground his jaw — Omega was proving to be about as tough a candidate as expected.

But Two Gun and Two Pulsar Squadrons were coming in fast to support Badger's wing, and as the long-range heavy pulsars and cannon shot from those two flights of boats opened up on the interrupting Battlecruiser's hull, the rest of Three Gun Squadron burst around the ship and dove back into formation, focusing again on the dancing Dreadnought.

"Wait for a good shot, guns…" Badger's eyes narrowed at his battle plot as the Dreadnought unleashed another salvo of missiles towards *Renown*, and two more of his boats were smashed aside by laser fire.

"Almost…"

But then the Genesis-built capital ship seemed to slide sideways, turning to bring its bow to bear on Three Gun.

"Break off! Scatter!"

The boats came out of formation and drove frantically in different directions, and just in time — the space they'd been advancing through was rapidly filled with energy.

Damn this wasn't going to be easy…

"He's keeping our boats occupied," Varnia frowned at her plot and allowed a very deep sigh. "They're not getting through."

"I've never seen Genesis ships move quite so fast," Narosh said solemnly, but as he made the comment his gaze drifted through the plot to Graham, who's face remained set.

"Master, can we get *anything* to bear?" Varnia turned away from the holo tank, and *Renown's* venerable old lead ship-handler shook his head.

"Sorry ma'am, every time I get a broadside to bear they're gone…"

Varnia offered a short, jerked nod in reply and looked back to the plot. Omega had their number, it seemed… So she'd just have to try something new.

"Alright then, let's start herding," she turned to *Renown's* First Lieutenant.

"They keep getting out of the way, that means we can start pushing them into the sights of the boats. Have Lieutenant Grange get a gun squadron ready for a target."

She glanced back to the plot, then nodded to herself, "Alright Master, turn fourteen degrees to port and begin rolling. Signals, get Third Gun to follow off our starboard quarter."

It was perhaps the most confusing set of orders Varnia Broadpaw had ever given, and without the benefit of telepathic communication, Narosh couldn't quite follow them. But *Renown* quickly shifted in space nonetheless.

And as Three Gun Squadron reformed and came up along the ship of the line's starboard quarter, the threat of their combined shot became obvious to the Omega Battlecruiser they were turning to target. It moved off to *Renown's* port side, turning fast to present its bow tubes for a shot on *Renown*...

Then Vern Grange's First and Fourth Gun Squadrons slammed right into its rear with a concentrated volley of shot.

Omega seemed not to have had time to do any major upgrading to these ship's protection systems, and as had always been the case, energy armor buckled under the weightless hammer of energy shot. The ship writhed, and as whatever damage-control teams Omega deployed were unable to stop the surges that pulsed through its drive systems, it rapidly exploded.

"Now that's more like it," Varnia nodded to herself, and then glanced to Narosh with a bob of her eyebrows. "Just a little learning from the–"

The Omega Dreadnought came up right alongside *Renown*, and its lasers focused directly on the *Venerable*-class ship of the line's bridge.

Garth Badger saw the concentration of laser fire crack *Renown's* shields and his eyes widened as the plating around the ship's bridge seemed to shear off. The explosion of the outer power relays flashed for a second before the void of space doused it, and then someone at *Renown's* helm put the ship into a roll and got the bridge out of Omega's sights.

But... the bridge?

"Two Gun come with us, Two Pulsar get ready for point defense — let's get that Dreadnought off *Renown's* back."

They absolutely couldn't lose *Renown* out here — they had to protect their mothership...

But a bridge hit didn't put *Renown* out of action, no matter how much damage it did, because there were Earther Gun Captains sitting behind each of the massive ship's 250 cannon, and as the roll began, the gunners to starboard saw a Genesis Dreadnought in their sights at point-blank range.

They didn't need any order to fire as their guns came to bear.

Badger let out a breath, and as the storm of shot leapt from *Renown's* broadside and incinerated the Dreadnought's port side, the Genesis-built ship seemed to evaporate. Though human lasers could be deterred by the very strength of Earther hulls, energy shot was more than a match for Genesis construction.

The Dreadnought was batted aside, with some of the shot meeting so little resistance it burst out the human ship's opposite side to speed off into space and dissipate.

But *Renown* was still rolling, and just when what was left of the plague ship might have gotten some emergency power and tried to drift away, the Earther capital ship's port guns came up.

The Dreadnought ceased to be.

"Scratch that last, then…" Badger blinked away any reaction to the exploits of his control ship. "Get us onto the tail of that Battlecruiser. We'll engage at point-blank from the rear, Two Gun get above and rain down."

The bridge was in a shambles as Graham hauled himself to his feet. Narosh's freshly-attached hand was lying on the deck next to him, but the human ignored it. As the ArcGeneral climbed again to stand next to the now-flickering plot, he realized just what had happened — they'd sustained point-blank laser shot to *Renown's* bridge, and even though the beams had gotten through the shields, *Renown's* hull had held fast.

This compartment hadn't decompressed, and it hadn't superheated to kill them all.

Narosh came to his feet shakily on the other side of the plot, and Graham nodded to him, "Your hand is over here."

The Larosian approximated a frown and then bobbed his head, using his remaining hand to cover the silver-bloody stump of his other wrist, "Seems I can't keep these intact… shrapnel?"

"Shrapnel alright…" Varnia sat up and avoided gritting her teeth. One of her ears had been chopped off near the base, leaving only one of the usually upright furry triangles atop her head as she struggled to her feet, "Never had this happen before. It bloody *hurts*…"

Graham nodded again, expression still neutral as he looked to the plot. Secondary circuits were taking over command of the holo display, so its flickering lessened and the image of the battle came through again.

The last two cruisers were being chased down by *Renown's* boats… of which eleven had now been lost, three with all hands.

"Graham?"

He didn't shift his gaze from the plot, "Yes?"

"You might want to get that looked at…"

His eyes moved from the plot to Varnia and Narosh, who both wore surprised expressions. He then glanced down at his torso. The piece of shrapnel that had carried off Varnia's ear and Narosh's hand was sticking out of his side, with the tip of Varnia's ear still dangling from its end.

Hmm.

"I don't expect it's too deep," he said quietly, eyes shifting back to the plot. "If some medics come up we can see about it."

Varnia raised an eyebrow, one of her hands covering the painful stump that had been her ear, "Yes, well we should get some of those up here then..."

She glanced to the First Lieutenant who was already nodding in reply to the order, then she looked to the Master, "You have helm?"

"Yes, ma'am."

The remaining Omega Battlecruiser exploded in the plot, and the boats now all closed in on the Heavy Cruiser... *Renown's* guns might not be needed after all.

"Bring us back alongside *Carnarvon* and dock."

The last defensive lasers from the Heavy Cruiser caught another boat in their fury, but on the whole Garth Badger wasn't displeased with the action. Three Gun was drawn up in claw formation and, with his boat at their centre, the squadron's craft were slashing at the ship from below.

Alongside them, Vern Grange's One Gun Squadron was hurtling upward as well, with the Lieutenant's boat in its center. They'd have this matter wrapped up in a moment...

"Closing to point-blank now... prepare to break formation..." Badger was frowning into the plot when the Heavy Cruiser exploded.

But nobody had hit it...

"Debris! That was a self destruct, we've got debris–"

The warning came from Vern Grange, and as it did the squadrons of boats surging towards the Heavy Cruiser scattered, avoiding debris they hadn't been expecting. The blast wave caught six of them, destroying two and disabling the others. Then the chunks of the ship followed the energy riptide.

Badger and his copilot struggled to heel their boat out of the maelstrom, and at a full 92 pls they managed to shoot out of the fray.

Fourteen more of *Renown's* boats didn't manage the feat. This Heavy Cruiser's dying booby-trap caught them, flattening nine and disabling five.

And one of the boats that got flattened was Vern Grange's.

As the conflagration cleared, Garth Badger's eyes scanned his HUD for the lead marker on any of the surviving boats, but there was none.

Which meant he was now wing commander... at least until they found Vern Grange, hopefully alive in the wreckage out there.

"*Renown's* bridge reports no fatalities," his copilot reported to him as he tried to blink away his surprise.

Badger nodded, "Tell them we've got significant losses. And our wing commander is missing..."

The HUD was filled with debris. They'd have to sift it all...

"Pulsar Squadrons begin search and rescue. Gun Squadrons, stand down combat systems. One and Four Gun, take up combat patrol flights over *Carnarvon*. Two and Three, let's get searching."

Renown's remaining gunboats began searching for Earther survivors.

CHAPTER 27

"You sure you're not light-headed?"

Sitting in the medical bay, Graham shook his head, and Celia Lazarus eyed him skeptically, "If you say so. It wasn't in deep, but you did lose a bit of blood there."

"I assure you, I'm quite alright."

Lazarus still didn't know what to make of Graham. She'd watched him closely as she'd removed the piece of chair-arm from his side, and pulled Varnia's ear off it. The human's face hadn't changed expression — not even when she'd had to detached a piece of the shrapnel that had hooked into his flesh.

It was just not natural.

Hell, before seeing it herself, she'd have argued that it was frankly impossible for anyone to so flatly stifle any sort of expression. It was disturbing. *Very* disturbing.

"Well, I've closed everything up, anyway. You won't have any complications — your regen will see to that."

"More than I can say," Narosh came to a stop next to Graham as the human slid off the edge of the medical bed onto his feet. The Larosian waved his stump at the ArcGeneral, "Apparently the old one got a little... cooked. They don't want to risk reattaching it, so I have to wait for another new one."

"That's unfortunate," Graham tugged his uniform back down over his waist. "And your ear, Varnia?"

The question didn't sound inconsiderate... just emotionless. Varnia's eyebrow raised slightly and her ear twitched.

"No twitching, it's almost back on..." the medic leaning over her head from behind gave the orders sharply, and she rolled her eyes.

"It still hurts, but they're regenerating it back on. Since it was dangling from you it didn't get cooked with Narosh's hand when the plot's relay blew."

"Glad I could help," Graham's tone remained somber, and his eyes drifted across the med bay. There were a few dozen Earthers in here, many of them crew members who'd been recovered by their fellows from disabled boats.

Aside from the bridge, there'd been no serious damage to *Renown*, and casualties had been pleasantly light for the ship. Fatalities in the boats, though, were still being counted.

"There. Now be careful with it... it might be ringing for a while," the medic leaned back from Varnia's head and turned off his regeneration stitcher-tool.

Standing and twitching her ear somewhat ponderously, she found herself trying in vain to look up at it when her husband stepped though the hatch.

"Did I hear you lost an ear?" Beckett Lupus headed straight for his wife as he came through the door, and she pointed at the freshly restored, twitching appendage, her eyes still climbing vainly to try to see it.

Beckett came to a halt and frowned, "Put it on backwards, did he?"

Varnia's eyes shot back to her husband and widened, and he grinned, "Oh wait, it's fine."

"You'll be missing an ear in a minute..." she grumbled and stepped past him towards Narosh and Graham, Beckett turning and following close behind.

The Larosian waved his stub to the General, and the wolf's eyebrows rose slightly, "They going to put a string on the next one so you don't lose it?"

Narosh bow-nodded and smiled, "I put in the request."

"How you can make light of missing limbs is beyond me," Varnia shook her head and sighed, and Beckett chuckled.

Garth Badger's boat came to a halt just beyond a floating chunk of the Heavy Cruiser, his HUD showing something odd about the piece of debris. These Omega vessels had mostly been made up of unaltered Genesis tech, with some Krogg-style enhancements to propulsion and weapons. Those high-energy systems seemed to have been obliterated in the explosions.

This piece of hull, however, contained a sealed compartment, and inside it was a very chaotic biosign. Part human, part Omega, and very much alive.

His boats had been incinerating any debris that showed signs of the Krogg-style biomatter, in case it carried the plague... but here was a full, living specimen of Omega.

Could they use it to test a cure?

"Let the bridge know, I've got a living infested human here. Please advise."

The intercom chirped just as Varnia began lecturing her husband about how serious losing an appendage could be, and he began listing off all the limbs he'd lost, the number of times he'd been paralyzed, and recalling that time he'd been blown up near *Harbinger Bishop's* survivors' camp.

"Ma'am, they've got a live Omega human out there," the report came to Varnia as she turned to face the comm panel.

The med bay fell silent.

"Lieutenant Badger wants to know whether he should bring it in."

Varnia looked from the panel to Beckett to Narosh to Graham and then to Celia Lazarus, whose ears had perked at the report.

"If we take him aboard, can he reveal our situation to Omega?" the Admiral asked.

Lazarus raised an eyebrow and shrugged, "I honestly don't know. If this one is alive, then presumably Omega can control it, and see through it... turn it into one of his nodes."

"If that's the case, he would be able to warn Omega of our disposition," Narosh said quietly.

"But if it's injured and alone, he mightn't have complete command of its faculties... or the ability to fully see everything it does," Beckett frowned thoughtfully. "We've killed many of his minions out here. Wouldn't that be like killing off many brain cells and just leaving one, Doc? Leave him able to only do so much?"

Lazarus shook her head slowly, "I really can't say. We just don't know enough about how he works yet."

Varnia nodded at both comments, "Either way it's probably a liability to have a fully functioning Omega human aboard."

"If we mean to find a cure, I think it would be rather necessary to have one," Graham's tone hadn't actually changed, but there was an edge that hadn't been there before. None of the assembled Earthers or the Larosian could read Graham's feelings or thoughts to confirm that he was hoping for a cure for his wife, but that was the assumption they all made.

Lazarus nodded, "I haven't been able to make a great deal of progress with Commandant Hodge's hand, as I have to keep the cells preserved. Scans of a living example could be crucial, and as a test case for a cure..."

Varnia's eyes drifted from Lazarus to Graham and then descended slowly towards the deck, "Well, if there's a way to get it aboard without endangering our operations."

"Stasis. If I can put it into full stasis, Omega won't be able to get anything from it unless we isolate it and deactivate the patch," Lazarus looked from Graham to Varnia as she made the statement.

It was quite an opportunity, on a number of levels, and Varnia knew it.

"Alright," she turned and paced back to the comm, keying its feed to the bridge. "Tell Garth to bring it into bay one."

"Aye, ma'am," the Second Lieutenant's tone was even, and the link cut.

"I'll get Cadmus down there with some marines. Doc, let's go..." Beckett moved to step out of the med bay, and Narosh, Varnia, Lazarus and Graham all moved to follow him.

The General stopped briefly and frowned, "I suppose we're all going then. Fair enough."

They left for the flight deck.

Garth Badger carefully hauled the piece of debris into *Renown's* largest landing bay, turning control of its heading over to the grav tractors built into the floor. With that done, he turned his boat around and headed back out of the ship, intent on continuing his search for Earther survivors.

The piece of Heavy Cruiser hung in the air above the deck as Cadmus Howler and Joyce Furgus' Company of 2/54th got to the bay. The envoy from the med bay had already arrived, and now the commanders stood and silently examined the charred piece of hull.

As Howler came up alongside Beckett, the General glanced at his old friend, "Somewhere in there is a living Omega human. We need to get him into stasis."

The Colonel nodded, "Fair enough. Any idea how to get in?"

Graham, standing on the other side of Beckett, spoke in what had become his familiar monotone, "Facing us is an interior bulkhead. Your rifles can punch through it."

Howler nodded, then turned to Furgus, "Joyce, punch us a hole. We've got a live specimen to get into stasis."

The lioness nodded, waving her company forward towards the floating debris, "Ellen, you and your squad get ready to catch it if it jumps out. Everybody else, let's get this hole made."

Veteran marines from 2/54th now took positions in front of the group of command officers, and as they did, the first shots rang out across the deck. Each was carefully placed, and soon the entire company was firing at the chunk of hull. The bulkhead began to split.

Lieutenant Ellen Arbear and her platoon set themselves up beneath the opening portal, rifles and swords in hand, shields on.

After only a few more seconds, a rough square of hull plating fell out of the debris, creating the desired gap. Everyone in the bay seemed to hold their breath, and the marines of Joyce Furgus' company — quite familiar by now with various forms of Omega — peered down their rifle sights, ready to pour fire into the opening.

But nothing came out.

They held fast, of course — the creature could be in there waiting to see if it could obtain some sort of advantage...

"Well... this is a bit eerie," Narosh looked sideways at Varnia, and just as he did, the thing launched itself through the hole in the debris.

And it didn't drop through into Ellen Arbear's waiting bear grasp — no, just the opposite. It hurled itself right over the marines, crossing a seemingly impossible distance, and dove to land on the one-handed Larosian.

The Earthers of 2/54th were already moving to respond as the thing hurtled through the air, but Narosh was unshielded and on the other side of Graham.

Beckett was the closest, and in the second that he had to act, he began to step sideways to get into the way of the hissing Omega human. He reached for his sword with one hand, keying his shield with the other...

But his sword wasn't at his hip where it should have been — it had been taken without him noticing, which shouldn't have been possible...

Someone on the deck yelled, "Get down!"

But the leaping Omega human was too fast. Narosh began to turn away, aware that his neck was about to be snapped by the intruder's landing, and that there was no one close enough to–

Graham stepped forward and got a loose hand onto the Omega minion's foot. As it toppled abruptly forward, he drove Beckett Lupus' short sword through its neck.

"Bastard."

The thing dropped to the deck, not dead but momentarily paralyzed as its Omega cells rerouted control of the nervous system around the interruption in the spinal column. It was all the time about twelve bears needed to pile on top of the bulging, flailing, almost-human creature.

Narosh, Beckett, Varnia, Howler, Furgus, Arbear, Lazarus, the deck hands... just about everyone had let their jaws drop. Graham didn't pay any attention, nodding instead to the doctor, "Good luck with it."

Lazarus nodded slowly, and as the creature was subdued by three stasis patches, one of the marines stood with Beckett's sword and presented it to the General. He bobbed his head in thanks, taking it in hand briefly.

"My apologies for not asking," Graham said simply. And then as the marines and the medics cleared up the mess, he left.

The assembled commanders exchanged glances, trying to figure out just how dangerous Graham Manchester had become.

CHAPTER 28

Vice Admiral Artemis Tigar leaned back in his chair and yawned.

Agamemnon's main officer's mess was quiet this afternoon, partially because picket duty had a lot of people at their stations for longer shifts (just in case) and partially because the old First Rate currently had about only two thirds of its Krogg War crew complement.

Well, the quiet suited him fine — he was used to this ship being quiet, having spent so many years aboard it when it was a museum. And since there wasn't a great deal happening here at New Halifax, it didn't actually feel wrong to be doing nothing.

Nothing but eating, that was, and getting ready for a meeting...

"Sorry I'm early," Minnie Maximane came to a stop next to Tigar's table and he looked up in surprise.

"Oh no worries, I'm just timing my yawns. Have a sit down, I think the cook said we've got some fresh salmon up from the farms — the really good stuff."

The Rear Admiral nodded with a smile and took her seat opposite Tigar, "So why'd you need me over here, Artie?"

Scratching his neck absently and nodding to the mess chief behind the counter on the other side of the room, Tigar bobbed his head sideways, "Well, I'm thinking it's time we move up to the corridor."

As they'd first discussed, Artie and Minnie had kept their ships at New Halifax for the past days, but with the recommissioned reinforcements now in the system, they had more than enough ships to leave a screen in support of the colony's orbital defenses and still hold the hyperspace corridor.

That was the theory, at least. Based on what they were seeing in Jax Furgus' report from around Freetown, there was certainly action on the cards out that way, which meant threats to the space behind Earth seemed less likely... though they couldn't be ignored.

If Tigar was Omega, he'd be using Freetown as a feint for a raid on Earth, or maybe on the New Halifax corridor itself. The latter colony wasn't so important — Omega could probably deal with New Halifax whenever he liked... but why not take a quick shot at Earth?

That was what Artie would have done, but then he wasn't Omega. He'd once been right about the Kroggs in Genesis, but this was a different matter entirely — Omega probably wasn't as predictable. In any case, speculation wouldn't do him much good. The New Halifax corridor was his responsibility, and whatever his off-the-wall theories might be, he was keen now on defending that sector of space.

"You think Omega's more likely to play for the corridor than the colony, then?"

Maximane's question was answered with a confirming nod, "If I were him... aha."

The cook arrived at the side of the table with two plates of steaming salmon and potatoes.

"Very good of you — thanks for bringing it over!" Artie smiled as he took his plate, and the cook nodded.

As the Admirals started on their food, the cook returned to his place and got back to preparing for the upcoming dinner rush. Maximane began to poke at her fish with her fork, frowning as she did, "So how much force should we move up?"

Artie Tigar took a thoughtful breath and maneuvered a potato onto his fork, "I'd say all of your ships, and probably all six of our squadrons of 74s... and three of our squadrons of 44s. And me with *Agamemnon* too... we can leave the rest here just in case..."

"That leaves only forty ships to look after New Halifax. You're certain you want to leave it so thin here?"

Chewing on the potato, now, Tigar paused to nod thoughtfully, "Yes. Nothing else for it, I want to make sure the corridor is safe."

Minnie nodded as she shoveled some salmon into her mouth.

"Fair enough," she said between bites.

"Good, I'll let Lab know at Admiralty House. We should get ready to ship out immediately. I want to be on station by this time tomorrow," Artie began to work his utensils in earnest. "Sound alright?"

Minnie Maximane nodded, "Indeed."

The New Halifax Admirals ate quickly, and a few hours later most of their ships left the system under energy drive.

First Space Lord Fox Magnus tried to contain his frustration, but it was getting rather potent just now.

"A single black hole threw us this far off course?"

Chimera's Master nodded slowly, "Sorry, sir, it was so far out we didn't realize the shear had repositioned the starlight."

With a deep breath, Fox nodded, "Not your fault, Master. We're far out of the lanes..."

And that was the truth. Fox's convoy was still trying to reach Gibraltar, but Omega patrols and pickets were blocking all the normal travel lanes.

The damned plague had turned out just about every ship in Genesis space to establish a blockade, and since secrecy about these reinforcements was crucial, Fox couldn't gamble on trying to blow through any of them. These weren't Kroggs — Omega would probably know the instant any of his minions saw anything, even if that instant happened to be the last one of their existence.

So now the convoy was far out on the relative left of the space lanes, making an end run around pickets, but not without difficulty. Black holes and singularities that had yet to be charted had tangled their navigation three times, and they were somewhere well off course, out in the unexplored void beyond Genesis.

They'd end up at Gibraltar, but much later than intended.

And worse, they couldn't warn anyone they were going to be overdue, for fear of detection...

This mission to reinforce the Earther fleet base was getting more and more complicated.

But Jardaw and Kandam would need these ships, and Fox's old friend Chronos Claw certainly would. Somehow they'd have to get through.

"In time," Fox said quietly to himself, sighing as he turned from the Master to the plot. "Well, let's get back under weigh."

The Gibraltar reinforcement fleet crept through space unnoticed.

Ed Jeffries looked at the chrono and did some math in his head.

He'd been following Omega's decoy squadron for exactly nineteen hours. They were heading out into the depths of nowhere, well beyond Freetown, but presumably Omega was still trying to convince him that his attack fleet was going to come from this vector. Maybe the plague even thought the Allies would send a force out here to make a preemptive strike...

Yeah right.

No, Jax Furgus had been quite clear — he'd expected Omega to try a decoy like this, and that's why he'd sent Tom Locke's frigates out with the new Freetown Fleet, and why those frigates hadn't been allowed to assist *Republic* when the Carrier had been ravaged.

It had been a hell of a sacrifice, and Ed still wasn't entirely pleased with it, but it was hopefully destined to pay off. Because Tom Locke would be able to sniff out the real base for Omega's attack fleet, and Freetown would be ready for it.

Unfortunately, Ed might miss the show. He and his ships had to keep dogging this decoy group, or Omega might get wise to Jax's plan. It was a great feint and counter-feint... but if anyone could play that game on Omega's level, Ed Jeffries believed Jax Furgus could.

So aboard *Savanna Felix*, Ed Jeffries silently recommitted himself to keeping up his wild goose chase for at least another nineteen hours.

• • •

While the Battlecruisers of Freetown raced further out into open space, Commodore Tom Locke sat in his chair on *Charybdis'* bridge, watching the movements of the wounded Omega hauler.

There seemed little doubt after nineteen hours of cruising — the ship was heading for Ecclesia. Omega probably had the system already, meaning the latest threat to Freetown's survival was about to come from the same location it had a month earlier.

"Order *Cleopatra* to drop back and send dispatch pods. Warn Freetown and Sol that Ecclesia is probably in Omega's hands; Freetown should prepare to counter an advance on that axis."

The orders reached the last frigate in Locke's line, and that ship dropped back. It would wait to release pods with the appropriate warnings until it was sure it couldn't be detected by Omega.

The silent, secret chase continued.

CHAPTER 29

Orion came out of energy drive with a smoothness that harkened back to the old days of the Krogg War. The 175-gun First Rate still had all the agility of yesteryear, and its speed had been enhanced rather impressively post war through some re-tooling.

They'd made smart time from Earth on the trip, almost catching up to *Unity Genesis*, and as they arrived now in Freetown space, Ursla took a deep breath.

She had a strong formation with her — enough to ensure the defenses of the planet were organized and secure. Between her 115 ships, Jax's extra Battle and Flying Squadrons, and the Freetown and Genesis Fleets, she had a sizable force here... though she couldn't be confident that it was enough until she found out precisely what was going on. She'd need to talk to Jax and to Audrey, see if more pickets had vanished, and if there'd been any more intelligence on Omega's whereabouts.

He was playing games out here, and Ursla was willing to bet that meant he was going to attack. Isolate Earth, try to catch the Genesis refugees in-system and take them, weaken Earth's overall protection...

Well, there was lots to worry about, and Ursla imagined Jax had thoroughly analyzed most of it already.

"Signal coming in from *Unity Genesis*, Admiral," the Signal Officer reported as Ursla peered into *Orion's* main plot.

"I'll take it here," she nodded, and a screen appeared in the holo tank, Sarah filling it after a second.

"I see Lab decided to send us more help after all," the President smiled. "It's good to see you here, Andra. Strange that we're both back at it... but good to see you."

Ursla grinned, "Glad to be back on a bridge, believe me. And to be out wreaking havoc with you again, too."

Sarah's smile seemed to sag a bit as she fought off a pang of nostalgia — it was somehow hard to believe that the days of the Krogg War, when she'd *only* been fighting to give her home a new lease on life, qualified as the good old ones just now.

"Well, I'm guessing we should meet with Jax and Audrey, and your two ArcLieutenant-Generals... who was it, Togo and Rozhestveski?"

"I love how you imply you don't remember their names, but then manage one like 'Rozhestveski' off the top of your head," Sarah's smile tried to brighten a little, and Ursla chuckled.

"Bears never forget."

Sarah cocked an eyebrow, "Is that right?"

Ursla donned a frown, "Is what right?"

Sarah shook her head, sighing almost pleasantly, "I'll call Jax."

"Who's Jax?"

It had been a long time since *Orion's* main briefing room had hosted officers making plans for war, but the old ship seemed somehow aware of the circumstances as a group of officers, some veterans and some newcomers, gathered in its hull to coordinate for this new war. It was, of course, impossible for an inanimate vessel to have an inherent awareness at all, but somehow *Orion* seemed to know, and to project a serene confidence over the assembly. Ursla didn't question the comfort, she just trusted it.

Finding her traditional seat at the head of the briefing table, Ursla watched Sarah seat herself at the opposite end. In between sat the chief officers of the fleets in the system: Jax Furgus — with Ron Hobbes and Alix Tarkham just in case — along with Audrey DeBrooke, since Ed was out on his goose chase, and ArcLieutenant-Generals Togo and Rozhestveski.

Ursla had hoped to catch up privately with Jax and his Captains before the meeting, but the two young human flag officers had been uncommonly early, and had thus forbidden any frank conversation as to the Freetown situation before the meeting began.

Of course, Ursla's instincts picked up the high level of tension in the room as Audrey and Sarah had arrived. Those two, at least, had managed to catch up with each other in the landing bay, and Sarah had learned about the complications that were keeping Audrey from her ships, and about the youthful saber-rattling of her juniors.

For her part, Sarah was feeling more herself now than she had at any time in the past two weeks... though honestly, that wasn't setting the bar too high. The uniform helped more than it should have — it gave her confidence again. She was a combat officer at heart, a bureaucrat only by necessity.

Now she had to be a bit of both, but at least she got to do it from the front lines. The remnants of her people needed her protection, and the very survival of the Alliance now depended on battle with Omega.

Things were back in terms she could understand.

"Alright, let's get started," Ursla hadn't chaired a meeting in a while, but she slipped easily back into the role. "So, where do we think Omega's ships are?"

She'd expected the question to trigger some speculation, discussion and brainstorming.

"They're at Ecclesia, with Tom Locke heading there to keep an eye on them," Jax Furgus answered, sounding almost disinterested.

Ursla was getting ready to ask something about what information they could pool to try to figure out where Omega was, and to that end had shifted her glance to the young Genesis commanders. But now her eyes darted back to Jax abruptly, "You mean... oh, well. Very good then..."

Jax grinned, "I'm old and crotchety, Andra, but I know how to find the enemy. Now we just have to go clean out that infestation."

Ursla cocked an eyebrow, "Yes... well that's definitely a possibility, but I'm guessing you don't mean right now."

Jax leaned back, "Aye. That's why I've got Tom out there. We'll know as soon as Omega makes a move, and then we can make sure we're in the way. I'm pretty sure he'll come straight here, but if he tries something fancy we might be able to catch him from a good angle in open space."

"You're forgetting how powerful he is though," Togo spoke up abruptly, then as the eyes of all the Earthers at the table shifted to him, he paused and reddened slightly. "He took out Kari Peltier's Battlecruisers and Henry Lutjens' Dreadnoughts."

"And *Republic's* getting towed into a slip about five hours from now. Rammed in action, nearly blew up," Audrey's tone was dry and bleak. "They're right, Andra, Omega's not playing by the rules we're used to. But all the same, my Battlecruisers still did fine against a limited squadron — we're just going to have to be ready for unconventional tactics."

"Indeed," Sarah's eyebrow was raised as she shifted her gaze between her two subordinates. "I suggest we stay here for now, then, but be ready to cruise as soon as Commodore Locke sees movement. I imagine Lab will be doing the same, once word reaches him about Ecclesia. If they come for us, we might just be able to catch them in the open."

"And if they move against Earth..." Andra quietly delivered the words, then looked up to emphasize their ramifications with a grim expression, "if they move against Earth, we head there in support."

There were slow nods from most of the assembled officers, but Jax frowned, "You think he'd be fool enough to take on Lab and the Home Fleet with his band of misbegotten Genesis bastards? No offense to anyone here, but he'd have no chance against a line of *Venerables* with those buckets in the state they seem to be in."

Ursla failed to hide her surprise at the less than diplomatic comment — she was used to Jax Furgus being a bit... brash... but the death of his daughter had shifted his sharpness to a different level, at least for now.

"He's right..." Sarah took a deep breath and her eyes shifted to the table top. "He's only got what we had in Genesis — he hasn't had time to come up with anything else. So he wouldn't have a hope in a stand-up fight against

Earther units... otherwise he'd probably have attacked Gibraltar first. No, he wants this system, and I'm guessing he wants the refugee ships."

Ursla had begun to consider that possibility while cruising out from Earth. Varnon was having accommodations set up on Earth for those ships' human passengers — the survivors of Genesis — but if Omega somehow managed to infect them, he'd have a readily mobile army of hundreds of thousands. Freetown would be an easy capture with that sort of force, and Earth would be entirely isolated.

"That would be the end of Genesis civilization," Ursla's words felt inadequate. "The question is, are the refugees safer where they are, or moving through open space. Do we think we should get the survivors out now? Before Omega moves?"

Sarah tilted her head, "It might be for the best. We've got a lull — we should use it. We can upset his plans that much, anyway. And Audrey, if you want to evacuate some people, they could move too..."

Audrey shook her head, "Not yet. We're all immunized anyway... no, our defensive arrangements would be best served by keeping everyone in place. We have civil defense plans, and with this much force in orbit I think we'll be inclined to defend our home."

Sarah slowly nodded — she'd probably have had the same reaction had their roles been reversed and this threat had been facing Genesis. It didn't seem the time to give ground... spaceships full of refugees was one thing, evacuating a settled planet was quite another.

"Well, before we start dispatching ships, I suggest we wait for Tom to get to Ecclesia. Let's be certain Omega's where we think he is. As soon as we know that for certain, we can get the convoy moving," Jax leaned forward in his chair.

Ursla nodded, "Fair enough. Get the ships ready, we'll be able to dispatch them soon. Now, as to setting up for actual defense..."

As matters shifted to the purely military, the minds of officers at the table began to settle into a familiar rhythm. Simple tactics fell into something of a known category — it was calming.

The officers made their plans.

CHAPTER 30

Graham hadn't gotten a very good look at the Omega human when he'd dragged it out of the air in the landing bay, so now as he stood on the other side of the one-way mirror that made up one wall of *Renown's* bio-containment lab, he found the sight mildly intriguing.

Evidently, the reason he'd not dislocated his shoulder during his abrupt maneuver came in the fact that the infested human was... or had been... a freshly recruited spacer. Before being taken, she couldn't have been more than eighteen, and she couldn't have weighed more than 115 pounds soaking wet. That small size and light weight now contained inhuman power... but somehow Graham had wrenched it to the deck without difficulty.

They'd managed to identify this woman as Livia King from some of the DNA they'd collected, but there wasn't much left of her humanity, at least not visibly. She had protruding spots of black bone in seemingly senseless places across her face, arms and legs, as well as patches of faded-black shiny skin, a bulging set of subdermal torso bone armor, and so many swollen glands and veins that her neck was about twice as thick as it should have been.

And yet her weight was unchanged — she was light and yet explosively strong. She probably fought in an ape-like manner, as had the Omega minions they'd met on *Genesis One*. Her leap seemed evidence enough of that.

In any case, Graham saw two possible paths emerging. This woman would either be cured — and thus his new life's quest would be to find and cure his wife — or she would be incurable, in which case his life would be over, save for his quest for vengeance.

In either case he would end up killing Omega — he would just have to wait and see which way circumstances took him. His future was very much predicated on the fate of this spacer.

But he didn't really feel anything particular about that predication, because he truly didn't feel much at all. He refused to feel. Being without emotion would make his abridged, revenge-filled future much easier.

Celia Lazarus stepped up beside Graham as he continued to impassively study the infected spacer.

"Have you had the chance to learn anything about it, Doctor?" Graham glanced briefly at the wolf, and she shook her head.

"Still running the deep spectral scan. It'll finish in about an hour, and after that I can get to work. I'm really not sure what to expect, Graham. It could be very positive news, or very bad news. I doubt there'll be middle ground, though."

"Why's that?" Graham's cool question drew a quick reaction from the doctor.

She glanced from Graham back through the glass to the Omega patient, "Omega has Krogg defenses, and he's sentient. Now, if we can find something that can crack his Krogg protection, there's nothing he can do to save himself. But if we can't find a way to specifically break through his defenses, the only way to kill him might be to wipe out the surrounding tissue. Like your ancestors' old treatments for cancer… kill everything that bears his mark. We do that and the patient will probably die."

"Many of the Larosians died," Graham commented with a slightly tilted head. "Even targeted cures might be too much."

Lazarus nodded once, "There's that too. They'd been forty years in that ship, of course, so their systems were extremely weak… But you're right, if Omega's gotten himself wound tight into the biology of his host, we won't be able to restore one without the other. I hope it doesn't come to that."

"Indeed."

The pair stood silently in front of the glass for a moment longer, Graham's eyes focused on the body of his enemy, Lazarus scratching her brow uncomfortably.

"Anyway, this isn't the reason I wanted to talk to you right now. While I've been waiting for the scan to finish, I had another look at Christine's condition."

Graham turned away from the glass slowly, "A solution?"

Lazarus' head titled and her ears twitched, "After a fashion. I can't cure the problem here — it's going to require some careful reengineering, like I said before. But I think I have a way to control the symptoms until then."

Waving Graham back into another of the med bay chambers — the one now holding Christine's static body — Lazarus stepped quickly to a table near the medical bed and lifted a stiff garment, "Recognize this?"

Graham offered a single nod, "It's her fencing skinsuit."

"I thought so. Well, I've had it scanned for measurements and I'm getting another one tailored in the ship shop right now, but I've changed the design a bit. The new one won't have all this armor wire, instead it'll have strands of the filament we use in stasis patches running through it," she rounded Christine's bed and handed the stiff garment to Graham.

He took it gingerly, "I was under the impression that you didn't need to cover the entire body to apply a stasis field… isn't a patch enough?"

Lazarus bobbed her head, "Usually. But this isn't just going to be a steady field. I'm going to get this suit to strobe the stasis — it's going to pulsate, for all intents and purposes. Within a fraction of a second it'll go from on to off to on in different areas — never all on or all off. If I can get the timing program right, she'll be able to operate despite her nerves. She'll have some sensation but only about ten percent of the signals her nerves are sending will get through so she won't be in agony."

Graham looked down at the suit in his hands and then at Christine's frozen form, "What of her head? It won't be covered."

"Well, it's a relatively smaller area, I should be able to get a patch or two tuned to do the same from her neck up. I've got the engineering section working on that right now. If all goes to plan, she'll be up and moving around tomorrow. Then we'll just have to figure out a set of atmospheric and liquid cocktails that will allow her to bathe and whatnot without the suit. We can probably set up her cabin as a closed system for her, load the air and the water with non-invasive dermal suppressor or some such thing. I'm still working that out."

Graham walked to the table and laid the fencing suit back down, "It sounds promising, Doctor. Do let me know when you've got it set up. I should be on hand when you wake her."

Lazarus nodded, "Of course."

"Thank you," Graham again offered a single nod, and with that he turned and left the room.

Lazarus stared at his back as he left, shaking her head slightly at the human's clinical reactions. He was either going to be killed by this whole mission, or he was the strongest human she'd every run across.

Or maybe he'd be both strong and dead.

"Did I just read his thoughts correctly? Might there be a solution for Christine's problem?"

Lazarus looked up abruptly as Narosh appeared in the doorway, "I couldn't tell you what he thought, but that's what it's looking like."

The Larosian stepped into the room and inclined his head thoughtfully, "This comment might seem strange coming from a Larosian, but maybe that'll put some life back into him."

Smiling at the words, Lazarus rounded the bed, "You're right, it does sound strange coming from you."

With an approximation of a shrug, Narosh delivered a smile, "I suppose all the bits of Earther biology you've pumped into me to keep me alive have had an impact. Just as they did in poor Christine..."

"Sobering thought for me," Lazarus' smile began to fade. "Anyway, what can I do for you?"

Narosh held up his stump, "I want to see my new hand!"

They left Christine's room to look at newly-grown appendages.

CHAPTER 31

Setter Caine sat across from his old desk and nodded as Lab Forepaw briefed him.

"And like I said, Artie's moving the stronger part of his fleet up to the corridor, just in case. He's thinking Omega won't make a play for New Halifax, but that he might come here or hit that corridor instead," Lab was frowning unconsciously as he leaned back in his chair. There was a lot going on...

"Fair enough. So we're pretty sure Omega has ships at Ecclesia?" Setter scratched his chin and matched Lab's frown.

The First Lord nodded in reply, "Yes. Not certain what that gets us, but we're pretty sure that's where his ships are. And Jax and Sarah are convinced he's going straight for Freetown — that he's going to want the Genesis refugees as a force of his own."

"I can see that being a problem. Are we bringing the refugees down here then?"

Lab nodded again, "As soon as Tom Locke reports for certain that Omega's at Ecclesia — we'll try to move them out before he gets rolling. Problem for them will be speed. It's a mixed convoy of refugee ships, and many of them are probably only good for about 2,000 pls. Andra will provide them with an escort, but they're going to be in open space for a while."

Setter continued to scratch his chin, "Aye... well there's nothing else for that, I suppose. We'll do it quietly and hopefully Omega won't even notice." He paused — *hopefully* the plague would just stay put, but hopes and wishes weren't horses just now...

Caine halted those thoughts, then raised an eyebrow at his old friend, "What about the Home Fleet?"

Lab shrugged, "Here they stay. I'm actually planning to head up to *Venerable* this afternoon... given the situation I'm going to have to run the show from there. With Fox out, I'll have to take command of the fleet myself, even if we move out of the system."

"Hmm... yes, that's the best way... speaking as the fellow who pioneered that particular system," Setter smiled. "What about the recomms — sending any more out?"

Shaking his head, Lab tapped up a holo of fleet statistics, and both Earthers shifted their gazes to the display. "Dran brought in Zed Dune, and the yards are working *miracles*, even by our standards. I honestly hadn't expected to be able to send Andra's force out until next week, but they're unpacking ships so fast I had to see it to believe it."

Setter remembered Zed Dune from the Krogg War — the brilliant engineer and frigate skipper who'd pioneered the work on spatial charges, and had helped initiate the blockade of the Krogg home systems. He'd been retired, as Setter understood it, but evidently Dran Nightclaw had brought him back in, and now the white wolf's engineering brilliance was proving critical. If anyone could build a ship in half the time it was supposed to take, it was Zed Dune.

Thinking of that, Setter's smile broadened a little, "I'm glad to be hearing so many familiar names again. Gives a little hope."

Lab nodded, "Zed? Yes, it does... Within another three days we're going to have almost 200 recommissioned ships active in-system to serve as a supplement for Home Fleet. Once I hit 200, I'm going to designate it 'Second Fleet' and get Kylie Peregrine to take it over. Whatever comes out of the yards after that will be the 'Third'... I think I've got Ami Dune lined up to come out of the Consulate for command of that one."

More familiar names from the Krogg War, and Setter nodded in recognition. Kylie Peregrine had been one of his best squadron commanders back in those days, and no one needed to be reminded of the exploits of Ami (Cairn) Dune, now one of the Consuls leading the planet, and of course, wife of Zed Dune. It was a very good sign that they were recrewing the fleet with so many veterans. And because the Navy was markedly smaller than it had been, they weren't running out of people... not yet, anyway. While there were sharp new officers like Minnie Maximane among the flag ranks of the fleet, the majority were hardened veterans with combat experience.

This war might be different than the last in its particulars, but it was still a war, and those with experience fighting an interstellar campaign would be important.

"So with them here in reserve, you looking to take Home Fleet out after Omega?"

Setter's question caught Lab slightly by surprise, though really it shouldn't have, because he'd been asking himself that very same thing. The Home Fleet was the most powerful combat formation in the galaxy, and that wasn't an exaggeration. The Gibraltar Fleet was a close second, but Home Fleet was still superior. If Lab took it to space and went hunting, he could potentially end the plague's offensive in a single action.

But, if he got caught out and Omega crushed him, the defense of Freetown, New Halifax and Earth might be irrevocably hindered.

Decisions, decisions.

"I think I'm going to elect to wait and see. If Tom can tell me where Omega's heading once he leaves Ecclesia, I'll probably move the fleet to get in the way... but if I do that I'm going to want everyone with me — Genesis, Andra, Freetown... maybe even part of the Second. It'll have to be all or nothing at that stage. We'll have to catch him in the open and blast him, or get between him and his target," Lab was almost thinking out loud, but Setter nodded in understanding.

"Indeed," the Supreme Consul replied quietly.

They had to wait and see.

Scratching behind his ear now, Lab exhaled deeply and leaned back in his chair, "I don't like waiting, Setter. I'd much rather know precisely what to do and then just do it... but that's not the way this works, is it? You never told us so, but you were never really certain about what to do against the Kroggs, were you?"

A sad smile crossed Setter's face and he slowly shook his head, "I knew I had to do my job and win a war. But strategy's always a best guess. Some years everything seems to be clicking, some years it all goes wrong. Ask Andra sometime, I nearly lost hold of myself after we found out the Kroggs were coming for Gibraltar and that I'd left the door to Earth wide open."

"I noticed that then," Lab observed, and then as Setter leaned forward with a questioning frown, the First Lord shrugged, "We were best friends then too, remember? I saw many things."

Setter opened his mouth to reply, but closed it for a moment. Friends they had been... friends they still were... "You'll do right, Lab. You'll make decisions and you'll lead, that's all that any of us can expect of you. That's all everybody seemed to want from me. Just do your damnedest and if things go well we all get to stand around after it's done to shake your hand."

"And the fate of the universe?" Forepaw asked the question with just a little resignation. "I'm seemingly responsible for that too..."

Setter took his turn to shrug, "There's no one else to do your job, Lab. You're First Lord because you're our best and brightest... if you can't do it, then we can't do it. Don't step out of your own shoes and try to live up to the role of universal arbiter. Make the decisions you'd always make... that's what we hired you for. And my guess is that's the only way you'll be able to beat Omega."

Leaving his eyebrow cocked, Lab met his friend's eyes, "You could take this job back, you know. You're the best of us, we both know that."

Setter shook his head, "I did a good job, but I was fighting my war in my time. And Omega got to watch all that anyway — to see what I was doing, and why. No, Lab, even if it were true that you weren't every bit my equal at the Admiralty, this would have to be your posting. Your vision is different than mine, you'll act differently than I would. If anything, *that* will save us."

A deep breath escaped Lab Forepaw, and then the First Lord agreed, "Fair enough. I'm either good enough or we're dead, and that actually means I don't have to worry so much."

"Makes sense to me," Setter sat back in his own chair and Lab donned a joking scowl.

"Great, makes sense to the guy who generally can't finish a philosophical discussion without turning everything into an 'equation'. Why did you keep doing that, anyway?"

Setter grinned and shrugged, "Foresight I suppose. Pat needed good titles for his books, after all…"

"Sounds cheesy to me," Lab shook his head and tried to hide a smile.

With a chuckle Setter shrugged again, "The humans don't seem to mind… but then they also enjoy blood sports. I'm going to stop talking about it now."

The old friends laughed.

CHAPTER 32

Narosh gingerly flexed his new hand as he held it behind his back. It felt just about the same as the last transplant... it just seemed to itch now and then, as if to remind him it wasn't the original.

But he knew that already, and given what had happened to Christine after she'd started itching, he really wished the sensation would stop.

The good news was that *Carnarvon* was slowly being pulled back together. It was an aged Battleship to be sure, but already Narosh was beginning to see its real potential as a combat vessel. With Earther engineering crews working alongside Larosians, the reactors had been reactivated and the ship's mains had been brought back online.

It was just a matter of time now before Narosh would be able to take command of the battlewagon. *Renown's* machine shops were turning out components for the rebuilding process, the wear and tear of forty years in space was being put to rights.

The question that remained, though, was what to do with *Carnarvon*.

The Admiral-of-a-Fleet tilted his head at the thought, and standing as he was on the vast but dimly-lit bridge of the ship, he considered the question yet again. His first instinct was obviously to rejoin this ship, to rally the Larosian forces at home, see them inoculated, and establish control in preparation for a counterattack against Omega.

And yet somehow that option did not seem the correct one. It was logical enough, *sensible* enough... but Narosh's blood seemed to have a different opinion.

Yet again the Earther DNA's impact was manifesting itself, and he knew it.

So what was the opposing case — why shouldn't he go home? Could there be a reason?

He would have to make that determination soon enough — *Carnarvon* would be ready for travel in only another day, and thereafter, *Renown* would be heading for the New Halifax corridor, only five days away.

Narosh would have to be on one ship... but which one?

"Admiral Narosh, Doc's calling for you in *Renown's* med bay."

Lifting his head in surprise, Narosh turned to find an Earther marine behind him.

"Thank you," he turned and left the bridge.

• • •

"This isn't good news, folks."

Celia Lazarus stood before a glowing holo as she spoke, and Varnia, Beckett, Graham and Narosh all shifted their weight uncomfortably at her words.

"I finished running my scans on the infected human... there's nothing left in there I can save. I don't know about killing Omega's cells yet — we'll have to get back to Earth and have a look at Fengate's labs... I want to see what Elandra Caine makes of this... but as to saving her, we can't possibly kill all of the Omega in her without killing her in the process."

Lazarus' words drew no verbal response, though all eyes shifted to Graham.

This was a death sentence for his wife...

"And Graham," Lazarus pressed on in quiet tones, "there's no indication that Gillian's case would be any different, despite her special situation. I think... well, the way Omega used your child's cells to act as a Trojan horse probably meant it took longer for him to settle in... but by now he's surely integrated."

It was a cool and frank assessment, and standing next to Graham, Beckett took a deep breath and brought his hand to rest on friend's shoulder.

The ArcGeneral was calm as death.

"Graham?" Varnia ventured the question first, leaning forward around her husband to view the human. "Graham, are you..."

Her voice trailed off as Graham turned his head and caught his Earther counterpart's eyes, "I am. Thank you, Doctor Lazarus."

He stepped back, pulling out of reach of Beckett's hand, but the wolf caught his eye and frowned, "Graham, maybe we should talk..."

Stopping abruptly at the words, Graham turned slightly to stare at his friend, "No need for that I think, Beckett. It seems I know precisely what I have to do now — Omega must be destroyed. And there's nothing to stop me or any of us from doing what we must."

Beckett blinked once and then his eyes drifted away. He offered a single jerked nod before looking over to Lazarus, "Is that it then, Doc?"

With a slow nod, she deactivated the holo behind her, "I suppose for most of you... I will keep working. I'll see if there's an unconventional way to get through the defenses... maybe given a lot of time and resources we could come up with something. But really... I wouldn't bank on it..."

"I should hope there isn't, Doctor. We cannot afford pity now, just vengeance," Graham turned back to Lazarus, and his words were hard and icy.

Beckett and Varnia both struggled to keep from frowning at the statement, but Narosh answered with a single nod, "That is quite true."

As a doctor, Lazarus just had to overlook that statement, "Well. Um. I'll still keep looking. Meantime, I do have something for you to help me with, Graham. We got Christine's suit back from the shop, I'm getting ready to wake her."

"Let us know how that goes," Varnia said quietly as Graham took a step forward. "We have to get *Carnarvon* ready."

Lazarus nodded, and Varnia and Beckett turned quietly and left. Graham nodded to each of them in turn, but as Narosh turned to leave he left a private message in his wake: *Graham, if you wish to discuss more about how to gain revenge, speak to me. It is not an unfamiliar tradition to Larosians, I might be of some help.*

The ArcGeneral didn't visibly react to the comment, but his mind relayed a positive impression that was all the answer Narosh needed. The Admiral-of-a-Fleet left med bay.

"What precisely do you need, then, Celia?"

Lazarus moved towards the door to Christine's room, "The orderlies are suiting her up right now. What I want to do is teach you the controls first."

Graham fell into an easy walk alongside the doctor, and she continued. "I'm going to be giving Christine a primer on the controls, of course, but there are no guarantees as to how well this is going to work. You're to be the failsafe — if something goes wrong, you put her up to full and get her here immediately."

"Me? I'm not sure that would be the wisest choice, I don't spend a great deal of time–"

Lazarus's head tilted slightly as they arrived at the doorway, "I think you're going to have to start. I know Christine gets along well with everyone, but she's your aide, and your species. In my experience that always counts for something..."

"And after the Earther-related complications, you'd prefer to have a human standing by with a failsafe. We're most aware of our own frailties," Graham's words weren't bitter — they held no emotion at all — and Lazarus somehow knew they weren't meant to accuse her of something.

"Indeed."

"Very well," Graham stepped through the door into Christine's room just as a pair of orderlies finished zipping her skinsuit from the back and laid her back to rest on her medical bed. The garment's high collar stopped shortly below her jaw line, and as the orderlies applied a stasis patch to the back of her neck, Graham silently studied the suit.

It looked the same as the white fencing garb Christine was well accustomed to wearing. Hopefully she would find it comfortable.

"Here," Lazarus held a slim silver remote up before Graham, and he took it carefully. The doctor produced one of her own and then walked to Christine's side, "It works the same as a regular patch control, but you get the extra option to set it to 'Current'. That's the pulsating field I mentioned to you before. Higher frequency means less feeling for her, lower frequency means more. I'm thinking her frequency should be around sixty per second... at least to start with."

Graham held the controller up closer to his eyes and offered a slow nod, "Understood."

"Any questions, just ask..." Lazarus let her offer fade as she watched Graham activate his controller, cycle through its settings, and then turn it off again.

He didn't exactly need coaching.

One of the orderlies nodded to the doctor, and as the two junior Earther medical staff stepped away from Christine's bed, she stepped forward and reached down to Christine's neck, "I've got it rigged so that the system's activity is governed by this patch. It goes on when you activate it, but it'll only go off if you deactivate it and the remote at the same time. Just make sure it doesn't get pulled off."

Graham slowly nodded again, lowering his controller, "Will she be able to spend time out of the suit?"

Lazarus shook her head slowly, her hands finding the patch and her forefingers hovering over its key, "Not until I get the atmospheric cocktail right. I realize bathing and sleeping and those sorts of things will require it, so I'm looking into a couple of chemical mixes that can partially sedate her nerves if she's saturated."

"No simple topicals?" Graham stepped forward, standing opposite Lazarus on Christine's other side.

Lazarus head continued to shake, "Her nerves are far too badly mutated. Don't worry, I'll sort it out..." she looked up at Graham. "Ready?"

Again he nodded, and with a deep breath, Lazarus keyed the patch active, then reached to the console over Christine's head and deactivated the field that was locking her in place.

The young human didn't move. Not at first.

And then her eyes slowly dragged themselves open.

"That's sixty per second... I think it'll be alright once she gets used to it," Lazarus straightened up.

Christine's eyes opened the entire way, turning first to the doctor, then to Graham. She opened her mouth, but she wasn't yet able to speak.

It took a few moments, but she was able to at last activate her voice, "What... happened...?"

"The doctor's come up with a solution, albeit one with complications. You can function, but with some difficulty," Graham replied evenly.

"Oh."

Christine's simple statement drew a smile from Lazarus, and then the doctor looked up at Graham briefly...

He stared back unemotionally.

Looking down to Christine, Lazarus nodded, "It'll take a little while for your system to adjust, but I'm hoping you'll be able to move normally in a few hours."

"I should hope so," Graham's eyebrow went back down. "I'll need you to teach me some wisdom of the sword when you're back on your feet."

Christine took a long blink. "Oh."

And they continued to converse that way.

Christine managed to sit up ten minutes later.

CHAPTER 33

Christine stood silently in front of her mirror and stared at herself.

Well, she still looked normal... normal if she was heading for her morning saber practice, that was. The suit was a dead ringer for the actual one she wore when fencing, though it felt different... and not because of the difference between Earther and human fabrics.

No, it was the almost-tingling sensation that made her and the garment feel odd.

"Gee, wonder why that is..."

As she muttered the question to herself, she realized she hadn't slurred any of it — that was an improvement, certainly. She'd been having a hard time forming words in the hour since she'd gotten on her feet — her brain was still adjusting to what felt like a slight, unnatural lag between its commands and the resulting muscle reaction.

The lag didn't seem to be manifesting in her actions, though; despite feeling sluggish, Christine didn't appear to be slowing down. Some other side effect of all the Earther DNA floating in her system... it was hard to piece together exactly what was going on under her skin.

But at least I don't have any fur to show for it...

The thought actually drew a small smile from Christine, but she halted the expression with some force as it tried to take over her face. Just didn't seem the right reaction to be having when she'd just been confined to life in a fencing suit.

Bright side: no helmet...

"Will you shut up..."

She stopped herself as she said it — her mind's commentator had evidently woken up from stasis refreshed and sharpened.

"I hadn't said anything, actually."

Christine blinked, her eyes shifting from the mirror to the source of the voice. Graham's face was, well, impassive. Nothing new there, despite the fact that according to the information shared quietly by Lazarus the ArcGeneral had learned that his wife was a total write-off...

Not such a diplomatic way to put it...

"Um... sorry," Christine turned awkwardly from the mirror, "didn't realize I wasn't the only person I was talking to."

"Quite. My apologies, anyway, I knocked twice and heard no reply... I thought the suit might have malfunctioned," Graham said evenly, no hint of concern in his tone.

Christine shrugged, making a gesture that encouraged him to move away from the door to her bathroom and back to the living room. As he stepped to a chair and seated himself, she lowered herself gingerly onto the couch opposite him, "Thanks for the concern. I was trying to figure out what I could wear over this thing... my uniform restricts too much. Think the Earther auto-tailors could cut me a new one?

"I expect so, yes."

Christine smiled at the frank remark, but Graham's terse response caused her to sober rather quickly.

"When you feel up to it, I'd appreciate some instruction with the sword. Preferably before *Carnarvon* is ready to leave, if at all possible..."

Christine let a curious frown cross her brow as Graham made the request.

"Really? Well... um... may I ask why?"

Graham turned his head slightly, "I should think skill with the sword could be of some use when we run across more infected Larosian ships, or ships with infected humans aboard."

Christine slowly began to nod, eager to do something that would reawaken her muscle memory and perhaps lessen this awkward tingle.

"Doc Lazarus did say I could return to normal physical work as soon as I saw fit... how about we head down to the gym now?"

Graham bobbed his head in agreement.

Renown's gyms were rather busy. With the ship anchored alongside *Carnarvon*, there was little for most of its crew to do, so a number of Earthers were taking advantage of the opportunity to polish their venerable hand-to-hand and blade-to-blade skills.

Cadmus Howler was even in one corner of the cavernous gymnasium, crossing swords with Sergeant Cuttar.

As Christine stepped into the gym, her well-blooded saber hanging in its scabbard at her hip, her mind retrieved the memories of her fight at Darymanis City. She'd fought alongside many of the Earthers in this gym — marines of 2/54th — when she'd been down there.

Christine had killed a girl with the sword she now held in her hand. She'd done that before becoming one of a very small minority to survive Omega's arrival on the Genesis. Her parents had not been so lucky...

How did I put that out of my mind?

Her heart rate was starting to rise as she began to think about all that had happened. She let her left hand slide off the grip of her sheathed saber... why exactly did she want to practice this now?

"Shall we, then?"

Graham's hand was suddenly on the small of her back, and through the strange tingle of the suit her mind recognized that she was being pushed to one of the two empty sparring circles in the gym.

She opened her mouth to protest, but Graham's push became more insistent, "It'll do you good. Keep your mind from taking you to places you'd rather not visit."

His quiet comment took a moment to process, but as it did Christine took two long blinks — how had he noticed?

With no ready answer to that question, she stepped inside the sparring circle, and Graham nodded to an Earther near the master shield panel. An energy barrier rose up and formed a dome over the pair. Graham keyed his personal shield and drew his own sword — the same somewhat intimidating mortuary-hilted weapon the Admiralty had presented him with years ago.

His own blooded sword.

"If you please, Christine," he said simply.

Christine opened her mouth to protest but Graham had already raised the point of his sword toward her. She blinked several times, then her mind grudgingly released direct control of her actions.

She keyed her own shield and bent at the knees, her saber coming smoothly from its sheath. Quickly unclipping that scabbard, she tossed it to the corner of the mat, then raised the point of her blade toward Graham.

I don't want to do this right now...

Graham surged smoothly forward — his motions far more controlled than anything she remembered seeing from him in past. His sword was coming at her point-on, so she batted it aside and slipped past it, drawing her curved blade back alongside her as he passed, preparing to turn on his undefended back...

But as she turned, so did he, and the flat side of his sword knocked her slash aside. They backed away from each other after that opening exchange, Graham's face the same impassive mask Christine was starting to get used to, Christine's displaying her surprise at his vast improvement.

"How?" she asked quietly.

Graham settled himself a few meters from her, his sword point back in position, "Practice against holos. The observation lounge's holo projector is good for more than just star charts."

"It's paid off," Christine moved as soon as she said it, and Graham's blade was there in time with hers.

A tight slash for his neck was avoided as he dipped beneath it and lunged forward, aiming for her midriff. She slid aside gracefully, marveling at the fact that her body was reacting as she was asking it to.

Then her shield crackled as his blade drew across her shin.

She shifted her weight to her untouched leg, hoping to rapidly turn and connect with Graham's arm as he drew away from the strike, but as she did his blade met the shield over her thigh, then traced its way up her stomach to her breastbone.

Christine's eyes widened slightly, drifting from the point of the sword now testing her shield to her own saber — hanging quite useless out to the left of Graham's shoulder — and then to Graham.

"Earther sims seem effective training tools, then," the ArcGeneral said quietly and stepped back, drawing his blade away.

"And you learn fast. I thought Beckett was training you before... with mixed results," Christine didn't bite back the comment in time. "I mean, you did fine on *Genesis One*... but..."

Graham sheathed his blade, "I was motivated to be good aboard *Genesis One*. I'm even more motivated now."

Christine frowned and sheathed her own blade, "More... but..."

She stopped herself just before adding 'your wife is dead'... hardly seemed like something she could say as a young woman who'd lost nothing of consequence.

Except your family.

She blinked again. He was keeping her mind off that... Was he consciously trying to help her? Perhaps he wasn't so devoid of emotional interest as he seemed.

Before she could pursue the question, the mat's shield fizzled twice — someone had knocked on it as if it were a door. Both humans looked to the source of the interruption, and Beckett Lupus responded to their simultaneous and intense gazes by twitching his ears, "Uh... sorry."

"Not at all," Graham turned fully to face his friend. "Is there something going on?"

Beckett shook his head, "No, they're eight hours from having *Carnarvon* ready, but Cadmus commed me and told me you were down here. Everything... alright?"

Graham offered a single nod, while Christine still struggled for words, "He's... ah... he's..."

"Much better," the junior Manchester looked from his aide to the General. "Care for a round, Beckett?"

The General raised an eyebrow. That was an uncommon offer.

"Might as well," Beckett nodded to an Earther near the control panel and the shield dropped around the mat. With her eyes fixed on Graham, Christine picked up her sheath and stepped out of the ring while the venerable wolf stepped in.

His two short swords were slung in his belt — Christine had learned in a rather comical mistake that those were *very* dangerous, especially in the hands of someone with Beckett Lupus' skill.

He wasn't a General because he was good at paperwork — though he'd gotten pretty good at that too.

As the ring shield went back up, Graham drew his sword. Christine's eyes flickered over the blade, then shifted abruptly to Beckett as his two short swords slid from their sheaths. Both officers now settled into their distinct dueling stances.

And almost immediately, Graham lunged.

Beckett had sparred with Graham for a solid year before the coup on Genesis, and he'd never once felt threatened by the junior Manchester. Indeed, few humans ever displayed the skill needed to really make Beckett Lupus uncomfortable. While the General wouldn't say Graham was threatening him now, he *was* somewhat uncomfortable. It felt as though Graham's motions were hiding something...

Graham surged. The attack was extremely controlled, and as it erupted, Beckett's instincts detected the current of rage driving it. It was as if death was coming for him — skill seemed irrelevant, because Graham almost *scared* the General...

Not the time for melodramatic observations — by the Earth!

Beckett nearly lost his balance as he slid sideways and batted the attack away. He was certainly in no condition to offer a counter in that second — his non-parrying sword was fully masked by his body, and as he turned to drive its tip towards Graham, the human's sword slashed down to push it aside.

They parted just long enough for Beckett to begin reassessing his approach to this bout — he definitely wasn't fighting the same old Graham Manchester.

Graham's sword was now held up at his side as he slowly paced the outside circle of the ring — it wasn't ready or on guard.

The junior Manchester didn't have Earther speed, so why was he opening himself up to attack?

Beckett was concerned. His instincts were picking up a silent rage in the Manchester, one that was well concealed off the sparring mat, but that was being revealed through the sword in Graham's hand. So focused, so cold, so potentially deadly. The wolf had never before seen that sort of anger in a human.

They'd have to talk about it later. For the moment, though, no more toying around.

The General surged ahead in a sharp, direct burst of motion, his right-hand blade sweeping towards Graham's unguarded side, his left-hand sword preparing to block the junior Manchester's inevitable swing from the other direction...

Graham dropped the point of his sword.

As soon as he walked ribs-first into the point of the weapon, Beckett realized what the human had done — clever, *very* clever.

Graham had denied Beckett the ability to properly gauge the range of his blade by keeping the sword up. Being distracted, the wolf had moved in just a little too close as he delivered his attack... and he'd been prepared for the wrong strike. Graham would thus have run him through, had this been a real, unshielded encounter.

"That wasn't particularly fair, nor will it work a second time," Graham said quietly as Beckett's shield crackled. "And we're both likely dead anyway. Impaled or not, you'd follow through, I expect."

The coolness of the words chilled Beckett, and Christine as she watched beyond the shield. They weren't just impassive... they almost sounded...

Hungry? As if he relishes the thought of dying in the moment he gives the killing blow.

As Cadmus Howler stopped alongside her, Christine absently rubbed her forehead. Her worries about her home were gone, her struggles with her suit for the moment seemed unimportant. Graham was so cold and impassive on the surface, but there was a new viciousness in his soul. And it cared very little about his well-being.

The same realization had filled Beckett Lupus' mind, and as he stepped back and sheathed his swords, his eyes fixed stoically on Graham's, "We're going to talk. Right now."

The ArcGeneral slid his own sword into his scabbard, "Very well."

A moment later, Christine watched Graham leave the gym with only a nod to her, and the shiver she felt had nothing to do with her new suit.

CHAPTER 34

Commodore Tom Locke narrowed his eyes as his ships edged towards the fringes of Ecclesia space. They were drawn out in a broad line abreast, eight 44-gun frigates with their fields stretched to almost 300 percent in order to avoid detection, and now their modern sensor suites began to probe the system

"Looks like Ecclesia's all Omega now, sir," the First Lieutenant was standing over the Sensor Chief's shoulder as she made the comment, and Locke nodded.

Slowly getting to his feet, he paced to *Charybdis'* plot and laced his hands behind his back. Omega had infested this system, alright... and he had a sizable force on hand here. More ships he'd taken command of — some in coherent-seeming fighting groups, others just a floating mob.

As the passive scans from the frigates stretched in and took note of each of them, actual numbers began scrolling up on the plot. Three hundred or so... no, almost 400 vessels... and quite a number of them were in fact ships taken from the mothball yards around Genesis. It was impossible to determine how many of those vessels had come from that system and how many were from Ecclesia... they were all now uniformly the hybrid ships of Omega's fleet.

Now it looked like there were *500* of them.

And it was edging towards *600*.

Locke took a deep breath as the number in the plot settled at 587, then turned to his Signal Officer, "Orders to *Outremont:* back out of detection range and send these numbers to Freetown and Earth immediately. We'll remain on station to keep everyone apprised of what's going on."

As the orders were given, one of the Earther 44s backed away from the system and cruised to a safe pod-launching area far away from Ecclesia.

It was seemingly unnoticed.

"Just got a pod from Ed, he's on his way back in with *Felix* now."

Jax Furgus had barely gotten through *Orion's* observation deck door when Ursla delivered her report, but he nodded and kept his pace. He was too preoccupied now with thoughts of *Republic*; he'd just seen the poor state of the Freetown flagship, which had essentially been decapitated. Even though just about every engineer Ursla could get her hands on was working on repairs, it looked as though the Strike Carrier might indeed be out of the fight for weeks.

"Nothing from Tom?" Jax came to a stop next to Ursla as the bear peered out *Orion's* windows.

"Not yet," Ursla replied in mid-sigh, and scratched the back of her neck uncomfortably. "I hope he finds every Omega ship at Ecclesia... and yet I hope he doesn't. Don't know, Jax, I'm just a bit uncomfortable being out here and not knowing."

The shorter lion Admiral offered a single understanding nod in reply, "Right there with you. But then I've also got it in for that bastard, so if he's at Ecclesia I'll be glad of it. I know Tom won't lose track of him, so between us and Lab I'm pretty sure we can lasso whatever plague ships are there, and remove this threat. Period."

"Think it's that easy?" Ursla's tone was quiet, and Jax took a deep breath, looking out at the Earther recommissioned fleet as it floated beyond the glass.

"Nothing's ever that easy. But we've got to start somewhere."

Sarah was continually impressed by the new bridge equipment mounted in ships like *Unity Genesis* — it was decades ahead of anything she'd had during the Krogg War.

Probably because the Krogg War had been four decades ago, she realized with the slightest hint of humor.

The ships still didn't mount Earther holo plots, but their screens were much more elaborate than the ones of old, and the interfaces were much more intuitive and better suited to commanding an entire fleet in intricate maneuvers in action...

Of course, right now, as Sarah and Pat hosted Audrey DeBrooke on *Unity's* bridge, there wasn't much to look at — save, unfortunately, for the half-wrecked hulk of the brave ship *Republic*.

"They'll have it back to fighting trim soon, Audrey," Sarah was trying to console her Freetown opposite as best she could.

Sarah recognized the dilemma of their respective positions all too well — she'd lost Genesis, Audrey had lost her husband of forty years, and yet both of them were required to be here and to serve as the leaders of their people. There was no alternative, there was no one else to do their jobs.

And so while Sarah had never thought of Audrey as more than a friend who happened to lead a distant colony, now they were depending on each other... two leaders trying to figure out a way to save their species from destruction. As such, Audrey had been invited up to *Unity* a number of times now, and Sarah down to Government House several times as well.

It was simple commiseration — as close to therapy as either was going to get, given the circumstances.

"Let's hope Omega doesn't get here first," Audrey's reply was so quiet Sarah almost didn't hear it, but as it processed she looked up and nodded.

There was little doubt in anyone's mind that Freetown was Omega's next target — with Tom Locke's suggestion that he was in Ecclesia, it seemed painfully clear that the plague was returning to its... *his* original imperative: kill humanity. A sense of dread seemed to have settled over every human with that realization, Audrey and Sarah included.

"Well, I wouldn't worry too much about that..."

Sarah and Audrey both blinked at the unexpected comment and Pat's eyebrows rose as the two women's gazes shifted to him.

The Irishman shrugged, "Someone's got to be the optimist, eh? And recall, Andra Ursla's in-system now. Not to mention the Genesis Fleet and soon the Freetown Fleet again. Omega comes this way and we'll break his head over something hard and toast to a good fight."

He was still putting on a brave front, and he hoped he was the only one who knew it...

"I left my toasting glasses in the house, Pat. Want to go back to Genesis and grab them for me?" Sarah replied sharply, and her husband's face darkened.

"We can use mine," Audrey offered quietly, and the three-way discussion died awkwardly.

"You think they're going to hold together?" Ursla's question was frank, and Jax's reply came in a half-hearted shrug.

"I can't speak for the humans, Andra... they've been through a lot more than I can conceive of. And as we both know, they don't operate like we do... I know I'm fine, daughter or no... I'm just focused on Omega now. But them... well, I can't say..."

Ursla was thoughtful as she turned away from the glass in *Orion's* lounge, "They've lost two crack squadrons already, they've lost their homeworld, and they've lost Graham. And now with Sarah taking command of the fleet, they've lost their government... but they *have* picked up a veteran fighting officer..."

"You know, I don't think we can really make too much of this... *human equation* again, Andra. They're going to struggle with this, I'm sure, but I don't think we can concern ourselves with how they're doing so long as they're still willing to stand with us. As a race of beings they'll either survive this or not, but what I'm concerned with right now is that they stick to their guns and fight as hard as before. Even if that's fighting unto death," Jax's words were sobering.

"How they're feeling is not our problem, is what you're saying. So long as they fight."

Nodding, Jax looked up to Ursla, "We need to stop Omega, Andra. And we've already lost Genesis... we can't worry about the survivors' state of mind until we're certain they're going to have a state of mind for longer than a few more weeks."

Ursla's sigh was her heftiest yet, and she looked down and met the eyes of her wily old friend, "I just hope they see it that way. Meantime, it's up to you and me to secure this system… as soon as we know where Omega is. Almost like the time we rode to Genesis, isn't it?"

Jax snorted a laugh, "Right about now I'd trade my bathrobe for the promise of Narosh and the Fourth Fleet-of-War."

"Indeed. But Omega has probably already killed them all."

Jax blinked at that comment, frowned, and was about to look up at his friend's dire revelation when the abrupt glow of a pod exiting energy-hyper appeared in the black space not far beyond the glass.

Without speaking, both Admirals turned and headed immediately for *Orion's* bridge.

CHAPTER 35

"So it looks like the next move will be coming soon," Varnon Broadpaw's tone was quiet as he drew the conclusion, and standing with him in Admiralty House's war room, Lab Forepaw and Dran Nightclaw nodded evenly.

Tom Locke's scans of Ecclesia were filling the massive holo plot in this Admiralty House bunker, and now they showed a picture that was particularly unpleasant. Some 587 'recommissioned' Omega ships appeared to be ready to move, and Freetown probably didn't have the necessary firepower to stop them if they came...

"Ecclesia... it lets him get the twist on us, just as those Churchers did..." Forepaw's somber comment prolonged the nods, then he looked from the First Consul of the Earther people to Dran Nightclaw. "Now it's just a question of when I take the Home Fleet out to handle our friendly intruder there."

Varnon seemed to stand up slightly straighter at that, "You think we should go in there and clean him out now?"

Lab shrugged and shook his head, looking back to the flashing black icons in the plot, "I don't think we'll catch him in there, even if we move out immediately... but as soon as he moves out of the system Tom will jump on his tail. We should be able to catch him in open space."

Varnon nodded again, "And so you want to know when to take the fleet out to wait for him."

"We could probably get to Freetown from here faster than his ships can from Ecclesia," Nightclaw submitted smoothly. "In case his target isn't Freetown, I'd suggest we wait to move out. It would not do well for us to pass him in space."

Nodding again, Forepaw looked to his two old friends from the bygone war, "Fair enough. We stay here until Tom warns us Omega is moving. Then we move to intercept..." he paused, then looked back to the plot. "That in mind, I think Dran and I should permanently shift our offices to ships in orbit. We may need to get out of system at short notice."

The panther frowned slightly, "It would be somewhat less efficient from an administrative standpoint..." Varnon and Lab both looked at him curiously, and the panther offered an uncommon shrug, "...but I will shift my flag to *Inferno*."

Lab nodded, "And I'll go to *Venerable*."

"And why not, I'll board *Guardian One*. If you two have to leave the system

I'll take over orbital defense," Varnon nodded to them both. "I'd rather be out there anyway, and Setter can take control of the government if needed."

The trio seemed to pause, having committed themselves to leave their London offices for ships and orbital stations. Something about that was gnawing at the back of Varnon's mind. He just couldn't tell what...

"This feel like a bad idea to anyone else?"

Lab shrugged, "Just about everything *feels* like a bad idea right now. But this makes sense, so let's do it."

With mutual nods, the old warriors of the Earther Navy left the Admiralty war room.

Each of them got the eerie feeling they would never return.

"So how do you sweat?"

The question was as frank as all the others Claire had asked, and Phealan smiled and shook his head a single time, "We pant, and only on rare occasions."

Claire was picking her way through some larger jagged slate rocks on the shore of the Caine estate's beach, watching as the rising tide swept in closer to them. It had been many days since Pat had left her to Phealan's care, and he seemed to be making progress — she was now speaking regularly.

Human psyches weren't always the most resilient, and while Phealan was fairly certain he could help this young woman, he wasn't going to sign any guarantees that she'd come out feeling alright.

"Seems like an easy way out to me," her words were a little softer as she made the comment, but her tone remained dejected. "Like whoever created you didn't want to deal with the hard details of drying your fur. Same with you not talking about sex — you're all too goody-goody to be normal..."

Indifferent to the rude probing, Phealan hopped up on a rock a little ways back from the advancing waves, "You're awfully quick to judge us by your own standards, aren't you?"

Claire looked at Phealan just as a brisk Atlantic wave reached between the rocks and wrapped itself around her ankles. She jumped with an abrupt cry of shock at the sudden cold, then retreated up the beach between the rocks.

"Well, I'm just saying what humans would think about you. I read about the whole 'Earthers are too good to be true' thing when I was young, and now I get it."

Watching her approach in squeaking wet shoes, Phealan twitched his ear, "If you want, I can arrange passage to Freetown for you. I'll bet they're not too good to be true up there."

Claire looked up from the rocks and scowled, "That's not what I said."

Phealan cracked a smile, "So we're not actually that bad to be around, are we?"

Shrugging, Claire turned to look back again at the waves swelling beyond the mouth of the cove, "You are too good to be true. But I guess that's better than Omega."

Phealan crossed his arms and withheld a smile. Any humans trying to deal with this young girl would doubtless have been frustrated by her tone and questions, but the junior Caine had more perspective. The very fact that young Claire was thinking and talking — bitter though she seemed — was progress.

She couldn't heal if she didn't talk, so Phealan would just be patient with her. She'd pull through yet.

Sitting even further down the beach was the Supreme Consul of Earth, leaning close to his wife and wrapping an arm around her waist as he watched his son work. Even from this distance he could see Phealan's wisdom at play — the young wolf was more clever and understanding than his elder, and Setter was proud to see that.

Phealan might well become the greatest leader the Earthers had ever seen... one day.

"He's really doing a good job down there," Elandra's comment was soft, and with a smile her husband nodded.

"He's letting her do all the work. I'd never have thought of that at his age, I'd have been plastering her with platitudes and ethics..." he let his voice trail off with that. Phealan was a properly bright young one.

Setter was *very* proud.

Now he just had to make sure he did his own part — ensure the Earthers would be in a position to defeat Omega, so Phealan's work with Claire wouldn't be a waste. The doom that was coming had to be stopped... or at least delayed.

So much had been lost already, he couldn't allow what remained to be destroyed.

For Setter, the largest incentives for making this fight were the same as they'd been forty years earlier. And they were both on this beach right now.

He'd defeat Omega for these people, his family. For all Earthers, in fact. And Setter knew every Earther alive would have made a similar pledge as Lab Forepaw distributed word of Omega's presence in Ecclesia.

They'd fight for their homes, their fellow Earthers, and their allies. Wouldn't be the first time, either...

"He's a lot like his father," Elandra seemed almost intent on breaking the cycle of her husband's darker thoughts, and he blinked and smiled at the comment. She continued, "You wouldn't be mister platitudes and you know it... you never were, or I never would've gone out with you in the first place."

Well, those happy mental pictures certainly served as a distraction. Setter so rarely thought of those early days of his life... so much time was focused on his duty that he often overlooked the day when Lab Forepaw, another Midshipman serving at Arctic Base, had introduced him to a rather fetching young science student who was working on a thesis on the evolution of non-Earther polar bears.

That *had* been a grand old time...

"Well, he still got some of your coloring," Setter said as he thought back to old days and his affinity then — as now — for Elandra's tan hues, so rare in Earther wolves.

Ah, the good times.

There was, of course, the temptation to feel nostalgic — to think of those times and wish they were back again... but alas, that wasn't for him. There was much to deal with in the here and now. Setter Caine wouldn't retreat into himself when others needed him.

"When do you head back to London?" he asked after a long moment's pause, watching his son and Claire Schaeffer as they talked in the distance.

Elandra let her head flop sideways onto her husband's shoulder, "This afternoon. And I'll be in for the long haul, I think. We're getting somewhere with the blood-cleaning compound — I think we'll be able to scrub the old Omega cells out of our bloodstreams soon. That's the first step, we think. And then I've got some ideas about a cure for the new one."

She said it so casually, so comfortably, and yet it was so significant. Setter smiled to himself as he thought of the possibilities: his wife, an Earther of peace and healing, finding a way to crush the greatest enemy he'd ever faced.

There'd be something poetic in that, and he looked forward to the experience.

So they sat for another hour, as a long way down the beach Phealan worked with Claire.

Waves continued to roll in.

CHAPTER 36

Christine Schaeffer was beginning to truly recognize the magnitude of the changes occurring within her. It struck her in some ways as absurd that it had taken so long for the gravity of what was happening to sink in. She'd noticed the changes, of course, during her battle alongside the Earther marines in Darymanis City, on Genesis One and when she'd come to this new galaxy...

But now, as her skin was caressed by a strobing stasis field, she stood still and recognized that her blood felt different. Whatever the UDRC dose had done to her had increased the effects of the regen. Her system was in *flux*, as Celia Lazarus put it, and for the first time she was really *feeling* what it meant to have one's DNA rewriting itself on its own terms.

She tried not to think about what would become of her. If Omega destroyed Earth, there'd be no chance of a cure, and there was no way of knowing what would happen if these changes were allowed to continue unchecked.

Continue? Celia said nothing about continuing changes, but I can feel them. The changes are happening all the time now.

Christine's thoughts came with frightening revelations. As she'd watched Graham and Beckett spar... as she'd realized that there was a dark fury driving Graham... she'd subconsciously begun to reflect on her own lack of fury.

After all that had happened to her, all she felt was despair, and a determination not to let that despair stop her.

That latter fortitude wasn't human. She had experienced human fortitude before... this was different. This was Earther fortitude. She was certain of it.

But she was human, wasn't she?

She didn't know anymore, and that terrified her. She couldn't even remember what it was like to be human —*just* human. The Earthers were wonderful comrades, but they weren't human. There was only one human here, and for all his troubles he was the only connection she had left to who she had been.

She didn't really want to lose Graham...

"What the *hell*, Graham? You're acting like you don't care about living. This *isn't* healthy..."

Beckett Lupus began his scolding as he dropped into his chair opposite the human ArcGeneral, but the junior Manchester's face remained maddeningly impassive.

"Graham, come *on*... I know you're hurting, but you can't stop living. You can't just give up everything you had. What will that accomplish?" Beckett kept pressing despite the lack of response, and Graham simply leaned back in his chair, letting the hand holding his sword by its sheath dangle over the arm of the seat.

Beckett stared into the human's eyes for a long moment, trying to use his instincts to get through Graham's wall. The rage and fury that had been so evident in the sparring circle was gone again, all emotion buried. The wolf had never seen a human so able to summon up and suppress his emotions at will.

That control was perhaps out of practical necessity — had Graham revealed to all the Earthers he met that he had such fury burning within him, and that he had no serious concern for his own survival, someone might well have sedated him. There was no question, as far as Beckett was concerned: here was a human dead set on dying, and on taking many down with him...

"Are you quite finished, Beckett?" those cool words forced an acknowledgment from the General.

The junior Manchester leaned forward again, "I understand that you don't do things my way, Beckett. You're an Earther — you can deal with emotional and spiritual crises in some enlightened way. You're a superior being. Savanna Felix once explained that to me, and I haven't doubted it since. But you still cannot understand *my* ways, because I'm still human. So don't bother to try. I appreciate your concern, but I won't suffer any interference on your part, or on the parts of any Earthers. Even though you're probably right, I'm still going to do this my way."

Beckett leaned back in his own seat as he listened, a deep frown crossing his face, "You're choosing a path of self destruction? You want to die?"

Graham did the nigh-unthinkable — he cocked an eyebrow, "Death might be required, I think. And as clichéd as it might sound, I'd be quite alright with that if it saw my duty fulfilled. I'll be ready to play any card I must. And don't ask me why, because you already know. You know or you wouldn't be sitting here talking to me."

Grinding his jaw, the Earther wolf let out an exasperated sigh, "You're going to try to make Omega pay. Revenge. He took your wife and your child, and you're going to do everything you can to end him."

Yes, Beckett understood that sentiment — he understood the desire, he'd felt something of it more than once in his life. The most memorable occasion had been on Krogg 'A', when Gillian Hodge, the wife Graham had just lost, was nearly eviscerated along with the rest of a human battalion who'd come forward to support his line.

For a moment that day Beckett had surrendered to his determination for retribution, and that had been fine — he hadn't been consumed by it, and in the end he'd done nothing he would regret.

But here was trusty old Graham, the funny doughnut man of the Genesis Fleet, the great friend of the Earthers, and he had surrendered everything to a singular quest...

"I'm not *me* any more, Beckett," Graham said very softly. "I'm aware of that, and I've accepted it. What I have left to do is avenge the death of who I was, and the loss of my family. To kill that godsdamned Omega *any way* I can. And to make sure no one and nothing stands in my way."

Graham's words had been cool before, but those last ones carried the deepest chill. The General let go a long breath as Graham delivered them, then looked away from the human to the window in his cabin wall.

Carnarvon was floating just beyond the glass.

Nothing... no one standing in his way...

"You're going in *Carnarvon*, then?"

Graham gave another single short nod, "I am. Narosh truly understands revenge, Beckett... I know that you understand the concept intellectually, but Narosh has lived it. I remember Setter telling me once just how willing the Larosians were to destroy all life on Krogg to see their own vengeance fulfilled. Well, he's peered into my mind. He truly understands, and he's willing to give me the resources to help me complete my own mission."

Beckett grew more serious as he listened to the comment, "At his own people's expense?"

Now Graham shook his head, "We'll go to Laros, inoculate the people and recommission the fleet. And then I'll find a way to use their fleet against Omega."

Beckett slowly shook his head, "But Omega's not in this galaxy."

"His old form is in the galaxy, Beckett, but you're right, the Omega I want to kill isn't. I'll find a way back to Genesis. The Larosians will help me because they understand what I have to do. They will help me eviscerate him."

So much of this conversation had been shocking to Beckett that he had no business being surprised by the *hunger* in those words.

"We're going to Genesis, we'll kill him... you can still come with us," the General tried again, and Graham shook his head a single time in reply.

"You will fight to save Earth, and to protect the survivors of Genesis. You aren't fighting to kill Omega, you're fighting to protect your homes, your families. Killing Omega is a way to achieve that goal, but in itself, it isn't your primary objective. I want to kill Omega. And that is *all* I want," the junior Manchester tried to make his explanation as clear as possible.

Beckett was beginning to see he really wasn't going to be able to crack the human's resolve, but he tried once more, "What about the Genesis Fleet? You don't care about your ships, your crews?"

"I would be of no use to them, Beckett. All I have left in me now is the desire to kill Omega. I want no other responsibilities. If I go back, Sarah and

Setter will try to give me responsibilities, duties. I want none of them. I know I am being selfish, Beckett. But I want Omega to *pay* for what he did to Gillian. Going with you would put me closer to him, but then I'd be in the company of those who didn't share my goal. So I go with *Carnarvon*, away from Omega but to a people who will help me find my way back, and then kill him."

Rubbing his head absently, Beckett sounded resigned, "I take it you wouldn't be telling me this if you weren't certain."

A final nod came from Graham, who then stood slowly, "I appreciate your concern, Beckett. And all of your help. And I'm sorry if I've offended you or any Earthers anytime over the last week. But I will do this, as I must. You understand?"

Coming to his feet as well, Beckett nodded slowly, "I get it. So good luck then."

There should have been more said, but Graham had no time for pleasantries. He just *left*.

Beckett turned to the comm and called his wife.

Graham didn't even see Christine as he walked quickly out of Beckett's cabin, but she called immediately after him, "Graham?"

Frowning, he came to a halt, then turned to face his aide, "Christine. Can I do something for you?"

She raised her eyebrows in surprise, "Um... are you alright?"

Though his face remained impassive, Graham shook his head, "Not as such, no."

"I... well... can I...?"

Graham's head tilted slightly at her seeming loss for words, "No, you can't, I don't think. Best thing for you will be to return to Earth with *Renown*, get yourself fixed up and find your sister."

He began to turn away again, seeming somehow rushed, but Christine took two steps toward him, a very deep frown settling on her face, "What do you mean *I* should — you're not–"

"I'll be leaving on *Carnarvon*," he didn't turn as he spoke. "Go back to Earth. Get fixed."

He then paced evenly down the corridor, leaving Christine baffled in his wake.

CHAPTER 37

Narosh settled himself in a chair in Varnia's day cabin, nodding to the wolf as she lowered herself into a seat opposite him.

"Well, *Carnarvon's* just about set?" she shifted in her seat and leaned forward to rest her elbows on her desk.

With an almost exaggerated Larosian-style bow-nod, Narosh confirmed the report, "Your engineering teams have been most productive, and Neytosh sends his sincere thanks."

"Glad to help, of course. So I'll be taking *Renown* back to Earth, by way of the New Halifax corridor, and you'll be taking *Carnarvon* to Laros. Once you get there, we'll need you to rally whatever you can. It's a good sign that *Carnarvon* could be put back to fighting condition, after a fashion, anyway. But we'll need as much as you can get ready to use against Omega, I think."

Narosh was nodding evenly, and Varnia let her voice trail off as the Larosian concurred with her. It seemed like they'd been together in this fight for years now, but in fact it had been only weeks since Genesis had faced the shadows of a Church coup. Only weeks since Narosh and the Larosians had been a distant memory from decades past.

Now they were getting ready to part ways again.

"I believe I should be able to rally a strong force to join you, thanks to the cure you're sending. Rest assured, Varnia, we will be coming to your aid in strength."

A genuine smile crossed Varnia's face, "Yes, I do appreciate that, and I know we'll all be glad to pass word along. But don't take any unnecessary risks with yourselves — we'll hold out well enough."

Narosh tilted his head slightly, "Risks seem to come with our duty these days, Varnia. But indeed, I take your point. Now, there is one other matter that would seem pressing... one more asset I'll be taking off *Renown*."

Another *asset*? Even Narosh didn't usually sound that stilted... "Um. Well, you've got half our boats and our new senior boat officer... I hear you're getting three companies of 2/54th under Joyce Furgus and Ellen Arbear... you want extra ratings to help run the ship?"

Offering his alien smile, Narosh shook his head, "I'll be taking–"

Of course, with something of that old Earther timing that had been so prevalent in the last war, the intercom chirped just as Narosh was about to say the important part, "Varnia? It's Beckett..."

Keying her comm, Varnia replied immediately, "I'm talking to Narosh, can this wait for a minute?"

"*Narosh*? Is he listening right now?"

Varnia's second eyebrow rose to join the first, "Um... yes — what's going–"

"What the hell did you fill Graham's head with Narosh? One minute he's chilling me to the bone and the next he's breathing fire — vengeance and not caring about surviving and such. What'd you say to him?"

Beckett's questions were pointed enough to shift Varnia's expression immediately into a frown, but she stopped herself and merely stared at the Larosian as he tilted his head somewhat awkwardly.

"Well, I was about to explain this to Varnia, Beck... I didn't put anything in his head, I just told him the truth — that I understand what is going on in his mind. We Larosians tend to have a fairly good grip on the principles of revenge, remember..."

Varnia's eyes hardened slightly, "Revenge? Ah right, your plan to blow up yourselves and Krogg 'A'. We had to talk you down from it."

Narosh offered a single, even nod, "Indeed. Graham is suffering now from a need for satisfaction. I believe his uncommon activities of late might suggest that much to all of you. He needs the opportunity to vent his hatred."

"And he can do that in your space? There's no Omega out here, Narosh, why are you suggesting he stay with you?" Beckett came back.

Varnia blinked.

"Excuse me, *stay*... wait a minute, that's the *asset* you're taking off *Renown*?" Varnia edged forward in her chair, leaning across the table to lock eyes with Narosh.

"I'm afraid so," the Larosian's reply was measured and showed no signs of consternation.

"Graham's argument was that his fleet wouldn't need him in the state he's in anyway, Varnia. He's taking much the same route Sarah did at Gibraltar... might well be a family trait. But he doesn't see our goal of stopping Omega and saving our homes and our race as compatible with his own of *eviscerating* Omega," Beckett's words of explanation made Varnia's ear twitch.

Graham was so bent on revenge that he was going to abandon his own fleet. The concept was alien to an Earther... hell, Varnia imagined it'd be alien to many humans.

But if that was what Graham was set on doing, then she couldn't force him not to. It wasn't the Earther way, for one, and what good would he be if she hauled him back with her against his will? First chance he got, he'd probably attack Omega and get himself killed... or worse, use his authority to lead the Genesis Fleet into a similar sort of attack and get hundreds of thousands killed.

Maybe keeping him a galaxy away would be better... but how could Varnia really know? The narrowly better of two bad options?

"You think this is *best* for him, Narosh?" Varnia's quiet question reflected the debate in her mind, and the Larosian nodded in silent reply.

"Is he nodding?" Beckett asked over the intercom.

"I am. It is best for him, Beckett. He'll never function as a human again if this is left to seethe within him. And I expect he'd be more inclined to send his fleet blindly at Omega in an attempt to gain satisfaction than he would be to mount a responsible defense," Narosh's words confirmed Varnia's thoughts. "We will honestly aid him. When our fleet is restored, and we return to your galaxy, he will come with us. And he will seek his revenge, with our help."

"You'll lead your fleet on a suicide mission, just for him?" Varnia's speculation halted at that thought, but Narosh shook his head.

"Beckett, I am shaking my head. Neither of you understand, because you are Earthers. Graham does not want a Larosian Fleet with him, he just wants a chance to confront Natosh... to fight Omega and be killed by him. Or to kill him. He has distanced himself from all of you because he knows this is a suicide mission, and he wants to do it alone," the explanation drew a dark stare from Varnia, but Narosh continued. "That is why he doesn't want to return to his fleet, because if he was put in command of them, he wouldn't be able to resist using them to further his mission. Part of him, a part he is not willing to acknowledge, cares for the fleet, so he is staying away from it. When we return to your galaxy, he would ask at most for one of our ships, to get him close enough. To give him a chance."

Varnia's eyes were firmly locked on Narosh's — she had no idea how to respond to that. Earthers didn't believe in seeking an avoidable death just to try to hurt something that had done you or yours harm. You died if you had to, but failing that you lived on, in honor of your fallen friends.

Narosh understood the difference between human and Earther mentalities, "You would deny him a ship to go to Genesis because you believe he could and should live on, and honor his family's memory. The humans would deny him that one ship, but would give him a fleet, and he would see them all killed. We will give him one ship, and volunteers to crew it who are willing to die on a noble mission of vengeance, and he will have his chance. We *understand* the honor in his fury. You never will."

None of this really made sense to Varnia — how could it? No Earther would ever let rage or pain consume them to the point where revenge was the only purpose. All Earthers would want to stop Omega, but not as an act of spite. Killing Omega was a necessity because it was the only way to protect their home, and to protect the human survivors of Genesis.

But here was a human Varnia thought of as a good friend, and he was ready to cast away his entire existence because Omega had taken his family.

He didn't want to honor his fallen loved ones, he wanted to avenge them, and ultimately, to fall with them.

Varnia couldn't dispute Graham's right to choose that course of action for himself... but the road to revenge would doubtless cost him more than any Earther could donate in support.

Graham would be restored or murdered by this quest.

"Trust me please, both of you. I will look after Graham. I will give him what vehicles he needs to find his revenge, but I will do my utmost to see him through the coming strife alive," Narosh's words carried some reassurance, but quite a lot of poorly hidden strain.

It seemed somehow unlikely that Graham was going to be easy to control.

"Fine."

Beckett's single word over the comm was followed by a distinct 'click' as he released his connection. Varnia took a deep breath and eyed the Admiral-of-a-Fleet.

"You keep him alive, Narosh. And if you can't do that, find someone who can."

"Christine! What are you doing back here so soon?"

Celia Lazarus laid a few pads down on her desk and came to her feet as the young human stepped into her office.

Christine, standing rigidly in her pseudo-fencing suit, set her jaw against any abrupt comments, and instead delivered a ponderous response, "I need to talk about my suit... namely, what do I do to make up for it in my quarters if I'm not wearing it?"

Lazarus' ear twitched and she rounded her desk, leaning against its corner as she stopped next to Christine, "Well, I'm working up an atmospheric cocktail of pain inhibitors that I think can take the edge off it for you. Other than that, I'm rigging up a shield generator to run a larger dampening field than the one you have now... between them, we should have you reasonably comfortable at home."

Christine nodded slowly — as she'd expected, the Earthers had already considered her problems. They'd soon have a way to make her life in her quarters tolerable.

"So... how would you jury-rig these systems into the cabin of... say, a Larosian Battleship?"

Lazarus wasn't certain she'd heard the question properly... but no, Christine's earnest eyes locked with the black wolf doctor's. This was no joke... what was she thinking?

"You realize I can't repair the damage before we'd part ways..." the young human nodded in reply to Lazarus' question, and a particularly deep frown formed on the wolf's face. "Christine... why? We're heading home... you have a sister, don't you? Surely you must want to return home... to see her..."

Christine nodded very slowly, "There's nothing I'd like better. When can you get a team to install the facilities on *Carnarvon*?"

Lazarus blinked again, "Um... give me half an hour to finalize things."

Christine offered a single, forced nod, then Lazarus stepped past her and out into the main med bay.

Listening distantly to the doctor ordering a team together, Christine indeed wondered just what she was doing. She was turning down her chance to go home. She was about to abandon a chance to go to Earth — where she could find many examples of the humanity she felt she was missing — so that she could stay alongside one man who barely still qualified as human...

No more 'about to' about it. It's done.

Indeed, it was. About forty-five minutes later, teams were prepped and sent to install special environmental controls in a cabin on *Carnarvon*.

CHAPTER 38

"I don't like having their refugee fleet lying overhead."

Audrey DeBrooke looked up abruptly as Ed Jeffries made the remark, her drawn eyes finding his almost immediately, "*Their* refugee fleet, Ed? That's all that's left of our home planet."

The large, dark-skinned Freetown Commodore tightened his jaw, "That's true, and that means we're essentially responsible for their safety. I'm not comfortable with that..."

Well, Audrey couldn't really grudge her Commodore his reluctance. She'd watched from the war room in Freetown's Capitol Building as the new ships of the Freetown Squadron had dragged themselves in after their wild chase, and she'd seen what had become of *Republic*.

Omega didn't fight by the rules, and because he didn't, their carefully designed and prepared squadron simply wasn't powerful enough to stand against him. So much planning, so much waste... she'd spent literally months pouring over the specs on those Battlecruisers and that Carrier with James, they'd worked everything out to perfection as they'd planned for how they could fight the Church...

James. Right, James.

Her dead husband.

Audrey swallowed hard as the image of his face filled her mind again. She'd deal with this later...

"I know we're not in the best condition to protect them. But they've got their own fleet in orbit, Ed. And Andra Ursla is out there. I don't think we could have asked for anyone better to help keep them safe."

"Yes, we'll be fine. But I'd be more worried about civil defense."

Neither Ed nor Audrey had offered that suggestion, so both turned to look at the door, and sure enough, Pat Conroy had stepped into the room.

With a bit of a wry smile, he held up a hand and offered a wave to both mildly surprised Freetowners, "Hi."

Ed cast a curious glance, but before either could question the Irishman, Pat stepped fully into the room and shrugged, "Sarah's busy up there, and I'm not going to any ship commands with her running the show. So I thought I'd come down and see if I could be of any use setting up Freetown's defenses."

"Sure you weren't sent to check in on us?" Ed's question was a bit cooler than it ought to have been, and it drew a silencing glare from Audrey.

"A lot of stress, I know," Pat nodded to the Commodore before Audrey could say anything. "Frankly, I'm sorry we've put you lot in the middle of this mess. But then I suppose we didn't... and it doesn't bloody matter much anyway. I think Sarah and Andra are planning to get the refugees out of system soon. What I'm worried about is your situation for dealing with landings."

"Landings... what?" Audrey frowned for a moment at the remark, then let her mind begin to process what Pat was saying. She hadn't really thought about it yet — a testament, perhaps, to her many preoccupations — but they might have to hold this planet against a concerted invasion from space.

"They already have Ecclesia. Maybe we need to start thinking about fortifications and militias. I hear the Earthers installed a good defense shield around the capital city... maybe you should round everyone up and make a stand here?"

Audrey grimaced, and Ed frowned, "You think the fleet isn't going to be enough to stop a landing?"

Pat's expression seemed to darken just a couple of shades, "After all you've seen, do you really want to take the chance?"

"I think we need to get them moving *now* Andra," Sarah's tone was remarkably even, and Ursla's gaze grew serious as her old human friend sat in one of the chairs at *Orion's* briefing table.

"The refugees?" Jax Furgus turned his chair to face Sarah, and she nodded.

"We have to get them out of this space before Omega arrives — they're all that's left of Genesis, I can't let them get caught in open space by his attack fleet. Not after the way he dealt with *Republic*. And we learned decades ago that it's virtually impossible to keep noncombatants safe during a battle..." Sarah's voice was filling with a new determination.

She'd fought many battles, now she just had to fight some more. This was no different than the Battle of the Asteroid Belt, or Genesis, or Krogg... she just had to be now like she'd been then.

And that meant she knew better than to leave a huge armada of defenseless ships anywhere near Omega's target. Freetown could protect its own, but not the Genesis survivors.

"I don't want to send them out until we know where Omega's headed," Jax offered his opinion in quiet tones, looking immediately to Ursla. "If he lines up against Earth, the refugees will be in just as much trouble."

Nodding, Ursla shifted her gaze from Sarah to Jax and back, "Indeed. Look, Lab isn't going to be taking the Home Fleet out until he hears of a specific deployment out of Ecclesia... we can wait until then to figure out what to do with the refugees."

That did make sense — Sarah could envision the carnage that might ensue if her civilian ships were caught between planetary systems by even a single Omega vessel. Inoculations had been distributed to some of the refugees, but if even a single human aboard a ship had missed treatment, Omega could probably take the vessel... Gods only knew what he would do then.

"Very well," she said after a moment, nodding to Ursla.

"Good. So all we need do now is wait to hear from Tom Locke..." Jax leaned back in his chair again with a frown. "I wish I was looking forward to that."

Tom Locke wasn't really eager to have news to report, but it was becoming evident that he'd have to send pods to Earth and Freetown soon. Omega's ships seemed to be preparing to move.

"Their drives are almost spun up... I *think*, skipper. They've got some readings there entirely unlike anything I've seen."

Locke turned from his plot to look at his Sensor Chief, "Any sign of changing formations?"

Well, if you could call the massive cloud Omega's ships were scattered through a 'formation'...

"Not as... wait a moment... I think we've got something..."

The holo plot was showing what the Chief was referring to when his voice trailed off. The Omega fleet was beginning to move — the great hordes of mismatched ships were sidling away from the planet they'd occupied, and they were certainly heading for deeper space...

"They're definitely moving now, sir. No question... heading our way too. Don't think they've seen us, it just looks to be their base course."

"To Freetown," Locke said quietly, then he looked to his First Lieutenant. "Let's get the field out fully to 300 percent. I don't want to get spotted. Signals, order the squadron to match our field density and scatter."

Locke's eyes settled on the great mass of ships moving through the plot. It had been quite a long time since so many vessels had been seen moving together in space. The Admiralty and Freetown needed as much warning as possible — at least both would know that the Omega fleet was on its way.

Then Ursla and Forepaw could do their jobs...

"Alright, Signals... send to Captain Uvar in *Siren*... have him get out of range and dispatch pods before rejoining. All sensor data and most up-to-date telemetry... we'll be tailing the Omega ships as they head out, and will make further updates along the way."

The orders were broadcast as soon as Locke finished speaking.

Unseen, Captain Lars Uvar maneuvered his handy ship out of sight, dropped from energy drive, and launched two pods.

Right, I didn't see that at all...

CHAPTER 39

"We're ready to weigh at your order, sir."

Lab Forepaw nodded to his Flag Captain as he took a seat on *Venerable's* bridge, his eyes narrowing as they settled again on the information from Commodore Locke's courier.

The pod had arrived at Earth forty minutes earlier, and based on the information *Siren's* Signal Officer had provided, it seemed that the Omega fleet — that armada of bastardized ships — was on its way into space, heading straight for Freetown.

"Think he's trying to misdirect us?" *Venerable's* Flag Captain, the veteran bear Arther Stowt, took his own seat next to the First Lord as he asked the question.

Forepaw offered a slow nod, "I imagine he's doing more than we're seeing... though I don't think Tom would be that easy to fool."

"Aye..."

Lab barely heard the acknowledgement; he was trying hard to get into Omega's mind. The plague was playing this conventionally, fighting ships with ships, taking planets and maneuvering in open space. This war, during which so many rules had been broken, seemed to be settling at last into a pattern the Earthers could handle.

They'd just have to stay on their toes...

Home Fleet would have to be ready, because this almost seemed too predictable.

"Fair enough..." the words were essentially out of place, but Lab followed them quickly with more decisive ones. "Signal Officer, orders to fleet: stand by for maximum sustainable cruising speed, at my order. Let's keep our eyes open for the next pod."

Setter stepped onto the C&C deck aboard the orbital station *Guardian One*. It had been about an hour since the pod had come in, and at Varnon Broadpaw's request, he'd taken his pinnace up from his estate to discuss the situation.

"What's going on, Varnon?"

Broadpaw was standing rigidly before the station's massive holo tank, his gaze fixed directly on Ecclesia, "Omega's moving... we're waiting to hear more from Tom Locke's frigates, but all indications for now are that he's headed for

Freetown."

Setter stepped evenly across the deck floor and came to a halt next to his old friend, "Indeed. Well, it would make sense... though I won't believe it until we've got things sorted out entirely."

"None of us will, I think. Lab just told me he'll be holding position until he knows more," Varnon glanced sideways briefly at Setter as he spoke, then looked back. "Either way, though, we're looking at action in about a day... maybe two."

Setter's shoulders straightened at those grim words. Soon enough they'd know just how powerful Omega really was. So far he hadn't shown them anything that was beyond their ability to deal with. He'd succeeded at Genesis, certainly, but there he'd faced unprepared humans, not Earthers who were expecting him. Now they'd find out if being ready to face him made any difference...

He was *Omega*, and something deep within Setter told him nothing would be simple in the war against this plague.

Nothing.

"Ami Dune just took command of the recommissioned Third Fleet, and Kylie Peregrine has the Second. I've got Zed Dune running the stations since he's still tied up with the recommissioning," Varnon pointed to each of the formations of forty-year-old ships in the plot as he spoke of them, then his finger moved towards Earth. "All those pennants are so familiar... hell of a good time for a reunion."

Indeed, those were all veteran names, and Setter was somewhat comforted to hear them again... but they were names that came with only 322 ships attached. They didn't have the numbers or the strength to confidently protect Earth if Lab took the fleet out and got caught in the open.

But what about Andra? There wasn't much chance of Freetown holding with only the 150-odd ships Andra and Jax Furgus could pull together, even with the Genesis ships making up for some of the difference...

Not my call any more. Omega watched me fight the last war, he's probably doing all of this with me in mind as his opposition. I need to let Lab make these decisions.

An almost painful sense of relief accompanied that thought as it crossed Setter's mind — Lab Forepaw was responsible for all this now, and even as Supreme Consul, Setter wouldn't attempt to overrule his old and trusted Flag Captain. The Home Fleet, the newest and most powerful force in space, would be the decider here, and it was in Lab's hands alone.

So maybe I can actually relax. He's not prone to making mistakes.

Setter's ear twitched, and his eyes narrowed at the plot.

"Times like these, I wish Fox hadn't taken all those ships out towards Gibraltar."

Jax's comment drew a cocked eyebrow from Ursla and she glanced sideways at him, "Fox? Right, I'd managed to completely forget about him... shouldn't he be there by now?"

The lion shrugged in reply, "I expect if he's late it's because he's avoiding a fight, not because he lost one. All the same, those *Chimeras* he took with him would be a nice addition to Lab's fleet."

Well, that was true.

Orion's trusty old main holo plot was showing the situation quite clearly — from New Halifax to Krogg, the Allies had something approaching 1,000 ships in service... but here at Freetown only about 350 were in position to deal with Omega's sortie of 500 plus. Earth was little better off, and the New Halifax corridor would be a writeoff if it got hit.

Omega had managed to spread them out, and now Lab was being forced to sit at the ready, to actively defend a nearly indefensible three-point perimeter...

"We'll just have to make do," Andra said it as much for herself as for Jax, and the lion nodded again.

"Looked worse at Gibraltar when the Kroggs came, I suppose," he added somewhat drearily. "Of course, the Kroggs never succeeded in wiping out Genesis, and killing my daughter."

Ursla ground her jaw and nodded, "But we beat Omega decisively... once."

Jax frowned and glanced up at his old comrade, "We did?"

With a mild shrug, Ursla looked down, "Right back in the beginning. We're the ones who trapped him in our blood, after all. So for all the tricks he pulls, he's trying a *comeback*. We're the incumbent power."

Scratching absently behind his ear, Jax looked back to his plot, "I think you mixed some metaphors there, but I'll buy it. He's broken out of jail... we just need to step on him now that he has."

Ursla managed a wry smile in the traditions of old, "See, that's the spirit."

They nodded to each other, trying to recapture some of the energy that had once guided their war efforts.

In two days or less, they'd need every bit of energy they could get their hands on.

"So they figure it's going to be Freetown," Artemis Tigar sat back in his chair and focused his gaze on the face of Minnie Maximane as she glowed in *Agamemnon's* bridge plot.

With a shrug, she nodded in reply, "They've got Tom Locke and a squadron of 44s watching the cruise; they figure two days or less and someone will be in action."

Artie offered a slow, understanding nod. For all the convoluted complications that had surrounded the past two weeks, they were finally seeing movement... and Omega was getting set to play them.

Having served with Andra Ursla, Lab Forepaw, Jax Furgus and all the rest,

Artie Tigar had a deep appreciation for their skill, but a nagging voice in the back of his mind suggested that Omega might just get them chasing the wrong way.

Perhaps he should get his fleet moving... secretly get it into position over Earth, just in case Omega was making a move with a strong feint.

That would leave the corridor and New Halifax wide open, but Artie was just about positive now that the plague wasn't after the conventional sorts of targets.

He had no idea why, but Artie believed he was getting a sense for this enemy... or something of a sense, at least.

But was it enough to act on? Was it, indeed...

"Artie? Artie you're zoning out on me," Minnie drew his attention back to the plot, and with a deep frown, Tigar came out of his chair.

"I've got an idea... tell me what you think."

CHAPTER 40

Captain Joyce Furgus slung her rifle over her shoulder and lifted her kit bag off her bunk. She had her sidearm at her hip, with her sword hanging in its proper place right behind that. She'd packed everything she'd need... right...?

Scanning her cabin once more for anything that looked important enough to bring, she nodded to herself. She was good to go, so she turned from her bed and stepped quickly toward the cabin hatch, keying it open smoothly and stepping out into the bustling corridor.

Joyce had three companies of marines preparing to join *Carnarvon* — just under 150 Earther marines would be reinforcing the Larosian crew, in order to provide extra hands in case work was needed, and to defend the ship in case of a boarding incident.

The assignment meant Joyce wouldn't be getting back to Earth for a while, but such was the nature of her job. When *Renown* got back home, her father would find out that she was alive and doing her job in this new galaxy. He'd be pleased, Joyce was sure of that. All of Joyce's marines' families would be similarly informed — these three companies were on a critical mission to Laros.

"We're all set to board *Carnarvon*, Joyce."

Furgus blinked and came to a stop in the hall, immediately tracing the report back to its source, and thus turning to face Lieutenant Ellen Arbear, "Alright then, let's get everyone moving."

Nodding evenly, Arbear turned away from the lioness Captain and nodded to the Sergeants and Corporals of 2/54th companies detailed to the operation. Movement began to spread quickly through the deck full of marines; a file of the veteran troops formed, and began worming its way out of the marine section towards the airlock.

Joyce watched as most of her marines marched away from their ship, then with a single flick of her ear, joined the long column.

The marines were boarding *Carnarvon*.

"This all seems a bit abrupt..."

Garth Badger held up his hand to stop the comment from one of his Boat Captains, then nodded to the assembled group of some sixty boat crews, "I know it's sudden. Believe me, I just took command of this wing after all... but Admiral Lupus assures me it's necessary that we put a strong boat force in

Carnarvon. The ship's own defensive systems aren't in great shape, and in order to turn it into an effective fighting vessel..."

There were somber murmurs of agreement from the assembled Earthers, and one followed with a question, "What sort of docking facilities will we have?"

Badger realized his hand was still raised, so he dropped it before replying, "Nothing fancy. The engineers have been working on *Carnarvon's* flight deck since we finished off the Omega squadron, so they'll have installed grav tractors on the deck and meshed some of our fly-by-wire kit. But we're not going to have all the amenities. Any of you here flown off one of the old Krogg War ship's decks? It'll probably be a lot like that."

There were nods amongst the large number of pilots and crew, as they began to get a sense of what was being asked of them. It wasn't a small commitment, that was for certain, but they were all needed for this mission. Unlike *Renown*, *Carnarvon* didn't have the heavy guns and shields needed to beat back any trouble it happened upon; the placement of boats with it was crucial.

Of course, Garth Badger wasn't exactly *eager* for this job — he'd just gotten command of this wing, so he was getting used to a great deal of change as it was already, and he'd lost friends not long ago.

He hadn't been to war before — unlike many of his fellow officers in the service, he wasn't accustomed to dealing with losses like these.

But he was quite used to doing his job. And that's what he would do now.

"Alright, we don't have much time. We're due aboard *Carnarvon* in under an hour, so get your kit together quickly, then get to your boats. We'll send off the pulsar squadrons first... we'll have to land them further back on *Carnarvon's* deck, because we're less likely to need them launch-ready before the gun squadrons. Yes that's right, one space door, so whoever's last to land is first out."

There were raised eyebrows of surprise as Badger explained the makeshift circumstances, but the pilots and boat crews gave their own signs of acknowledgement and then, after a moment, began to clear the flight deck briefing room.

About twenty minutes later, the first of the Pulsar Squadrons launched itself from *Renown's* deck.

The gunboats were transferring to *Carnarvon*.

"You're some piece of work, Narosh."

The Admiral-of-a-Fleet looked up abruptly at his cabin door — he hadn't heard it open, but sure enough, Beckett Lupus was standing and leaning into the Larosian's room, hands propped on the sides of the doorframe.

"Is that a good thing or a bad thing?" Narosh straightened up, closing the small kit that contained his treatment gear. Doctor Lazarus had quickly attached his new hand, but she wouldn't be able to do the post-operation procedures that would ensure healing, so he had to carry this kit with UDRC injectors and such things.

Beckett's eyes narrowed slightly, then looked the Larosian up and down, "I just need to know, Narosh... did you put this in Graham's head, or did he decide to go with you on his own?"

The Admiral-of-a-Fleet met the General's eyes and tilted his head slightly, "I would not manipulate him, Beckett. On my honor, I am only giving him a *safe* outlet for his anger and grief. We can keep his anger from doing damage, and by the time he returns with us to your galaxy, he will either have gained a measure of peace and self-control, or he will be given a Warcruiser, to go where he pleases."

A long sigh slipped from Beckett, and his narrowed eyes opened fully again, "Alright. You look after him though, my friend. He's not going to have any humans or Earthers around... I'm not sure if that'll be good for him."

"The only real human friend I had was alone with us for years, Beckett. And while I would not compare Graham to the Son in his spiritual stature, I believe he might be equally important to my people..." Narosh let the words trail off as a puzzled Beckett stepped fully into the room.

"You think Graham's going to make some sort of major contribution?"

Approximating a shrug, Narosh took his kit from his desk, "I could not say with any certainty. But he has the... constitution for it."

Beckett smiled sadly, "I hope it doesn't kill him. Alright then, you get over to *Carnarvon*. Got any messages for me to pass along?"

"We'll bring a strong force to the aid of our longtime allies. I pledge that," Narosh's confidence should have seemed out of place, but Beckett caught a hint of something in the Larosian's tone.

This was an Admiral who had been fighting wars for as long as Beckett had been alive. His word was neither light nor untrustworthy.

"Fox and Lab and Varnon will be glad to hear it, I expect," the General smiled and nodded to his comrade.

Then wolf eyes met silver Larosian ones, and somewhat uneasily, Beckett extended his hand, "Safe journey, my friend."

Without pause, Narosh bobbed his head and took the hand, "And to you. I'll see you soon."

And then Narosh released Beckett's hand, stepped past the General and exited his cabin.

The Admiral-of-a-Fleet was boarding *Carnarvon*.

Graham was traveling light, but then he would — he essentially had nothing to carry. His sword and sidearm were at his hip, he'd slung a rifle over his shoulder, and he had a small duffle containing the various Earther-manufactured pieces of clothing he might find useful.

With those necessities in hand, he was marching through *Renown's* corridors, heading for the lock to *Carnarvon*.

His expression hadn't changed. Every Earther he passed felt the chill that had settled on his soul, and as he found himself approaching the lock and the large body of marines and volunteer ratings who were now boarding the Larosian vessel, he earned himself some disturbed glances.

"All set, sir?"

He blinked and looked to his left.

Captain Furgus nodded to him again, "We're glad to have you."

Graham offered a very slim nod, "I appreciate that, Captain, but I expect I shall benefit more from your presence than you shall from mine."

Joyce opened her mouth to comment, but a more familiar voice interrupted, originating from beside the airlock just ahead.

"We'll miss you though, Graham."

Varnia and Cadmus Howler were standing by the lock to see the *Renown* volunteers off the ship, and the Admiral addressed him as he approached. With a quick acknowledgment to Joyce, he stepped away from the file of marines and came to a stop just before the pair of Earthers.

"You'll do better without me, I think. My compliments to the fleet. Tell them they shall do well without me, and that my own mission took precedence."

Varnia bit back any reaction — it was Graham's call to make, and she was alright with that... she just wished he'd chosen differently.

Oh well, wishes and horses and all that.

"I'll pass it along."

Graham nodded shortly in reply, both to Howler and to Varnia. The marines continued to file through the lock, and Graham stood aside from them, watching them walk, and remaining silent.

"Ah, I haven't missed your farewells, then..."

The words from Narosh were unexpected, but as the Larosian came alongside Graham and nodded to the Earthers, the human looked up, "No, you haven't."

"Well, I'll go ahead and board then," Narosh's voice maintained some enthusiasm, and he turned then and took Howler's and Varnia's hands in turn. "Look after yourselves. I'll have a fleet to your aid very soon — that is my pledge."

Varnia smiled, "I'll be glad of it. Be safe."

With a smile and a bow-nod, Narosh joined the last of the marines boarding *Carnarvon*.

Graham stood and watched the Larosian enter the lock ahead of him, then turned back to his Earther comrades.

"Hold up, don't board yet..." Beckett trotted down the hall behind Graham, and the human glanced back as the General slid to a stop next to the hatch, nearly bowling over Christine as he did. "Sorry about that..." he nodded absently to the young aide, then he held a silver box out to Graham, "This is for you... call it a care package."

Graham looked at the wolf General whom he'd assumed he'd seen the last of, then took the box and slowly opened its top cover.

It was full of shield belts.

"I know it's not exactly a gift basket, but those are Fox's thing. And I figure you might need these sometime... besides, I was passing an arms locker on the way down here," Beckett rubbed the back of his neck as he tried to explain just what strange reasoning had compelled him to provide the box.

"Well, I'm fairly certain the marines will have many of these, but I appreciate the thought," Graham nodded to his friend, then turned slightly so he could address the three Earthers standing with him. "And I... do apologize for my behavior. I hope it has not been too much of a trouble... I cannot even say this is the end of it. But you have all been of immense help to me. It's a saddening reality that we must part ways here."

Varnia and Beckett offered small smiles, and Howler offered a respectful nod.

"Go find what you need," Varnia's words were simple.

As much as everyone there might have liked Graham to smile at the sendoff, he didn't. He closed the box of shields and tucked it under his arm, managing with great poise to keep it and his rifle and duffle all in hand without difficulty. He locked eyes with each of the Earthers in turn, the trio of wolves each still feeling that chill from him.

It seemed that would never go away...

"We'll miss our flight," Christine warned absently, correcting the position of her own rifle on her shoulder and picking up a heavy looking case again. "Bye everybody."

With quick nods to the Earthers, she entered the airlock tube. A moment after that, Graham nodded as well to his friends, and followed his aide.

As the pair of humans crossed space and entered *Carnarvon*, Varnia keyed the panel beside the airlock, and the hatch shut. The trio stood and watched through the hatch window as *Carnarvon's* door closed as well, and then the docking arms retracted and the two mighty warships parted.

In only a moment, the Battleship's freshly-powered thrusters had fired, pushing it sideways, away from the ship of the line. The wolves watched as *Carnarvon* drifted further and further away, then began to maneuver as its main drives came online.

Preoccupied with dark thoughts about what would become of Graham, it took them long moments to realize precisely what they'd seen. Then Beckett Lupus blinked, and looked to both his wife and his friend, "Was that *Christine* who went aboard?"

The eyes of the three wolves simultaneously widened.

Graham and Christine had boarded *Carnarvon*.

Christine wasn't certain it had registered with Graham that she'd essentially smuggled herself — admittedly in full sight — aboard the Larosian Battleship.

The two humans were pacing through the freshly-lit, de-horrified corridors of their new ship, looking for the marker that would show their cabin assignments. She'd specifically asked the Larosian receiving personnel at *Carnarvon's* side of the lock for the location of the quarters Lazarus had converted for her. It had to be here somewhere.

Focusing on looking for it kept her from wondering whether her decision to join Graham on this mission was the right one. She was strangely calm about her choice — a choice that, either way, she would have expected to trouble her. Abandoning Graham or abandoning her sister... she had just repeated the decision she'd made when she went aboard *Genesis One* after Gillian.

And she felt perfectly calm. Steady, certain, convinced of what she must do. Like an Earther...

"I *have* noticed, you know."

She bumped right into Graham. He'd stopped in front of her and now she walked into him, dropping her heavy case in the collision. The Earther box pitched sideways out of her grip, and as she seemed prone to doing now and then, she littered the deck with her belongings.

Still clumsier than an Earther.

Field generators, atmospheric manipulators, and a small Earther auto-tailor.

Crouching immediately, Graham began to collect the fallen items and re-pack them as she stood and watched, and before she completely blinked herself out of her pondering state, he was standing before her and holding the case out to her, "You clearly planned this ahead of time. Why did you come aboard?"

She didn't really have a good answer for him, "Because... that's what I had to do, I suppose."

"I cannot ask this from you, Christine."

Listening to those words very carefully, Christine was almost certain she could hear some hint of emotion. Almost. *Almost* a hint. But then more cold words, "I believe I told you to get fixed."

Christine smiled at that, "Yes, you are quite a charmer, aren't you? I've made my decision, Graham. I'll stay broken for a while."

The confidence she felt as she said those words was new to her. She still questioned herself, and wondered whether her decision was correct, but not in an uncertain way. It felt as though, instead of panicking, different parts of her mind were having a calm discussion, assessing pros and cons, and coming to a decision. Simple. Now she'd move forward. Like an Earther would.

Graham's eyes softened, and for just a moment his brow seemed to lift in one of those defeated-sad-tired expressions. Then his face reset and he executed a single nod.

"Thank you."

He turned and kept walking up the hall.

Christine shifted her case in her arms and followed her ArcGeneral up the corridor.

The only two humans in the galaxy were aboard *Carnarvon*.

CHAPTER 41

"So based on their speed, I'd give it about... call it forty hours to arrival here."

Jax Furgus nodded as Ursla commented on the star chart hovering silently in *Orion's* main briefing room's holo tank. With them were Ron Hobbes, Alix Tarkham, Barty Stowt and the officers of Ursla's 'First Fleet', and they sat somewhat uncomfortably around the table, watching the flashing icons of the moving Omega squadron.

"Tom's staying close to them, keeping the edge of their formation in sight. As we said, it's a formation of 500 plus — it doesn't look as though they're leaving anything to hold Ecclesia. What we need to do is put together a good plan to meet them," Ursla leaned back in her chair as she said the last few words. "That may be a bit of a tall order, based on what we've seen."

There were slow nods from the individuals in this all-Earther assembly, and they exchanged glances as they tried to think through the problem.

"So we've got ourselves about 200 human ships — Genesis and Freetown — and our own fleet," Barty Stowt, the veteran bear of Ami Dune's old squadron, offered his own comments as he leaned forward.

"Aye. We're outnumbered... and after the action Ed Jeffries had against the Omega raiders, I don't know how confident we can be about the utility of human ships against him," Jax's frank words essentially vocalized the collected officers' concerns.

But what did that leave them?

Freetown was an open target — that was why Omega was coming here. There were only 150-odd Earther ships in the system, and many of the Genesis ships were still not fully inoculated.

"Lab will bring out the Home Fleet once we get absolute confirmation... he can make the trip in about thirty-six hours if he pushes it, so we can expect a pod from him in about four hours saying he's on his way," Ursla's words on reinforcement drew a few more nods, then eyes narrowed and darted to the plot again.

Even with the 128 modern ships of Home Fleet, they would be looking at close-to-even odds against Omega... and that was counting the human ships.

"Reminds me of Gibraltar all over again," Jax grumbled. "But our boats won't turn the tide this time."

Again there were murmurs of confirmation. There was a certain grim inevitability to all this — they were facing the wildly vicious Omega, and they were finding it difficult to rein in their uncertainty. The plague had them twisting their own conventions, trying to figure out what special piece of maneuvering they'd have to do to stay alive…

Ursla frowned as she recognized the uncharacteristic amount of pessimism in this room full of Earthers, then looked up, "Alright… so it looks bad. But like you say, Jax, we've seen bad before. I think part of Omega's plan has to include tying us in knots like this — listen to us, we're sounding like we don't believe we can win. And I'm willing to bet that the only thing that beats us in this circumstance is our own lack of confidence."

Looking through the plot at his veteran friend, Jax returned Ursla's frown. That was certainly an apt comment — they were definitely preoccupying themselves with uncertainties that could well be unwarranted. Then again…

"I think I've given similar advice in my day," Barty Stowt leaned forward in his chair, then vocalized the question on all the Earthers' minds. "So, how do we beat his fleet?"

Ursla's ear twitched at the question, and then for some reason a bit of the old energy seemed to pour into her blood. She smiled wryly, "I think that's what we're meeting about, Barty."

With some of his characteristic old flair, Jax leaned forward and nodded, "Indeed it is. I, for starters, would suggest we shoot at them."

Lab Forepaw stood at *Venerable's* main plot and watched the glowing holo in its corner tick through another minute. There wasn't much more for him to do *but* watch the clock right now — he couldn't move Home Fleet yet, not until he was certain.

"Come on, Tom," he said quietly to himself, and just as he did Captain Arther Stowt came up beside him.

"We've got another few hours, Lab. Want to get some lunch?"

Forepaw's ear twitched at the thought… well, he *was* a little hungry, and the mess was only a minute away.

In the old days he'd never gone into battle on an empty stomach if he could help it, and though he'd have to wait thirty-six hours for action after giving an order for Home Fleet to move, he'd still like to avoid a growling stomach while he decided when to strip Earth of its most powerful combat force.

"Yes, let's get some food," Lab turned to *Venerable's* officer of the watch, "Call us if you see a pod."

Hopefully one would be coming soon.

"They keep yo-yoing in and out of range, skipper. Their speed isn't constant, and I think if we match speeds precisely with them, they might notice we're back here."

Tom Locke nodded to the Master as she delivered her report. *Charybdis* and the squadron were having quite a difficult time keeping hold of Omega's force — it would surge just out of range and then slow again, then bend slightly and veer right back...

And based on everything Tom Locke had seen in the Krogg War, that probably meant Omega was trying to misdirect anyone who *happened* to see his force. He was undoubtedly hoping the wrong target would be warned, so he could blindside Freetown the way he had Genesis.

Unfortunately for Omega, he had a squadron of crack frigates sitting on the back end of his fleet.

"Coming back into range now, skipper."

Locke looked from his Cruising Master to the main holo plot, narrowing his eyes as three ships... now four... from the rear end of Omega's squadron appeared in the plot. Now five... six... ten..."

"Ease off our speed, Master... watch them..." Locke turned back to his veteran ship-handling officer, and she nodded in reply, passing more specific orders on to her helm crew.

The Earther frigates slowed again, just slightly, and waited for the Omega ships to pick up speed... and there they went, doing it again.

Tom's brow creased in a frown as the Omega ships lurched away, then he looked to his First Lieutenant, "Problems handling engines maybe?"

The Lieutenant cocked an eyebrow, "Could be... though misdirection is still more likely..."

Nodding again, Locke turned back to the plot, "But for all his zigzags, he still looks like he's taking that fleet toward Freetown..."

Yes, but Omega could turn at any moment, so how could Tom tell Lab Forepaw that the target for Home Fleet was Freetown when he couldn't be certain?

Well, he'd just have to tell the First Lord what he *did* know and let the Admiralty decide what to do about it. Lab would need this information as soon as possible, because if the Home Fleet was to move, they'd need sufficient time to travel from Earth to Freetown before Omega arrived.

With that in mind, Tom turned to his Signal Officer, "Order *Siren* back out of range, have them send pods to Earth and Freetown alerting them that Omega appears to be holding course for Freetown, but we can't give final confirmation... afraid that Admiralty will have to deploy based on own instincts. My bet is still Freetown."

The Signal Officer was keying in the message as Locke spoke, and then as the Commodore turned back to the plot, the frigate *Siren* began to drift backwards out of the line-abreast formation of his squadron. Moments later the muted spikes of energy-hyper pods appeared on deep-range sensors, and

Freetown and Earth were duly warned.

Hopefully someone in one of those places would have a more concrete feeling about this operation than he did.

"Well, I honestly don't have any idea what to expect, Arther. Omega's biggest advantage right now is that he's got us second-guessing ourselves," Lab Forepaw laid his tray of food on one of the mess tables and took a seat, his Flag Captain sitting opposite him with a much longer tray that suited the bear's greater size.

"That's true," Stowt began as he hefted his pitchfork, "but I still—"

The intercom chirped with its usual bad timing, "Bridge here, we've got a pod coming in now from Commodore Locke. Just opened it, sir, and... and he says they're still making for Freetown, and that's his best guess on the ultimate target for Omega, but he can't be sure. He says he hopes you have a better feeling about that than he does."

The whole ship's complement in *Venerable* heard the update over the intercom, but Lab was the one who'd have to make the ultimate decision. It looked like Freetown — more humans in the sights of a plague who'd demonstrated his uncanny skill for killing and absorbing them. Could he risk pulling the Home Fleet out of Earth space to help them?

Actually, the question that settled in Lab's mind was *how could he not?*

This would be a hell of a gamble...

"Stand by for a moment please, bridge," Forepaw avoided directing his gaze up at the ceiling speakers as he replied, instead looking across the table to his trusty Captain Stowt.

The bear's expression was studied, "I'd... do whatever I would have done against the Kroggs. I wouldn't let Omega twist us into not acting just because of who he is."

Lab nodded slowly at the comment — it did make sense. Omega's strategy to beat the Earthers was as much psychological as it was Naval, so the Earthers would have to deal with this the way they would have a Krogg force. They had to trust their instincts.

"Indeed," Lab Forepaw sighed and laid his fork on his plate, then addressed himself to the speakers in the ceiling, "Alright Lieutenant, relay orders to the Home Fleet, weigh anchor and stand by to make for Freetown, maximum cruising speed. I'll be up in..." he looked briefly at his plate "...eight minutes."

"Aye, sir. All hands, stand by to weigh anchor."

The intercom cut after the order, and with a certain resignation, Forepaw took hold of his fork.

In silence, he and his Flag Captain ate a quick lunch, then returned to their bridge.

About eleven minutes later, a pod was sent to Freetown, informing Ursla that the Home Fleet was coming, and about three minutes after that, Lab Forepaw ordered his fleet into energy drive.

Freetown was about to get reinforced.

CHAPTER 42

"I'm heading back to the office, then…"

Elandra Caine turned back through the doorway and waited for her son to say his customary goodbye as she headed out for a few days of solid work in London. He was chatting with Claire, trying new techniques in an effort to get the young human to open up. Phealan's persistence and patience impressed his mother — he was dealing with the young Schaeffer with a maturity Elandra normally would have expected of a 100-year-old wolf.

Perhaps it was just motherly pride, but Elandra got the feeling that her son was going to grow up to be just like his father — a real patriarch fit to lead the Earther people. Time would tell.

For now, she was due at the office, "*Phealan*… going to work for the rest of the week…"

This time his ear twitched and both he and the human looked to Elandra, "Sorry mom, see you!"

"Yes, you will," Elandra smiled a last time and slipped out the door, leaving Phealan to his project.

While he tried not to see Claire Schaeffer that way, she truly was becoming his great undertaking… impersonal as that might have sounded. He wanted to help her, but it was clear to him that it would take time to help move her through the pain, bitterness and anger that were tightening around her soul. Every time he talked with her, she spent most of her time slinging questions and criticisms at him, mainly about his own Earther nature.

Those questions were challenging for the young Caine. He knew what it was to be an Earther, but trying to explain the tenets of 'Eartherness' to a human forced him to reflect on just what being an Earther meant. Claire had trouble understanding how Earthers could move past loss, and be so committed to their own beliefs that they didn't succumb to bitterness or hate, even when facing Omega.

She seemed to think the reason the Earthers didn't share her hatred and bitterness was because they didn't care about humanity. No matter how many times Phealan told her that wasn't the case, she couldn't believe what he said.

Perhaps, in time, she'd understand that the Earthers didn't get tied up in fury because it served no good purpose. Perhaps she'd realize that the reason you smiled in the face of doom wasn't because you didn't care about living, but because if doom was coming, you weren't going to have many more opportunities to smile. You had to seize every chance you got.

In time she might understand... but not now.

Phealan continued to talk with Claire.

"There's something on your desk you need to see!"

Elandra had taken exactly four steps into the Thames River Genetic Center when the abrupt call came from behind her, so she slowed to a halt in the entry way and frowned, "What's up, Haley?"

The cat in the lab suit smiled and shook her head with uncommon excitement, "We think we might have the genetic key to the Krogg defenses keeping us out of Omega."

Now that wasn't bad news at all... about time, too, Elandra had been close to becoming very slightly concerned that she wouldn't find a way to crack this plague.

Well, now she had something to work with, anyway!

"Let's walk and talk... what exactly are you looking at, Haley? A cure?"

The doctor shook her head and fell into step next to Elandra as the wolf proceeded down the corridor again, "Not quite. It's the new sequences you started last week, they're showing an opening. We're thinking we might be able to create some sort of energy field carried in immune cells... something that can irradiate the Krogg defenses and weaken Omega enough to give UDRC a chance to kick in."

Elandra frowned, "A genetic weakness that leaves the cells vulnerable to non-lethal radiation?"

Haley nodded again, "Indeed! Your idea about fluxing the cells so the defenses can't recognize them, it might be the key! We just need to find a way to keep active Wyndhymn energy in immune cells as they go in... something residual that can keep them in flux long enough to launch their attack on Omega's controlling nodes in each body..."

Elandra nodded slowly and walked quickly. She'd been married to the leading strategist of the Earther people for almost 150 years, and in that time she'd gained more than a little aptitude for tactical thinking. The first question that had to be answered was *how* one could implement this treatment...

But that was putting the cart before the horse: she needed to know exactly what she was looking at before she proposed it to those who'd have to implement it. She'd let Setter and the Admiralty know she was on to something, and then she'd get to work.

Hopefully, they'd be able to give Omega a nasty surprise — and soon.

"That's it, Lab's just shipped out with the Home Fleet," Jax turned from the screen in the holo tank to Ursla, "We're getting *big* help."

Nodding, Ursla let her eyes shift back to the plot. They had a fairly strong plan in the works as it was: the Genesis Fleet — its crews still being inoculated — would stay over Freetown, combining its firepower with the Freetown orbital defense grid to stop landings... and to avoid being taken by Omega. As they did that, the Earther ships in-system would be taking a page out of standard tactics — buzzing around, in-and-out of energy drive either by squadron or division, aiming to destroy Omega ships in the same way so many Kroggs had been eliminated.

Boats and the Freetown Fleet, hopefully with *Republic* restored to modest fighting condition in time, would hold position just within the system's asteroid belt, ready to dive in as a concentrated force when the moment was right.

Now it looked like the Home Fleet would be in position to do the same.

"Alright, then we have a good thing going here," Ursla nodded evenly. "Let Sarah know... what do you think, send the refugees out now?"

Jax's eyes narrowed, then he gave a slow nod, "Indeed."

It made sense, they'd move the humans.

"Call it in, and then we'll finish this plan..."

Sarah turned from Jax's message on her chair display to the main bridge screen on *Unity Genesis'* command deck. The Home Fleet's information was scrolling up over the monitor now, with notes on ship classes, armament, speed, and commanders. It was a hell of force.

So that took some of the pressure off Freetown, and admittedly added a little more to Earth. Unfortunately, she'd have to increase that pressure, with another gamble of the sort that she didn't like to make, but had to.

Turning to *Unity's* ArcColonel, she offered a single solemn nod, "Pass word to the refugee fleet, they're to form convoy and make for Earth at the next order."

The ArcColonel nodded and turned away, while Sarah returned to the console attached to her chair arm. It was far more sophisticated than the one she'd had on *Joseph Barron's* bridge, and one of its many controls allowed her to open signal channels on her own, without the Comm Officer's help.

She tapped a hail to the Freetown Government House, and waited as her personal screen went through the switchboard panels and located Audrey DeBrooke.

Unity's main bridge screen switched back to a display of the Freetown system, and silver dots began flashing next to the icons of the refugee ships that had received their orders and were cycling up their flux drives.

A convoy of about a thousand ships, it was no mean flotilla...

"Sarah..." it was Audrey's voice from the screen, and Sarah looked down again, "...I see your refugees are powering drives. Ready to make for Earth, then?"

The President-ArcGeneral replied with a nod, "Lab Forepaw just led the Home Fleet out of the system. The hand's been dealt. Omega seems to be coming here... and I want the survivors long gone first. Can you spare ships to escort them?"

DeBrooke's brow creased, "I think my fleet's a bit *smaller* than yours."

Sarah ignored the sharpness of the reply, "I'm sending an understrength Dreadnought group and fourteen Destroyers... perhaps your older ships could go as well, under *Sword*. I'll give your officer overall command."

Audrey opened her mouth, then closed it for a moment. Sarah could almost read her counterpart's mind — this wasn't a real escort force, this was a force being put together to get the weakest ships out of Freetown before Omega hit.

It wasn't an obvious ploy, but to these two women, who had already lost much, it was painfully evident. All that would be left for Omega to face — and kill — in Freetown space would be those most able to fight.

"I see your point..." Audrey's mind, despite the ever-present weight of grief, grasped the concept, "I'll shuffle crews around as quickly as I can. Give me... an hour?"

Sarah nodded, "Certainly. And thank you."

Audrey wasn't sure whether to thank Sarah in return, so she just cut the link.

Sarah sat back in her chair and watched the clock. Soon she wouldn't have to worry about the survivors of the world she'd lost... but she would be facing the possible loss of another world to Omega.

She'd have to stand in his way... and hope...

CHAPTER 43

At Gibraltar, on the far side of Genesis and well away from threats of immediate Omega attack, Admiral Garvin Jardaw frowned deeply as the latest update from Admiralty House scrolled up through his screen.

"They've taken Home Fleet out of Earth space and are getting ready to make their fight at Freetown... looks like the Genesis refugees are on their way to Earth, too..." Karl Kandam narrowed his eyes thoughtfully as he spoke, his gaze sweeping across the provided information.

"They're hoping they can win that battle at Freetown... I surely hope they can," Jardaw let a short sigh escape as he spoke. "So what's that leave us?"

Kandam looked sideways to Lang Sandpelt. The young Rear Admiral merely shrugged in reply.

Jardaw continued to frown at various elements in the plot as he thought about that question himself. There was still no sign of Fox Magnus' reinforcement force — at this rate the First Space Lord was going to be declared missing in action.

And ships were still coming back from their survey posts all across this side of space. The Gibraltar system was fast filling with reasonably vulnerable vessels, and all Jardaw had at his disposal was the admittedly powerful Gibraltar Fleet...

He was tied to this base, then — he couldn't risk a sortie to attack Genesis while Omega's ships were committed to an attack on Freetown. There were too many civilian ships here to leave unguarded.

"I could take the *Venerables* and reconnoiter Genesis in force, that's about all I'd suggest..." Sandpelt looked to the Genesis system in the holo tank as he spoke. With over 500 of his ships out to attack Freetown, it seemed unlikely that Omega would have much left in the Genesis system.

"Just the *Venerables*?" Kandam frowned. "Only fifteen ships?"

Sandpelt offered a half shrug, "If Omega left the back door open, that'll be more than enough firepower to smash anything productive left in the system... and if he didn't, we'll have enough teeth to beat back his garrison, and we'll be fast enough to show him a clean pair of heels."

The holo map *was* showing Genesis to be a giant information hole... any intelligence they could gather about what the plague had brewing in there could be most useful.

But Jardaw couldn't send his strongest unit out to check, not with all the frigates and sloops busy collecting the civilians.

"Not yet, Lang. I'm sorry, but I'm more inclined to wait until we have more solid indications of what's going on at Freetown... and until Fox arrives with his force. Right now the *Venerables* are too important an asset," the polar bear Admiral looked through the plot to Sandpelt, and the Commodore offered an understanding nod.

"Not a problem, Garv... just let me know if you want me to go snooping around once Fox's ships arrive. I don't think we should use any of those for a recon mission like this — they're too slow."

Nodding again, Jardaw looked back to the plot for a moment, his eyes drifting along the route from Earth to Gibraltar. Where *was* Fox Magnus? That convoy could make the difference out here...

"Let's hope Fox finds his way here soon," Kandam's words mirrored Jardaw's thoughts.

The trio of flag officers stared at the plot.

Fox Magnus visibly relaxed and smiled at his wife as *Chimera* smoothly exited energy drive.

They'd *finally* reached Gibraltar.

After dodging all too many Omega pickets, and running so far out into deep space they'd almost gotten lost, they'd finally found their way back to the greatest of Earther Naval installations. Gibraltar was still every bit the military base it had been during the Krogg War — there was no chance Omega could have defeated it...

"Sir, no power emissions... no stations... nothing..."

Fox stiffened in his chair, his head whipping to the plot as he came rapidly to his feet and virtually lunged towards the holo tank. The system was empty, with the glowing orbs of the planets appearing devoid of Earther presence.

Had Omega been able to...

Wait a minute, *planets?*

"Master, confirm that we're where we should be," it was Thena Magnus who voiced the order as she moved to her husband's shoulder.

Frowning as he did, the Master began to key up a number of star charts, along with the system maps they had of Gibraltar. The main plot filled rapidly with information, and dozens of pairs of Earther eyes shifted between it all...

"Well, I'll be. Nearest planetoid is made of the same stuff as Gibraltar, and has a very similar orbital pattern. Guidance computer misidentified it," the Master was speaking softly as he keyed through some glowing holo displays.

Fox let out a much more relieved sigh, "Okay, not so bad then. Do you know where we are?"

The Master looked up at the First Space Lord with a raised eyebrow, "I'll get a court martial if I say 'we're here', will I?"

The First Space Lord grinned at the prospect, "Shut up and tell me where we are, Mister Gunth."

With a chuckle, the Master began speaking to his helm crew, and calling down sensor technicians from the nearby consoles. Fox glanced at his wife as the Master examined the situation stoically. Mister Gunth had been with Fox since the first days on *Flame* and *Atlas* — with his experience, he could have figured out their location had they drifted into a different space-time continuum... and surely they hadn't.

"I don't know how much more lost we can get," Thena said quietly, and Fox chuckled. She'd been with him back in the days of *Atlas* too, so she knew Mister Gunth as well as he did.

"That's a matter of opinion, at least we didn't end up in Genesis," the smile that came with Fox's retort was a little sadder — neither of these two was keen to think about the human plight just now.

"Sir, ma'am..."

Both flag officers turned at the summons, and the Sensor Officer keyed up a map in the main holo tank as they did, "I don't know exactly where *we* are... but that looks an awful lot like the deep-range beacon for Gibraltar to me. It puts us about three days away from the system."

The Master looked up at the map and then nodded through the plot to Fox and Thena, "That'd definitely be it then. Omega can't have copied that beacon this quickly, and it's in about the right place... based on my dead reckoning anyway."

Fox paused, "If your dead reckoning's that good, why are we out here in the first place?"

Gunth frowned at the remark, "Because you're using up your bad luck before we have to do something important, skipper."

Fox smiled at the sentiment, and at being called 'skipper' again. It was rare for him to be referred to as anything but the First Space Lord these days, and something about the old word put a bit of wind back in his sails.

"I hope you're right. Alright, Master, take us to top cruising speed. Signal Officer, have the convoy fall in behind us. Let's get to Gibraltar. Hope they don't mind us being really, really late."

Chimera accelerated back into energy drive.

Somewhere across space, Omega noticed Earther ships near him.

Ooh, clever — they were trying to keep tabs on him, no doubt, and Lab Forepaw probably had his ships moving around somewhere to try to catch his flank.

Well, these ships wouldn't get what they wanted...

Omega-Gillian smiled to herself, watching in her mind's eye as two or three frigates tried to slide silently along without detection.

He'd let them think they had a chance... and then the convoy would pay.

I love being me... but then to say that makes me sound like an egotistical bastard...

Wait a second, I am one.

Soon Earthers will die.

Omega's wasn't where anyone thought he was.

CHAPTER 44

Varnon Broadpaw had done his share of fighting during the Krogg War, and forty years away from combat had done nothing to dull his instincts. Unfortunately, while time may not have left his instincts confused, Omega had. As much as Varnon was *certain* that Omega was heading towards Freetown, he still had his doubts.

For the past thirty hours he'd waited and wondered. Based on all the intel they had, Omega was now only six hours out of Freetown. Lab would beat him to that colony by at least half an hour... or that was the plan, anyway.

Could Omega's ships fly faster than they realized? Could the plague somehow shake Tom Locke's frigates, or misdirect them?

In the old days, Varnon would never have been so tormented by such questions. He would have worried, of course, but never would he be shaken to the very core by them.

This bastard killed Varnia, Beckett... Genesis. Of course it's different.

Varnon tried to still his concerns, but again didn't quite succeed.

He focused on the plot he was standing beside in *Guardian One's* Command and Control Center, staring at the icons of the local defense forces. Kylie Peregrine was commanding one formation from *Captain*, a 74, while Ami Dune had the other with her flag flying from the 80-gun *Foudroyant*. Kylie was out on the Pluto Orbital Plane, Ami sitting in lunar orbit. If Omega turned up at Earth, those two Admirals would have to stop him.

Here? He's going to Freetown. Or is he...?

Varnon felt like smacking himself on the forehead, but managed to refrain from doing so. All he could do now was guess and hope...

"Guessing and hoping... I seem to remember that being a large element in the strategy of the last war."

Varnon raised an eyebrow and turned from the plot as the voice crossed the command deck to him.

Without a uniform, Setter looked slightly out of place on the bridge of an orbital platform — the picture so often associated with the Supreme Consul was that of him standing firm in his First Lord's tunic, even though he hadn't worn it in decades.

But that wasn't particularly important right now — Setter's instinctive connection to Varnon was strong, and he'd evidently picked up the First

Consul's doubts.

"Yes," Varnon nodded as his fellow wolf approached the plot. "We did do a lot of guessing, Setter. But back then I knew we'd do fine when we guessed. Today... well, I'm not so sure. You said it yourself, the rules of the game have changed."

Setter looked into the plot, watching the same dance of Sol-based defensive squadrons that had distracted Varnon, and then he nodded slowly, "That's true enough. Omega's done a good number on us, I think. He's managed to seize the momentum and keep us from finding our usual footing. We were caught out, and his very nature is abhorrent from our perspective, so we're having a hard time getting back to fighting trim."

Varnon nodded to his wiser friend, offering a resigned reply, "That he did."

Setter's ear twitched. Varnon knew better than most...

"He didn't *kill* Varnia, though. Remember that, Varnon — she died, and *Renown* died, thwarting him. So it's possible to defeat him... we just have to finish off what she started."

Varnon's eyes fell blankly to the base of the holo tank. His only daughter was indeed gone... Omega had broken the rules, and she'd broken them back to stop him.

So if there was such a thing as an afterlife, and he got to see her again, he'd have to tell her how proud he was of what she'd done. In the meantime, he'd have to follow the path she'd laid down: beat Omega, no matter the cost.

"We're Earthers, we do what we say we'll do, in a way that reflects us..." Varnon quoted the familiar words in a very soft tone, and Setter looked sideways at his old comrade. Tilting his head slightly, Varnon looked back, "Tell me what we've said we'll do, then, Setter."

The Supreme Consul looked from his friend to the plot, then back, "We're going to stop Omega, Varnon. Or at the very least we'll die to the last trying."

Yes... yes that was just about it.

Varnon looked pensively back at the plot.

Lab Forepaw sat alone in his darkened cabin, gazing silently at a holo of *Orion* and the First Fleet in orbit over Genesis after the Krogg War battle there. The holo file had been included in the Earth release of Pat Conroy's *The Alien Equation*, illustrating that first titanic struggle with the Kroggs.

It had been a remarkable day, and the old First Fleet had fought like the elegant and masterful combat formation it was. Some 600 ships, all working together in perfect harmony as the Kroggs broke and fled...

That had been one of the best days of that war.

Of course, it had been followed by a to-the-death blood match at Gibraltar, and the slaughter around the Krogg star systems... but those *had* been the so-called good old days. Back then, the Earthers had been fighting a war to keep their word to the humans, and they'd been facing an enemy with a similar animalistic nature.

Now?

Lab Forepaw was probably the greatest Naval officer the Earther Navy had ever seen — Setter would even concede that title to Forepaw were he asked. But in four hours, when he reached Freetown, he'd be in a situation unlike any they'd faced in the days of the Krogg War.

This would be altogether more vicious, because Omega wasn't just out to win, he was out for revenge. This wasn't going to be a strategic fight for the fate of the cosmos, this was going to be Omega doing everything he possibly could to gut the Earthers.

And the plague knew that every human who died would weigh on the Earther conscience, because he'd used Earther blood as a Trojan horse for so long. The Earthers had ultimately proved much better than cattle for him: they'd given him a vehicle to the stars, and an opportunity to find aliens to infect...

If Lab let his mind review everything they currently knew about Omega, he'd spend many hours deciding just how completely the plague had managed to drag the Earthers out over a barrel.

But as First Lord, Lab could not allow himself to surrender to that unnecessary introspection.

He would be doing battle in the old style, and in several hours, he'd either win or die.

That thought settled his mind.

"Well... say something profound, Andra. Give me that positively Earther sense of control that'll let me do my job well."

Ursla looked up from her pad — she'd been alone in *Orion's* conference room, going over status reports, and she'd assumed it was Jax coming in for a final talk when she'd heard the door open.

But it was Sarah standing at the opposite end of the table, her face reasonably impassive, but her tension evident to Ursla's instincts. The *understandable, remarkably controlled* tension — Sarah was, for all the stresses on her, handling this as well as she'd handled herself at Krogg 'A', after she'd sorted herself out...

Right, well that wasn't really a surprise — it was Sarah, after all. Longtime war leader, and President of a now-dead planet...

Ursla stopped thinking, because everything 'good' was coming out sharply backhanded in her head.

"You want me to say what?" she laid the pad she was reading on the table and looked across it to her old human friend.

Sarah didn't quite know what she was even doing over here on *Orion*. She'd gone through all the plans already, and now she just wanted reassurance. And since Pat was down on the planet helping sort out civil defense, and since he wasn't a big, strong, reassuring Earther, she'd just boarded a pinnace and come to *Orion*.

There were only two hours left until Lab Forepaw arrived, and once he did there wouldn't be time for this sort of drivel...

Ursla let out a long sigh, "You know, all I can say is we'll fight... and we'll either win or die. Pretty straightforward."

The door had opened again as Ursla spoke, and as Jax stepped through with Barty Stowt in tow, the grizzled lion scowled, "That's the undramatic way to put it."

Frowning at the unexpected remark, Sarah turned and nodded to the Earther Admirals as they stepped in, "Yes... well... it was something..."

Jax smiled thinly, "Mind if I breathe some fire, Andra?"

The lion had directed the question to Ursla over Sarah's shoulder, and now the kodiak Admiral grinned and shook her head, "I know better than to try to stop you."

Shifting his gaze back to Sarah, Jax took a step forward and narrowed his eyes, "You lost a world, I lost a daughter, and Omega's thinking he can get the best of us. Well, maybe he can, maybe he's going to kill every last one of us. But if that's the way it's going to be, we still get the chance to hurt him every time he does. We get to fight back, and while he's trying to get his revenge, that's ours... or mine, at least. Not revenge the way you humans define it, probably, but it's revenge to us. He's trying to stop us from being what we are, so we'll continue to be exactly who we are. That's revenge for us. Earthers don't give up. We'll win or we'll die."

The typically direct words did swell some confidence within Sarah — not much, frankly not enough to help her shake off the feeling of dread. But it was about time she got back to her job.

"Well, I could've done without the 'he'll kill each and every one of us' bit, but he's right," Barty Stowt shrugged from over Jax's shoulder, and Sarah smiled at the comment.

"Alright. Death or glory it is... I'm going to go get something to eat."

Sarah nodded to each of the Earthers again, and left.

"Damn, now I'm hungry," Jax grumbled as he took his seat.

Ursla, Furgus and Stowt, Krogg War veterans all, began to speak for the last time of their tactics for the battle.

Audrey rubbed her forehead and gritted her teeth against the rather immense pain that seemed to be stabbing through her skull. The tropical-like sunshine of Freetown's capital city was damning today... it was so beautiful it made her heart ache.

It was as though the planet they'd settled and cared for didn't even realize what they were all about to lose...

In the distance, Audrey's eyes fell on the last pinnace as it began to lift from its launch pad. That was Ed Jeffries, heading up to *Savanna Felix* at the last possible moment. Lab Forepaw's Home Fleet had appeared over Freetown just fifteen minutes ago, and Omega had to be close, so the Commodore had left her side.

Audrey stood alone on the main balcony at Government House, and watched as the pinnace lifted up into the sky and shrunk to a dot in just seconds of acceleration. She wished that she could just be up there in *Grendelsbane City*... but no, the old Heavy Cruiser was escorting the Genesis survivors to Earth, and her place as leader was with her people.

As the last pinnace had now left for orbit, and the few civilians from other parts of Freetown had all been moved to the capital island, the security grid began to activate around the city.

Audrey watched silently as it turned on — she'd only seen it activated twice, both times as a test...

It was a massive Earther-built grid, with a shield network that formed a complete energy dome over half the island, and backed it with long carronades and Freetown's only Earther-built energy cannon.

Those guns began to come to life across the city, crewed by civil defense teams and capable of shredding any ships in orbit over this hemisphere of the planet... it seemed an impressive and powerful defense.

Hopefully it would be enough.

"Those things get bloody loud when they fire, take it from one who knows."

Audrey's frown deepened as she looked to her right. Sure enough, Pat was on the other side of the balcony, leaning on the rail and watching the grid come to life.

"Of course, the one I was witness to was from the old days, these new ones might be library-quiet, as they say..."

Audrey turned away from her city and looked at the scruffy Irishman, "Shouldn't you be on *Unity* with Sarah?"

Pat shrugged, "She's not too keen on having me around now that she's in the uniform. And I'll do more good here, I think — your Naval staff isn't exactly overflowing."

"Neither is our fleet. You should go up to be with Sarah..."

The twinge in those words made Pat clench his jaw. There was nowhere he'd rather be, but he knew that just being in the room with his wife would put him in her way. She needed to become the cold, tactical sorceress of old, and she wouldn't be able to do that if he was sitting next to her on the bridge of *Unity* — he'd be too much of a reminder of what she'd already lost... and he'd make her cautious.

And as much as he hated her taking foolish risks in command, those risks were the Allies' best shot at surviving this day.

So Pat shrugged and made it look casual enough, "Meh, the shield's already up. Now we best get back to the war room."

They left the balcony. Freetown waited for the maelstrom.

CHAPTER 45

Venerable sat silent at a dead stop under energy drive, with its mighty field out to a formidable 300 percent. Like the rest of Home Fleet, this new, massive-sized First Rate had been designed with all the lessons of the Krogg War in mind. It was able to lie in wait like this, and as Lab Forepaw stood at its main plot and watched a blank spot in the plot's display come closer and closer to Freetown, he ground his jaw.

They'd gotten here with an hour to spare, and now after talking to Ursla, he'd decided to keep Home Fleet right at the edge of the system, to wait for Omega to arrive. His fleet would come out of energy drive as soon as the first Omega vessels decelerated, destroy those infected human ships, and then join Ursla's guerilla-style attacks.

They might not have numbers on their side, but Omega still wouldn't know what hit him.

The blank spot came within fifteen minutes of the system, and Lab's eyes narrowed. Omega was hiding behind some pretty powerful stealth — seemingly based on what the Faithful had used against Freetown before this mess had started. According to *Venerable's* long-range scanners, he only had ten ships coming in.

Fortunately for the Allies, though, the eight faint icons of Tom Locke's squadron were still tailing the empty spot as it advanced towards Freetown. Omega's ruse wouldn't work — not with those 44s sitting unnoticed on his tail.

"All ships, ready for action," Lab turned from his plot to his Signal Officer. "And give me Fleetcomm."

There was a brief pause and an announcing whistle through every ship in the system as Lab turned back to his plot, and then the Allied Fleet waited, for the first time, to hear what Labrador Forepaw would say before a great battle.

Setter Caine had set the bar high...

"Omega is on his way, and he thinks his victory is a foregone conclusion. He thinks that, by sitting in on the last war, he knows how to win this one. My brave fellows, I think we all know better than that. He's come far since his arrival, and he's done great harm, but his momentum is about to come to a halt. We're about to finish his drive — this is the first place we've made a stand, and he will not take this system from us. Not today. So stand to your posts, my friends, let's remind this *plague* just what it means to deal with us. We're all creatures of Earth: we beat him once, we'll do it again. War has returned. The most significant war in our history."

There was a silent pause as Earthers and humans took in the words — Lab was definitely up to the Caine standard, and now, as his words sunk in, the familiar and deafening cacophony of Earther roars reached out across Fleetcomm.

The humans of the Genesis and Freetown Fleets were much less sure of themselves than the Earthers, but they took up cheers of their own, if only to try to fight their fear.

The destroyer and enslaver of Genesis civilization was on his way in...

Lab Forepaw's eyes narrowed as he stared into *Venerable's* plot, "Captain Stowt, beat to quarters."

Arther Stowt nodded, and *Venerable's* crew prepared their ship to fight.

Tom Locke turned from the plot and walked quickly to his chair. As he sat his First Lieutenant came to the seat beside him, "We're cleared for action, sir. Freetown in two minutes and counting."

Tom nodded evenly. He'd been a Carrier officer for much of the last war, but he'd cut his teeth in frigates, and now he'd be fighting in trusty old 44s again.

That suited him just fine.

"Signal Officer," Locke looked to the bear at the communications console, "Orders to squadron, we're to drop out of energy drive behind the last ships in the formation — the ones that aren't hidden under that jamming field. Squadrons to break into divisions as we do; we'll do as much damage as we can before they realize we're back here."

The Midshipman nodded and immediately transmitted the orders through energy comm to the rest of the frigates in *Charybdis'* squadron.

"One minute now, sir," the Cruising Master announced from his station on the other side of the plot from Locke. "I'm guessing the first of the Omega ships are hitting Freetown... *now.*"

Tom nodded evenly, "Alright Master, take us out right behind the last ones. Guns at the ready... bring the field into 100 percent... *now.*"

"Here they come," Arther Stowt's low comment seemed to punctuate the moment, and Lab Forepaw nodded in reply.

The plot told the story: the first ten ships of the Omega group decelerated from flux rather unevenly, in no particular formation, but clearly present to spring any traps the Earthers had waiting for them.

Unfortunately for Omega, the Home Fleet was a big enough trap for Lab to let loose on these first arrivals — even though the pathfinders would warn the main fleet van, it was better to destroy them now, when even one ship could infect much of the Genesis Fleet.

"Fleet to follow First Battle Squadron to action," Lab's words were cold. "Master, take us to normal drives. Captain Stowt, destroy those ships. Squadron to line ahead."

"Aye, sir," Arther Stowt said the words with a certain crispness, and *Venerable* appeared in normal space well above the Omega vanguard.

As the great ship rolled and presented its starboard broadside, *Charybdis* surged out of energy drive alongside one of the attackers, *Guerriere* appearing on the other side. The two 44s loosed four broadsides in scarcely six seconds, and the Omega ship came apart.

The rest of the 44s appeared, and two more Omega ships took damage before they could begin their maneuvers.

And then the Home Fleet's guns spoke in anger for the first time.

Venerable's 100-gun starboard broadside was just about enough — the Omega ships were battered to hulks by its tide of energy.

Then *Invincible* and *Indomitable* added their own 100-gun salvoes, and the hulks of those first ten ships ceased to exist.

The First Battle Squadron of eight *Venerable*-class ships surged forward, forming an even line ahead while the Second Battle Squadron turned upwards in its own line ahead, ready to cover the alternate flank.

Tom Locke's frigates copied the maneuver, and falling into a line ahead of their own, they darted out at another angle, while the first of the much newer *Cerberus*-class frigates slipped from energy drive.

In the veritable *avalanche* that had in the last war come only from Carriers, boats began to soar by the hundred from the bays of the *Venerables*. Over 1,600 of the lethal craft — they weren't leaving reserves on the decks now, they'd need every ship.

Home Fleet was ready.

Standing at his plot, Lab took one last deep breath...

"Signal from Commodore Locke in *Charybdis*."

Not even looking to the Signal Officer, Lab nodded, "In the tank."

Tom Locke glowed to life in the massive holo plot, and the Commodore nodded to him, "Good to see you here, sir."

Lab nodded in reply, "And you. Well done Tom, join Andra's forces."

"Aye, sir. And well done eliminating the rest so quickly, sir. Looks like Omega won't be so tough after all."

Lab actually started to nod.

Then he stopped.

"I'm sorry... what *rest*, Tom?"

The frigate Commodore opened his mouth, "We exited behind the last ten in line..."

Then he realized there was no debris on his scanners.

His eyes widened, as did Lab's, and Arther Stowt's. And all the Earthers in the system were shocked into stillness as they realized the implications of what Locke had said.

"By the Earth…" Arther Stowt managed to gasp.

Lab Forepaw's eyes flew to the tank, and counted again every ship in the Home Fleet he'd brought out here with him.

By the Earth, indeed.

CHAPTER 46

"At present speed, we'll be in Earth space in just over half an hour."

Captain Claudia Cummings, now flying her flag in place of Audrey DeBrooke on *Grendelsbane City*, nodded with a good and deep sigh of relief at that report.

It was the last thing she ever did.

Grendelsbane City was incinerated in flux the very next second, as an Omega ship flew into its path.

The escort for the convoy of hundreds of thousands of surviving Genesis humans was suddenly under attack.

Vice Admiral Kylie Peregrine's Second Fleet had just returned to lunar orbit after its time on maneuvers, so it was Ami Dune and *Foudroyant* that now dropped out of energy drive on the Pluto Orbital Plane.

"Alright, let's run this one by the numbers folks," she nodded to her Flag Captain, and then looked to the Signal Officer. "Let's have a line abreast maneuver, fleet level and–"

"Admiral!"

It was a yell of surprise — not a common thing for an Earther sensor technician, so Ami Dune's eyes immediately whipped around to plot.

Foudroyant was a veteran 80, and with it was a force now of about 145 ships. That was what she had been looking at in the plot just a moment prior, but now a black haze was strobing about ten minutes beyond the border of the system... well, fifteen minutes in these older ships.

"I'm seeing energy readings that look like a fight, ma'am... a big fight..."

The Sensor Officer was quickly over the shoulder of her surprised rating, "Confirm that... flux disintegrations!"

Ami stiffened instantly. The refugee convoy — it was supposed to be coming in today... if it was out there and under attack...

"All ships, make for the battle area, maximum possible speed! Inform Admiralty House as we go — Master, *move it!*"

The escort was dying fast, that much seemed evident.

And while all but a dozen of the convoy had managed to decelerate from flux before Omega ships could fly into them and disintegrate them, now a herd of vulnerable civilian ships was trying to scatter before the stars.

From the window of one of the passenger liners, a young boy watched.

Some of the civilian ships tried to rush back into flux, and one or two made it away from the view of the window, but many exploded as they were rammed in flux by Omega hulls.

And many more ships were fired upon.

Random-seeming missiles and lasers hurled themselves through space, and caught luxury yachts and cargo haulers all in the drive sections. Engines died, generators overloaded, and ships blossomed into immense fireballs.

The boy stood with eyes wide — he'd seen this sort of thing in the movies, he'd seen the Earthers and the Navy fight the Kroggs in the movies, and he'd said it was awesome and that he'd have liked to have been there...

But now where were the Earthers? They always came to save the day in the movies. They were great, and his mom had told him he'd meet one now that they had to go to Earth.

They had to come soon...

But at least there was a Genesis Navy ship, a big and strong Dreadnought. His class had taken a trip on one before, and now next to it were three Destroyers. He knew his ships — the Navy was cool, and these were cool ships.

They were shooting back, and jerking side to side really fast. Missiles were going all over the place, and lasers too. The armor of one of the Destroyers was glowing red, and there was an Omega ship trying to ram it, but it got out of the way because it was faster and better.

Now the boy's ship was turning towards those vessels, and as the window direction changed, the boy could see eight... nine... ten other ships like this big liner he was on, all turning the same way.

He knew what that meant, they were getting closer to the Navy ships because the Navy ships were fighting back, and that meant they'd be safe.

Beyond those ten ships, the boy could see many bad ships. Like his mom told him, they'd once been Genesis ships, but now the bad guys owned them... there were a lot more of them than Navy ships.

But mom said they'd been close to Earth so the Earthers would be here soon...

"Come on, come on..."

Ami Dune was perched on the edge of her seat, grinding her jaw and watching the range in the plot tick down.

The Master was moving rapidly between the consoles at helm, checking numbers. He looked up, "That's 3,024 pls, ma'am... I'm going to redline the last reactor, that'll get us to 3,075 or so!"

Ami nodded, "Do it..."

They were nine minutes away.

•••

The Navy ships kept fighting, but as the window turned back the boy noticed that two of the Destroyers were hanging limp in space, and were really beaten up bad.

So now the Dreadnought was doing a lot of fighting, like a bigger kid owning the yard at school. The last little Destroyer was whooshing around the Dreadnought, keeping missiles away from it.

Then a bad ship came rushing towards the Dreadnought, and it shot the Destroyer so the Destroyer couldn't fight back. So the Destroyer turned really fast and rammed right into the bad guy, and the two ships went all limp in space.

The Dreadnought was by itself.

Then the liner the boy was on rocked sideways and there was a clanging thud, but the boy kept watching the Dreadnought. It was fighting real hard, and even though there were holes in it from missiles and lasers that had hit it, it didn't slow down or anything.

The boy was proud of the Navy ship, and now all that he needed was for the Earthers to come save the day.

Because that's what they did.

"Receiving a long-range transmission... it is the convoy ma'am," the Signal Officer's voice was weak. "Visual signal from the escort now."

Ami nodded and looked at the chrono — they were six minutes out...

"Put anything you can up in the plot," she said quietly.

And the Signal Officer complied; the visual feed from the bridge of the Dreadnought *Saint Edward Holmes III* appeared in the tank, and the ship's ArcColonel wasn't even paying attention.

The ship was clearly bucking, and he was holding himself in his chair. The monitor that would normally have shown Ami's face to the bridge of that Dreadnought might not even be working — she could see the humans, but could the humans see her?

"Hold on..." she said under her breath, and then there was a static-laden buzz, and sound was restored to the feed.

The ArcColonel was screaming at his bridge crew over a deafening roar as his ship jerked back and forth: "Target that one on the left! Fire — fire *now*! *Anything you have! We must protect the survivors! Stand at your posts! We must save them — save the civilians! Bearing three thirty two... don't let them near that liner. Watch out above... we must save the refugees! Get us between that one and the liner — move! Where are all these small craft coming from? Stop them from getting to the transports! We have to buy the Earthers time, they're coming to save–"*

The ArcColonel didn't see the piece of shrapnel that ripped off the front half of his head, but the entire bridge crew of *Foudroyant* did, and they watched his body fly out of the chair before another piece of flying debris killed the communications relay.

Ami Dune slid back in her chair, letting out a very long, shaky breath.

They were still five minutes away.

The boy watched as the big Dreadnought stopped firing. The Earthers would be here soon, then, because it wasn't fighting any more. The Earthers always came just in time in the movies, so now they'd come.

Behind the boy, the door to his cabin opened, and he turned, "Mom! The Earthers are coming soon, aren't they?"

Mom stepped into the cabin, but because of the dim lights the boy couldn't see her properly. Then she stepped right up to her son, and he saw that her eyes were black, and that her skin was bulging.

The boy's eyes widened, and he tried to scream, but his mother put a stop to that.

And so as Omega began to drink the blood out of this limp body, this 'mother' watched through the window as the liner, and all the other ships in the convoy that had been successfully infected, turned away from Earth and reentered flux drive.

Only proper Omega ships remained around the debris, and soon they would be moving again.

So much for Genesis civilization… I'm so good…

CHAPTER 47

Ami Dune's jaw set.

She'd narrowly missed the end of Genesis civilization. Omega had killed them all just short of safety. *All* of them. Because they were close enough now that *Foudroyant's* sensors could see Omega's fleet sniping any surviving hulks of metal holding survivors. He and his 500-odd ships... damn him.

Damn him.

"Admiral Peregrine signaling, ma'am... she's coming right up behind us with Second Fleet. She says take them, ma'am. She says kill them all."

Ami Dune's eyes narrowed. She'd seen more war than she'd ever thought would have been necessary during the struggle against the Kroggs, but this... this was like nothing she'd ever witnessed.

The death of a society. The near-death of a race.

And so close to her, so close to Earth.

Omega.

Omega would pay.

It was rage — true, blind and righteous that surged through Ami's blood in that instant. And through the veins of every Earther, every last Earther, in every ship in nearby space.

And even though between Ami's force and Kylie Peregrine's there was only about 360 ships to Omega's 500, the plague, the creator, was about to bloody well pay for what he'd done.

Because Earthers *never* angered, unless things like this happened.

"Master, take us in. All ships, *kill* them."

Omega had expected a reaction, and it looked like he was about to get one. The Earthers had emptied Earth space for this, and he supposed that made sense. Now they'd see just how well they could do against him...

Ooh, this'll be fun...

Foudroyant surged out of energy drive and immediately fired two broadsides. Though the eighty cannon erupted into space filled with Omega ships, none of the energy shot hit anything, and the next two ships in the squadron line were rammed by infected Destroyers and torn to shreds.

But the rest of the recommissioned fleets arrived in the following seconds, and energy filled space. Earthers had no compunction now about fighting at their basest level — they were predators, pushed to fury by the savagery they had just witnessed.

Omega ships began to blossom and burn.

Well, they've got it in for me now... oooh.

They were giving just as good as they got, it seemed — for every ship of theirs he destroyed, they killed one of his. That was fair enough...

So he was essentially tying up the entire Earth defense fleet in one-on-one fighting, and he had the edge of about 150 ships.

Well, he'd love to stay and eviscerate, but that wasn't on the cards.

Let the Earthers boil and win here...

Separating 150 ships from his armada, Omega began his run to Earth.

Ami was holding onto the sides of the plot to stay upright as *Foudroyant* blazed its way through the Omega formation again, its veteran guns hammering away at the infected ships of Genesis. Even if they died to the last, these Earther veterans would see this fight ended here.

"Ma'am! About... call it 150 Omega ships are breaking contact... making for Earth!"

But... by the Earth. Ami's eyes were struck wide, and she twisted immediately to the Signal Officer, "Get me Admiral Peregrine, right now!"

Vice Admiral Peregrine began to glow to life in *Foudroyant's* plot, but just as her holo stabilized, she vanished.

Ami frowned and looked back to the Signal Officer, who shook his head in confusion, but then the Sensor Officer clarified, "Her ship's gone, ma'am. No survivors on scope."

Unaccustomed to rage, Ami didn't quite feel it when her fist went through the console before her, and came out bloody.

"Any ships that can disengage, get back to Earth right now. We'll hold as many of his ships as we can here."

They'd been baited, trapped, and bested.

Varnon's mouth hung open as he watched the long-range feeds.

The C&C of *Guardian One* was silent, and all eyes were fixed on the images in the main holo tank. What they'd seen was unthinkable... the end of the Dreadnought's ArcColonel, and now the end of Genesis civilization, the trapping of Ami Dune's fleet, and the end of Kylie Peregrine.

And no one moved. Mouths hung open for long seconds as the Omega ships detached to Earth came soaring towards the planet, faster than Ami's ships could ever hope to disengage and return.

This wasn't the way things were supposed to happen — things were never supposed to be able to get this bad. How was this possible, how had they been so–

"Stations, beat to quarters. Signal Officer, send to Io, Mars, and the asteroid bases to hold their boats close for local defense. Send to Luna and to all orbital and ground stations, launch boats and deploy to the patterns of Defense Plan Twenty-One."

No one quite processed the cool and even words from Setter Caine's rich and familiar voice — at least not at first. Eyes slowly began to turn from the ghastly death in the plot to the great Earther wolf standing before it, his arms clasped behind his back.

Setter was their leader, and as much as the horror of what he'd just seen tried to tear his brain from its grasp of reality, something deep within drove him to his old ways.

This would *not* happen to Earth. He had just failed Sarah and the humans, he would not fail his own home as well.

No, Omega would not get the best of him again.

He ground his jaw at the thought. The Earthers would make their stand here. Once and for all.

Varnon, still trying to control his disbelief, looked to his old friend, and tried to rally himself.

But it was not so easy.

And yet, while all the Earthers who saw the destruction of the Genesis survivors in real time stood aghast, the crews of over 15,000 gunboats in the Sol system ran to their small, deadly ships.

Earth was the best fortified system in the Alliance, and that wasn't just because of its Home Fleet.

As gunboats lifted off their fields at the Arctic and Antarctic Bases, and as they poured from the orbital stations and the lunar pads, and as the local defense boat groups took up their positions around the key planets of the system, Setter Caine stood tall and watched in the plot.

His confidence, feeling so misplaced just now, was all that bolstered the strength of his Earthers. He was their leader, absolute and undisputed, and now they threw their trust totally into his hands.

The last eight minutes before Omega's arrival passed slowly.

As was Earther policy, the feeds seen by the crews of the orbital stations' C&Cs were beamed to holo tanks all across Earth, and Earthers everywhere stopped and watched in horror as the survivors of Genesis were massacred.

Phealan Caine managed to get Claire out onto the deck before she saw most of what was there.

Elandra Caine looked from the image of a dead fleet of Genesis ships back to her scanners, and worked with a new urgency. She was close to something here — it might save the infected Genesis survivors... one day...

And the rest of the Earther population stopped dead, disbelieving, finding it altogether too hard to accept what they were witnessing...

• • •

And then Caine turned to a camera, and instead of giving orders, spoke to his people. *His* people.

"Omega ships are on their way. Ami Dune is delaying or destroying many of them, but more are coming. We will fight them. We *all* will fight them. Hundreds of thousands of humans have died in these last minutes, we cannot honor their memory if we share their fate. We cannot do anything on their behalf, in their memory, if we *die*. Stand fast as Earthers, for now we must *fight*."

And then he looked away again, and his words slowly began to imprint on the shocked Earthers who watched. They began to move again — most to find their way home to be with their families.

"They're entering the system now… sir, they're not slowing at system's edge."

The voice of *Guardian One's* Sensor Officer was restored to miraculous calm, and as the warning came in, Caine nodded. Omega was coming right for Earth, it seemed. He was going to try to end two civilizations in a row.

"General Kudlee reports she's got six brigades ready for hopping to landing sites, and the rest of the corps mobilized for transport in support," the marine Colonel who was the liaison between fleet and ground command for *Guardian* Command added after word came through her comm.

"All city shields have been activated to repel falling debris," one of the Lieutenants along the command deck added quickly. Energy shields had been installed around all of Earth's cities to give them added security in case of a space attack like this one.

Earth was ready. Not as ready as it could have been, but ready enough…

"Twenty seconds — they're moving *fast* sir…"

Caine nodded, "All stations, run out your guns."

As they had when once threatened by the Church, the Earth defense stations now prepared their great cannon.

"Ten…nine…eight…"

Varnon tried to draw himself up to full height, and to prepare himself with calming breaths. He'd never thought it would come to this…

"Three… two… one…"

Varnon winced, Setter stood calmly, and breath caught on the bridge…

"One ship decelerating… the rest are passing right over us!"

What?

What?

Caine stiffened — they weren't coming for Earth… well, one was but–

Artie.

They were a day away from the corridor.

"They're heading for the New Halifax corridor, sir. Making high speed!"

Of course — that had been Omega's first objective after taking Genesis, to get through the corridor to get to the Larosians again... to use them to create those powerful Earther-killer warriors. That's what Omega would need for an invasion of Earth — infected humans were only so strong, but...

"Setter!"

Varnon grabbed Caine by the arm and pointed at the holo tank.

The one ship that had decelerated was redlining its drives. It was a ram.

And though boats immediately swarmed it, they couldn't concentrate enough firepower on any one side to knock it off course.

The nearest platform put a broadside into it, but the thing was moving at 98 pls. Half its hull flaked off, but it had evidently been a Superdreadnought — it was too big to be blasted away outright. And all it needed was some of its mass to make it a ballistic weapon...

As Setter Caine and Varnon Broadpaw watched, and as Elandra Caine looked up to see what the noise was, the lone Omega ship struck London, England, at near-light speed, its reactors exploding as it disintegrated. London's city shield didn't have a hope of stopping that kind of force.

The British Isles were shattered.

CHAPTER 48

Phealan saw the explosion. It was visible from across the Atlantic.

A tidal wave kilometers high was flung out by the impact, and while the shockwave flattened everything in Scotland and sunk Wales and Ireland into the sea along with the south of England, the English Channel beached itself all over France.

Most of Europe, in about five minutes, was absolutely devastated... but at least it was still there. Tsunami damage could be repaired, and Earthers could be fished out of the water. The British Isles weren't so fortunate.

The tidal wave was set to cross the Atlantic, and to absorb islands like Newfoundland. Phealan somehow knew to expect that as he grabbed Claire and flung her to the deck after seeing that initial explosion. The shockwave careened over them both, and drove him down hard on top of her, cracking two of her ribs in the process.

But as soon as that passed, Phealan hauled himself to his feet, realized he had a broken arm, and dragged Claire — stunned and silent as she was — into the house. He turned on the house shield, knowing it'd save them from the wave, and hoped that the crews at the Climate Control Center in Sydney were on their game.

Despite horror and shock that might have paralyzed human personnel, those Earthers at C3 reacted just as their training demanded. From Sydney, Australia, their command center monitored Earth's weather, and in case of major catastrophe, took steps to control damage.

The lead technician saw the mega wave, and knew precisely what to do.

Keying up the Atlantic Ocean shield grid, he activated all of the 4,000 grids that had been sewn across the ocean over the previous eight decades. Shields rose up every five kilometers across the Atlantic, angling both north-south and east-west. A literal grid of energy walls, each a kilometer high, ruptured the wave short of land.

The damage from the impact was therefore contained to the eastern side of the North Atlantic ocean. What destruction it was...

Setter Caine stood frozen on the bridge of *Guardian One*, staring at the remains of England that were being shown in the main holo plot. Sensors were already reaching out to scan for survivors — both Earthers, and Omega humans who might have sought to infest the planet. Even if they couldn't infect Earthers, they could doubtless wreak havoc.

Setter was attempting to process the fact that London was gone, but battle instincts were forcing his mind to remain detached as he continued to react to the realities.

"Prep an energy-hyper pod for Admiral Tigar, send it immediately with our best estimates of the Omega force," he sounded as if he actually hadn't noticed the missing island in the North Atlantic.

The Earthers at the appropriate stations didn't respond or jump quickly to action. It took very long seconds for them to clear their own minds, and trusting their instincts, to begin doing their jobs again.

Setter looked then to the Signal Officer, "Send to General Kudlee, we should deploy wide scanning teams, make sure Omega didn't land anyone on the surface as he did at Genesis. And send to Admiralty House, have them begin coordinating search and rescue efforts."

The Signal Officer was typing more ponderously than usual, but with the last order she looked up slowly, "Sir?"

Varnon looked away from the plot for a moment to correct Setter, "Send the last order to Antarctic Base, he means."

Frowning, Caine turned to his friend, "The Admiralty–"

"Admiralty House was in London, Setter," Varnon's quiet words came with the staggered cadence that counted for shock in Earther circles.

And with those words, Setter's battle instincts finally stilled.

Admiralty House was gone. London was gone. Most of England was gone.

Elandra.

Elandra.

Ami Dune collapsed into her chair, clutching the bloody gash in her stomach with a wince of pain. She'd be passing out pretty soon if the medical team didn't get to the bridge...

Foudroyant tipped sideways and another Omega ship strafed the starboard broadside, tearing away more of the 80's outer hull. Structural energy fields were keeping the veteran ship together, and over sixty guns remained in action. She'd win this yet...

Or maybe that was the blood loss talking. Optimistic, that blood loss...

The plot, however, was agreeing with her, because the Earther fury had begun to simmer, and they were fighting with clear heads again. They were now killing three Omega ships for every two Earther ships that fell.

Foudroyant lurched in the opposite direction, and Ami gritted her teeth as the force of the movement pressed her sideways into the arm of her chair.

Then *Foudroyant's* guns hummed, and on the plot another Omega ship winked out.

Omega ships were dying now... it was as if the plague was losing interest in the battle, and his inattention was muting the previously lethal coordination of his forces. The kill ratio was climbing towards two-to-one against him.

"Send to *Roanoke*, *Rodney* and *Saints*," Ami chewed out the order. "Form on us and return to Earth space."

They had to get *something* back to help defend their home. If Omega was losing interest in this fight, it was probably because he had another, more important one going elsewhere.

The 80-gun *Foudroyant* and the 74s *Roanoke*, *Rodney* and *Saints* slid into energy drive moments later.

Phealan grimaced as he applied the stasis patch to his broken arm — he'd need a good dose of UDRC for a clean break like that one. Drawing a second patch from the household med kit, he turned to Claire, who sat, still rather stunned, on the couch, hunched slightly to one side.

"Sorry I landed on you so hard," he said distractedly, kneeling in front of her, "Lift your shirt for a second."

She complied without ceremony, and he gently pressed the stasis patch onto the area of broken ribs and keyed it on.

"We should get you some UDRC... though I don't know if it'll work as well without you having been given full regen... I'll have to ask mom. Anyway, I think you'll be alright for... now..." his words trailed off as he realized what he'd said.

His mother had gone back to the office just hours ago... had she... was she...

Standing in a sharp jolt, Phealan turned quickly to the arm of the couch and keyed the living room holo to life, tapping it to tie in with the planetary news grid.

The sensor logs from the orbiting stations were on one side, a number of reporting officials were along the other, and right in the middle was a holocam shot, evidently being taken live by a circling gunboat.

All that was on screen was a frothing Atlantic... and a caption that said simply: 'England is gone'.

Phealan's knees seemed to weaken, and as they did he shifted sideways and half-sat, half-fell onto the couch next to Claire.

He... couldn't... believe this. This sort of thing didn't happen, couldn't happen. Why would it happen now? How did Omega get through all the defenses... what had he managed...?

"Isn't that where your mom was going?"

Claire's question was honestly quite innocent — she wasn't too well versed in Earth geography...

Phealan's nod was barely visible. His mouth hung open as he felt his mind slipping loose of its moorings..

Claire took his hand silently, and he continued to stare at the holo.

What could stop this Omega?

Because the Earthers weren't doing so well so far.

CHAPTER 49

"And this happened six hours ago?"

Vice Admiral Chronos Claw was still holding his squadron's position over Krogg 'A', chaperoning the Allies' old alien enemy while an even older foe ravaged his home and his friends.

The Lieutenant delivering the news to the conference room in *Formidable* simply nodded, "Yes, sir. Pod just arrived."

Claw let out a groan, trying to force a balance between his disbelief and his horror. How had Omega managed to accomplish these things?

"It would seem that this new enemy is... quite adept," Peacelord Kragran had been lunching with Chronos again, talking about general security and other routine matters. Now this. The Earthers — the wardens of Krogg 'A' and his people's new pattern for existence — were being handed defeats on a crushing scale.

The Peacelord began to sense an opportunity.

"Thank you, Lieutenant, we'll have a look ourselves," Claw's words were relatively calm, and the young wolf in the doorway nodded before departing quickly.

Turning to the conference table, Claw tapped up the main holo tank and watched with a deeply furrowed brow as holo recordings taken by ships of the Earther recommissioned 'Fleets' showed the old 74s and 80s arrive too late to save the Genesis refugee convoy.

"He seems to have defied all prediction," Kragran said with almost — *almost* — a hint of admiration. The Kroggs had never managed so complete a victory against the Allies... here was an enemy, perhaps, whose unorthodox strategy might serve as an example for the Kroggs.

But that was not a thought for now, the Peacelord knew.

"Indeed. He was a spectator during the whole last war, remember. And he's had momentum and surprise at hand so far... but look there, Kylie Peregrine and Ami Dune severely battered him."

The holo was glowing with the arrival of Dune and Peregrine's forces on the site of the Genesis slaughter, and it clearly showed their high rate of casualties as they dealt with the Omega ships.

And then some got past Ami Dune.

Claw winced as he watched more and more recommissioned ships wink out of existence. What distressed him more, though, was the huge wave of some 150 ships that drove right towards Earth. What made him close his eyes in horror was the Superdreadnought that annihilated London.

"The Omega vessels seem to have combined with the survivors of the action against Ami Dune's ships... some 200 ships are heading for the New Halifax corridor. Admiral Tigar holds that place?"

Claw wasn't quite listening to Kragran's words — at least not at first. But as the query registered, the cat Admiral nodded, "Indeed. With recommissions and Minnie Maximane's blockade force. He'll put a stop to them..."

"If he fails, though, *our* flank will be severely exposed."

Nodding absently, Claw leaned forward and propped his elbows on the table, watching the route of the Omega ships again. They'd blown right past...

Wait a moment.

"*Our* flank?" Chronos wasn't expecting an answer to his abrupt question. Instead his eyes drifted to the corridor at New Halifax and then shifted to the corridor his own ships were defending... oh so close to Krogg 'A'.

Omega wouldn't go into the other galaxy just to harvest Larosians as soldiers for his armies... though he might do that too. No, the primary reason the plague would have for going through the corridor at New Halifax would be to get to Krogg 'A'. Omega could do an end run around Garvin Jardaw's defenses at Gibraltar and appear *behind* Krogg 'A', leaving the system vulnerable. If Omega could harvest the Kroggs themselves...

"He has demonstrated the ability to use raw Krogg DNA as a tool... were he to absorb my world, Chronos, he would be essentially unstoppable. And with all the Larosians infected with his earlier form, and unable to stop his progress in their galaxy, he could come here without difficulty."

Claw clenched his jaw. The Peacelord was seeing things with all-too perfect clarity. It made sense. Omega could benefit from the resources of two alien races this way, taking the Larosians left in their own universe as soldiers, and coming unopposed through the other galaxy to Krogg for a massive source of biomatter.

All the while avoiding the powerful defenses at Gibraltar, effectively rendering the station useless. A Maginot line.

Sitting upright again, Claw nodded quickly and looked through the plot to Kragran, "That's a brilliant insight, my friend... I wish it were to our advantage."

Kragran tilted his head in an alien manner, and bobbed his head, "True. But recall, you might make *use* of my people, Chronos. Arm us again, and we will protect our home."

Despite the haze that clouded part of Claw's senses, his eyes still shifted immediately to his counterpart, "I can't go that far, Krag, you know that. But we'll look out for you. I just need to pass this warning on to Garvin and Lab...

your insight might just have saved us all."

Kragran straightened in his seat, offering a less enthused nod, and silently decided to make his own preparations.

The Earthers have a strong enemy now, and we will learn from that enemy and become stronger ourselves. Our new Lords will have to come to understand their mistake in dealing with us in this way.

Claw couldn't hear Kragran's thoughts, and he didn't really need or want to. He just keyed the intercom, "Claw to Signal Officer."

There was a pause, before the Lieutenant running *Formidable's* comms reported in reply, "Here, sir."

"Prep two pods, one for Earth, one for Gibraltar."

"I'll take *any* good news right now," Karl Kandam glanced at Lang Sandpelt as Gibraltar's flag officers stood on the command deck of its main station.

Sandpelt shrugged at the panda's comment, "I'm not going to hold my breath. Any word on survivors?"

Jardaw was staring into the plot as the images of London's destruction played through, and he shook his head slowly, "Nothing as yet. They're still hoping."

Sandpelt and Kandam both nodded evenly at their commander's grim words, then quieted for another few moments while more of the holo feeds rolled.

The destruction was thorough... it was true devastation.

"That's 200 ships he has running towards New Halifax, and one he crashed into Earth. He can't have brought many more than those online since he took over Genesis... he *must* have weakened his Genesis defense fleet to launch the attack," Lang said rather abruptly after a moment. "Can I go have a look now? *Audacious* can be read for space in four hours. We can see how many ships he has in reserve."

Jardaw looked up through the holo, his mind processing. It wasn't the polar bear Admiral's first or most comfortable option... but what he was seeing in the plot seemed to demand an unusual response. They had to show Omega they could shuffle the deck just as well as he could — he wouldn't expect a counterattack to hit Genesis so quickly.

"Have both *Venerable* squadrons make preparations for space. I'm not giving the final go-ahead, but I'll recommend a reconnaissance in force in my next pod to Admiralty House," Jardaw's tone was as dry as it was dark, and Sandpelt replied with a solemn — though contradictorily eager — nod.

Kandam was opening his mouth to remind Jardaw that Admiralty House was gone when the plot flashed and a sector of it off to the side shifted from light blue to red.

"Picket buoy bearing 145 by 111 by 211, sir. Deep-range one — a day out. It's detecting a large number of ships on the way in..."

The report from the Sensor Chief was played out in the plot as dozens of icons floated from the abyss towards Gibraltar. The picket pods were handy remotes — they gave the base a good heads up when any unusual traffic was coming in.

Lately that meant any large group of ships. Like this one they were seeing. Omega...?

Then a pennant blinked to life over the lead ship.

Four colored tabs, green-blue-red-white... the pennant of the First Space Lord.

"It's Fox!" Sandpelt grinned immediately. Beyond just the promise of reinforcement, Lang was glad of the chance to see his old friend and once-commander again.

Kandam's ear twitched and he allowed a minor smile of relief to creep onto his face. He looked from the edge of the plot, which was now recoloring itself blue again, to his fellow bear Jardaw, "Well, I said I'd take any good news."

Jardaw nodded, "Indeed..."

And then a white strobe appeared in the plot — the sign of an approaching energy-hyper pod.

"Do I hear another shoe dropping?" Kandam's voice sobered again as the pod from Krogg 'A' arrived.

"It's from Vice Admiral Claw... patching the data through to the plot now," the Signal Chief was enough of a veteran not to need orders to take that action.

A star chart appeared in the holo. Text scrolled up in one corner, and Jardaw, Kandam and Sandpelt watched with dark expressions as the black-markered group of Omega ships rushed through the New Halifax corridor, crossed the defenseless Larosian Empire, entered the Krogg hyperspace corridor, and appeared next to Krogg.

Below the simulation, Chronos Claw's message appeared, "Look up the Maginot line."

The reference didn't make sense to anyone standing nearby save for Jardaw, who grimaced. During the Second World War, the mighty French fixed defenses built to stop a German invasion had proved useless, because the Germans had invaded right around them. In point of fact, the Maginot line had become a trap for the French, keeping all their best forces tied to fixed defenses and leaving them unable to meet the attack that ended up coming from their flank.

"Good historical sense, Chronos," he muttered to himself. Omega wouldn't even have to hit Gibraltar, not until he'd infected many more Larosians, and had taken Krogg, *and* gotten access to all the Krogg biomatter he could dream of.

Jardaw's eyes shifted up to Sandpelt, "We better hope Artie's ready to stop them at New Halifax. And we'll definitely need to know what Omega has left to strike us with. If he's shot his whole bolt at the attack on Earth, counting on us to sit still, I want you there to surprise him in Genesis."

"Aye, sir. I'll return to *Audacious*," Sandpelt nodded.

Walking tall and with determination, Sandpelt left the command deck.

Kandam looked to Jardaw, "And if they get through Artie's defenses?"

Jardaw released a long sigh, "I'm not going to make the mistakes of Maginot, Karl. We're going to meet him wherever we must, even if we have to abandon Gibraltar."

CHAPTER 50

In the wake of epic destruction came a beautiful evening. A smooth, cool breeze crossed the Caine estate, traveling from the west, as though the world were sucking fresh air in to fill the vacuum left as the sea swallowed most of the British Isles. On most days, the fresh breeze would have been enough to still any worry in Phealan Caine's mind. Peace was in the wind, he liked to think.

Now, it obviously wasn't enough. Phealan wasn't certain anything could ever halt the dark feeling of loss that had closed over his soul.

He had never felt like this, and he suspected that few Earthers ever had. No force had ever struck Earth with such power — not since the Earthers had taken custody of the world. This was their planet to protect, and today Omega had managed to get past them. Earth had been scarred, and millions of Earthers had been obliterated.

Millions, including a certain Elandra Caine.

The stab of grief that pierced every nerve in Phealan's body as he thought about his mother was again overwhelming. He sat on the steps of the Caine house's deck and looked east at the horizon, and his mind seemed to stall. Over the waters of the Atlantic had been his mother. Now she was gone.

He didn't know how to deal with this. He just didn't know. Perhaps some Earthers had experienced a feeling like this one before, but he didn't have that experience to rely on. How was he supposed to act? What was he supposed to feel?

Rational questions like that helped him understand his reactions. He had to figure out what he was feeling — had to understand how deep this grief went. As an intellectual sort of wolf, he knew he couldn't consciously come to terms with all the pain by just thinking about it. He knew that he would feel this epic loss for the rest of his life, in one way or another. Time would reveal just how that loss manifested itself. For now he had to get past the shock.

I have to get past the shock. I can't let this paralyze me. Claire needs my help, and she lost more than I just did. Dad will need my help, because he lost more than I just did.

Setter had lost his wife *and* millions of Earthers, or so he would believe. Phealan knew there was nothing his father could have done to stop Omega's wildly unorthodox attack. Though not a military wolf, Phealan just *knew* that. But Setter would blame himself for the lost souls, and for his lost wife most of all.

Phealan had to be strong and insistent. While he could never make his father accept, deep down, that this couldn't have been foreseen or stopped, he could force Setter to agree with that intellectually. He could help Setter get over his own shock.

Nothing would take away the deep pain. Elandra had been torn from the Caine family, and on so many levels that would wound both Phealan and Setter. But as the young Caine sat and stared at the eastern horizon, he knew he had to compartmentalize the wounds. Until Omega was gone, he had to help his father, continue to help Claire, and help the Earther people.

No longer did he have the luxury of waiting to discover who he was, and what his life direction would be. Now, more than ever before, the Earthers needed leaders to stand tall. They needed his father. And that meant it was his job to support his father, in any way possible.

And his mother...

Elandra's face seemed to fill the sky before Phealan's eyes, and the stabs of grief returned again. His determination would not waver, but he could no more forget that his mother was dead than he could abandon his father.

He had to live with the pain. That's what he had to do. That was the Earther thing to do, and he was his parents' son: a quintessential Earther.

Watching Phealan through the glass from the living room couch, Claire Schaeffer enjoyed the sight of the wolf's sunken head as much as she had the ability to enjoy anything. How would *he* like it? It was so easy for him to say things to try to make her feel better when he didn't know what it felt like. And he'd gotten off easy, he still had his father.

Not that the old wolf had called since the explosion. No, hadn't even bothered. Some family these Earthers were.

Their enlightened principles were bullshit, Claire just knew it. They'd soon learn that there was no escaping the darkness. They'd soon learn the pain and the anger and the bitterness. Maybe then they'd stop trying to get her to laugh and be happy and move on. She didn't want to. They didn't understand that. They expected her to be able to turn it all around, move on...

"Yeah, now we'll see how well you move on, won't we?" she asked the question under her breath, glaring at the back of Phealan's head.

Stupid Earthers. The movies always lied. She'd known they were too good to be true... now they'd be bad and real. They'd be human. When it came down to it, all life in the universe had to be like humans — Claire was sure of it.

How could any feeling creature get over the grief Omega inflicted? It was impossible. It was inhuman.

Claire looked forward to Phealan learning that, so he'd leave her alone.

Setter Caine stood in one of *Guardian One's* observation lounges and stared at the surface of his homeworld. The station was over Europe now, and while search and rescue teams hopped up and down over the European countries, fishing out Earthers who'd been swept up in the tidal wave, Setter's eyes locked on the blue water where England should have been.

There were no survivors in England. Some Earthers who'd been protected by city shields in Dublin, Belfast and Glasgow were found floating alive in the newly cleared ocean, but Wales, Ireland and Scotland were destroyed.

London was gone.

Elandra, of course, was gone.

Along with millions of Earthers who hadn't been ready for what Omega had done.

Setter hadn't been ready for what Omega had done.

Of course it wasn't his job to be ready — not officially. As Supreme Consul, no one really knew what Setter's job description included, but planetary defense was generally in the hands of the Admiralty. And the Admiralty was gone.

Whether it was in his job description or not, though, Setter felt responsible. Omega was his responsibility, his fight to make. He was uniquely qualified to wage a war on this scale, against this sort of malevolent enemy. He should have realized this would happen. Somehow, some way, he should have known Omega would fight with this level of senseless brutality.

I should have found a way to know.

"You couldn't have known, any more than I could have."

Varnon Broadpaw sounded hoarse as he trudged into the observation lounge, and without looking back at his friend, Setter simply shook his head, "None of us could have known... I understand that. But it can't change how I feel, Varnon. I should have found a way..."

"I should have too," Varnon let out a long sigh as he stopped next to Setter, his chin dipping and his eyes closing. "I'm sorry about Elandra."

Setter had been filling his mind with the millions of Earthers he'd failed, specifically because he didn't want to picture that one face. That one beloved face.

But Varnon was right to bring her face to Setter's mind. It felt to Setter as though he'd been stabbed, and physically he found himself clutching his chest, his breathing coming for a moment in rasps.

Elandra's smiling face eclipsed his thoughts — all thoughts but one: *she's gone*.

For 150 years, Elandra had known Setter as no other Earther ever would. Friends like Andra Ursla had understood him as a commander, and friends like Lab Forepaw had understood him as a wolf. Elandra had understood his soul. He'd taken that for granted for all these years, failing to see a day when she would no longer be there.

That was the nature of love. For it to work, you had to take it for granted. You had to lose all perspective of consequences and time and fate. You had to lose yourself to it… and that wasn't easy for a wolf like Setter.

Setter had spent his life knowing he was a leader, and he'd spent the Krogg War with the weight of millions of deaths on his shoulders. He felt the responsibility of leadership in all things. He considered the consequences of every action he took, and every decision he made.

Only Elandra had known how to take that weight off his shoulders. Only she had seemed to understand why he took it on… or perhaps only she had understood that he *had* to take it on. And somehow, with her incredible skills as a healer, she'd helped him find peace when they were together.

Setter knew an old adage that said it was 'lonely at the top'. Among most Earthers, it was a defunct saying: Earthers stood together at the top all the time. But for Setter, with his unique history of leadership and his unique sense of responsibility, it could have been true. Elandra had helped him down from the top, though. She'd given him moments of great peace.

And now she was gone.

Omega had taken her, and millions of Earthers, in a bid to destabilize the Earther will to fight.

Setter knew what the plague was doing, but knowing what was happening didn't make it any less difficult to stop. The plague was showing the Earthers that their power wasn't as grand as they'd hoped. He was challenging their utopian ideals and way of life. He was hoping to demoralize and destroy them… to torture them with their own failures and inadequacies.

Worse, he was trying to change the way Earthers fought. He wanted Setter, Varnon, Lab and everyone else second-guessing themselves, wondering what was coming next. He wanted them afraid, unable to respond with their inherent prowess.

Elandra's face slowly faded from Setter's mind. As he straightened and released his grip on his chest, he closed his eyes. Her face would come back, but for now he had a moment to think.

Omega was determined to change the way the Earthers fought. Setter had to seize on that. The fact that Omega didn't want them on game was a sign that, perhaps, the Earthers were a threat to him when they were fighting at their best.

He had to hold on to that. He had to.

Elandra's face floated back into his mind, and his eyes screwed tightly shut.

"He killed my wife, Varnon. He killed her and millions of others so that we'd be afraid of him," Setter's words came through gritted teeth.

Varnon's voice was still hoarse, "Yes, he did. And I'm terrified of him."

It was a plain admission, and Setter nodded in agreement, "We all are."

The two remained silent for a moment. Setter dwelled on his words, and focused longingly on the image of Elandra's face he held in his mind. Omega had taken her, and there was nothing Setter could have done to stop that.

Omega had a great deal of power, and it was *terrifying*.

But Setter couldn't be governed by that fear. He had to let that go. Grief wouldn't leave him, but fear... either the Earthers would survive their war with Omega, or they wouldn't. Those were the two options. He had to isolate those... he had to abandon the fear.

After losing Elandra, what else could hurt him? What else could Omega do?

Phealan.

Setter opened his eyes.

"He's taken a lot from us, Varnon. He'll take more if we let him. I don't intend to let him. Not without a fight."

The choppy sentences drew Varnon's gaze to Setter's face.

"We can't let him change who we are or the way we fight. We can't. He's hoping we'll crumble. Perhaps he's too used to harvesting humans, or perhaps he knows we won't fold and is just torturing us for amusement. But... we have to..." Setter stopped and swallowed.

Varnon nodded once, not needing the sentence to be finished aloud.

We can't let him change the way we fight, or more will be lost. We must stand.

Setter's gaze moved back to the ocean where England had been.

We have to fight.

The pain hit him again, as he knew it would. It didn't change his resolve. He couldn't let it.

CHAPTER 51

Artemis Tigar sat in his chair on the bridge of *Agamemnon*, glad he'd listened to Minnie Maximane. She'd told him not to leave the corridor to reinforce Earth, even though he'd guessed rightly that Omega was going to strike there.

The fact that London had been incinerated almost twelve hours earlier was obviously not what made him glad he'd listened. No, he was glad he'd listened because now he had a powerful fighting force waiting here to crush that bastard Omega for his insolence.

The plague had done unimaginable harm — killed the British Isles and wiped out the Genesis convoy. There was nothing Artie could have done about either event — even had he been in-system, he'd probably have been as surprised and unable to assist as Ami Dune had been.

But now a bruised Omega was going to meet *Agamemnon* with the recommissions and Minnie's fleet under *Galahad*. And that plague was going to regret its actions out amongst the stars. This was the choke point, after all. It was where Omega would be made to pay — even if it turned into Thermopylae in the process.

The New Halifax Squadron was *waiting* for Omega, and this time he couldn't play games.

"Long-range pickets have him now, sir — the whole fleet we saw at Sol. He's about six hours out, and coming on in open order."

Artie nodded as the report came from the watch officer, and he turned to his First Lieutenant, "Pass that along to the crew."

"*Galahad* signaling, sir."

Artie nodded without looking to the Signal Officer, "Very good. Put her in the main tank."

There was the briefest of pauses as Minnie Maximane's holo visage glowed to life in the main battle plot, and Artie stepped towards her as the feed stabilized.

"So, six hours?" she half-asked, half-commented.

"Indeed. Now here's how we're going to handle him..."

Omega was... well... damned near elated. So far things had been going pretty much as he wanted — the plan was coming together and the Earthers were being put into the most vulnerable state they'd ever been in.

So now he just had to deal with the small blockade force at New Halifax's corridor, and then it would be on to the Larosians and the Kroggs, all in one fell swoop.

And he hadn't even used black wave yet.

"I'm so good..." Omega-Gillian purred as her ship floated in the depths of space far beyond the trade routes but reasonably near Freetown. Omega-Natosh, standing on the surface of Genesis, laughed at the comment as though he was in the same room as Hodge.

The Earthers would try to stop him, and maybe they'd manage to block his wave of quickly-infected Genesis ships, but they had no concept of the war that was about to close in on them.

While he knew *exactly* who they were and how to deal with them...

Ooh, revenge was *sweet*.

Next up: the New Halifax corridor.

Artie Tigar was watching the chrono silently. He'd stepped off the bridge for only fifteen minutes in the past six hours, and that had been to get something to eat. At least his stomach wouldn't be growling when he faced the coming onslaught...

Well, 'trap' might be a better way of putting it.

Minnie Maximane's *Champion*-class ships of the line — sixteen fairly new, powerful fleet units — would be the bait, along with their frigate and sloop escorts. Minnie would move to intercept Omega's 200-odd ships with that meager force, and she'd inflict as much damage as she could in the opening exchange.

The jaws of the trap, though, would be Artie's six squadrons of 74s and eight squadrons of frigates and sloops. He'd completely stripped New Halifax — he'd left nothing there in reserve, and as such he could count on 112 veteran ships and veteran crews.

Which meant Omega's 200 were going to get jumped by just about 150 fresh Earther warships that had chosen their own time and place to attack, and that already knew how this plague fought a Naval war...

Yes, yes, it all looked quite reasonable on paper — just like a number of traps in which the Kroggs had been caught. But Omega wasn't going to be easy prey, that was a certainty.

So standing quietly on *Agamemnon*'s bridge, Artie held his hands behind his back and counted the minutes.

There were only ten to go now. How marvelously fast time seemed to have moved since the pods had begun to come in.

Soon they'd fight.

•••

In a different galaxy, Varnia Lupus dropped somewhat gingerly into her chair on *Renown's* bridge, "We're *how far* out?"

The stodgy old Master smiled and tipped his head to the side, "Well ma'am, looks like Narosh's estimates on travel time were based on a Larosian ship at hyper... we're considerably faster than that. We should be at the corridor in... oh, call it an hour."

"The grav eddies are already registering on long-range scans — it's definitely the right corridor. Another ten minutes and we should see the warning buoy," the Sensor Officer concurred, and Varnia smiled.

Home *very* soon, and she'd get to see her dad and family again, and carry word of Narosh's promise of support...

Well, hopefully Omega hadn't carried the fight to Earth yet. If he'd moved out of Genesis by now it would probably have been against Freetown, and the Earthers might well have turned him back. It would be very difficult for the plague to get a drop on the whole Earther Navy, and it'd be even more difficult for him to succeed when this ship got home.

Renown's cargo of data on Omega would be shared with leading Earther minds, and in no time Elandra Caine, working with the likes of *Renown's* own Doctor Lazarus, would find a way to kill the plague.

Before he managed to launch a force out of Genesis, they'd have him beaten...

I just thought all that 'out loud'. Wow, I guess I didn't learn much from the last war...

Varnia's bright lines of thought persisted despite her superstition about luck.

Home soon.

"Outer pickets are rejoining the blockade fleet... *now*. Omega is two minutes out, sir."

Artie nodded at the report and allowed himself a deep, centering breath. He hadn't seen action for a long time, but at least he'd have the comfort of his same old ship as he made this stand — *Agamemnon* was the only ship in which he'd ever gone to war.

"Here we go again..." he said to himself quietly. Then he looked to his Signal Officer, remembering his place as commander of this fleet. "Alright, give me Fleetcomm. I don't care if Omega intercepts it... Actually, Master, field to 100 percent. Signals, order all ships to full emissions, and give me a general broadcast. I *want* him to hear me."

So much for the *trap* part of the equation, but for some reason this was more important in Artie's book right now.

There was some surprise on the bridge as the veteran tiger's plan went out the window, but Artie stood tall at the plot and let his eyes narrow.

"One minute to combat range, sir... and you've got broadcast *now*."

Artemis Tigar smiled, "Omega, nice of you to join us."

Well, this *was* a surprise.

Just about 150 fresh Earther ships to his 200 battered Genesis beasts...

It would have been a tough trap to fight through, but now what was this commander... it sounded like Artie Tigar... what was he up to?

"Hope you enjoyed your flight out here, Omega," Tigar persisted over the comm, his tone smacking of a confident *arrogance* that wasn't common in Earthers. "See, we're not under any illusions that we're going to smash you the same way we did the Kroggs, and then all go for the same sort of pleasant post-war chat. But we're still going to screw your plans right up, my dear boy. Hope you like watching things fail on you... but wait, you must have gotten used to seeing that when we castrated you the first time. So you'll know what to expect from this."

Omega-Natosh, Omega-Gillian, and Omega-Thomas Paine — now the three chief avatars — all gritted their teeth at the goading.

Artie Tigar would be taught a lesson for his hubris.

"I know, you're thinking you'll teach me a lesson for my hubris. But I'm not whipping the Hellespont here, Omega. You're about to lose as much as I can take from you. See you in a minute."

The link cut, and Omega's ships surged forward with more purpose.

This would be *fun*.

CHAPTER 52

Omega's lead ship didn't slow down as it came out of flux — as Artemis Tigar expected, it was set to ram *Agamemnon*. Despite its size, the great old 150-gun First Rate still knew how to move like a dancer, and move it did.

A broadside ripped through the ramming Omega ship as it slipped past the side-stepping *Agamemnon*, and then the rest of the Omega ships exited flux before a great wall of Earther veterans.

What followed was like a war between animals, fighting on instinct and for the most primal reasons.

Earther squadrons, refreshed with their familiar ships and keen on maneuvering as they had in the old days, swept forward in jagged fits of determined anger, while clouds of Omega vessels threw themselves into a frenzy and lunged with all the might they could muster.

Each side hit the other in the middle of space.

Minnie Maximane's eyes narrowed as *Galahad's* Captain, Mel Ramsay, ordered the powerful First Rate forward into the fray, with fellow *Champion*-class ships *Lancelot* and *Hector* following on the flanks.

The newer ships powered right through the melee — while 74s rolled and shot and rolled, the *Champions'* quicker recharging guns just cut swathes out of Omega's formations, and moved to interrupt his attacks on the veteran vessels.

"Keep us together, fight by half-squadrons at least. Look for concentrations of Omega — we're going to rupture his formations. All ships *forward!*"

As Minnie gave the orders with the confidence that came from being a member of the family Maximane, the entire New Halifax Squadron raced from its station at the corridor, throwing itself wholesale into the fray.

"Admiral Maximane has committed her force forward–"

The report was cut short as *Agamemnon* slid sideways hard under the orders of its Cruising Master, and a wild Omega Destroyer barely missed the front end of the massive vessel. Carronades tore the Omega ship apart as it tried to circle again, but Artie was ignoring it even as it was turned to debris.

"Signals, send to all ships — keep the pressure on, don't let Omega get past us."

So far he'd lost nineteen ships, and Omega had lost twenty-four... it was better than it could have been, and Minnie was coming into it now.

They just had to keep Omega from the corridor...

"Looks like he's trying to set up an end run, sir!" the plot shifted immediately to show about thirty Omega vessels pulling out of the rear of the fight and collecting themselves. Artie gritted his teeth at the sight.

He didn't really have a tactical reserve...

"Fine, *Mjollnir, Thor, Loki, Grendel, Calypso, Brazil*, fall into line astern of us. Let's go break them up ourselves."

"About to hit the corridor... four minutes."

Varnia cocked an eyebrow, "That really *wasn't* an hour, Master."

Renown's veteran chief cruising officer shrugged, "The grav shear made it look as though it was farther than it was. I can't get a lock on the beacon buoy for the same reason, but we've got the entry point targeted... this is a real mess of a corridor entry over here. Sure glad the other side isn't so distorted."

"Indeed, we'd never *find* it... alright, all hands stand by for hyperspace corridor translation," Varnia sat back in her chair and activated her personal shield... just in case...

Renown hurtled towards home.

"*Mjollnir's* gone... and *Brazil*... rammed sir..."

Artie's eyes narrowed and he held fast to the side of the holo tank as *Agamemnon* swung sideways again to avoid collision.

The end-run group of Omega ships was just ahead... and they were still trying to get away — to go up and over his fleet, and reach the corridor unchecked.

Well, he'd see about that...

"Range in four seconds, sir!"

Artie nodded to the First Lieutenant, "Let's work our way down their line, see whose shields are *tougher*."

Tigar knew the answer to that question: this was his ship, and he wouldn't suggest testing the matter if he didn't believe he'd win.

Agamemnon erupted into the clear behind the battling fleets, only to dive into the group of thirty Omega ships. The plague-controlled vessels all tried to turn on this great First Rate, but *Agamemnon's* mighty guns and carronades began tearing the formation apart as it drove through. Four ships were crushed outright by the fire, and as the rest of the 74s drove in behind their flagship, they killed six more...

Before three of the 74s were destroyed entirely.

"Damn, not enough..." Artie leaned forward and glared into the plot. "Bring us around again."

"They're moving, sir — moving *fast!*"

The Omega ships had begun their acceleration towards the rift now — twenty ships, followed by ten more from the fray. That many ships getting to the Larosian universe... they could re-infect all the Larosians who had Type 1 Omega, take what remained of the Larosian Fleet as their own... and still overpower Chronos Claw's blockade force at Krogg if they didn't.

He couldn't let them reach the other galaxy.

"Send to Minnie, she needs to put a Battle Squadron on the doorstep of that corridor!"

Minnie Maximane was already seeing what was going on, and she nodded to *Galahad's* Captain as the order came in, "Take us back there. Signals, we need as much of the Eighth Battle Squadron with us as we can get. Stand by all boat reserves for launch."

Most of the relatively meager allotment of gunboats that the New Halifax Squadron had were in space and fighting, but Minnie had held almost 100 back in her ships. Perhaps they could be of use right now.

"Take us to 300 pls — get us there first!"

Galahad and *Hector* were the only two ships of Eighth Battle Squadron, New Halifax station, able to break action and fall back to the corridor... Not enough. Not nearly enough.

"Order... damn, who's left?"

Artie bit off his words as his gaze fluttered through the plot. The numbers scrolling on the sides of the holo projection showed that his force was at even numbers with the Omega formation, some eighty ships each now. But Omega had one concentrated unit to show for it, and all Artie's ships were split apart...

"Any ship that can, get there. We *must* hold the corridor shut."

Or close it the hard way.

Artie blinked at the thought — he hadn't wanted to collapse the corridor as Varnia had at Genesis, but he *could*...

"And all ships stand by with hyper charges. If any Omega ships get into the corridor, *blow* it."

There was no reply from anyone, but a half-dozen Earther vessels slipped away from the battle and chased the Omega fleet towards the corridor.

Galahad slid to a halt in front of *Hector*, and the two lone ships of the line sat before the mouth of the corridor as the first Omega ships hurtled in.

"Stand by for violent maneuvers," *Galahad's* Master warned evenly, and Minnie Maximane braced her hands on the sides of the holo plot and waited just another second.

"Let them have it!"

Galahad fired, rolled fast, fired, rolled fast, fired... *Hector* fired, rolled fast, fired, rolled fast, fired...

Boats spewed from both.

The shot ravaged the first three Omega ships in line as they barged their way towards the corridor, but they were big vessels, and despite the weight of shot from the two newer ships of the line, the plague ships seemed set on collision courses.

So the Masters of the two great *Champions* moved their ships from the path of danger, and created an opening for the rest of the Omega ships to get through.

"Get us in there!"

Agamemnon slid into and out of energy drive in a flash, *Thor* and *Calypso* the only 74s left to join the great First Rate in its run. Guns sung and loosed deadly shot that crushed another Omega ship, but *Thor* paid for the kill with death by ramming, and then twenty-two Omega ships dove straight towards the corridor.

A number of frigates had managed to get themselves in the way, and now they tried to stop the rush with broadsides, but they were too few.

"They'll be through in a minute, sir!"

Artie ground his jaw and nodded, "Get the hyper charges ready — send to Minnie, tell her to close that rift right now."

"Sir!"

That word stopped Artie's thoughts, even though it didn't explain to him quite why he should pause.

"Ship coming *through* the corridor!"

Artemis Tigar straightened slightly. By the Earth, he hadn't given Omega enough credit — a fantastic pincer operation, a new plague ship, perhaps Larosian, to hold the corridor open...

"Exiting in twelve seconds... *Galahad* is moving to intercept."

Artie nodded. One new Omega ship wouldn't change the fight now anyway.

"Get us into them... ram them if you have to!"

They had to buy Minnie time to shut the door, and so *Agamemnon's* Master gritted his teeth and nodded, then keyed the intercom, "All hands stand by for some impacts. Engineering, slave Reactor Six to shields, and deploy a deck shield around it in case it blows."

There was a change in the hum of *Agamemnon's* electronics, and then the great First Rate, still spewing energy to and fro in a tremendous show of gun power, literally hammered into the Omega end-run group.

Literally.

The massive bow of the ship was like a sledgehammer, and while Destroyers of Omega's horde could be deadly when they did the ramming, they crumpled like paper as the First Rate drove into them at almost 90 pls.

Shields flared and seared, but they held — a whole reactor had been slaved to holding them intact now. And the great aged hull of *Agamemnon*, built to Earther standards laid down oh so long ago, more than held the force of the strikes in space.

Six ships died in a moment either from being shot or rammed, all killed by *Agamemnon*.

But still more dove towards the corridor.

A Destroyer caught *Hector* in the rear, and the powerful First Rate's engines shut down, casting it adrift. Frigates rushed to its side, huddling around it to keep the Omega rams away, but they weren't needed.

No, Omega had tunnel vision now — only *Galahad* stood in the mouth of the corridor, and eighteen ships were rushing towards the lone First Rate.

Minnie Maximane took a very deep breath and watched as just over twenty gunboats swirled into claw formation just off her ship's bow. They'd add their fire to the very last... and then they and *Galahad* would likely be crushed by the collapsing corridor.

They would, in the end, die as Earthers, just as Minnie's father had...

"The newcomer will be translating in nine seconds, Omega will be in range in just over a minute."

Minnie nodded and ground her jaw, "Prepare the port guns for–"

There was an awkward, high-pitched squeal as interference was cleared on the comm, and then the Signal Officer came abruptly to his feet in surprise, speaking into his headset without concern for the rest of the bridge, "Yes *ma'am*, we're under heavy attack. Clear for action if you can..."

Minnie frowned and turned from the Signal Officer to the plot, noting with an abrupt sense of calm that a pennant had appeared over the newcomer's icon in the corridor. *ENS Renown*, Rear Admiral Varnia Lupus.

"I can't believe this... he's hitting New Halifax? Are we cleared for action yet?" Varnia turned to her First Lieutenant, and the lion listened in his headset for a moment and then nodded.

"Boats ready for launch, guns crewed... that's got to be a new record time..."

Sensors couldn't operate at their full capacity within the corridor, but *Venerable* had the most advanced scanning gear the Earthers had ever developed. Halfway between galaxies, they were able to detect the explosions on the far side of the corridor, and as they grew nearer the picture got clearer. It was a grim one.

So *Renown* would do what it could to help.

"Translating!"

Varnia nodded, then gritted her teeth, "Run out the guns."

It was a sight worth seeing, because as grand as a *Champion*-class ship of the line was, a *Venerable* was even greater.

Renown dove out of the corridor at full speed, venting the 50-odd remaining boats of its strike wing and loosing broadsides immediately.

Agamemnon burst from the side of the Omega force as *Renown* appeared, and the First Rates of different eras — alone now with the loss of all the nearby 74s — cut great swathes from Omega's formation.

Eighteen plague ships rapidly became twelve, and *Galahad* slipped forward out of the mouth of the corridor to deliver more shot...

One of the Omega Destroyers just clipped the stern of Minnie's ship. The force of the impact in the strange grav eddies that dominated the corridor mouth drove the First Rate off station, and gave one... two... *three* Omega ships a moment to get through.

Artie slammed his fist into the side of the plot, "Send to Varnia: close the corridor with hyper charges if you can."

He wasn't even processing what it meant that Varnia Lupus and *Renown* were alive. Not yet, that was for later...

"Signal from *Renown*, closing it won't do any good — they could survive and the path for our pursuit would be cut off."

Artie's ear twitched... they'd have to give chase.

The plot was showing that just about all of the rest of Omega's formation was gone — the New Halifax Fleet was down to... by the Earth, twenty-one ships, but after a hard fight, all that remained of Omega's force were the last seven ships now heading for the corridor.

"Get us in their way, then, and signal all ships to reform and prepare for travel in the corridor. We can't let them get far."

"Aye, sir. Moving us to..."

There was a pause, and Artie looked to the Master, who looked to the helm, and then grabbed the back of a chair as quickly as he could, "Fourteen points starboard, up thirty-six and make speed 98 pls. All hands stand by for collision!"

Artie's eyes jerked back to the plot. Damn. And they'd had such a charmed fight so far too — not one single bit of damage...

The Omega Destroyer angling for them slammed into the shields above the bridge at full speed. Reactor Six tried to cope with the massive overload, but exploded instead, and while on the engine deck shields confined the force of the blast, the power surge ruptured relays all across the ship.

The plot exploded in Artie's hands, and then the bridge depressurized as the point of the Omega Destroyer's nose drove into it.

• • •

Varnia's eyes widened — this wasn't the homecoming she'd wanted...

One of *Renown's* carronades tore *Agamemnon's* adversary to shreds, then Varnia ordered her ship to get in the way of the rest.

But it was too late. Five more ships slid into the corridor, though *Galahad* managed to get control back in time to shatter the sixth with a powerful broadside.

And that was the end of the fight... here.

But Omega was in the Larosian galaxy with eight vessels.

"Signal to all ships, I'm taking command of the... battle group. All capable ships are to translate immediately, on our lead. Master, take us back into the corridor."

So much for going home.

Renown drove into the corridor with unsafe speed, followed by *Galahad* and the frigates that had been guarding the wounded *Hector*. Then came a scattered band of 74s and 44s, just under a minute behind.

Varnia looked at the ragged line in her plot, and she knew it'd be a match for any eight Omega ships...

But if even one plague ship got away... what could happen if Omega re-infested a ship like *Carnarvon*? Narosh had said there were thousands of such vessels around out there.

The trip seemed short.

"Translating in four, three..."

Varnia took a deep breath and steadied herself at the plot. *Renown* was doing very well today.

"Translating."

The breath of every Earther on the bridge caught... the exit point would be a perfect place to stage a ram.

But none came. *Renown* emerged back in the Larosian galaxy, and there was no sign of Omega.

"No ships in the local area."

Varnia frowned, then turned to her Sensor Officer, "Where are they then?"

"Getting a cluster of eight flux markers from right here... but I can't see trails, and I can't see them. It's the grav eddies ma'am, they could've gone anywhere..."

Varnia stiffened. They'd lost Omega. They could go out and look everywhere, try to find him... but what if he'd split up... what could they do like this? The rest of the New Halifax force was limping out of the corridor. If she split her haggard 'battle group' up to go hunting, the ships could be picked off one by one.

Omega had gotten away. The Earthers were in no condition to chase.

"Signal from *Galahad*. Rear Admiral Maximane is requesting orders."

Varnia blinked and looked up from the plot, "Tell her to lead her ships back through the corridor. We'll follow directly. Signals, prep an energy-hyper pod. Get bearings on Laros, and dump our scans from the action into it. Tell them we'll be sending reinforcements through presently, but for now we... we have to collect our dead."

The Signal Officer nodded grimly and began to compile the pod.

So, moments later, as the last of the battered New Halifax ships slipped back through the corridor, an energy-hyper pod lunged out of *Renown's* side, and leapt through space towards the Larosian homeworld.

"*Now* we go home," Varnia said as she watched it go. "Master, take us back."

Omega had fought his way through the blockade.

CHAPTER 53

ENS Chimera exited energy drive in Gibraltar space, and as the familiar myriad of stations and planetoids appeared in the First Rate's plot, First Space Lord Fox Magnus let out a long sigh of relief.

"Now we're getting somewhere," he said in low tones, and as he made the comment his wife, the ever-intrepid Thena Magnus, grinned at him.

"We're not *getting* somewhere," she said quietly. "We're here."

"Minor detail," Fox smiled, then looked across *Chimera's* bridge to the Signal Officer, "If he's not already calling, let me talk to Garvin Jardaw."

There was a pause as the Signal Officer turned from one console to the next, and then the Lieutenant nodded, "Signal on its way now."

"Main tank," Thena didn't look away from that main plot as she gave the orders, and Fox merely nodded in confirmation.

It took just about fourteen seconds for the signal to hit *Chimera's* receiver and to glow to life in the tank — an unusually long time because the two computers behind the signals had to compare time stamps after one had been off the charted routes for weeks — and then Garvin Jardaw glowed to life in the holo tank.

"Good to see you, Garvin. I come bearing a fleet, need one by chance?" Fox's pleasant greeting seemed to be swallowed by the dark expression that clouded the polar bear's features.

Fox slowly began to frown — what had he missed...

"Sorry Fox... I'm sending the data now. Can you come aboard *Gibraltar One* to debrief, or should we join you in *Chimera?*"

Fox glanced sideways at his wife. As First Space Lord, it was Fox's prerogative to choose the host of any meetings, but Garvin had really bad news. Best that Fox went to him, then.

"We'll be over in half an hour... how bad is it, Garvin?"

The bear's face seemed to stretch taught, and Fox let go a long breath, "Alright, coming over in a few minutes then."

Jardaw nodded and vanished, and then the plot began to fill with scans. A refugee fleet slaughtered, London destroyed, the New Halifax corridor breached...

Fox stared in silence.

•••

Lab Forepaw had to admit feeling some comfort in boarding *Orion* again. Esther Arbear was really looking after his old ship, and it was good to be back aboard. *Venerable* was a great ship, but the soul at the core of *Orion* knew Lab Forepaw like no other... save, perhaps, for Setter himself.

So as he walked the decks to the conference room, Lab felt as if the ship was welcoming him back. His instincts seemed to hum with soft approval, his mind eased and for a few brief moments he managed not to reflect on the losses. There was no need to repeat them to himself or anyone else now — they were gruesome, and they were in great part his responsibility.

He might just have surpassed Setter when it came to number of deaths on his watch as First Lord. Many millions had been in England, and hundreds of thousands more had been in the refugee fleet...

Steeling his mind against that thought, Lab let the fingers of his left hand trace the panels of the corridor bulkheads as he passed them, and he allowed the memory and the spirit of mighty *Orion* take him in, comforting him just a bit.

Jax Furgus was very much angered by Omega's moves — by the refugee fleet strike, by London and by New Halifax.

But he was elated, too, for a different, very good reason: his daughter was *alive*. Joyce Furgus was with some damned Larosian Battleship in a different galaxy right now, but she was *fine*. In fact better than fine, she was distinguishing herself in the tradition of the family.

Well, that was giving himself a lot of credit, and he wasn't ready to go *that* far...

"You wanted to see me?"

Turning quickly, Jax found a newcomer in *Orion's* main observation lounge — a tall, broad officer by the name of Esther Arbear. Jax didn't know *Orion's* new Flag Captain that well — not beyond her reputation as a fighting Captain from the last war, anyway.

But he didn't need to know her well to tell her the news...

"Esther, hi. Got a few messages from the last Admiralty... er... Antarctic Base pod. They didn't have time to pool proper reports for everyone yet, but I know a couple of the cats there..." he was drifting so he mentally kicked himself. "*Renown* arrived at New Halifax just in time for the fight... you know that right?"

Arbear nodded, "I checked the manifest as soon as I saw... neither of our daughters survived the trip."

Jax shook his head quickly, "Neither made the trip *back*, Esther, but Joyce and Ellen are together, running the marine detail assigned to a Larosian ship that Varnia and Narosh put back in action. They should reach Laros soon... they're alive and well!"

There had been a reserved but persistent grimace on Esther Arbear's face, but it melted instantly, "Seriously?"

Jax grinned and nodded, "Damned straight. The Larosians are about to get back in it, and your cub and my cub are helping them."

Esther Arbear smiled.

"We're going to deactivate the city shield for now."

The report, from wherever it came in the room, drew only a simple nod from Audrey DeBrooke. She stared at the footage of the refugee fleet being raped in space, of her trusted old ships getting incinerated in almost incidental butchery, and of Ami Dune and the Earthers dying by the thousand trying to stop Omega... and failing.

London and most of England had been incinerated, reportedly killing Elandra Caine and breaking the back of most of the anti-Omega research in the process.

At some point this all was going to break her mind.

"Artie stopped all but eight of them getting through... I imagine Varnon will be sending ships after them, but then I don't know what returned with Varnia," Pat leaned back in a chair opposite Audrey and let out a long sigh as his words trailed off.

On the monitors now, he could see the Freetown shield lowering itself, and he could imagine just what was going on in the space above.

He probably should get back up there. Sarah might not let him in at all... but at least he would be there if she did.

"You should go back up," Audrey's tone was dead, her words exhausted and worn. Looking up at the Irishman abruptly, her sunken eyes shocked him for a moment.

The poor woman had very little left for a personal life, and the world she'd worked for more than half her life to build seemed next on the list of planets to be shredded.

There was no telling for certain where Omega was going next... but it seemed predictable that it'd be either Freetown or Gibraltar... or perhaps Krogg or Earth...

Right, well that was just about everywhere. So chances were it'd be one or more of those places.

"I... well, yes. Yes, I'll sit in while Lab and Andra figure out how to win this," Pat's words tried to be confident, but it was increasingly difficult for him to hide his worry.

Audrey looked down at the table for a moment, doubt filling her mind. The Earthers had done so much for Freetown... hell, they'd made the colony possible. But now the great patrons were being defeated.

"I don't know if this can be won, Pat," Audrey's eyes shifted back up to Pat's, and any attempt at optimism dropped immediately from his face.

He looked from Audrey to the table and back, then slowly came to his feet, "Probably not, now that you mention it. But I don't mind deluding myself, so I'll let you know how things shape up, unless you want to come with."

"I'll wait for the official briefing. My people need me here."

With a slow nod, Pat waved a low hand and then turned from the table.

Audrey watched him go and then shifted her eyes to stare at the table again.

Sarah sat in Ursla's cabin, waiting for her old Earther friend to return from the kitchen with waters for them both, and thumbed through the list of *Renown's* crew and passengers one more time.

Graham wasn't on it.

Which, she decided, was fine. Because she'd come to terms with his death — bringing him back to life now wouldn't actually help her mental strength. She was still suffering enough to keep Pat from tearing her out of a strategic haze... she couldn't sacrifice any more of her warring abilities to her family.

Not until Omega died for his crimes.

Ursla came out of the kitchen just as Sarah closed the crew file again, and as the ArcGeneral laid the pad on Ursla's coffee table, the Earther handed her an icy glass of water.

"So... how are you holding up?" Ursla took a seat opposite her human friend, and Sarah stared at the Admiral in response to the question.

That well, eh? Ursla hadn't expected Sarah to be particularly cheery, but... well, she'd hoped that Sarah was handling things as well as it seemed she had been before the refugee fleet had died...

"I don't blame you, or the Admiralty, or anyone, Andra. It wasn't foreseeable, and if anyone in my fleet tries to blame you for it, they'll deal with me," Sarah punctuated her cold remarks with a gulp of ice water.

Ursla leaned back in her seat, "I... appreciate that. But that's not what I'm worried about right now. I've got news for you, from Jax through a friend at Antarctic Base."

Sarah didn't make eye contact with Ursla, but her expression reflected her grim curiosity, "Very well. News that got held up because of the London chaos, I expect?"

"Indeed," Ursla sipped her water before going on. "Communications are a bit more dicey than usual with Admiralty House gone. But what you should know is that the reason Graham isn't on that crew manifest for *Renown* isn't that he's dead."

Stiffening instantly, Sarah's eyes shifted to lock with Ursla's, "What..."

Ursla held up her hand, "He left the ship to join Narosh in a reactivated Larosian Battleship, *Carnarvon*. He's going to help them get their fleet back online and then he's going to help lead them back here to-"

"He's *what?*"

Putting her glass on the coffee table, Ursla leaned forward to repeat herself, "He's in the Larosian galaxy helping them restore some of their fleet. He's got Christine Schaeffer with him, and a small crew of Earthers, and Narosh."

Sarah's mouth hung open for a moment. So he was alive... but he was... what... "What the devil is he thinking — his place is with this fleet... he's out with *Narosh* helping revive a dead fleet because *why*, Andra? He's not responsible for them... he's supposed to come here and help us. If he was here then I could have been with my people... they wouldn't have... or I wouldn't have... I mean... you know..."

Ursla frowned and caught Sarah's eyes with her own, "You wish you'd died with your people."

The ArcGeneral-President's eyes grew wider at the sharp observation, and she stopped babbling for just an instant, reliving again the horror of what she'd seen. So complete was her failure of her people, so utterly complete.

By those terms she had nothing to live for — as President she was a great failure, so all that remained for her was the Navy, and trying to bring this fleet to battle, and to find some revenge, perhaps.

But that wasn't what she wanted to do...

"He should be here, Andra... he should be handling the fleet, *he* should go after Omega. Because... he'd be better at it than me. But he's running from his duties, waiting for revenge out there... Omega killed his *wife* and he's out there waiting for revenge... I just don't... don't..."

"You're all your fleet has. And you've still got Pat, if you stop trying to shut him out of your life. So whether you should be or not, you have to do this job. Your people are relying on you."

Sarah opened her mouth to object, but saw no point in trying. Andra was right, her duty was all that was left to her.

"Right."

Her weak word didn't convince Ursla she'd accepted the reality, but the wise bear Admiral decided not to press the question. Sarah was on a knife edge right now, after all that she'd lived through. Hopefully she could come back from the edge again.

Perhaps Pat could bring her back...

"Anyway, the meeting with everyone is in ten minutes," Ursla took her water and gulped down the last of it. "Let's get down there."

Fox and Thena stared at the projections, and on the opposite side of the plot, Garvin Jardaw and Karl Kandam stood silently reconsidering the conclusions they'd drawn... only to concur.

Omega was going after Krogg 'A', and Gibraltar wasn't going to do a damn bit of good in stopping him.

"You're... right," Fox was frowning as he looked up through the plot at the two bears. "This... this is too plausible to ignore, and we can't take the chance and give him that much Krogg biomatter."

The bears exchanged nods with the foxes, and Thena's eyes narrowed as they drifted to the icons of Lang Sandpelt's fifteen *Venerables*, "I take it Lang is getting ready to run out and check on Omega's force count at Genesis."

Fox's eyes shifted to the glowing pennant of his former Midshipman's squadrons — they were cleared for the week-long cruise to Genesis.

Garvin nodded in reply, "He's been itching to have a look since we pulled out... now it seems rather crucial."

Nodding slowly, Fox looked up at the polar bear Admiral, "Fair enough, send him. And then... damn, let's start packing up the system. Move everything to Krogg 'A'... tell Chronos we're coming to him with lots of firepower..."

Jardaw let out a long breath and nodded, "Alright. But just so you know, Fox, we've probably got a couple of weeks yet to wait before the last of the survey teams gets back here. We can't leave the system completely until they're all here to convoy out."

Well, that complicated things.

"Yeah. Yes alright, we'll start moving out what we can now, though. Pack up the portable yards and send them along with all the packed ships I brought... that way Chronos can start building fast. And we'll wait here with the stations and everything that's in fighting condition, just in case. I'm guessing we'll have enough breathing room to wait a week."

As he spoke, Fox realized just what he was saying.

After four decades of Gibraltar being the greatest Naval base in the *galaxy*, they were about to pack up and leave it behind.

Because Omega had thoroughly outflanked them.

The First Space Lord's voice had dropped off, and all eyes shifted curiously to him. Thena leaned over quietly, "What's up?"

Blinking, Fox looked from his wife to Kandam and Jardaw, "Sorry. Just... have any of you ever heard of the Maginot line?"

Jardaw cocked an eyebrow, "Chronos already told us about it."

Fox half shrugged, "Figures, he's the one who first told me... but here's the good news, we won't repeat that mistake."

Kandam frowned, "Extending the analogy... we're hoping to head them off before Dunkirk?"

Fox nodded: in 1940, the British and French had failed to maneuver to effectively counter the German invasion, in part because the French had tied themselves to the Maginot line. That had led the British to withdraw their army at Dunkirk, a miraculous evacuation that prevented total loss. In the modern context, Fox hoped that by abandoning the Maginot line of Gibraltar sooner, they might prevent the need for a miracle, though he certainly wouldn't turn one down if it was offered.

"Yes, we are. But I never learned to speak French..." Fox blinked his memories away. "We're not going to get trapped here. We'll maneuver and meet Omega, from wherever he comes. Preparations will need to be made."

And they were. Gibraltar would be abandoned.

CHAPTER 54

Carnarvon, despite its age and its lack of recent use, was still a powerful and fast Battleship. After only six days in hyperspace, the once-mighty ship of war reached its home star, and on the ship's alien silver bridge, Graham, Christine, and Captain Joyce Furgus stood with Narosh.

Everyone was intensely anxious — had Omega, old or new version, infiltrated the last Larosian world in the absence of its Admiral-of-a-Fleet? Would this be a happy homecoming or a tragic reminder of the cruelty of Omega, and a crushing of the last hopes?

Christine was appreciating a certain Earther-like calm about these questions. She was still learning to get comfortable with her new perspectives, but this was definitely one that she approved of. It might be beyond human to be reasonably philosophical at a time like this, but that's what she was. If they found an infected Laros, they'd have to go somewhere else. If they didn't, their new mission could begin.

Either way, she'd have to keep watching Graham. He hadn't changed at all over the days of travel, it seemed. It was as though he'd completely shut everything out, and that the alien environment here on this ship gave him more excuse not to be human.

His quest for revenge... there was nothing Christine could do to stop it. The best she could do was keep him alive through it.

So that was what she'd do.

Admiral-of-a-Division Novash, filled with anticipation, stepped onto the bridge of the Larosian Navy's flagship.

Novash was a great old Larosian warrior, and the first Larosian to meet an Earther. He'd drawn much wisdom from his time with the Earthers, and though that had indeed been decades ago, he still felt better for it.

Now, as he took his seat on *Lycrotar's* bridge, his mind interfaced with the ship's systems, and with the minds of the crew who filled the small ship. While vessels were in short supply for the Navy, Laros was still producing ample Naval personnel. They had no resources left in system for shipbuilding, so they'd made up for quantity of ships with quantity and quality of crews...

Which meant Novash had a complete picture of his ship, his crew and the solar system as the new hyper point on its outer rim ejected its occupant.

Sure enough, it was *Carnarvon*.
Take us out to meet them, helm.

Narosh smiled as his minded filled with images of his home, "Just as I left it."

Though the Larosian crew of *Carnarvon* took orders telepathically, they recognized his English, just as the assembled humans and Earther did. A collective sigh of relief — in the tone of three different races — filled the large bridge, if just for a moment.

Move us towards the planet. Broadcast our banner, and prepare to answer any challenges. They will not be expecting us. Narosh's orders, delivered in his smooth telepathic voice, set *Carnarvon* moving again.

Lycrotar is coming out to meet us, sir, one of the bridge crew reported, and Narosh physically nodded as he acknowledged the report.

"Novash is coming out in *Lycrotar* to investigate us," Narosh explained to his non-telepathic guests. Then he looked to Graham and Christine, "If you like, I can let you see the conversation as we contact him. I'm afraid I cannot allow the same for you, though, Joyce."

The lioness smiled and shrugged, "Not your fault."

"We'll be glad to listen in," Graham's tone and expression didn't reflect any gladness whatsoever, but Narosh ignored that.

"Very well..."

Coming into range now, sir.

"Here we go," Narosh settled himself back in his chair and tapped into the minds of both humans on his bridge.

Before she knew it, Christine was seeing something in her mind's eye... *Lycrotar*, with Admiral-of-a-Division Novash seemingly floating in space over its forward hull.

Weird mental imagery... I thought I was messed up.

Novash looked curiously at her — yes looked at *her*. In this vision thing... oh damn, had he *heard* that?

You didn't exactly whisper it, Novash donned an amused half-smile. *It is good to make your acquaintance Christine, and to see you again Graham. And Narosh, sir, it does me great good indeed to see you with us again.*

Narosh smiled — Christine turned and saw him floating over *Carnarvon*, and realized she and Graham were floating over the ship too. It wasn't like a dream state, it felt as though they'd just walked out there.

Indeed... though I must say, Novash, you don't seem at all surprised to see us.

Christine frowned at that comment — how could he know whether Novash was surprised based on just a few lines of dialogue?

Can hear you thinking, remember, Graham nudged her with his mind and she frowned.

Novash was smiling fully now, *I have missed humans... and Earthers. I see some*

Earther bio signs on your ship. That is good... and in answer to your question, Admiral-of-a-Fleet, we received an energy-hyper pod from Renown *three days ago, detailing the situation with Omega.*

Aha, Narosh folded his arms before him as they all floated in space above their ships. *So Varnia went and stole my thunder... what news did it bring, Novash?*

The Admiral-of-a-Division paused and then looked briefly to the humans, *Forgive the abruptness of this, but you should see it too, since you are here.*

Christine opened her mouth to say something but it was too late. She was somewhere else, watching a fleet of Genesis refugee ships... being flayed. She was watching Earth... being hit. She was watching the New Halifax blockade... being breached.

Gods... Omega? her thoughts would have come out as a mutter had she spoken them, but Novash nodded.

Indeed. And eight of his ships slipped beyond detection range of Renown *when they reached our galaxy. A message from Setter Caine arrived just yesterday, suggesting that Omega will be attempting one of two things: he will either try to capture our already infected ships to use as his own, or he will run straight for the Krogg corridor, in hopes of getting to that system before it can be reinforced.*

Novash's explanation drew a look of mild shock from Christine. Narosh's eyes narrowed very slightly in a sign that very much betrayed the amount of Earther DNA swimming in his veins, and Graham, until now very quiet, tilted his head slightly.

Excellent, the junior Manchester thought coolly. *We'll have our chance at revenge, then, Narosh. All we need do now is make ready for war and find him.*

Narosh and Novash tilted their heads simultaneously and looked to the human, the latter speaking first, *That is a tall order, Graham.*

Graham's expression, even here in this strange telepathic vision, was cool. But in this mental form of communication, the ArcGeneral let some fury slip, and a sharp, hot vibration seemed to shake the void around him.

Christine's eyes widened as she felt it, but she did all she could to ignore it. The Larosians simply looked to each other and then back.

In any case, Novash pressed on in his report, *I've turned out the fleet, and made everyone ready to receive UDRC inoculations. The Laros central labs are ready to reproduce the compound for widespread distribution, so the blockade fleet can now be put at your discretion, sir.*

Narosh bow-nodded, *Excellent. We will go hunting for Omega very soon then, and now that he must face us on our preferred terms, we shall see how he fares.*

Christine held in a bit of a sigh, and Graham's eyes narrowed just barely.

We're going to make him pay, the ArcGeneral thought sharply.

The assembled officers in the telepathic conference nodded and concurred.

CHAPTER 55

Well, the Earthers had fucked him… but only a little.

Just eight ships got through the corridor, but there was plenty of Larosian junk out there to re-infect. He'd upgrade all those plague ships from the Type 1 Omega infection to his own Type 2, and then he'd use them to take Krogg.

Well, not them alone, because he was planning too much to rely on pathetic Larosian ships to carry the campaign.

But the Earthers wouldn't so much as be able to find him — they'd never locate his eight ships before they returned to the site of that thousands-strong, plague-ridden Larosian Fleet. No, he wouldn't leave them any trail, so they wouldn't even see him.

And hell, even if they did, he had the black wave.

Yeah, it sounded like a pretty cheesy name, but no 1,200 Krogg-augmented ships could be dismissed as just *cheesy*… well, perhaps unless he ate them with cheese. But that wasn't the same as eating toddlers with cheese, which was much more fun.

Especially if they were still squirming and squealing… ah the life of luxury.

Though, Omega reminded himself quickly, he had to start worrying about getting his human slaves to reproduce, because he couldn't afford to run out just now. He'd used a billion of the people of Genesis as raw material to create the black wave fleet, and billions more had been set aside to serve as his army. All those commitments in mind, he couldn't afford to run low now.

He probably had to cut back on the pleasure killing.

So only one evisceration a week… okay, and some sort of Marquis de Sade style murder-rape a week too… after all, no one's made of stone. Everyone needs a weekly bit of entertainment.

Yum, skinning…

So, as the black wave continued to grow and coalesce in Genesis space, and as Omega-Gillian sat silently in a blackened cabin in the depths of space, and as Omega-Paine sat in his office in Ecclesia and waited for commands, Omega-Natosh laughed to himself, and watched the growth of his minions.

The Earthers hadn't seen anything yet.

And they would all fail and die.

In a fun and tasty way.

· · ·

"Can you stop hugging me now, dad?"

Varnon ignored his daughter, just smiling and squeezing her a little tighter to him. They'd been standing like this for... well, about five minutes now, and all the Earthers on the flight deck of *Guardian One* politely ignored them.

All save for Beckett Lupus, who stood aside as he waited for his father-in-law to step back.

He'd be waiting for a while.

Understandably, though — Varnon had thought... no, had been absolutely *certain* that his daughter was dead. So now he'd take his time in welcoming her back, because it wasn't every day that a dead loved one came back...

And Setter.

Damn, Varnon had managed to forget entirely that Setter had come down to the flight deck with him, to welcome Varnia back to Sol and to get the short version of *Renown's* long story of survival.

It had to be piercing Setter deeply, Varnon realized, to see a friend reunited with lost family.

Beckett was having similar thoughts as he watched the lengthy hug, and he edged sideways towards the Supreme Consul. A great sadness seemed to radiate from Setter, and yet with it there was a great determination to continue the struggle. Varnon knew well how much losing Elandra and the millions of Earthers had affected Setter. The wound was deep, and it was the sort that might never heal.

But Setter Caine could fight wounded. Perhaps, like wolves before him, he would actually be more dangerous when he was wounded.

That would be a good thing, because the Earthers needed all he had to offer now. As far as Beckett was concerned, Setter Caine was the Earther leadership. Now as before, everyone else was merely in position to help make his vision work. Supreme Consul wasn't going to be an undefined title for very long.

Varnon drew back from his daughter, and while Varnia still smiled, Varnon sobered as he looked to Setter, "I... ah. Hm. Sorry to... I mean..."

Varnia's own expression sobered as she too recalled just what Setter was dealing with, but the Supreme Consul merely donned a polite, sad smile, "No, don't apologize. It's the best news we've had in days that you're back, Varnia, Beck. I'm happy beyond words for you all... I just need time. You understand."

Setter met the eyes of each of the three wolves as they nodded in reply, and then he nodded to each in turn, "So welcome back. I want you all to get some time together to catch up before the debriefing... how about we meet in the conference room in an hour?"

"We can go now Setter — really, we can," Varnon was stopped by Setter's raised hand.

"Go on, please."

Varnon locked eyes with his friend, and then after a moment, the First Consul conceded the point, "In an hour."

With another quick nod, Setter turned and left.

Setter stood on the observation deck again, and looked at Earth while the pain billowed within him. It wouldn't go away. He kept telling himself that, so his mind could move from hoping for relief to adapting to the situation. If pain was going to be a constant, then he needed to learn how to lead and fight when he was feeling pain.

He needed to learn how to focus on the holo plot even when Elandra's face filled his mind.

It wasn't going to be easy.

"Well, that's no surprise," he muttered to himself.

"What, me sneaking in here? They installed quieter doors on all ships about a decade ago."

Setter turned to see Varnon advancing from the door, "Ah, I was wondering about that. You never struck me as stealthy."

With a smile, Varnon shrugged, "To each his own. We're ready for you in the conference room. You're going to find a lot of this interesting... *Renown's* got an Omega human aboard for study. Doctor Lazarus will be working round the clock to make up for what we lost."

Varnon wanted to kick himself the moment the words came out of his mouth.

"Good," Setter smiled a bit sadly, "Elandra wouldn't have wanted us to give up on that side of things... and don't walk on eggshells around me, Varnon. I lost my wife, but you lost your daughter. You know how this feels, just as well as I do. We're better off if we just accept the pain and keep working through it."

Varnon shook his head narrowly, "But I got my daughter back, Setter. And you can't be carrying the load for us all the time — you're the greatest of us, but you're not invulnerable. If you need to take time, then take it. We'd all be better off for it..."

Nodding, Setter looked back out the window, "I'm going home after the debriefing. Phealan and I will sort this all out... as best we can. But don't feel bad about Varnia — it's been a good month for daughters. I hear Esther Arbear and Jax got theirs back too. Just been a bad month for spouses..." The last words carried no bitterness, just sadness. Gillian Hodge, James Stanton, Elandra Caine... "Well, depends on who you are, I suppose. For our inner circle it's been that way. But people like Sarah have lost so much more."

Varnon's reply was soft, "That they have. And I still think Omega might get the twist on us — after he's done all this, bringing back just one ship from the dead isn't enough. We're all going to have to learn this new reality of war, I suppose."

Setter's eyes fell on the stars just beyond Earth, and his ear twitched, "The keystone to reality is *self*, Varnon. We can't let him change us, or we'll have done his work for him."

The words drew a blink from Varnon, "Um. Yeah."

Turning back to his friend then, Setter cracked a broader smile, "Alright, if you were Ursla, we'd have an equation by now. So forget it, let's go to our meeting."

With a short chuckle, Varnon nodded, and the pair of wolves left the observation deck.

EPILOGUE

Phealan Caine sat silently on one of the big rocks on the beach at his family estate.

The waves were rolling in again, and it was intermittently foggy and raining. But it was the most peaceful place he could be right now, and he was glad to be there.

Pain continued to stab through him. It didn't go away, it didn't dim. It seemed as though every second thought that crossed his mind reminded him that his mother was gone. He'd think about something mundane, like what to have for supper, and immediately he'd wonder what his mom would be in the mood for after a day in the lab. Things like that were excruciating.

But the pain was something he had to live with, work with. Phealan was young for an Earther, but he'd listened to what his father had told him about the old war, and about being an Earther. And perhaps Phealan was himself a wise wolf, despite his youth.

If the pain wasn't going to leave him, then he'd have to learn to work with it. Grief was in some ways a gift: it reminded him of how wonderful his time with his mother had been. It was a constant reminder of why he had to somehow join this fight against the plague.

Others would suffer even more grief than they were already feeling, if he didn't help stop Omega.

"Hey."

Setter Caine appeared behind Phealan, and seated himself on another large rock near his son. It had been a day since the attack, and this was the first contact the two had had. Claire had hissed to Phealan that this proved Setter didn't love his son. Phealan knew better: his father knew he didn't *need* to immediately talk about Elandra being killed. Setter had so many responsibilities to so many Earthers, and Phealan could deal with his own woes.

In other words, Setter had known that Phealan could handle his own grief without Setter trying to tell him how to. The younger Caine took it as a compliment, whatever Claire thought.

"Hey," Phealan's reply echoed his father's.

The two wolves were silent for a moment, staring out at the sea.

"Lovely day..." Setter said quietly, and a sad smile twitched onto Phealan's face.

"It really is."

They sat there for the longest time, just staring out at the rolling waves, and intermittently feeling cool drizzle on their fur. The wind just washed over them with the comfort and confidence that only a real sea-breeze wielded, and for a time there seemed to be nothing — no universe, no consequences, just a small window of much-needed peace for the Caines.

"How're they holding up out there?" Phealan asked after that period of silence, and Setter frowned and shook his head.

"They're holding up the best they can, I think. But Omega... well, he knows how to hurt us. He's hoping he can intimidate us, *scare* us, into losing our edge."

Phealan frowned in a mirror of his father's expression, "He's worried about us having our edge? That means he's probably worried about *us*."

For the first moment in a long time, Setter felt a genuine smile come to his lips, "That's what I thought."

Again mirroring his father's expression, Phealan smiled too, "I learned from the master."

Setter looked his son in the eyes, still smiling, "I think you'll surpass the master, if you can call me that."

The comment was plain and honest, and Phealan took a breath and looked back out to sea, "Maybe one day. But for now, I'm ready to help. You lost in mom the one person who knew how to take the weight off your shoulders, didn't you?"

Setter nodded again, looking down at his hands, "I did."

"Well, I can't do that. I don't know how to take that weight off your shoulders. But I can help you carry it," Phealan's words were earnest, and they came with a wisdom and maturity that struck Setter as well beyond forty years of life experience. The young wolf then continued, "It's time I stopped trying to decide what to do, and just do what needs doing. I'll help lead this fight."

He could do that. Earthers believed firmly in self-direction: one became a Consul by one's own appointment. If you thought you were capable of leading, you went to the individual who was presently leading, discussed it, and if the incumbent leader agreed that you were better suited to the job, that Earther stepped aside. It was a system that baffled humans, but one that worked with the inherent cooperation the Earthers always enjoyed.

If Phealan was to appoint himself Deputy Supreme Consul, no one would question it. No Earther would believe that a Caine — even a young one — would overstep his abilities at a time like this. Humans would wonder how one so young could know what his skills truly were, but Earthers simply *knew* sometimes.

Setter understood this — he had simply *known* that he should lead the fleet to meet the Genesis Quest, and the Consulate at that time had trusted him, though no Earther had ever fought in a war at all. He could see the same certainty in Phealan now. The junior Caine had learned much from the elder's stories of life, death, and responsibility in the Krogg War.

Letting out a long breath, the father nodded at his son's pledge, "Two sets of shoulders is better than one."

The relief that came as Setter said those words was as unexpected as it was dramatic. In that moment he didn't feel the same peace he had felt when Elandra released him of his burdens, but he felt a new, different calm.

For the first time ever, he didn't feel alone at the top.

"Claire thinks we should be bitter. I don't think she can get past her own hurt, so she wants me to feel as much agony as she does," Phealan observed, narrowing his eyes against a gust of wind. "I can't imagine what it must be like for her. I told her about Christine staying with the Larosians, and she didn't even react. Her pain is so deep that I don't know if she can feel anything at all."

"Something we're both becoming familiar with," Setter said quietly.

Smiling sadly, Phealan looked at his father, "We'll be more familiar with it when one of us gets killed."

That was true enough, and Setter nodded, "Indeed."

"I don't understand how the humans cope with their pain, though. They wish it on others, on people who had nothing to do with the hurt they're feeling. Doesn't make sense to me..." Phealan shook his head.

With an ironic chuckle, Setter rubbed his brow, "Humans often don't. Graham Manchester is out with the Larosians seeking cold revenge right now. He's turned his back on his duty in hopes of getting a Larosian ship to ride into Genesis, for a suicidal fight to the death. Young Graham..."

Phealan leaned back and looked at his father, "I can understand revenge, I think... though I doubt my definition and Graham's would match up too closely. I want to stop Omega. I heard the signal Artie Tigar sent to Omega at New Halifax too — that sounded to me like our kind of revenge. I think revenge is something we understand."

"Ours is different," Setter agreed quietly, almost not loud enough to be heard over the waves. "The humans don't understand what we'd call 'revenge'. What Artie wants, and what Jax wants, and what everyone who lost someone today wants, is to deny Omega the satisfaction of getting his way. We may not be able to beat him, but even if we can't, we can have our own kind of revenge. He wants us to change, so we won't."

"We defy him. We don't give him his satisfaction. We die our way, fighting him with everything we have. And if we can manage it, with smiles on our faces — just to spite him," Phealan smiled as he said it.

With a laugh, Setter nodded in agreement, "He wants to make us feel fear. He wants to change us. We'll deny him his pleasures. We'll either beat him or we'll lose, but we'll do it on our terms. That's our revenge. That's..."

An absurd thought entered Setter's mind as he repeated those thoughts to himself, and instinctively Phealan knew precisely what his father was about to say. In that instant, both Caines saw the smiling face of Elandra in their minds, and they both felt the warmth of her presence deep within them, driving out the chill of the North Atlantic breeze.

The waves crashed in, so loud that neither wolf actually heard the words that finished Setter's quiet sentence. It didn't matter, though, because they both knew.

It was...

"...the vengeance equation."

APPENDIX A: CHARACTERS

The threat of Omega is looming. Here's a reminder of who stands against the plague, and who's become *part* of it.

Arbear, Ellen – Lieutenant
A marine with Cadmus Howler's elite 2/54th stationed aboard *Renown*, Ellen is the daughter of venerable Krogg War Captain Esther Arbear. While her mother returns to service in the Earther Navy, Ellen is in *Renown*, marooned outside the Earth galaxy.

Arbear, Esther – Captain
During the Krogg War, Esther Arbear was one of the Earther Navy's finest Captains. Having retired after the end of that conflict, she has rejoined the service in order to help battle Omega. She has been posted as Flag Captain aboard *ENS Orion*.

Broadpaw, Varnon – First Consul
Varnon Broadpaw is the First Consul of the Earther people. One of the most respected veterans of the Krogg War, he has a keen military mind and a bad sense of humor — though the latter quality has been considerably dampened by the grizzly successes scored by Omega at Genesis.

Caine, Elandra – Doctor
Elandra Caine is the wife of Setter and mother of Phealan, and is the greatest genetic scientist the Earther people have yet seen. Her successes in adapting Earther drugs to aid human patients saved millions of lives between the Krogg War and the arrival of Omega, and now her expertise will be essential in defeating the plague.

Caine, Phealan – Citizen
Phealan is over forty and about ready to move out on his own, though he is only beginning to decide what to do with his life. The writing of history had appealed to him before the rise of Omega, but facing the plague's threat to his home, he is contemplating what other roles he might fill.

Caine, Setter – Supreme Consul of Earth
Setter Caine is the patriarch of the Earther people, having led them to wartime victory and peaceful prosperity. With the rise of this new threat, he is ready to take control of the Earther government, though he is not eager to do so, fearing that by watching the Krogg War, Omega will have learned to out-think him. Trusting in his friends Lab Forepaw and Varnon Broadpaw, Setter continues to wait in the wings, hoping his leadership will not be necessary for victory to be earned.

Claw, Chronos – Vice Admiral
A veteran (and subsequent Commander) of Fox Magnus' *Flame*, Chronos Claw finished the Krogg War as one of the Earther Navy's most distinguished sloop officers. Electing to stay out at Krogg 'A' after the war, he moved up through the ranks and now commands the Earther force overseeing the non-military development of the Krogg race.

Conroy, Pat – Historian
Pat Conroy finds himself with no formal role. With Genesis taken by Omega, his life as a historian is either on hold or over, and with his wife Sarah isolating herself in order to focus on her duties, he cannot even serve to comfort or advise. He is determined to remain the most positive voice in Sarah's inner circle, refusing to be overwhelmed by the horrors he's seen, though he's not sure how long he can keep that brave face up as Omega surges.

Cuttar, Ernile – Sergeant Major
Ernile Cuttar is the Sergeant Major commanding the elite Recon Squad attached to 2/54th and General Beckett Lupus. Having fought alongside both Beckett and Colonel Cadmus Howler in the Krogg War, he is acknowledged as one of the most elite marines in the Earther service.

DeBrooke, Audrey – Admiral
Now a widow, Audrey DeBrooke finds herself as commander of the Freetown Navy that she helped build, and disputed ruler of the Freetown colony itself. Thanks to a poorly-conceived constitution, there is no clear line of succession that gives her control of the colony now that her husband, the official Governor James Stanton, has been killed. Dealing with questions about the constitution and with the imminent threat of attack from Omega, Audrey finds herself in an unenviable position.

Dune, Ami – Rear Admiral
Ami (Cairn) Dune was one of the Krogg War's best-known officers, her exploits having been covered extensively by Will Rust and the Genesis Free Press. After the war she married Zed Dune, her fellow wartime Commodore, and joined the

Earther Consulate. With the rise of Omega, she has returned to the Navy to assist in the defense of Earth.

Dune, Zed – Rear Admiral
One of the most innovative thinkers in the history of the Earther Navy Engineering Corps, Zed's fingerprints can be found on the first versions of Earther hyper charges and energy-hyper cutters. He is also an experienced frigate officer. With this unique blend of talents, Zed has been drafted by Dran Nightclaw to assist with the recommissioning of Earther Krogg War ships for the battle against Omega.

Forepaw, Labrador – First Lord of the Admiralty
Lab Forepaw is probably the best officer ever to serve in the Earther Navy, and recognizing this, Setter Caine has expressed absolute confidence in his overall command of the campaign against Omega. Trusting in his judgment, and bringing a slightly different perspective to fleet command than Setter did, Lab hopes to meet and defeat Omega before the plague can do any more harm.

Furgus, Jax – Admiral
During the Krogg War, Jax Furgus had many ships shot out from him. Now he commands the recommissioned 74-gun *Aboukir*, and heads up the Earther ships stationed at Freetown. Believing his daughter, Joyce, to be dead, he has lost his usual crotchety sense of humor, and his patience with human eccentricities. He intends to stop Omega, or to die trying.

Furgus, Joyce – Captain
Commanding a company of Cadmus Howler's elite 2/54th based aboard *Renown*, Joyce Furgus is marooned outside the Earth galaxy. An excellent marine, she will be relied upon during any boarding operations conducted by the ship as it attempts to find a way home.

Hobbes, Ronax – Captain
A carrier skipper during the Krogg War, Ron Hobbes returned to the service when Lab Forepaw asked him to serve as Flag Captain of *Aboukir* on a run to Freetown. He now serves with Jax Furgus aboard that ship, and sits at Freetown preparing to counter whatever moves Omega attempts to make.

Hodge, Gillian – Avatar
Gillian Hodge isn't herself anymore: her body belongs to Omega. The plague was able to infect her (despite the protection of Earther regen treatments) by infesting her unborn fetus, and now she is one of his favorite avatars. Omega-Gillian has killed many innocent humans in unspeakable ways.

Howler, Cadmus – Colonel
Cadmus Howler had commanded Beckett Lupus' old recon squad on Krogg 'A', and since then he's remained at Beckett's side, turning the recon squad into a special escort unit for its former Sergeant, and eventually taking over command of 2/54th. Now marooned with *Renown* in another galaxy, his expertise will be useful in dealing with any boarding operations that occur.

Jardaw, Garvin – Admiral
Formerly the Flag Captain of Draco Maximane's *Engadine*, Garvin has assumed rotating command of the Earther forces on the far side of Genesis, including the fleet at Gibraltar and the ships at Krogg 'A'. He remains in the service partly in honor of his fallen friend Maximane, and he is one of the most respected commanders in the new Navy.

Jeffries, Ed – Commodore
A veteran of Pat's Pirates, Ed went to Freetown after the Krogg War, and rose to command of *Savanna Felix*, one of the colony's new Earther-hybrid warships. He remains one of the senior officers in the Freetown service, and with Audrey facing constitutional problems on the colony, he will have to take on more command responsibilities to compensate for her divided attentions.

Kandam, Karl – Vice Admiral
Karl Kandam has been the commanding officer at Gibraltar intermittently over the years since the Krogg War. Having assumed that post shortly after the base's activation, he is the leading expert in its operation. Though he rotates home to Earth for breaks on a regular basis, he remains something of a fixture in the Gibraltar system.

Kragran – Peacelord
The leader of the new Krogg people, Kragran committed to developing his race in a new direction unaffected by the evil of their Queen. He works closely with Chronos Claw — so closely that Claw has come to trust him. Kragran intends to take advantage of this trust, and to show the Earthers precisely what the Kroggs have learned during the Earther trusteeship.

Kudlee, Karyn – General
A distinguished veteran of the Krogg War campaigns at Avalon and Amaratsu, Karyn has worked her way up from her old command of 2/49th to her current post, General commanding the defenses at Earth. Karyn is decidedly aware of how her last name is pronounced, and she uses her considerable body size to make sure no humans give her grief for being a 'cuddly' bear.

Lazarus, Celia – Doctor
During the siege of Krogg 'A', Celia Lazarus was a medic aboard *Orion*, and it was she who stabilized Narosh after his crash landing on that ship's deck. Her actions saved his life then, and the injections of Earther drugs she gave him spared him from infection by Omega forty years later. Now serving as chief physician aboard *Renown*, she is determined to learn all she can about Omega, hoping to help Elandra Caine cure the plague — if the ship can find its way home.

Locke, Tom – Commodore
Having skippered carriers during the Krogg War, Tom Locke is an experienced Earther officer. When the first call for reserve officers went out during the Church coup crisis, he was quick to answer, and as such took over the frigate squadron attached to Jax Furgus' command. He remains with Jax at Freetown, preparing to meet Omega.

Lupus, Beckett – General
Beckett Lupus has risen to the top of the Earther Marine Corps in the forty years since the end of the Krogg War, and is nominally in overall command of the service. However, trapped aboard *Renown* outside the Earth galaxy, Beckett's concerns are much more immediately tied to helping his wife and the ship's crew find a way home.

Lupus, Varnia – Rear Admiral
Varnia (Broadpaw) Lupus is the wife of Beckett Lupus and the daughter of Varnon Broadpaw, and up until the Church coup was the Earthers' senior ambassador to Genesis. She now commands *Renown*, and as that ship is trapped outside of the Earth galaxy, her duty is limited to finding a way home.

Magnus, Fox – First Space Lord
First Space Lord Fox Magnus is officially the commander of the Earther mobile forces — according to the job description, he commands ships away from Earth space while Lab Forepaw controls the Navy from Earth. Omega has forced Fox into a desperate mission to reach Gibraltar with reinforcements, so from the bridge of *ENS Chimera*, the dapper fox aims to slip a convoy of warships around Genesis undetected.

Magnus, Thena –Vice Admiral
After a distinguished career in 74s during the Krogg War, and after being one of Fox Magnus' key commanders in the 186th Battle Squadron, Thena married the First Space Lord. She remains one of the Earther Navy's elite flag officers. She is now with her husband aboard *Chimera*, as the two take ships to reinforce Gibraltar.

Manchester, Graham – ArcGeneral

Trapped outside his own galaxy aboard *Renown*, and with his wife under the sway of Omega, Graham has shut down the parts of him that allow feeling. The junior Manchester sibling has taken a page from his elder sister's book: he intends to deny his humanity until his objective is reached. He means to save his wife, or to hurt Omega. He doesn't care what it will cost him.

Manchester, Sarah – President, ArcGeneral

As President of Genesis, Sarah witnessed the destruction of her planet and of billions of her people. Holding onto faint hopes that the Earthers can save those humans infected by Omega, Sarah commands a rag-tag, fugitive fleet in its bid to escape the clutches of the plague. Attempting to again shut out her human emotions, she has isolated herself from her husband, Pat, and hopes that the Earthers will be able to offer her wisdom that might help her cope with the weight of what has happened.

Maximane, Minnie – Rear Admiral

Daughter of Draco Maximane, Minnie has followed in her father's footsteps and joined the Earther Navy. One of the fleet's rising stars, she is the officer commanding the blockade force at the New Halifax corridor when Omega appears at Genesis. She flies her flag from *ENS Galahad*.

Narosh – Admiral-of-a-Fleet

Narosh was rescued from the clutches of Omega by *Renown*, and he now remains aboard that ship, trapped outside the Earth galaxy. Recovering from the wounds inflicted on him by Omega-Natosh, Narosh intends to help Varnia Lupus' ship find its way home.

Natosh – Avatar

Natosh is no longer himself, but is instead the chief avatar of Omega. He was the vehicle through which Omega captured Genesis, and his physical and telepathic prowess is considerable. He is one of the plague's preferred vehicles for torture and mutilation.

Nightclaw, Dran – Comptroller of the Navy Board

Acknowledged by one and all as the greatest frigate officer who ever lived, Dran is the Comptroller of the Navy Board. As the Navy races to recommission the many Krogg War ships that had been packed in crates in case they would ever be needed again, his skills as an organizer will prove critical to the success or failure of Earther operations against Omega.

Omega
The creator of the Earthers, Omega is coming for his revenge. The Earther immune system that he created in the twenty-first century was so powerful it defeated him, but now that he has been spliced with Krogg DNA, he's ready to show the Earthers just how nasty he is. He was in their blood during the Krogg War, watching them fight, and at times terrifying aliens with his telepathic might. Now he knows how the Earthers make war better than they do, and he's going to use that against them.

Paine, Gregory – Grand Chancellor
The leader of the Commonwealth of the Faithful, Paine's ambitions of defeating Freetown have been crushed by the Earthers. With the failure of the coup on Genesis, he is forced to try to develop a new plan for victory, with the help of the Gods.

Peregrine, Kylie – Vice Admiral
Another retired veteran of the Krogg War, Kylie returns to fleet command when Omega appears at Genesis. Her experience will rapidly be put to good use by Lab Forepaw and the Admiralty.

Ramsay, Mel – Captain
Mel Ramsay's parents both served with Draco Maximane over their careers in the Earther Navy, though both survived the destruction of *Engadine* at Krogg 'A'. Forty years later, Mel serves as Flag Captain for Draco's daughter, Minnie, at the New Halifax station. She commands the *Champion*-class *Galahad*.

Sandpelt, Lang – Rear Admiral
Lang Sandpelt was one of the intrepid officers aboard diminutive little *Flame* during the Krogg War, and he has remained with the fleet over the interceding forty years. Stationed now at Gibraltar, he commands two squadrons of *Venerable*-class ships of the line, and he's eager to use them against Omega.

Schaeffer, Christine – ArcLieutenant
Christine Schaeffer was just another cadet in her fourth year at the Genesis Naval Academy, working at a Panatorium to pay her tuition. Then she'd met Pat Conroy, who'd introduced her to Graham Manchester, who'd hired her as his new aide on a whim. In a freak accident on *Genesis One*, she'd been critically injured, forcing Doctor Celia Lazarus to give her a rapid regen treatment, and when she'd gone home to explain that necessity to her parents, the Church had launched a coup. Remaining with Graham, she'd been aboard *Renown* when Omega arrived, and had joined Graham in a failed bid to rescue Gillian Hodge. Now trapped aboard *Renown*, Christine is feeling strange side-effects from her

crash regen treatment, and is trying to help Graham even while he denies his humanity.

Schaeffer, Claire – Citizen
With her parents dead and her sister lost, Claire Schaeffer is virtually catatonic, and under the care of Pat Conroy. Pat hopes to find this teenage girl some help, but the trauma she has suffered is considerable. Perhaps Earthers can help Claire, but only with great patience and fortitude.

Stowt, Arther – Captain
One of Ami (Cairn) Dune's skippers from the Krogg War, Arther has taken on the job of Flag Captain for the First Lord of the Admiralty aboard *ENS Venerable*.

Stowt, Bartemius – Vice Admiral
Barty Stowt was Ami (Cairn) Dune's Flag Captain through the Krogg War, and continued on in the Navy for some years during the peace before retiring. With the rise of Omega, he has returned to the fleet, offering his experience wherever it is needed to stop the plague.

Tarkham, Alix – Captain
Alix Tarkham developed a reputation as one of the fleet's best hand-to-hand combatants before the Krogg War, and then served with distinction as a fleet officer during that conflict. With the rise of Omega, he returned from retirement to command one of the 74s attached to Jax Furgus' force, and is now stationed at Freetown.

Tigar, Artemis – Vice Admiral
Artie Tigar was Andra Ursla's Flag Captain through the entirety of the Krogg War, serving with her aboard *Agamemnon*. After the war, Artie preserved many of the great ships that had fought at Krogg 'A' in a museum at the New Halifax colony, and it is there that he takes over when Omega appears. Restoring *Agamemnon* to fighting form (from its status as a museum), he takes command of the New Halifax station, and the defenses of that colony's hyperspace corridor to the Larosian galaxy.

Ursla, Andra – Admiral
Andra was a civilian when Omega arrived at Genesis, but the rising threat of the plague has led her back to the command chair. Her massive experience — and massive body — are ready to go wherever Lab Forepaw needs them. Wherever Andra is, Omega best be wary — she is, of course, one of the great fleet commanders of the Krogg War.

APPENDIX B: FIVE TENETS OF EARTHER CAMPAIGN STRATEGY

With Omega setting himself up at Genesis, the Earthers are facing a number of serious tactical and strategic challenges. As the First Lord of the Admiralty, Lab Forepaw has to deal with some grave questions about what to protect, what to abandon, and how to meet Omega's impending onslaught. This appendix will provide a brief introduction into the kinds of strategic ideas held by officers who've come up through the Navy. These five points are essentially the lessons that the Earthers drew from the Krogg War, and right or wrong, they guide any decisions that will be made in the fight against Omega.

I. The Centers Of Gravity

The great human military thinker Carl Von Clausewitz identified 'centers of gravity' as the locations in a country that maintained its ability to fight. If they were destroyed, then the country would fall. These were places you could *not* afford to lose. Sometimes these centers are easily identified — capturing Paris tends to win wars against France, for instance — and other times they're difficult to locate. For the Earthers, Earth is the ultimate center of gravity. Because of the potential power of the Kroggs, Krogg 'A' is also a center of gravity in the conflict against Omega. Freetown, and its population of humans who the Earthers are committed to defend, is another.

New Halifax and Gibraltar are important posts, but they are *not* centers of gravity. Each of those bases was established to command the approaches to one of the centers of gravity, and thus to limit potential enemy access to a center of gravity. If you lose one — say New Halifax — your concern as a strategist won't be that you lost that base, but that your center of gravity is now more vulnerable.

II. You Can't Protect Everything

There is an old adage in military circles that says "if you try to protect everything, you'll keep nothing". When Stalin tried to resist German invasion during the Second World War, he lined all his forces on the eastern front up along the German-Soviet border, their deployments actually following every zig and zag on the map. Hitler's troops overwhelmed the Soviet forces by concentrating forces against selected points against that front line, and thus the adage was proved right.

The point that this brings up in the Earther context of space warfare is simple: you have to choose what places are most important to defend. New Halifax, Earth, Freetown, Gibraltar and Krogg 'A' are all held by the Earther Navy, but with their relatively small number of available ships, can they afford to protect them all? Consider the hypothetical: if Lab Forepaw had 1,000 ships and Omega had 1,000 ships, and Lab tried to defend each of those systems, he'd have to deploy into five fleets of 200. Omega could then hit any one of those systems with his full fleet and have a 1,000 to 200 (5:1) advantage.

This is where understanding which planets are centers of gravity comes in: you know which ones need the most defense. However, that doesn't actually simplify things too much, since Gibraltar and New Halifax are both posts that were built to help defend the centers of gravity — each commands one of the approaches to one of the centers. Should they then have smaller forces... or larger ones? Part of that question depends on how *well* these posts command the approaches they sit on, and that's the next matter to consider.

III. Covering Your Rear — In Space

Here's a question: can you simply jump around from target to target in space, or do you have to attack in a linear fashion? To make those two choices clearer, consider an example from the Krogg War. Setter Caine's plan for pushing the Kroggs back after the Battle of Genesis was to attack in a linear fashion — the Earther and Genesis Fleets advanced on a line towards Krogg 'A', and cleared every system along the way. They didn't skip any systems to get to the Kroggs' homeworlds... so why not?

In land warfare, you usually need to secure everything behind you as you advance. That's not to say you can't bypass enemy strongholds, but you have to contain them, to make sure that they don't cut you off from your base and reinforcements, or that they don't cut your communication and supply lines. Does this hold up in space?

If Omega launched an attack at Krogg 'A', he'd need to go through Gibraltar... or would he? Space is rather *big*, so couldn't he simply go around Gibraltar? The Kroggs did just that when they raided Earth and Genesis during the Krogg War, so it's possible. However, Earther strategy still relies on Gibraltar, because if an attack was to bypass that base on its way to Krogg 'A', the assumption is that the Gibraltar Squadron would either be able to counterattack the source of the strike — Genesis — while Omega's fleet was out attacking Krogg 'A', or that they'd be able to disrupt Omega's supply lines.

This assumption is based on Earther experiences during the Krogg War — a war that was slow and attritional, when the Earther and Genesis fleets on the front lines relied on secure supply lines to keep up their assaults. Whether the lessons of that war will apply to a war against a sentient plague is anyone's guess.

Ultimately, the Earthers have learned from experience that having a major base sitting on the way to a major target is a good way to keep that target safe. An enemy will think twice about leaving his or her rear and home base exposed to counterattack if they bypass it. When considering how to deploy limited numbers of ships against Omega, this philosophy would likely play an important part.

IV. Initiative

The bottom line when it comes to this sort of grand space campaign strategy is simple: being on the defensive sucks. While the Earthers would say that more eloquently, it remains the fundamental reality of their experience in the Krogg War. Trying to defend planets is difficult because you have to identify centers of gravity, decide how to defend them (keeping ships at them or at posts commanding their approaches), and have to face the possibility of 'end run' attacks that bypass those posts. You're almost forced to try to defend everything.

As the Earthers discovered in the Krogg War, the only antidote to these problems is to get onto the offensive — to force your enemy into a corner, so that she or he is compelled to use all her or his forces for defense. The Allied advance during the Krogg War had this effect: though they faced a counterattack in strength at the Battle of Gibraltar, and though there were raids on Earth and Genesis, none were in the strength of thousands of ships. The Kroggs were being pressed hard back through their own territory, so they simply couldn't put aside enough forces to launch a devastating attack anywhere.

Initiative is thus critical in space combat strategy. In the military sense, 'initiative' essentially means holding the momentum — you have it when you're attacking and dictating where and when the battles will be fought. It's an intangible thing, but when you have it, you can control the pace of the conflict.

V. Intelligence

Not smarts, but reconnaissance telling you where your enemy is and what he or she is doing, is critical to all of these other factors. You can get the initiative from an enemy by knowing what he or she is planning. If you know that Omega is going to attack Freetown, then you can concentrate your forces there — you're no longer trying to protect everything. Intelligence is thus the most important defensive and offensive tool in grand strategy.

Historically, at the Battle of Midway in 1942, the Americans used intelligence to discover that four Japanese carriers were going to attack one of their bases (Midway Island). At the time, the US had three serviceable carriers, the Japanese more than twice that many, but by knowing where and when the attack was coming, the Americans were able to seize the initiative, and sink four Japanese carriers in one battle. The course of the war in the Pacific changed instantly, and the Americans went on to victory.

No matter how many places you have to defend, or how few ships you have to do it, superior intelligence always gives you a fighting chance. If you can concentrate your best forces against the enemy — particularly when he or she wasn't expecting serious resistance — you can meet with success. This happened when Setter Caine held Gibraltar against that massive Krogg attack, and that lesson of relying on good intelligence is one that would be foremost in the mind of any Earther strategist.

Conclusion: The Utility Of Lessons

These five points are some of the cardinal rules behind Earther strategy when it comes to space campaigns. When you read about the decisions Lab Forepaw has to make in his campaign against Omega, keep these points — these lessons from the Krogg War — in mind. In human history and in the ranks of the Earther Navy, veteran military officers always try to take the lessons of past battles and adapt them properly to new circumstances and enemies.

Douglas Haig, a veteran cavalry officer who fought numerous successful small wars for the British Empire, learned many lessons during his years on campaign, and tried to apply them when he took command of the British Empire's forces during the First World War. He has been roundly dismissed by most popular remembrance as a fool for not realizing that some of those lessons he learned during his combat experiences didn't apply to the trench war of the Western Front — an unfair condemnation, to say the least.

Once the experiences of the war showed him the errors of his old tactics, Haig struggled and adapted as quickly as anyone could have been expected to. Though he didn't understand new innovations like tank warfare, he fully supported junior commanders (like Canada's Arthur Currie) who could effectively introduce new weapons to the field. Popular memory often believes the opposite — that he refused to adapt, which is untrue. Millions died in the trenches of the Western Front, and Haig and the Army's other general officers became scapegoats to anyone who wanted to condemn that war. They were often said to not have cared about the men who died.

Lab Forepaw would sympathize with Haig. Responsible for so many lives (that he certainly did care about), he had to try to make decisions in a war unlike any other before it, based on his experiences from past conflicts. The rules of war he'd learned when he'd led soldiers in combat had changed, and contrary to what people might like to believe in hindsight, the only way for him (or anyone) to learn the new rules was the hard way — by getting people killed. Of *course* he made mistakes: he didn't have a crystal ball. He still adapted as best he could, and though some people mightn't like to admit it, he was successful in commanding the British Empire's forces in the Allies' victory over the fierce German Army.

After the war, Haig was overwhelmingly popular with former servicemen. During the decade that followed the conflict, he helped popularize a campaign to have November 11 marked as a day of commemoration for the Great War, and to make the poppy a symbol of remembrance. When he died in 1928, the streets of London were filled by veterans and their families paying their respects — it was one of the largest public funerals in British history. One might safely suggest that the men and women of the time recognized that Haig had done the very best he could. History and popular memory simply twisted that understanding as the decades wore on, and bitter hindsight set in.

Haig and the war's other Generals were condemned by most histories.

Will Lab Forepaw be?

ABOUT THE AUTHOR

Born in 1984 in St. John's, Newfoundland, Kenneth Tam holds both a Bachelor's and Master's degree in history from Wilfrid Laurier University in Waterloo, Canada. His MA thesis examined the creation and operation of the Caribou Hut, a hostel for Allied servicemen in St. John's during the Second World War.

In 2006, Kenneth received a prestigious Canada Graduate Scholarship from the Social Sciences and Humanities Council of Canada. He was also awarded a Balsillie Fellowship at the Centre for International Governance Innovation during 2006-07. In that capacity, he worked for Mr. Paul Heinbecker, Canada's former ambassador and permanent representative to the United Nations. He presently serves as a Communications Consultant for Kitchener–Waterloo's federal Member of Parliament, Peter Braid.

Since releasing the first *Equations* novel in 2003, Tam has promoted his books across Canada, speaking with junior and high school students, delivering writing workshops, and doing book signings at bookstores and Iceberg-organized events. He frequently appears as a guest author at science fiction events across the country.

Kenneth is a partner in Iceberg Publishing, the company he and his family started in 2002. He has authored many of the company's existing titles, and is also responsible for graphic design, including the company logo, website, banners, advertisements, and other marketing materials. He acts as a primary contact with printers and suppliers, and is also key in new author development and recruitment.

He remains very lazy about writing his author bios. When they told him to make this one longer, he mostly copied and pasted it together from the Iceberg website, www.icebergpublishing.com.

www.ingramcontent.com/pod-product-compliance
Lightning Source LLC
Chambersburg PA
CBHW031601240626
47153CB00002B/589